THE PASSENGER

The novels of the American writer Cormac McCarthy have received a number of literary awards, including the Pulitzer Prize, the National Book Award, and the National Book Critics Circle Award. His works adapted to film include *All the Pretty Horses*, *The Road*, and *No Country for Old Men* – the latter film receiving four Academy Awards, including the award for Best Picture.

ALSO BY CORMAC McCARTHY

Stella Maris

The Road

No Country for Old Men

Cities of the Plain

The Crossing

All the Pretty Horses

The Stonemason (a play)

The Gardener's Son (a screenplay)

Blood Meridian

Suttree

Child of God

Outer Dark

The Orchard Keeper

THE PASSENGER

Cormac McCarthy

PICADOR

First published 2022 by Alfred A. Knopf,
a division of Penguin Random House LLC, New York

First published in the UK 2022 by Picador
an imprint of Pan Macmillan
The Smithson, 6 Briset Street, London EC1M 5NR
EU representative: Macmillan Publishers Ireland Ltd, 1st Floor,
The Liffey Trust Centre, 117–126 Sheriff Street Upper,
Dublin 1, D01 YC43
Associated companies throughout the world
www.panmacmillan.com

ISBN 978-0-330-53551-9

1 3 5 7 9 8 6 4 2

A CIP catalogue record for this book is available from the British Library.

Printed and bound by CPI Group (UK) Ltd, Croydon, CR0 4YY

THE PASSENGER

It had snowed lightly in the night and her frozen hair was gold and crystalline and her eyes were frozen cold and hard as stones. One of her yellow boots had fallen off and stood in the snow beneath her. The shape of her coat lay dusted in the snow where she'd dropped it and she wore only a white dress and she hung among the bare gray poles of the winter trees with her head bowed and her hands turned slightly outward like those of certain ecumenical statues whose attitude asks that their history be considered. That the deep foundation of the world be considered where it has its being in the sorrow of her creatures. The hunter knelt and stogged his rifle upright in the snow beside him and took off his gloves and let them fall and folded his hands one upon the other. He thought that he should pray but he'd no prayer for such a thing. He bowed his head. Tower of Ivory, he said. House of Gold. He knelt there for a long time. When he opened his eyes he saw a small shape half buried in the snow and he leaned and dusted away the snow and picked up a gold chain that held a steel key, a whitegold ring. He slipped them into the pocket of his huntingcoat. He'd heard the wind in the night. The wind's work. A trashcan clattering over the bricks behind his house. The snow blowing out there in the forest in the dark. He looked up into those cold enameled eyes glinting blue in the weak winter light. She had tied her dress with a red sash so that she'd be found. Some bit of color in the scrupulous desolation. On this Christmas day. This cold and barely spoken Christmas day.

I

This then would be Chicago in the winter of the last year of her life. In a week's time she would return to Stella Maris and from there wander away into the bleak Wisconsin woods. The Thalidomide Kid found her in a roominghouse on Clark Street. Near North Side. He knocked at the door. Unusual for him. Of course she knew who it was. She'd been expecting him. And anyway it wasnt really a knock. Just a sort of slapping sound.

He paced up and back at the foot of her bed. He stopped to speak and thought better of it and paced again, kneading his hands before him like the villain in a silent film. Except of course they werent really hands. Just flippers. Sort of like a seal has. In the left of which he now cradled his chin as he paused and stood to study her. Back by popular demand, he said. In the flesh.

It took you long enough to get here.

Yeah. The lights were against us all the way.

How did you know which room it was?

Easy. Room 4-C. I foresaw it. What are you using for money?

I've still got money.

The Kid looked around. I like what you've done with the place. Maybe we can tour the garden after tea. What are your plans?

I think you know what my plans are.

Yeah. Things dont look too promising, do they?

Nothing's forever.

You leaving a note?

I'm writing my brother a letter.

A wintry summary I'll wager.

The Kid was at the window looking out at the raw cold. The snowy park and the frozen lake beyond. Well, he said. Life. What can you say? It's not for everybody. Jesus, the winters are confining.

Is that it?

Is what it.

Is that all you have to say?

I'm thinking.

He was pacing again. Then he stopped. What if we packed up and just skedaddled?

It wouldnt make any difference.

What if we stayed?

What, another eight years of you and your pennydreadful friends?

Nine, Mathgirl.

Nine then.

Why not?

No thank you.

He paced. Slowly rubbing his small scarred head. He looked like he'd been brought into the world with icetongs. He stopped at the window again. You'll miss us, he said. We've come a long way together.

Sure, she said. It's been just wonderful. Look. This is all beside the point. Nobody's going to miss anybody.

We didnt even have to come, you know.

I dont know what you had to do. I'm not conversant with your duties. I never was. And now I dont care.

Yeah. You always did think the worst.

And was seldom disappointed.

Not every ectromelic hallucination who shows up in your boudoir on your birthday is out to get you. We tried to spread a little sunshine in a troubled world. What's wrong with that?

It's not my birthday. And I think we know what it is you've been spreading. Anyway, you're not going to get in my good graces so just forget it.

You dont have any good graces. You're fresh out.

All the better.

The Kid was looking around the room. Jesus, he said. This place really sucks. Did you see what just crossed the floor? What, are we completely out of Zyklon B? You were never exactly Mama's little housekeeper but I think you've outdone yourself here. Time was you wouldnt be caught dead in a dump like this. Are you seeing to your person?

That's none of your business.

One more in a long history of unkempt premises. Yeah, well. You dont know what's in the offing, do you? If you'll pardon the pun. Ever thought about taking the veil? Okay. Just thought I'd ask.

Why dont we just make what amends we can and let the rest go. Dont make it worse than it is.

Yeah yeah sure sure.

You knew this was coming. You like to pretend that I have secrets from you.

You do. Have secrets. Christ it's cold in here. You could hang meat in this fucking place. You called me a spectral operator.

I what?

Called me a spectral operator.

I never called you any such thing. It's a mathematical term.

Yeah. Say you.

You can look it up.

You always say that.

You never do that.

Yeah, well. It's water under the bridge.

Is that what it is? What, you're worried about a low grade on your job report?

Call it what you like, Princess. We did the best we could. The malady lingers on.

That's all right. It wont linger much longer.

Yeah, I keep forgetting. Off to the bourne from whence no traveler whatever the fuck.

You keep forgetting?

Figure of speech. I dont forget much. Of course you dont seem to have all that much in the way of recollection concerning the state we found you in when we first showed up.

I dont have to recollect it. I'm still in it.

Yeah, right. Correct me if I'm wrong but I think I remember a young girl on tiptoes peering through a high aperture infrequently reported upon in the archives. What did she see? A figure at the gate? But that aint the question, is it? The question is did it see her? A small bore of light. Who would notice? But the hounds of hell can pass through the weem of a ring. Am I right or what?

I was fine till you showed up.

Jesus you're a piece of work. Did you know that? Still, I've got to hand it to you. As the trick said to the blind hooker. Hell's own, drooling and leering, and she's trying to look over their shoulder. What's out there? Dunno. Some atavism out of a dead ancestor's psychosis come in out of the rain. Over there smoking in the corner. Well what the hell. Let me get the lights. No good. Shut off the projector. Who the fuck ordered this anyway? Roll up the screen and the fucking things are on the wall. The other thing you called me was a pathogen.

You are a pathogen.

See?

Are they coming in or not?

Is who coming in?

Cut it out. I know they're out there.

The horts, that would be.

That would be.

All in good time.

I can see their feet under the door. I can see the shadows of their feet.

Feet and the shadows of feet. Just like in the real world.

What are they waiting for?

Who knows? Maybe they dont feel welcome.

That never stopped them before.

The Kid arched one mothgnawn eyebrow. Yeah? he said.

Yeah, she said. Pulling the blanket about her shoulders. No one invited you. You just showed up.

Okay, said the Kid. Someone in the hallway, right? Well let's take a look.

He skated to the door in a long glissade and stopped and pushed back his sleeve and gripped the knob with his flipper. Ready? he called. He hauled the door open. The hallway was empty. He looked back over his shoulder at her. Looks like they flew the coop. Unless—how do I put this—it was your imagination?

I know they were there. I can smell them. I can smell Miss Vivian's perfume. And I can certainly smell Grogan.

Yeah? Could just be somebody cooking cabbages down the hall. Anything else? Any sulphur? Brimstone?

He shut the door. Immediately the crowd outside was back. Shuffling and coughing. He rubbed his flippers together. As if to warm them. All right. Where was I? Maybe we should bring you up to date on some of the projects. You might stabilize a bit if you saw some of the progress we've made.

Stabilize?

We ran the stuff we got from you and so far everything looks good.

What stuff you got from me? You didnt get any stuff from me.

Yeah, right. We're still getting one hundred leptons to the drachma which is okay in the sense that it's not really wrong but we hope that most of this classical stuff will come out in the wash and we can get down to the renormal. You're always going to see different shit once you get everything under the light. You just differentiate, that's all. No shadows at this scale of course. You got these black interstices you're looking at. We know now that the continua dont actually continue. That there aint no linear, Laura. However you cook it down it's going to finally come to periodicity. Of course the light wont subtend at this level. Wont reach from shore to shore, in a manner of speaking. So what is it that's in the in-between that you'd like to mess with but cant see because of the aforementioned difficulties? Dunno. What's that you say? Not much help? How come this and how come that? I dont know. How come sheep dont shrink in the rain? We're working without a net here. Where there's no space you cant extrapolate. Where would you go? You send stuff out but you dont know where it's been when you get it back. All right. No need to get your knickers in a twist. You just need to knuckle down and do some by god calculating. That's where you come in. You got stuff here that is maybe just virtual and maybe not but still the rules have got to be in it or you tell me where the fuck are the rules located? Which of course is what we're after, Alice. The blessed be to Jesus rules. You put everything in a jar and then you name the jar and go from there à la the Gödel and Church crowd and in the meantime real stuff which is probably some substrate of the substrate is hauling ass off down the road at deformable speeds with the provision that what has no mass has no volume variant or otherwise and therefore no shape and what cant flatten cant inflate and vice versa in the best commutative tradition and at this point—to borrow a term—we're stuck. Right?

You dont know what you're talking about. It's all gibberish.

Yeah? Well just remember whose hand is on the nandgate Ducky. Because it aint the cradlerocker and it aint the dude in the runic tunic. If you get my drift. Hold it. I got a call. He rummaged in his pockets and produced an enormous phone and clapped it to his small and gnarly ear. Make it quick, Dick. We're in conference. Yeah. A semihostile. Right. Base Two. We're on fucking oxygen up here. No. No. Tough titty. Two wrongs dont make a riot. They're a pack of dimpled fuckwits and you can tell them I said so. Call me back.

He rang off and pushed the antenna down with the heel of his flipper and shoved the phone back into his clothes and looked at her. There's always somebody that doesnt get the word.

Who *doesnt get.*

Right. Back to the charts. I know what you're thinking. But sometimes you just got to go for the equivalence. Run a montecarlo on the motherfucker and be done with it. For better or worse. We aint got till Christmas.

It is Christmas. Almost.

Yeah, well. Whatever. Where was I?

Does it make any difference?

Your number one lab device is going to be the servomechanism. Master and slave. Hook up a pantograph. Put the stylus in the dilemma and rotate. Count to four. Sign to sign. Repeat until the lemniscate appears.

The Kid did a little buck and wing and another long slide across the linoleum and stopped and began to pace again. They're going for the big Kahuna. Boom boom time on the savannah, Hannah.

Plenty of broads in the mix too in spite of all the whining from the sci-fems. I had my people check it out. You got your Madam Curry. Your Pamela Dirac.

Your who?

Not to mention others nameless for the nonce. Jesus will you cheer up? You need to get out more. What was it you said? After the math comes the aftermath? Tell you what. Comic interlude. Okay? Stop me if you've heard this one. Mickey Mouse is filing for divorce and the judge looks down and he says: I understand that it is your contention that your wife Minnie Mouse is mentally deranged. Is that correct? And Mickey says: No, Your Honor, that's not what I said. What I said was she's fucking nuts.

The Kid stomped around the room holding himself at the waist and laughing his yukking laugh.

You always get everything wrong. What are you laughing at?

Whooh, he gasped. What?

You always get everything wrong. It's Goofy. It's not nuts.

What's the difference?

She was fucking Goofy. You dont even get it.

Yeah, well. We got you. Anyway the point is that you need to snap out of it. What do you think? At the last minute little Bobby Shafto is going to wake from the dead and come and rescue you? Silver buckles on his shoes or whatever the fuck? He's out of the loop, Louise. Since he duffeled his head in his racing machine.

She looked away. The Kid shaded his eyes with one flipper. Well, he said. That got her attention.

You dont know what you're talking about.

Yeah? How long's he been snoozing now? A couple of months?

He's still alive.

He's still alive. Oh, well shit. If he's still alive what the hell. Why dont you come off it? We both know why you're not sticking around vis-à-vis the fallen one. Dont we? What's the matter? Cat got your tongue?

I'm going to bed.

It's because we dont know what's going to wake up. If it wakes up. We both know what the chances are of his coming out of this with his mentis intactus and gutsy girl that you are I dont see you being quite so deeply enamored of whatever vestige might still be lurking there behind the clouded eye and the drooling lip. Well what the hell. You never know what's in the cards, do you? You'd probably have wound up back in Chitlinland. Just the two of you. Dining on fatback and harmony grits or whatever the fuck it is that they eat down there in the land of the mammyjammer. Not exactly hobnobbing around Europe with the motorcar set but at least it's quiet.

That's not going to happen.

I know it's not going to happen.

Good.

So where do we go from here?

I'll send you a postcard.

You never did before.

This will be different.

I'll bet. Are you going to call your grandmother?

And tell her what?

I dont know. Something. Jesus, Jasmine. There's lots left to do you know.

Maybe. But not by me.

What about the nightgate and the lair of the unspeakables? Not scared of that?

I'll take my chances. I'm guessing that when I trip the breaker the board goes to black.

We really put ourselves out for you you know.

I'm sorry.

What if I was to tell you stuff I'm not supposed to tell you?

Not interested.

Stuff you really would like to know.

You dont know anything. You just make things up.

Yeah. But some of it's pretty cool.

Some of it.

How about this: What's black and white and red all over?

I cant begin to think.

Trotsky in a tuxedo.

Great.

Okay. How about this one. A farmer finds two boll weevils in his cotton patch.

You told me.

I never.

He chose the lesser of two weevils.

Yeah. Okay. Look. I'm putting together some new acts. I got some of the old Chautauqua stuff lined up. You always had a taste for the classics. A little costume repair. Couple of weeks' rehearsal.

Good night.

I even got a lead on some more eight millimeter. Not to mention a shoebox full of snaps from the forties. Los Alamos stuff. And some letters.

What letters?

Family letters. Letters from your mother.

You're full of it. All the letters were stolen.

Yeah? Maybe. What are you going to do?

Go to sleep.

I mean long range.

I'm talking long range.

All right. Save the best for last. Of course.

Dont put yourself out.

It's all right. It's not like I didnt know where all this was going. Who knows? You might want to see how you'll be spending your time. The past is the future. Close your eyes.

What if I dont want to close my eyes?

Humor me.

Yeah, sure.

All right. We'll do it the oldfashioned way. What do I know? This should be rich.

He pulled a large silk square from somewhere about his person and fluffed it aloft and caught it and stretched it and turned it both sides for her to see. He held it out and shook it. Then he snatched it away. In a canebottomed chair sat an old man in a dusty black clawhammer coat. Striped trousers and gray waistcoat. Black kidskin ankle-

top shoes and moleskin spats with pearlydink buttons. The Kid took a bow and stepped back and looked him up and down. Well. Where did we dig him up at, hey? Yuk yuk yuk.

He slapped the old man on the back and a cloud of dust billowed. The old man bent forward coughing. The Kid stepped away and fanned at the dust with his flipper. Jesus. Been a while since this one's seen the light of day, what? Well, Pops, how's the world look to you? We could use an outside opinion.

The old man raised his head and looked around. Pale and sunken eyes. He adjusted his cravat with a lurching upward motion of the knot and squinted and peered.

That suit's a classic, hey? said the Kid. A bit the worse for the ground damp. He was married in that outfit. Little wifey was sixteen. Of course he'd been banging her for a couple of years so that would put her at fourteen. Finally managed to knock her up and hey, here we all are. The dirty bugger was older than her father. Well the wedding bells did ring summarily. Eighteen and ninety-seven I believe was the year. A formal do. White shotguns. Anyway that's pretty much it. I thought the old fart might have something to say but he seems somewhat confused. Isnt he sort of listing a bit to the starboard?

The Kid straightened the old man in his chair and stepped back and measured him with one eye for verticality. Holding up an oarlike flipper and squinting. Maybe we could use a spirit level, what do you think? Yuk yuk yuk. Well, what the hell. So he's not a bundle of laughs. Wait a minute. It's his teeth. He's missing his goddamned teeth.

The old man had opened his leather mouth and was at pulling wads of stained cotton from his cheeks and stuffing them into the pocket of his coat. He cleared his throat and stared about bleakly.

What's he doing now? said the Kid. Something in his waistcoat pocket. What is that, his watch? Jesus. Dont tell me he's winding it? He's listening to it? It cant be fucking running. Nope. He's shaking it. Nicelooking watch actually. Half Hunter. Deadbeat escapement no doubt. Attaboy. Give it a shake. Nope. Nothing doing.

The old man clacked his gums. Wait for it, said the Kid. It's com-

ing. News from beyond the something. Damned little thanks I get for all this shit I do for you.

Where, wheezed the old man, is the toilet?

The Kid straightened up. What the fuck. Where's the toilet? That's it? I'm a son of a bitch. How about you get your cheesemold ass out of here? Where's the toilet? Bloody Christ. It's down the fucking hall. Just get the fuck out.

The old man rose from his chair and slouched toward the door. A fine dust sifted to the floor behind him. Some small creature fell out of his clothes and scurried away under the bed. He fumbled with the doorknob and got the door open and lurched out into the hallway and was gone. Christ, said the Kid. He went to the door and slapped it shut and turned and leaned against it. He shook his head. Well. What ya gonna do? Bad idea, okay? Fuck it. Some get rained out. Why dont we just bring in a few of the old gang. Maybe cheer us up a bit.

I dont want to bring in some of the old gang. I'm going to bed.

You said that.

Good. Watch me.

Look, Ducklet, I dont want to belabor anything here but you're on fast forward to fuck-all.

And you're here to torment me.

You all right? Not feverish? You want a glass of water?

She curled up in the bed and pulled the covers over herself. Douse the lights when you leave.

The Kid paced. Your name didnt get pulled out of a hat, you know. I dont know what it is that you're supposed to know and what it is you aint. I just work here. I'm an operator? So I'm an operator. And maybe somebody knows what's coming down the pike but it's not yours truly. Come on. I cant talk to you with your head under the bloody covers. You're not even going to say goodbye?

She pushed the covers back. Open the door and I'll wave.

The Kid stepped to the door and opened it. They were all there. Peering in to see, waving, some on tiptoe. Goodbye, she called. Goodbye. The Kid ushered them away with a shooing motion. Like a nun with schoolchildren. He pushed the door shut. Okay, he said.

Are we done now?

I dont know, Sweets. You're not making this easy. I'm not coming with you to the bin you know.

Good.

Concentrated populations of the deranged assume certain powers. It has an unsettling effect. You spend some time in a nuthouse and you'll see.

I know. I have. I did.

Choice is the name you give to what you got.

Stop quoting me.

You dont want to talk to me.

No.

Anything at all here? Any last words of advice for the living?

Yes. Dont.

Jesus. That's cold.

Let's just turn out the lights and call it a life.

We'll miss you.

Will you miss yourself?

We'll be around. There's always work to be done.

He looked a bit slumpshouldered standing there but he roused himself. Okay, he said. If that's it that's it. I can take a hint.

He folded one flipper across his small paunch and made a sort of bow and then he was gone. She pulled the covers over her head. Then she heard the door open again. When she looked the Kid had come in once more and he stepped quietly to the center of the room and hefted the canebottomed chair by one slat and shouldered it and turned and went out and pulled the door shut after him.

She slept and sleeping she dreamt that she was running after a train with her brother running along the cinderpath and in the morning she put that in her letter. We were running after the train Bobby and it was drawing away from us into the night and the lights were dimming away in the darkness and we were stumbling along the track and I wanted to stop but you took my hand and in the dream we knew that we had to keep the train in sight or we would lose it. That following the track would not help us. We were holding hands and we were running and then I woke up and it was day.

He sat wrapped in one of the gray rescue blankets from the emergency bag and drank hot tea. The dark sea lapped about. The Coast Guard boat that had pulled up a hundred yards off sat rocking in the swells with the running lights on and beyond that ten miles to the north you could see the lights of trucks moving along the causeway, coming out of New Orleans and heading east along US 90 toward Pass Christian, Biloxi, Mobile. Mozart's second violin concerto was playing on the tapedeck. The air temperature was forty-four degrees and it was three seventeen in the morning.

The tender was lying on his elbows with the headset on watching the dark water beneath them. From time to time the sea would flare with a soft sulphurous light where forty feet down Oiler was working with the cuttingtorch. Western watched the tender and he blew on the tea and sipped it and he watched the lights moving along the causeway like the slow cellular crawl of waterdrops on a wire. Strobing faintly where they passed behind the concrete balusters. There was an onshore wind coming up past the western tip of Cat Island and there was a light chop to the water. Smell of oil and the rich tidal funk of mangrove and saltgrass from the islands. The tender sat up and took off the headset and began to rifle through the toolbox.

How's he doing?

Doin okay.

What's he want?

The big sidecutters.

He hooked a set of shears to a carabiner and snapped the carabiner over the workline and watched the shears slide into the sea. He looked at Western.

How deep can you use acetylene?

Thirty, thirty-five feet.

And after that it's oxyarc.

Yes.

The tender nodded and pulled the headset back on.

Western drained the last of the tea and shook out the dregs and put the cup back in his bag and reached and got his flippers and pulled them on. He slipped the blanket from his shoulders and stood and zipped up the jacket of his wetsuit and bent and got his tanks and lifted them by the straps and pulled them on. He fastened the straps and pulled on his mask.

The tender slid the headset back. You care if I change stations?

Western lifted the mask up. It's a tape.

You care if I change tapes?

No.

The tender shook his head. Helicopter us out here in the freezing-ass cold at one oclock in the morning. I dont know what the hurry was.

Meaning that they're all dead.

Yeah.

And you know this how?

It just stands to reason.

Western looked out at the Coast Guard boat. The shape of the lights unchained in the chop of the dark water. He looked at the tender. Reason, he said. Right.

He pulled on his gloves. The white beam of the spotlight raced over the water and back again and then went dark. He pulled on his belt and hooked it and fitted the regulator into his mouth and pulled down the mask and stepped into the water.

Dropping slowly through the dark toward the intermittent flare of the torch below. He reached the stabilizer and dropped down onto the fuselage and turned and swam slowly along, tracing the smooth aluminum under his gloved hand. The bead of the rivets. The torch flared again. The shape of the fuselage tunneling off into the dark. He kicked past the hulking nacelles that held the turbofan engines and dropped down the side of the fuselage and into the pool of light.

Oiler had cut away the latching mechanism and the door stood open. He was just inside the plane crouched against the bulkhead. He gestured with his head and Western pulled up in the door and Oiler shone his light down the aircraft aisle. The people sitting in their seats, their hair floating. Their mouths open, their eyes devoid of speculation. The workbasket was sitting on the floor inside the door and Western reached and got the other divelight and pulled himself into the plane.

He kicked his way slowly down the aisle above the seats, his tanks dragging overhead. The faces of the dead inches away. Everything that could float was against the ceiling. Pencils, cushions, styrofoam coffeecups. Sheets of paper with the ink draining off into hieroglyphic smears. A tightening claustrophobia. He doubled under and got himself turned around and made his way back.

Oiler was swimming down the outside of the fuselage with his light. The light made a corolla in the airspace of the double glass. Western went forward and pushed his way into the cockpit.

The copilot was still strapped into his seat but the pilot was hovering overhead against the ceiling with his arms and legs hanging down like an enormous marionette. Western shone his light over the instruments. The twin throttle levers in the console were pulled all the way into the off position. The gauges were analog and when the circuits shorted out in the seawater they'd returned to neutral settings. There was a square space in the panel where one of the avionics boards had been removed. It had been held in place by six screws by the holes there and there were three jackplugs hanging down where the pigtails had been disconnected. Western wedged his knees against the backs of the seats at either side. Good stainless steel Heuer watch on the copilot's wrist. He studied the panels. What's missing? Kollsman altimeters and vertical speed indicators. Fuel in pounds. Airspeed at zero. Collins avionics otherwise. It was the navigation rack. He backed out of the cockpit. The bubbles from the regulator sorted themselves along the dome of the roof overhead. He'd looked in every possible space for the pilot's flightbag and he was pretty sure it wasnt there. He pushed out through the door and looked for Oiler. He was hovering over the wing. He made a circling motion with one hand and pointed upward and kicked off toward the surface.

They sat on the small deck of the inflatable and pulled off their masks and spat out the regulator mouthpieces and leaned back into the tanks and loosened them. Creedence Clearwater was playing on the tapedeck. Western got his thermos out.

What time is it? said Oiler.

Four twelve.

He spat and wiped his nose with the back of his wrist. He leaned past Western and twisted shut the valves on the gas bottles. I hate shit like this, he said.

What, bodies?

Well. That too. But no. Shit that makes no sense. That you cant make sense out of.

Yeah.

There wont be anybody out here for another couple of hours. Or three. What do you want to do?

What do I want to do or what do I think we should do?

I dont know. What do you make of this?

I dont.

Oiler stripped off his gloves and unzipped his divebag and got his thermos out. He took the plastic cup off the bottle and unscrewed the cap and poured the cup and blew on it. The tender was pulling up the workline and the basket.

You cant even see the damn plane. And some fisherman is supposed to of found it? That's bullshit.

You dont think the lights could have stayed on for a while?

No.

Probably right.

Oiler dried his hands on a towel from his bag and got his cigarettes and lighter out and shucked a cigarette from the pack and lit it and sat looking out over the black and lapping water. They're all just sitting in their seats? What the fuck is that?

I'd say they had to be already dead when the plane sank.

Oiler smoked and shook his head. Yeah. And no fuel slick.

There's a panel missing from the instrumentation. And the pilot's flightbag is missing.

Yeah?

You know what this is, dont you?

No. Do you?

Aliens.

Fuck you Western.

Western smiled.

What do you think the range is on one of these things?

The JetStar?

Yes.

Probably a couple of thousand miles. Why?

Because you got to wonder where it was coming from.

Yeah. What else?

I think they've been down there a few days.

Fuck.

They dont look all that well kept. How long does it take for bodies to come up?

I dont know. Two or three days. Depends on the temperature of the water. How many are there?

Seven. Plus the pilot and copilot. Nine in all.

What do you want to do?

Go home and go to bed.

Oiler blew at his cup and sipped his coffee. Yeah, he said.

The tender's name was Campbell. He studied Western and he looked at Oiler. That's got to be some ugly shit down there, he said. That dont bother you?

You want to go down and take a look?

No.

Hell. I'll tend for you. Western'll go with you if you want.

You're shittin me.

I aint shittin you.

Well. I aint goin.

I know you aint. But if you aint seen what we seen maybe you ought not to be so quick about tellin us what we're supposed to think about it.

Campbell looked at Western. Western tilted the leaves in his cup. Hell, Oiler. He didnt mean anything by it.

Sorry. The point is I dont have a story about how that plane got down there. And every time I think about all the things that are wrong the list gets longer.

I agree.

Maybe the good doctor Western here can come up with something like an explanation.

Western shook his head. The good doctor Western dont have a clue.

I dont even know what we're doin out here.

I know. There's nothing about this that rattles right.

So what have we got, two hours till daylight?

Yeah. Hour and a half maybe.

I'm not bringin em up.

I'm not either.

Survivors. What the shit is that?

They sat with their faces shadowed by the lamp, the raft lifting and tilting in the swells. Oiler held out the thermos. You want some of this, Gary?

I'm all right.

Go ahead. It's hot.

All right.

I didnt see any damage at all.

Yeah. It looked like it just left the factory.

Who makes it? The what, JetStar?

JetStar, yeah. Lockheed.

Well. It's a hell of a plane. Four jet engines? How fast will that thing go Bobby?

Western shook out the leaves and screwed the cap back onto his thermos. I think right at six hundred miles an hour.

Damn.

Oiler took a last draw on his cigarette and flipped it spinning into the dark. You've never brought up bodies, have you?

No. I just figured anything that you didnt want to do I'm probably not going to like either.

You bring em up with a rope and harness but you still got to get them out of the plane. They keep wantin to put their arms around you. We brought fifty-three up out of a Douglas airliner off the coast of Florida one time and that did it for me. That was before I went to work for Taylor. They'd been down there a few days and you damn sure didnt want to get any of that water in your mouth. They were all swollen in their clothes and you had to cut them out of their seatbelts. Quick as you did they'd start to rise up with their arms out. Sort of like circus balloons.

These dont look like corporation guys.

Yeah? They got on suits.

I know. But they're not the right kind of suits. Their shoes look European.

Well. I wouldnt know. I aint had on a pair of regular shoes in ten years.

What do you want to do?

Get the hell out of here. We need to take showers.

All right.

What time is it?

Four twenty-six.

Time flies when you're havin fun.

We can hose off on the dock when we get back. Hose out our suits.

I'm goin to be hard to find, Bobby. I aint comin back out here.

All right.

You think there's already been somebody down there, dont you?

I dont know.

Yeah. But that aint an answer. How would they get in the plane? They'd of had to cut their way in the same way we done.

Maybe somebody let them in.

Oiler shook his head. Damn, Western. I dont know why I even talk to you. All you ever do is spook the shit out of me. Gary, you want to fire this thing up?

You got it.

Western tucked his thermos into his divebag. What else? he said.

I'll tell you what else. I think that my desire to remain totally fucking ignorant about shit that will only get me in trouble is both deep and abiding. I'm going to say that it is just damn near a religion.

Gary had gone to the back of the inflatable. Western and Oiler raised the two anchors and Gary stood with one foot on the transom and hauled on the starter rope. The big Johnson outboard started immediately and they burbled along till they were well clear of the orange float and Gary cranked the throttle open and they set out across the dark water toward Pass Christian.

Coming downriver an antique schooner running under bare poles. Black hull, gold plimsoll. Passing under the bridge and down along the gray riverfront. Phantom of grace. Past warehouse and pier, the tall gantry cranes. The rusty Liberian freighters bollarded along the docks on the Algiers shore. A few people along the walkway had stopped to look. Something out of another time. He crossed the tracks and went up Decatur Street to St Louis and walked up Chartres Street. At the Napoleon House the old crowd hailed him from the small tables set out before the door. Familiars out of another life. How many tales begin just so?

Squire Western, called Long John. Up from the murky deeps is it? Come join us for a libation. The sun's over the yardarm if I'm not cruelly mistaken.

He pulled up one of the small bentwood chairs and set his green divebag on the tiles. Bianca Pharaoh leaned and smiled. What have you got in the bag, Precious?

He's off on a trip, said Darling Dave.

Nonsense. The Squire wont abandon us. Waiter.

It's just my gear.

It's just his gear, said Brat to the table at large.

Count Seals turned sleepily. It's his diving gear, he said. He's a diver.

Ooh, said Bianca. I like that so much. Let me see inside. Anything kinky?

The man goes to work in rubber apparel, what do you expect? Here my good fellow. A flagon of your stoutest for my friend.

The waiter moved away. The tourists passed along the walk. Threads of their empty conversation hanging in the air like bits of code. Underfoot the slow periodic thud of a piledriver from somewhere along the riverfront. Western regarded his host. How have you been, John?

I'm well, Squire. I was away for a while. A slight contretemps with the authorities regarding the legitimacy of some medical prescriptions.

He detailed his adventures in an offhand way. Pads of forged prescriptions from a printshop in Morristown Tennessee. Real doctors, but their phone numbers replaced with numbers from payphones in supermarket parkinglots. Girlfriend a few feet away in a parked car. Yes. That's correct. His mother is terminal. Yes. Dilaudids. One hundred sixteenths. Three weeks of this in the small towns of the Appalachian south and then pacing up and back in a room at the Hilltop Motel on Kingston Pike in Knoxville. The room paid for with a stolen credit card. Waiting for the connection. Half a shoebox full of Schedule II narcotics with a street value of over a hundred thousand dollars. He'd stripped out of his clothes in the heat and was pacing naked save for a pair of ostrichskin boots and a widebrimmed black Borsalino. Smoking his last Montecristo. Five oclock came. Then six. Finally a knock at the door. He snatched it open. Where in the hell have you all been? he said. But he was staring down the barrel of a .38 caliber service revolver and there was a backup man off to the side with a pump shotgun. The TBI agent was holding up his badge. Looking up at this tall and totally naked felon. Old buddy, he said, we got here just as quick as we could.

You're out on bail, said Western.

Yes.

I thought you werent supposed to leave the State?

Technically true. But in any case I'm here but for a few days. If that will put your mind at ease. The old town was beginning to wear on me. When they finally sprang me I went home and showered and changed and was on my way down Jackson Avenue to see if I could cadge a drink when I ran into an old girlfriend. Why John, she says, is that you? I havent seen you in ages. Where have you been? And I said: My dear, I have been in durance vile. And she said: Really? You know my sister married a boy from Winston-Salem. And I thought to myself: I really need to get out of this town.

Western smiled. The waiter brought the beer and set it on the table and went away. The long one raised his glass. Salud. They drank. Brat was in conference with Darling Dave. Seeking counsel. In this dream, he said, I climbed through a window and beat this old woman senseless in her bed with a meatmallet. She had these waffle marks on her head.

Dave brushed something unseen from the tabletop. You're reaching out for help, he said.

What?

It may be that your body's not getting something it needs.

It's always about freedom, said Bianca. Lifting all that stuff off of you. Like a parent dying.

Seals roused himself. A bird person he. In his bathroom brooding raptors hooded like hangmen shifted sullenly upon their perches. A saker, a lanneret.

A parrot? he said.

Bianca smiled and patted his knee. I love you, she said.

Various of them looking for work. John gestured with his glass. Brat very nearly secured a position, he said. But of course at the last moment it all came uncottered.

I just blew it, said Brat. Something came over me. This breather kept going on about this policy and that policy. Finally he said: And another thing. Around here we dont watch the clock. And I said well I just cant tell you how happy I am to hear you say those words. I've had a lifelong habit of being up to an hour late for just about everything.

What did he say?

He got sort of quiet. He sat there for a minute and then he got up and left. And it was his office. After a while the secretary came in and she said that the interview was over. I asked her if I'd gotten the job but she said she didnt think so. She looked kind of nervous.

Have you found another place to live?

Not yet.

What about the arson charges?

They dropped them. They found some of the cats.

Cats?

Cats. Yeah. The problem was that the fire had started in about six different places so that looked sort of suspicious to them but then they started finding the cats. It was just a matter of putting two and two together.

The cats knocked over a can of my paint thinner, said Bianca. Then they rolled around in it. Then they all ran up under the heater and caught fire. And then they just ran all over the studio.

Cats.

Kittens. You know. Little cats. She measured a length between her palms. I said why would I set fire to my own apartment? And anyway, we're only renting for God's sake. How are you going to collect on that? I mean anybody should have been able to figure it out that the cats were on fire. What did they think, they were just sitting around waiting for a fire to start so they could throw themselves into the flames? Obviously the cats caught fire first is what started the whole thing. They're just so fucking dumb.

The cats?

No, not the cats. The fucking insurance people.

It was pretty much fun, said Brat. When the bailiff raised his hand to swear her in she reached up and slapped him a big high-five. I dont think they'd seen that before.

I suppose the genetic predisposition must vary with the breeds, said John, but in any case the selfimmolatory tendencies of cats does seem to be a known factor in the feline equation. Noted in the writings of Asclepius, among others of the ancients.

Jesus, said Seals.

It would seem to contradict Unamuno, though. Right, Squire? His dictum that cats reason more than they weep? Of course their very existence according to Rilke is wholly hypothetical.

Cats?

Cats.

Western smiled. He drank. A cool and sunny day in the ancient city. The noon and early winter light soft in the street.

Where is Willy V?

He's set up his easel in Jackson Square. Hopes to peddle his daubings to the tourists of course. He and that mooncolored hound of his.

That thing will bite some tourist in the ass and he'll be in a lawsuit.

Or jail.

Long John had set about unwrapping a large black cigar. He bit the end and spat and rolled the cigar along his tongue and gripped it in his teeth and reached for a match. I had a dream about you, Squire.

A dream you say.

Yes. I dreamt you were wandering in your weighted shoes over the ocean floor. Seeking God knows what in the darkness of those bathypelagic deeps. When you reached the edge of the Nazca Plate there were flames licking up from the abyss. The sea boiling. In my dream it seemed to me you'd stumbled upon the mouth of hell and I thought that you would lower a rope to those of your friends who'd gone before. You didnt.

He ran the match crackling along the underside of the table and fell to enkindling his cigar.

Are you really a diver? said Bianca.

Not the kind you had in mind, Darling, said Dave.

He's every kind of diver you can name, said Seals, struggling partially upright and placing one fist on the table. Every goddamned kind.

I'm a salvage diver, said Western.

What do you salvage?

Whatever we're hired to. Whatever is lost.

Treasure?

No. It's more commercial stuff. Cargoes.

What's the weirdest thing you were ever asked to do?

You mean of a nonsexual nature?

I knew I liked him.

I dont know. I'd have to think about it. Some guys I know raised a bargeload of batshit one time.

Hear that? said Seals. Batshit.

How did you happen to get into this?

Dont go there, my dear, said John. You dont want to know. How he secretly hopes to die in the deep to atone for his sins. And that's only the beginning.

Oh this is getting interesting.

Dont get too excited. You may have noticed a certain reticence in our man. It's true that he does dangerous underwater work for high pay but it's also true that he's afraid of the depths. Well, you say. He has overcome his fears. Not a bit of it. He is sinking into a darkness he cannot even comprehend. Darkness and immobilizing cold. I enjoy talking about him if he does not. I'm sure you'd like to hear the sin and atonement part. That at the very least. He's an attractive man. Women want to save him. But of course he's beyond all that. What say you, Squire? How far off the mark?

Rave on, Sheddan.

I think I'll rest my case. I know what you're thinking. You see in me an ego vast, unstructured, and baseless. But in all candor I've not even the remotest aspirations to the heights of self-regard which the Squire commands. And I'm not unaware that it even lends a certain validity to his views. After all, I'm merely an enemy of society, while he is one of God.

Wow, said Bianca. She turned toward Western with a hungry look. What did you do?

Sheddan's thin cheeks caved as he pulled at the cigar. He blew the scented smoke across the table and smiled. What the Squire has never understood is that forgiveness has a time line. While it's never too late for revenge.

Western drained the last of his beer and set the mug on the table. I've got to go, he said.

Stay, said Sheddan. I take it all back.

I wouldnt dream of it. You know how I enjoy your chatter.

You're not off on one of your overseas jobs are you?

No. I'm on my way home to bed.

Just getting off the graveyard shift is it?

That's pretty much right on the money. I'll see you.

He reached and got his bag and rose and nodded to the assemblage and set off up Bourbon Street with the bag over his shoulder.

I like your friend, said Bianca. Nice ass.

You're digging a dry hole, my dear.

Why? Is he gay?

No. He's in love.

Pity.

It's worse than that.

How so?

He's in love with his sister.

Wow. Is he part of that upriver crowd that shows up here on Sunday mornings?

No. He's from Knoxville. Well, again, it's worse than that. He's actually from Wartburg. Wartburg Tennessee.

Wartburg Tennessee.

Yes.

There is no such place.

I'm afraid there is. It's near Oak Ridge. His father's trade was the design and fabrication of enormous bombs for the purpose of incinerating whole citiesful of innocent people as they slept in their beds. Cleverly conceived and handcrafted things. One-off, each of them. Like vintage Bentleys. Western himself I met at the university. Well, actually the first time I ever saw him was at the Club Fifty-Two out on the Asheville Highway. He was up on the stage playing the mandolin with the band. Bluegrass. I'd never met him but I knew who he was. He was a mathematics major with a four point grade average. Somebody at our table invited him over and we got to talking. I quoted Cioran to him and he quoted Plato back on the same subject. And he had this beautiful sister. I think she was fourteen. And he would take her to these clubs. They were just openly dating. And she was even smarter than he was. And just drop dead gorgeous. A flat out trainwrecker. He got a scholarship to Caltech and he went there and studied physics but he never got his doctorate. He came into some money and went to Europe to race cars.

He drove racecars?

Yes.

What kind?

I dont know. Those little things they race over there. He'd raced dirt-track cars at the Atomic Speedway at Oak Ridge when he was in high school. Apparently he was quite good at it.

He raced Formula Two, said Dave. He was good at it, just not good enough.

Yes. Well. He has a metal plate in his head for his troubles. A metal rod in one leg. That sort of thing. He has a slight limp. Still, it may have been just an ugly piece of luck. I think he was probably a pretty good driver. They're not going to strap you into one of those things if you cant drive, I dont care how much money you have.

Does he still have the money?

I was waiting for you to ask. No. He pissed it all away.

And all the while he's banging his sister.

That's my considered opinion.

I'm surprised you never asked him.

I did ask him.

What did he say?

He didnt take it well. Denied it, of course. He thinks I'm a psychopath and he may well be right. The jury is still out. But he's a textbook narcissist of the closet variety and, again, that modest smile of his masks an ego the size of downtown Cleveland.

He seemed awfully straight to me. I was wondering how this crowd even knew him.

The long one looked at her. Straight? You must be joking.

What else has he done?

What else? God. The man's a seducer of prelates and a suborner of the judiciary. He's an habitual mailcandler and a practicing gelignitionary, a mathematical platonist and a molester of domestic yardfowl. Principally of the dominecker persuasion. A chickenfucker, not to put too fine a point on it.

John?

What.

You're describing yourself.

Me? Not at all. That's nonsense. An eiderduck perhaps. Once.

An eiderduck?

The bridal duck so called. *Somateria mollissima,* I believe.

Jesus.

A minor peccadillo alongside the enormities rightly laid at the door of your man. Dreams haunted by the complaints of poultry. A restlessness in the roost, a squabbling. Then the ensuing wingwhack, the shrieks. It's a sobering thing. Just his daily list of things to do. Pick up cleaning. Call mother. Fuck chickens. I'm surprised to see a woman of the world such as yourself so easily taken in.

He pulled reflectively on his cigar. He shook his head almost in sadness. Still I suppose they might be willing to endure these indignities if it meant being snatched from under the poulterer's boning-knife at the eleventh hour. And of course the question does arise as to whether it's proper to eat them afterwards. Islamic law is quite clear on this point, if I'm not mistaken. That it would indeed be wrong. But your neighbor can eat them. Assuming he's of a mind to. The Western Church I believe is silent on the matter.

You cant be serious.

Couldnt be more in earnest.

Bianca smiled. She sipped her drink. Tell me something, she said.

Of course.

Does Knoxville produce crazy people or does it just attract them?

Interesting question. Nature nurture. Actually the more deranged of them seem to hail from the neighboring hinterlands. Good question though. Let me get back to you on that.

Well he seemed very nice to me.

He is very nice. I'm enormously fond of him.

But he's in love with his sister.

Yes. He is in love with his sister. But of course it gets worse.

Bianca smiled her odd smile and licked her upper lip. Okay. He's in love with his sister and . . . ?

He's in love with his sister and she's dead.

He slept until evening and then got up and showered and dressed and went out. He walked down St Philip Street to the Seven Seas. There was an ambulance parked in the street with the motor running and a couple of police cars at the curb. People standing around.

What happened? said Western.

Some guy croaked.

What happened? Jimmy?

It's Lurch. He took the pipe. They're bringing him down now.

When? Last night?

Dont know. We havent seen him for a day or two.

Harold Harbenger was looking over Jimmy's shoulder. We havent seen him cause he was dead. That's why he wasnt around.

Two medics were bringing the gurney out. They lifted the wheels at the threshold and wheeled Lurch into the street. They'd covered him with a gray rescue squad blanket.

Here he comes and there he goes, said Harold.

He's under there all right, said Jimmy. You can take that to the bank.

We smelled the gas. This morning it was real strong.

He'd taped up all the doors and windows.

He stuffed his socks under the door. You could see em stickin out in the hall. That's what gave the game away.

You didnt think you should check on him?

Fuck him. Live and let live, I say.

There he goes, said Harold.

They loaded the gurney into the back of the ambulance and shut the doors. Western watched them pull away down the street. When he walked into the bar a city detective was talking to Josie.

Was he sort of a quiet person or what?

Quiet? Hell no he wasnt quiet.

Was he a troublemaker?

Josie sucked on her cigarette. She thought about that. Look, she said. I'm not one to speak ill of the dead. You dont know where they might be or whose ear they might have. You follow me? You run a place like this there's always somebody you got to make allowances for. Up all night drunk and hollerin or whatever. And some other stuff I'd as soon not get into. All I can say is that he never done nothin like this before.

The detective wrote that in his book. Did he have any kin that you know of?

I dont know. They always seem to have a sister somewhere.

Western got a beer from Jan and went to the rear of the bar. Red and Oiler came in and got beers and came back. Old Lurch, Oiler said.

You wouldnt take him for the type.

People will fool you.

Western nodded. Wont they though. Did you tell Red about our little job this morning?

Yeah.

I wonder if maybe we shouldnt keep it to ourselves.

Might not be a bad idea.

What about you, Bobby? How long do you think that plane had been in the water?

I dont know. A while. At least a couple of days.

Who's going to do the salvage?

Oiler shook his head. Not us.

By us you mean Taylor's.

Yeah. Lou says they sent the check over by courier.

Who's they?

Dont know.

There must have been a name on the check.

It wasnt a check. It was a money order.

What do you think this is about?

Oiler shook his head.

How could there have been somebody in the plane?

No idea.

Well somebody has got to have the data box. The pilot didnt just throw it out the window.

I dont have an opinion about it. I dont want to have an opinion about it.

Western nodded. It doesnt make any difference. We havent heard the last of it.

Why is that?

You dont think we're going to be asked about this?

I dont know.

Sure you do. Think about it.

He walked out back to the men's room on the patio. When he came back Red had already left and Oiler was sitting at one of the little tables.

Where was he going in such a hurry?

Oiler kicked back the chair. Sit your ass down. He's got a date.

He's got a date?

That's what the man said.

A date.

Yeah. I asked him if he meant he was going to pick up some skank he'd met and go get a blowjob in a parkinglot somewhere. You know what he said?

No. What?

He said yeah. A date.

Western picked up the beer Oiler had brought from the bar. He shook his head. Jesus.

Yeah.

Let me ask you something.

Ask away.

You guys talk about Nam. Or maybe it's Vietnam to an outsider. But when I'm around you shut up. It's like when you walk into a room and everybody stops talking.

I suppose you get that a lot.

I'm serious.

It's just the way it is. If you werent there you werent there. It doesnt make you a bad person.

Red told me once that you won a bunch of medals.

Won.

Wrong word.

I dont know anybody that went to Nam that ever won anything. Other than a wooden overcoat.

What did you get the medals for?

For being stupid.

I'd like to hear about it.

About being stupid.

Come on.

What's the point, Bobby?

You were a gunner on a helicopter.

Yeah. Doorgunner. On a gunship. You cant get much dumber than that. Look, Western. You can make up your own story. You wont be far off.

I doubt that.

You dont even know enough to know what to ask.

What's the most significant thing that has ever happened to you in your life.

In my life.

Yeah.

Okay. Nam. So?

So what's the most significant thing that didnt happen to me.

Christ.

Just tell me anything. Or something. Try and pretend that I'm not just some dumb fuck.

I dont want to have to explain stuff.

You wont have to. I'll pick it up.

All right. Fuck it. We were trying to pick up some guys in an LZ and we took rocket fire and went down and I shot a bunch of gooks but the only guy I got out was me. Well, I got one other guy out but he died anyway. I took a few rounds. That's all. The other guys are still there. Just some bones scattered around in a triple canopy jungle. They damn sure didnt get any medals. What else?

I guess I'd just like to know what it was I missed.

You didnt miss shit.

You know what I mean.

What's the point, Bobby? You were the smart one, not me. And I pulled two tours. And a tour was thirteen months for Marines. That's the sort of thing you do when you're eighteen or nineteen and dumb as a box of hammers.

He picked up his beer and drank and leaned back in the chair and picked at the label with his thumb. He looked at Western.

Go ahead.

Fuck you, Western.

How many times were you wounded?

Anything can be a fucking wound. I got shot five times. How's that for dumb? Wouldnt you think two or three would be enough? You ought to be able to figure out by then that it probably wasnt good for you. There were guys that just simply walked out of the war. You never hear about them. I dont know how many of them made it. Some guys walked out through Laos to Thailand. I know one guy walked to Germany.

To Germany?

Yeah. A buddy of mine got a letter from him. He's still there. As far as I know.

Like I wasnt some dumb fuck. All right?

All right. They had a radar-controlled cannon in the triborder area and we sailed through there like we didnt have a fucking care in the world. The first round came through the front of the gunship and exploded in the pilot's chest. The second round took out the main rotor. Very quiet all of a sudden. Just some grinding noises. The motor had already shut down. I remember thinking as we started down, well you knew this shit was coming and now here it is and you dont have to worry about it anymore. And then I realized we were taking fire from the side of this hill and I looked over at Williamson and he was just hanging in the straps and about that time an RPG came through the tail of the ship and carried that off and I picked up a bunch of metal fragments and I'm unloading this beltfed M60 with a hundred-round belt but we're wobbling around and half the time I'm just firing at blue sky. I finally quit because the barrel was getting red and I knew it was about to jam and by now we're dropping like a fucking rock. The copilot was still alive and I looked over at him he had his sidearm out and was chambering a round. And then we hit the canopy.

As in jungle canopy.

Yeah. We hit pretty hard but we were all right. We broke down through all that shit and finally came to a stop about eight feet off the ground. I pulled myself up to the cockpit and asked the lieutenant if he thought he could walk and he said he was damn sure going to give it a try and for me to get him out of there. So I pushed the release on his belt and dragged him down to the door and rolled him out. He just disappeared through a bunch of grass and I got my ammo vest and my weapon and went out after him. Spooky quiet. When I got to the lieutenant he still had hold of his .45 and he looked a little pissed off but I thought that was probably a good thing. He had a lot of blood on him but I figured most of it probably belonged to the captain and I got him up and we went hobbling off through the jungle. And we did that for three days until we finally got picked up at an LZ. Just dumbassed luck. There were gooks everywhere and we never even fired a shot. We got picked up by this Huey and we got back to base and they loaded the lieutenant onto a stretcher and put a blanket over him. He was a ballsy guy. Probably younger than me. Or as young, anyway. I knew he was in a lot of pain. He looked up at me and he said: You're one good motherfucker. He got rotated stateside and I never saw him again.

You werent hurt.

They picked a bunch of metal fragments out of me from where the RPG took out the back of the gunship. I hadnt eaten in three days but I wasnt even hungry. All I wanted to do was sleep. About a week later I went on R and R and three weeks after that I was back in an AC-130 all strapped in and ready to die all over again.

Did you kill a lot of people?

Jesus.

Western waited. Oiler shook his head. You go to war you're not really mad at anybody. You're just trying to keep alive long enough to learn how to stay that way. It's only when you start to see a few of your buddies get wasted that you really get a hard-on for those sons of bitches. The reason I signed up for a second tour was to try and get even. That's all. Nothing complicated about it. Well. Not really all, I guess.

What's the rest of it?

You get a taste for it. People dont want to hear that. Too bad. I thought our outfit was pretty much a bunch of pussies and then we got a new CO. Wingate. Lieutenant Colonel. And he started kicking ass and taking names. Day one. Everybody knew the war was shit. By late '68 the whole thing was sliding off into the toilet. Drugs used to be just at the rear but by then they were pretty much everywhere. Guys shooting civilians. You got a new platoon leader and the first thing you had to decide was whether or not you were going to have to frag his fucking ass to save your own. The real problem was you couldnt get to the field grades. Cocksuckers hanging medals on each other for engagements they couldnt find on a fieldmap. I got back to headquarters and it took them a few days to get me reassigned. Which was fucked up. They never got it that you wanted to be with your buddies. You didnt want to be moved around. Just dumb as shit. I'd made E-6 by then so they couldnt have me mopping floors. But the colonel used to have me run errands for him. Then one day I heard him on the phone and I found out later that he was talking to a bird colonel up in operations and he told this guy that he didnt give a fuck. He said let me tell you something, Colonel. I'm here to kill people. And if I dont get to kill people I'm going to be a hard motherfucker to live with. And if you're not here to kill people you need to let me know. Because I dont want to work for you. And then he hung the phone up. And I knew that he was my kind of guy. He was a warmongering motherfucker. And I was there to inflict painful death myself and that's the only reason I was there. And you wont like this either. Did I kill a lot of people? I been asked that question a few times. But never before by a man. I told this one girl I was seeing that yes I had killed a bunch of gooks but that I hadnt eaten any of them. So what do you think? You had enough of this shit?

Go ahead.

I used to go up every afternoon to the patch-em-up. You couldnt make any sense out of the ward there. It was just a big plywood room with a bunch of sawhorses. No beds. They brought the litters in and set them on the sawhorses. That was it. I saw it full a few times. Like something out of the Civil War. One nurse told me that the guys who stepped on land mines you would think they would bleed to death with their legs blown off like that but that the blast cauterized the stumps. That's handy, aint it? I'd lay on a table with just a towel over me while she picked pieces of aluminum out of me. Or steel. She was a damn goodlooking girl and I knew she didnt mind seeing me walk in there. I was a bufflooking motherfucker. But she was an officer and I knew that wasnt going anywhere. I asked her one time if she ever felt like calling me anything other than by my paygrade and she almost smiled but she didnt.

What did she say?

She didnt say anything. She'd seen so many of me it didnt even compute.

Did it hurt?

Pulling chunks of metal out of my ass with a pair of longnose pliers?

Yes.

Well. You would of had to of seen her. I'm going to say that it felt just about right.

Western smiled.

Anyway, mostly I just slept my ass off. There was a psyops soundship would show up about three oclock in the morning, just oaring away out there in the dark. Broadcasting the sound of a baby crying. Over and over. They knew that we werent going to send anybody up about that. If you shot it down it would probably just fall on you. After a while I got to where I kind of liked it. I'd just drift off back to sleep.

He looked toward the bar and held up two fingers and after a few minutes Paula brought over a couple of beers. Oiler held his beer up to the light and studied it. I can tell you this shit. But it's not going to mean anything. I'm not even sure what it means to me. If I think about things that I just dont want to know about they're all things that I do know about. And I'll always know them. Too fucking bad. Somebody next to you takes a round and it sounds like it's hitting mud. Well. It is. You could have gone your whole life without knowing that. But there you are. You know every day that you're someplace that you aint supposed to be. But there your young ass is.

Rich boys went to college and poor boys went to war.

Yeah, well. I didnt really think like that.

Tell me about where you shot a bunch of gooks.

I shot a bunch of gooks.

You were in another helicopter crash.

I was never in one that didnt crash.

Is that true?

Yeah. That's true. In this case we got called into an LZ where a Huey had been shot down going in. There were four guys in there that they were supposed to bring out. Lurps. You wouldnt think they'd of got theirselves into such a fucking mess. Two of them had stepped on punji sticks. We didnt make out much better than the Huey. Well, as it turned out we did make out a bit better because the Huey pulled up and wobbled off into the jungle and crashed and caught fire. We never saw any of those guys again. We found out later that there was a slick coming in behind us but when they saw all this mess they just pulled up. Smart guys. We'd had to dump a bunch of fuel for the weight in order to load our guys and I kept thinking what if something hot comes in here? Anyway, the tail hit the tops of the trees first and we nosed down. Rotors whacking the shit out of everything. The other doorgunner was a guy we called Wasatch and I jumped out and he just kept on firing and the ship was tipped sideways and one of these hot shellcasings went down the back of my flightsuit and it hurt like a motherfucker. What followed was four days in the jungle and a bunch of running firefights and I came out of there with only one guy left and he died in the chopper going out. You get a fucking medal for that? Gimme a break. That's it, Bobby, I'm done.

What's the most scared you ever were.

I was scared all the time.

The most.

I think the most worthless feeling was when you were being shot at by something really bad. In the air that would be SAMs. You took one of those your only hope was reincarnation.

Did you get fired on by them? SAMs. Missiles. Right?

Yeah. They came at you in pairs. The captain jerked the ship over and we went down damn near into the canopy. That's it.

What else.

Jesus.

What else.

We had a 106 recoilless rifle home in on our base. We figured the thing was about two miles out. After the first round hit we just started running. Complete evacuation. Even the FNGs knew what that fucking thing was. That's it.

What do you regret? Can I ask you that?

Regret.

Yes.

All of it.

How about some of it.

All right. The elephants.

The elephants?

Yeah. The fucking elephants.

I dont understand.

Where we flew out of Quang Nam we'd see these elephants in the clearings and the bulls would back off and raise their trunks and challenge us. Think about that. That's pretty fucking bold. They didnt know what we were. But they were taking care of the old lady. The kids. And here we come along in this gunship armed with these 2.75 rockets. You couldnt fire them too close because the rocket had to travel a certain distance in order to arm itself. To arm the warhead. They werent even all that accurate. Sometimes the fins wouldnt open right and they'd go wobbling off like a goddamned balloon. They could go anywhere. So maybe we thought what the fuck. They've got a chance. But we never missed. And it would just blow them up. They'd just fucking explode. I think about that, man. They hadnt done anything. And who were they going to see about it? So that's what I think about. That's what I regret. All right?

He didnt know that he'd be asked so quickly. He walked back through the Quarter. Past Jackson Square. The Cabildo. The rich moss and cellar smell of the city thick on the night air. A cold and skullcolored moon driving through the skeins of cloud beyond the roofslates. The tiles and chimneypots. A ship's horn on the river. The streetlamps stood in globes of vapor and the buildings were dark and sweating. At times the city seemed older than Nineveh. He crossed the street and turned up past the Blacksmith Shop. He unlocked the gate and entered the patio.

There were two men standing outside his door. He stopped. If they could get inside the gate they could get inside his apartment. Then he realized that they had been inside his apartment.

Mr Western?

Yes.

I wonder if we could have a word with you?

Who are you?

They reached into their coat pockets and produced leather fobs with badges and put them away again. Maybe we could go in and talk for a minute.

Vault the gate. Run away.

Mr Western?

Sure. Okay.

He put the key in the lock and turned the deadbolt and pushed open the door and turned on the light. The apartment was a single room with a small kitchen and a bath. The bed folded up into the wall but he always left it down. There was a sofa and an orange rug and a coffeetable piled with books. He held the door for them.

You didnt let my cat out did you?

Sir?

Come in.

They entered with a studied deference. He shut the door and then knelt and looked under the bed. The cat was crouched against the wall. It whined softly.

You hang on, Billy Ray. We'll eat in a minute.

He rose and gestured toward the sofa. Have a seat, he said.

I have to say that you dont seem particularly surprised to see us.

Should I be?

It's just an observation.

Of course. Would you like some tea?

No thank you.

Sit down. Let me just put the kettle on.

He went into the kitchen and lit the gas burner and filled the kettle from the tap and set it on the burner. When he came back they were sitting on the sofa one at either end. He sat on the bed and took off his shoes and dropped them over the side and pulled his legs up under him and sat looking at them.

Mr Western we'd like to ask you about the dive you were on this morning.

Go ahead.

Just a few questions.

Sure.

The other man leaned forward and put his hands on the edge of the coffeetable, one folded over the other. He patted the lower with the upper a few times and looked up. Actually we dont have a lot of questions. Just one pretty goodsized one.

All right.

There seems to be a passenger missing.

A passenger.

Yes.

Missing.

Yes.

They watched him. He'd no idea what they wanted. Do you have any identification? he said.

We showed you our identification.

Maybe I could see them again.

They looked at each other and then leaned and produced the badges and held them out.

You can write down the numbers if you like.

That's okay.

You can write them down. We dont mind.

I dont have to write them down.

They werent sure what he meant. They flipped the badges up and folded them away.

Mr Western?

Yes.

How many passengers were in the aircraft?

Seven.

Seven.

Yes.

You mean plus the pilot and copilot.

Yes.

Nine bodies.

Yes.

Well apparently there should have been eight passengers.

Somebody missed the flight.

We dont think so. There were eight passengers on the manifest.

What manifest is that?

The manifest for the flight.

Why would there be a manifest?

Why wouldnt there be?

It was a private aircraft.

It was a charter.

If it was a charter there would have been a stewardess.

They looked at each other.

Why is that, Mr Western?

FAA regulations require a stewardess on all commercial flights of more than seven passengers.

But there werent more than seven passengers.

You just said that there were eight.

They sat looking at him. The one with his hands on the table leaned back. How do you happen to know that? he said.

About the stewardess?

Yes.

I dont know. I read it somewhere.

Do you remember everything you read?

Pretty much. Excuse me. Let me get my tea.

He went into the kitchen and took down the tea cannister and spooned the dark chopped tea into a halflitre lab-beaker and poured in the hot water and set the kettle back on the stove and turned off the burner and came back and sat on the bed again. They didnt appear to have moved. The one who had been speaking nodded. All right, he said. Maybe manifest is not the right word. What we have is a list of the passengers from the corporation.

You may have a list. I dont think there's a corporation.

Any why is that?

I dont think it was a corporate flight.

You seem to have a lot of opinions about the flight.

I dont think so. I have questions about the flight. The same as you.

Would you like to share them with us?

Or maybe I have just one pretty goodsized question.

Go ahead.

Could I see those badges one more time?

Excuse me?

I'm just pulling your chain. Sorry.

All right.

We thought that the aircraft had been in the water a while. And we didnt think it was called in by some fisherman. You couldnt even see it. And we think that there is a somewhat better than zero probability that somebody had been in the plane before us.

Some other diver.

Some other somebody.

Well it would have to be a diver wouldnt it?

Would it?

You thought someone had been in the plane before you.

That's what we thought.

Before you and your partner.

Yes.

Of course if you'd taken something from the plane it would make sense for you to claim that you were not the first people there.

How many salvage divers do you know?

They looked at each other.

Why do you ask?

Just curious. We dont take things from planes.

Maybe you could tell us a little about what you found when you reached the site.

Sure. The plane was sitting in about forty feet of water. It looked pretty much intact. When we put the divelight through the window we could see the passengers inside sitting in their seats. We just had the one tender and he was pretty new on the job so I went back up and left Oiler to get into the plane.

And how did he get into the plane?

He cut out the doorlatch with a torch.

The plane was intact.

Yes.

There was no breakup on impact.

We didnt see much sign of an impact. The plane was sitting on the floor of the bay. It didnt even look like there was anything much wrong with it.

There wasnt anything wrong with it.

Not that we could see. Other than the fact that it was in the water.

After your partner entered the plane, did you dive again?

Yes. We didnt spend a lot of time in the plane. We'd been dropped out there to see if there were any survivors. There werent.

Has anyone been in contact with you concerning this incident?

No. Are you sure you wont have some tea?

We're sure.

Is that a regulation?

Is what a regulation?

Nothing. I'll be right back.

He went into the kitchen and got out the icetray and filled a large green glass with icecubes and poured in the tea through a colander. Then he stood looking at the leaves in the colander. Who are you guys? he said. He went back and sat on the bed and took a drink of the cold tea and waited.

Have you ever salvaged an aircraft?

Yes. One time.

Where was this?

Off the coast of South Carolina.

Were there bodies in the aircraft?

No. I think there were four or five people aboard but the plane had broken up. They found a couple of bodies washed ashore a few days later. I dont think they ever found the others.

Do you fly Mr Western?

No. Not anymore.

When was this? The South Carolina thing.

Two years ago.

Are you familiar with the JetStar aircraft?

No. That's the first one I'd ever seen.

Nice aircraft.

Very nice aircraft.

Did you guys open the luggage bay?

Why would we do that?

I dont know. Did you?

No.

Do you know what a Jepp case is?

Yes. We dont have it.

But it was missing.

It was missing. Yes. That and the black box. The data box.

You didnt think that was worth mentioning?

I didnt think it worth mentioning something that you already knew. Why dont you tell me what your interest is in this, what you think has happened. What you know.

We're not at liberty to do that.

Of course.

But you didnt take anything from the aircraft.

No. We dont take things. Oiler said we should get out of the water and that's what we did. The water was full of dead bodies. We didnt know how long they'd been dead or what they'd died of. We didnt take the Jepp case. We didnt take the data box. We didnt take the luggage. And we damn sure didnt take any bodies.

Are you bonded, Mr Western?

Yes.

Is there anything else that you'd like to tell us?

We're salvage divers. We do what we're paid to do. Anyway, I'm sure you know more about this than I do.

All right. Thank you for your time.

They rose from the couch simultaneously. Like birds leaving a wire. Western eased himself from the bed.

Maybe I really should look at those badges again.

You have a peculiar sense of humor, Mr Western.

I know. I get that a lot.

When they were gone he closed the door and knelt and reached one hand up under the bed and talked to the cat until he could get hold of it. He rose and stood with it in the crook of his arm stroking it. A solid black tomcat with teeth outside. Its tail twitched from side to side. He was well disposed toward cats. They to him. Where is your dish? he said. Where is your dish? He carried the cat to the door and stood in the doorway. The air was cool and damp. He stood there stroking the cat. Listening to the quiet. Under his sockfeet he could feel the dull hammer of the distant piledriver. The slow beat. The measure of it.

II

She said that the hallucinations had begun when she was twelve. At the onset of menses, she said, quoting from the literature. Watching them write on their pads. Reality didnt really much seem to be their subject and they would listen to her comments and then move on. That the search for its definition was inexorably buried in and subject to the definition it sought. Or that the world's reality could not be a category among others therein contained. In any case she never referred to them as hallucinations. And she never met a doctor who had the least notion of the meaning of number.

This then would be in the little room under the eaves of her grandmother's house in Tennessee in the early winter of nineteen sixty-three. She woke early in the morning on that cold day to find them assembled at the foot of her bed. She didnt know how long they'd been there. Or if the question itself had any meaning. The Kid was sitting at her desk going through her papers and making notes in a small black notebook. When he saw she was awake he put the notebook away somewhere in his clothes and turned. All right, he said. Looks like she's awake. Good-O. He rose and began to pace back and forth with his flippers behind his back.

What were you doing going through my papers? And what were you writing in that book?

One question at a time, Princess. All in due course. Book: Book of Hours, Book of Yores. Okay? We got a certain amount of ground to cover so we need to get going. There could be a quiz on the qualia so keep that in mind. True false on the interalia, four wrong and we fail ya. And no multiple choice on the multiple choice either. Pick one and move on.

He turned and eyed her and then continued to pace. He paid no attention to the other entities. A matched pair of dwarves in little suits with purple cravats and homburg hats. An ageing lady in pancake makeup smeared with rouge. Antique dress of black voile, graying lace at throat and cuffs. About her neck she wore a stole assembled out of dead stoats flat as roadkill with black glass eyes and brocade noses. She raised a jeweled lorgnette to her eye and peered at the girl from behind her ratty veil. Other figures in the background. A rattle of chains in the far corner of the room where a pair of leashed animals of uncertain taxon rose and circled and lay down again. A light rustling, a cough. As in a theatre when the houselights dim. She clutched the covers up under her chin. Who are you? she said.

Right, said the Kid, pausing to make an encouraging gesture with one flipper. We'll get into the core questions as we go so no need for twisted knickers on that score at this juncture. All right. Any other questions?

The left dwarf raised a hand.

Not you, fuckhead. Jesus. Are you trying to give me gas? All right. If there are no further questions we're going to kick this thing off. Got some great acts lined up. If anything gets too spicy for your taste feel free to make a note of it and then fold the paper longwise and stick it where the sun dont shine. All right.

He traipsed over and sat in her chair again. They waited.

Excuse me, she said.

The question period is over Olivia so no more questions period. All right? He hauled a large watch from somewhere about his person and pressed the button. The cover sprang open and a few bars of music tinkled feebly and ceased. He closed it and put it away. He folded his flippers and sat tapping one foot. Christ on a crutch, he muttered. It's like pulling fucking teeth around here. He raised one flipper to the side of his mouth. Places, he called.

The closet door flew open and a small benchjumper in a plaid hat and reachmedown breeks sprang into the room clapping his hands.

He leapt onto the cedarchest. He had a smile painted onto his face and his waist was hung with tinware and he did a little clanking dance and held up a pair of pans by their handles.

Jesus, said the Kid, rising and coming forward. God's bleeding piles. No no no no no. For the love of Christ. What the fuck do you think this is? You cant come in here hawking this crap. We ask for straightforward acts and we get some fucking tinker minus his fore-lobes? Good God. Out. Out. Jesus. All right. Who's next? Christ. Where do you have to go for a little talent? To the fucking moon?

He stood flipping through his notebook. Whadda we got? Punch and Judy? Ferretleggers? Animal acts of a suggestive nature? Well, what the fuck. Bring it on.

Excuse me, she said.

What is it now?

Who are you?

The Kid raised his eyebrows and looked at the others. You get that, people? Pretty rich. All right, listen up. This is pretty much the sort of thing you can expect so if you're standing around waiting for anything like a little gratitude you might as well make yourselves comfortable. Okay? Okay. Whadda we got. Yeah, this is good. We know this guy. Let's do it.

A small man in a shrunken suit and a stained white shirt with a green tie twisted around his neck shuffled from the closet and began to recite in a dull monotone: You got your classical clockworks to tote up. The timelets in your seanet. Let everything drain. You may have to hang the hydrocephalics from the rafters overhead but that's okay. Dont worry about the floor. Everything will dry. The thing we're really talking about is the situation of the soul.

Saturation, said the Kid.

Saturation of the soul. The wood is old and a bit dry and there may be some creaking. A light drift of wood-dust is normal. Dont become noxious.

Anxious.

Dont become anxious. Try not to get worked up. A word to the wise. Bird in hand.

Bird in hand?

A stitch in time. We're not out of the woods.

What the fuck. Where's it say that?

Penny wise and pound foolish. Honesty is the best policy.

Jesus. Enough already. Where's he getting this shit? Will someone get his dippy ass out of here? Where's the hook?

Excuse me.

He looked at the girl in the bed. She was actually holding up her hand. What, for God's sake?

I want to know what you're doing here.

The Kid rolled his eyes upward. He looked at the other entities and shook his head. He turned to the girl. Look, Presh. At bottom it's pretty much about structure. Something not all that thick on the ground around here, I think even you might agree. But you cant do anything until you lift the mood. Get everybody together. A little comity. Okay? We're trying for a baseline. Otherwise it all starts to unravel. You got to use your best judgment. Work with the materials at hand. There's a number of ugly scenarios here. Like what? Chalk outline? That's easy. Nothing to be done. But you been peekin under the door, Doris, and we dont have much of a file on that. So if you get the impression from time to time that we're sort of winging it here so be it. The first thing is to locate the narrative line. It doesnt have to hold up in court. Start splicing in your episodics. Your anecdotals. You'll figure it out. Just remember that where there's no linear there's no delineation. Try and stay focused. Nobody's asking you to sign anything, okay? And anyway it's not like you got a lot of fallback positions.

He turned to the others and gestured at her over his shoulder with one flipper. Birdtits here imagines she's got friends out there to fend away the inclemencies but she'll get over that soon enough. All right. Let's take a look. See what we got.

He went over and sat in the chair again. We're ready, he called. They waited. Anytime, said the Kid. Jesus. What do we need here? A fucking megaphone? Places.

Two blackface minstrels in overalls and straw hats came flapping out in enormous yellow shoes. They carried stools and a banjo. The stools were painted in red white and blue stripes with gold stars. The minstrels doffed their hats and put the stools down at either side of the room and sat. The interlocutor appeared behind them. His top hat and tails dusty from the road. He flicked his cane and smiled and bowed. The Kid leaned back in his chair and looked about with satisfaction. All right, he said. This is more like it.

Mister Bones, called the interlocutor. What do we have on the program for this evening?

Wellsuh Mistah Interlocutor we goin to do the menstrual dance for Miss Ann heah. We fixin to do the drylongso shuffle and we goin to dance the weevily wheat till the housecats take to the barn. And we got tapdancin on the menu so dont nobody leave early. You all fixin to see some genuine close to the floor work. Then we goin to have some repartee that Miss Ann can play the whole thing back on her stereo and while away the lonely evenins. Aint that right Miss Ann?

The Kid leaned back in his chair and put one flipper to the side of his mouth. Say that's right, he whispered hoarsely.

My name's not Ann.

Mistah Bones you ready to pick that thing?

Yassuh yassuh, called Bones. He sprang up and began to play the banjo. His eyes were blue and his strawcolored hair showed from under the brim of his hat. The two of them fell into step and danced sideways across the room and back.

Mister Bones, called the interlocutor.

Yassuh Mistah Interlocutor.

Papa mole comes along tunneling under the garden and he sniffs and he says: I smell rutabagas. And Mama mole comes along behind him and she sniffs and she says: I smell turnips. And Baby mole comes along and sniffs and what does Baby mole say he smells?

He say he dont smell nothin but molasses.

They fell over themselves hooting and guffawing. The entities chortled and the Kid grinned and took out his notebook and wrote in it and put it away again.

Mister Bones.

Yassuh Mistah Interlocutor.

What did Rastus say to Miss Liza when the tailboard fell off her wagon?

Say: Miss Liza, you want yo tailboard?

And what did Miss Liza say?

She say: Rastus you mindreadin fool get in this wagon.

They stomped around the room hooting and slapping themselves.

Excuse me, she said.

The Kid leaned back and looked at her. What is it now?

Those are the corniest most awful jokes I ever heard.

Yeah? So why is everybody laughing? What are you, a critic of some kind? Jesus.

I've no idea why they're laughing.

The Kid rolled his eyes toward the ceiling. He turned to his cohorts. All right. Take ten, people.

I want to know where you came from, she said.

You mean some place we were before we were here?

Yes.

The cohorts moved slightly closer. As if to hear. All right, said the Kid. Anyone want to take that?

It's a simple question.

Yeah, right.

How did you get here?

We came on the bus.

You came on the bus.

Yeah.

You didnt come on the bus.

We didnt? Well pardon me all to hell.

No. You didnt.

Why not?

You didnt come on the bus. How could you come on the bus?

Christ, Clarissa. The driver opens the door and you climb aboard. How hard is that?

Were there other people on the bus?

Sure. Why not?

And no one said anything?

Like what?

You didnt get any funny looks?

Funny looks.

Could they see you?

The other passengers?

Yes.

Who knows? Jesus. Probably some could and some couldnt. Some could but wouldnt. Where's this going?

Well what kind of passenger can see you?

How did we get stuck on this passenger thing?

I just want to know.

Ask me again.

What kind of passenger is it that can see you.

I think I know what we've got here. Okay. What kind of passenger?

The Kid stuck what would have been his thumbs in his earholes and waggled his flippers and rolled his eyes and went blabble abble abble. She put one hand over her mouth.

I'm just jacking with you. I dont know what kind of passenger. Jesus. People will look at you and they look surprised, that's all. You know they're looking at you.

What do they say?

They dont say anything. What would they say?

Who do they think you are?

Who do they think we are? I dont know. Christ. I guess they think I'm a passenger. Of course you could make the case that if they're passengers then I must be something else. But maybe not. I cant speak for them. Maybe they just see a small but pleasant fellow. Of no determinate age. Receding hairline.

Receding hairline?

The Kid rubbed his pale keloidal skull. What's wrong with that?

You dont have any hair to recede is what. I just want to know where you come from and why you're here.

It's all the same question. I thought we'd just been through this?

You're in my room.

So are you. That's why we're here. What room did you think we should be in? If we were in some other room we wouldnt be here at all. Look, we've got a certain amount of ground to cover and we're losing the light so if it's all the same to you can we just move it along?

It's not all the same to me.

The question is always going to be the same question. We're talking infinite degrees of freedom here so you can always rotate it and make it look different but it aint different. It's the same. It's going to keep coming up like a bad lunch. I know you're in the inquiry business but this is a little bit different. You're supposed to be this girl genius so maybe you'll figure it out before we all fucking faint from tedium.

She sat with her hands folded and pressed to her lips.

That's it? said the Kid.

No.

The Kid shook his head wearily. Yeah, well, he said. He dredged up his watch and opened it and checked the time and put the watch away again. He yawned and patted his mouth with one flipper. Look, he said. Let me put it to you this way. As the vicar said to the choirboy. To the seasoned traveler a destination is at best a rumor.

I wrote that. It's in my diary.

Good for you. When you carry a child in your arms it will turn its head to see where it's going. Not sure why. It's going there anyway. You just need to grab your best hold, that's all. You think there's these rules about who gets to ride the bus and who gets to be here and who gets to be there. How did you get here? Well, she just rode in on her lunarcycle. I see you looking for tracks in the carpet but if we can be here at all we can leave tracks. Or not. The real issue is that every line is a broken line. You retrace your steps and nothing is familiar. So you turn around to come back only now you've got the same problem going the other way. Every worldline is discrete and the caesura ford a void that is bottomless. Every step traverses death.

He turned in his chair and clapped his flippers. All right, he called. Places.

He walked down to the French Market in the morning and got the paper and sat on the terrace in the cool sun and drank hot coffee with milk. He thumbed through the paper. Nothing about the JetStar. He finished his coffee and stepped into the street and hailed a cab and went down to Belle Chasse and walked into the little operations room. Lou was sitting at his desk pulling at the handle of an oldfashioned adding machine. What do you want? he said.

I need to talk to you.

You are talking to me.

He sat down at the other side of the desk. Lou was scribbling on a pad. He looked up at Western. Can you tell me why they have such a thing as a long ton?

No.

I thought you were supposed to know everything.

I dont. What do you know about this airplane?

Lou scrolled the tape up through his fingers and studied it. That's fucked up, he said. What airplane?

Dont jack with me.

Western, what would I know? Stuff dribbles down from the front office. Who the fuck knows? Apparently a courier showed up here with a check and that was that.

No way to know who the check was from.

Apparently not.

Did you know there's nothing in the papers about it?

I dont read the papers.

You dont think that's odd?

That I dont read the papers?

Why would a planecrash not be in the papers? Nine people dead.

Maybe it'll be in tomorrow.

I dont think so.

Let me ask you a question.

Go ahead.

What the fuck do you care? Did you see any laws being broken?

No.

Because that's Taylor's policy. Halliburton policy, for that matter. If it looks wrong we walk.

Yeah, well it looks wrong.

So? We're out of it. Forget it.

All right. What time do you have?

What time do you?

Ten o six.

Lou rotated his wrist and looked at his watch. Ten o four.

I need to go. If you hear anything more about the mystery flight let me know.

My guess is that we've heard the last of it.

Maybe. Can I borrow a vehicle?

There's nothing out there but the boomtruck.

Can I take that?

Yeah, sure. When are you bringing it back?

I dont know. In the morning.

You got a hot date?

Yeah. Are the keys in it?

Unless somebody's carried them off. Dont bring it back empty.

All right. You dont have a pair of binoculars do you?

Jesus, Western. What else?

He opened the bottom desk drawer and took out an old pair of olive-drab army binoculars and stood them on the desk.

Thanks.

Red says that thing is actually great for picking up chicks.

The kind he picks up I wouldnt doubt it.

•

He drove to Gretna and took the highway north and then turned off on the road heading east to Bay St Louis to Pass Christian. On the far side of the bridge lay the marshlands at the lower end of Pontchartrain. Two graylooking Cajun boys with cigarettes hanging from their lips held their thumbs out in a desultory manner. One standing, one squatting. He watched them draw away in the rearview mirror. The one standing turned lazily and raised a finger after him. When he looked back again they were both of them squatting on their heels. Staring at the road where it lay motionless before them in the morning sun.

The truck had a top speed of about sixty. A faint blue haze of motorsmoke seeped up through the floorboards and he drove with the windows down. He scanned the marshes for birdlife but there wasnt much out there. A few ducks. On the far side of the Pearl River a dead otter in the road.

He drove into Pass Christian and down to the docks where he parked the truck and asked around about a boat. He wound up with a sixteen foot lapstrake skiff with a round hull and a twenty-five horsepower Mercury outboard. When he pulled out of the estuary it was almost one oclock.

Out in the bay he twisted the throttle open. The slap of the waves under the hull leveled out, the sun danced off the water. No horizon out there but only the whiteout of sea and sky. A thin line of pelicans laboring up the coast. The salt air was cool and he zipped up his jacket against the wind.

He'd slung Lou's binoculars around his neck by their strap and he raised them and scanned the open water. No sign of the Coast Guard boat. When he reached the cluster of offshore islands he turned to the east and ran along the south shore until he came to a small bay. He eased the throttle back and chugged on until he came to a beach and here he pulled in.

He cut the motor and ran the boat aground in the sand and went forward and climbed out and hooked his hand under the foredeck and hauled the boat up onto the beach. It was a pretty heavy boat. There was a small kedge anchor wedged in the bow and he lifted it out and dropped it in the sand and walked up the beach. Maybe a hundred feet of sand. Then grass and palmetto. Beyond that scrub liveoak. There were bird tracks in the hard sand above the tideline. Nothing else. He tried to remember the last time it had rained. He went back to the boat and pushed off and knelt aboard and took up one of the oars and poled out through the shallows and then shipped the oar and put his foot on the transom and hauled on the starter rope.

By late afternoon he'd pretty much circled the islands, putting in at every beach. He found the remains of a fire and he found fishing floats and bones and bits of colored glass ground dull by the sea. He picked up a piece of parchmentcolored driftwood in the shape of a pale homunculus and held it up and turned it in his hand. Late in the day with the light failing he put ashore in a small cove and beached the boat and climbed out and turned and saw almost immediately the tracks in the sand. Just above the thin dark rim of wrack. They looked to have been partly filled in by the wind, but that wasnt it. Something had been dragged over them. He walked out to the edge of the palmettos and here the tracks came back and went down the beach. Clean tracks. The rubber ribs of wetsuit bootees. He stood looking out over the gray water. He looked at the sun and he studied the island. Would the wildlife include rattlesnakes? Eastern diamondbacks. Eight feet long. Atrocious or adamantine he couldnt remember. He picked up a piece of driftwood and broke it to length across his knee and followed the tracks into the woods.

There was what looked to be a game trail running through the sparse parkland. The stunted liveoak. A scattering of down timber from Hurricane Camille. The two hundred mile an hour winds that had cut Ship Island in two. He could hear turkeys chittering in the ground cover but he couldnt see them. He followed the trail for perhaps a quarter of a mile until he came to a clearing and he was on the point of turning back when a bit of color caught his eye. He left the path. Separating the palmettos before him with his stick as he went.

It was a yellow two-man rubber raft that had been deflated and rolled up and wedged under a fallen tree and then covered over with brush. He dragged it out and stood looking at it. He turned and studied the parkland. A light wind among the oaks and the faint wash of the tide out there in the shallows. He squatted and unfastened the straps and rolled out the raft.

It was still wet. Seawater in the corners. He spread it out. Brand new. He ran his hands up under the bolsters where they joined the sheetrubber floor. He unsnapped and went through the pockets. There was a plastic inspection tag in one of them but that was all. He squatted there studying the thing. In the end he rolled it back up and rebuckled the straps and shoved it back under the tree and raked the brush and dead palmetto leaves over it and went back out the path to the beach. There'd been no oars with the raft but he'd no notion what that meant. When he got to the beach the sun was low over the water and he stood there looking out to the west, the slow gray swells and the thin bight of shore beyond and somewhere beyond that the city where the lights would be coming up. He sat in the sand and dug in his heels and crossed his arms over his knees and watched the sunset and the light on the water. The thin reach of land to the south would be the Chandeleur Archipelago. Beyond that the hydra mouth of the river. Beyond that Mexico. The low tide lapped and drew back. He could be the first person in creation. Or the last. He rose and walked up the beach to the boat and pushed off and climbed in and went to the rear to ballast it off the sand. He took up the oar and poled his way out through the shallows and then sat there watching the deep red of the sunset darken and die.

He motored slowly down the point and along the south shore of the island. The gulf was calm in the last of the light and lights had begun to come up along the shore to the west. He swung the boat around and twisted the throttle slowly forward and headed north, taking his bearings by the lights along the causeway. It was cold out on the water with the sun down. The wind was cold. By the time he got to the marina he thought that the man who'd gone ashore on the island was almost certainly the passenger.

When he pulled into the yard at Taylor's it was ten oclock. He sat in the quiet under the mercury lights and then he turned the key and started the truck again and drove back up to Gretna and across the bridge to the Quarter. He ate a bowl of redbeans and rice at the little cafe on Decatur Street and then drove up St Philip and parked the truck and let himself in at the gate.

He had another two days off before going on a job downriver at Port Sulphur. Late morning he walked up Bourbon Street to meet Debussy Fields for lunch at Galatoire's. She was already in line and she waved to him extravagantly. Turned out in an expensive dress and four inch heels. Her blonde hair piled on top of her head. Shoulderlength earrings. Everything was pushed just to the edge including the cleavage at the front of her dress but she was very beautiful. He kissed her on the cheek. She was taller than he was.

Nice perfume, he said.

Thank you. Can we hold hands?

I dont think so.

You're not any fun. I thought this was going to be a date.

When they got inside there was some conversation with the maitre'd about the table. I'm not sitting at the rear, she said. And I'm not sitting against the wall.

I can seat you here, said the maitre'd. But of course there's the traffic.

Traffic will be fine, Darling.

She took an antique silver cigarette case from her purse and fitted one of the dark little cigarillos she smoked into an ivory and silver holder and slid her Dunhill lighter across the table to Western. He lit the cigarillo for her and she leaned back and crossed her rather remarkable legs with an audible rustle and blew smoke toward the stamped tin ceiling with a sensuous and studied ease. Thank you, Darling, she said. At nearby tables diners of both sexes had stopped eating altogether. Wives and girlfriends sat smoldering. Western studied her pretty closely. In the two hours they were there she never once looked at another table and he wondered where she'd learned that. Or the thousand other things she knew.

I came by your club on the way down. You're headlining.

Yes. I'm a star, Darling. I thought you knew.

I knew it was just a matter of time.

You're looking at a woman of destiny.

She leaned to adjust the strap of her shoe. She was almost out of her dress. She looked up at him and smiled. Tell me your news, she said. You dont call you dont write you dont love me anymore. I dont have anybody to talk to, Bobby.

You've got your own crowd.

God. I get so tired of faggots. The things they talk about. It's so tedious.

The waiter came and placed menus before them. He poured water from the table carafe. She held the little black cigarette at shoulder level like a wand and reached and tipped open the menu with her other hand.

Tell me what to eat. I'm not eating that wretched fish in a bag.

How about the scallops? The Coquilles St Jacques.

I dont know. All the shellfish are supposed to be polluted.

I'm having the lamb.

You're having the lamb and I'm supposed to eat putrescent molluscs.

Well why dont you have the lamb as well.

Thank you.

You're having the lamb?

Yes.

Excellent choice. Would you like some wine?

No, Darling. It's kind of you to ask.

He folded shut the menu and placed it on top of the winelist.

It doesnt mean that you cant have a glass.

I know. I'm fine.

Do you have a new number?

Yes. Of a sort. Do you have a pencil?

No.

Let me see if I can get one.

It's all right. I can remember it.

He gave her the number at the Seven Seas. 523-9793. She repeated it to herself.

It's just the bar number, he said. But I'll get the message.

All right. I'm going to call you.

All right.

She leaned and tapped the ash from her cigarillo into the heavy glass ashtray. Do you remember the bicentennial minutes?

Those bits of history they aired during the bicentennial?

Yes. I heard a new one.

Okay.

Martha Washington and Betsy Ross are sitting in front of the fire sewing the first flag and they're reminiscing about the old days and all the parties and dances and everything and Betsy says to Martha: Oh and do you remember the minuet? And Martha says Lord honey I cant hardly remember the ones I screwed.

Western smiled.

That's it? she said. A little smile?

Sorry.

You're not going to be dour are you?

Dew-er.

Dew-er?

The preferred, I believe. You dont mind me telling you?

No. Of course not. Dew-er. Actually I like that better.

Good. I'll cheer up.

The waiter came and placed the silver. Another came with bread wrapped in a cloth napkin. When their waiter came back Western ordered for both of them. The waiter nodded and moved away. She took a long draw on the cigarillo and moved her head in a slow upward arc, exhaling. He couldnt even imagine what her life was like.

Do you think that it's more de trop to eat a cute little lamb or something truly disgusting like a pig?

I dont know. What do you think?

I dont know. Why do they have to call it lamb? Why cant they have a name for it? Like veal. Or venison.

I dont know. Have you ever thought of becoming a vegetarian?

Many times. I'm too much of a sensualist. I'm a gourmand. Gourmette? Can we get some mineral water?

Of course.

He flagged the waiter. She took the halfburned stub from the holder and tapped it out in the ashtray and laid the holder on the tablecloth. I've decided against Mexico, she said. She looked up at him.

I think that's smart.

I knew you would. I remember our conversation. It means waiting another year. At the least. That's not nothing. A year is a year. I'll be twenty-five. God it goes fast.

Yes it does. Are you scared?

No. I'm not scared. I'm terrified.

Understandable.

It gives you the willies, doesnt it?

I suppose. Yes.

I'm scared of everything. Every footing is frail.

It doesnt show.

Thank you. I work at it.

At not being afraid?

I think that's too charitable. I work at not letting it show. It's all a charade. But I dont know how else to go about it. Everything you see took work. A lot of work.

I believe you. Sorry. That was the wrong thing to say.

It's okay. Some girls are happy just to do the hormone thing and keep their you-knows. But gender has meaning. I want to be a woman. I was always envious of girls. Just a little bitch. That's pretty much gone. I know that to be female is an older thing even than to be human. I want to be as old as I can be. Atavistically feminine. When I was seven I fell out of a tree and broke my arm and I thought that since it was broken anyway maybe I could twist it around to where I could kiss my elbow because if you kissed your elbow you would change from a boy into a girl or vice versa and I suppose they saw me hauling on my broken arm and screaming and they strapped me down on the gurney because they thought I was hysterical. I really hope I do live to be old. I'll finally be able to tell everyone to kiss my ass. Well, maybe not. I'd probably get a lot of takers. Or not. I'd be old. Just as long as I'm not poor. Did I tell you my sister came to see me? No, of course not. My sister came to see me. She was here for a week. School break. We had such a good time. She's so great. She finally got to where she would walk around the apartment in just her panties. That just meant so much to me.

She turned her head and fanned her eyes with her napkin. Sorry.

I just get very emotional where she's concerned. I absolutely bawled when she left. She's so pretty. And smart. I think she's probably smarter than me.

How old is she?

Sixteen. I'm trying to get her to go to college. I told her I'd help her. God, I need money. Oh good. Water. I'm parched.

The waiter poured their glasses. She touched her glass to his. Thank you, Bobby. This is nice.

The waiter came with the plates. She ate slowly and with great attention to the food. You're watching me eat, she said.

Yes.

It's the only Zen thing I ever really got. Do the thing at hand. It's good for the waistline too. I love to eat. It will be my ruin. It's okay. You can watch. I dont even like to eat and talk at the same time.

She looked up at him and smiled. You can talk and I'll listen. For a change.

While the waiter was pouring the coffee she took out another of the little Cuban cigarettes and he took the lighter from the table and held it for her. Do you ever get to Greeneville? he said.

She blew a thin stream of smoke over her shoulder. You're not supposed to inhale these. Which is why I smoke them. That and the way they look of course. And smell. But I inhale them anyway. A little bit. They're contraband, naturally. From Mexico. Or from Cuba by way of. No. It's too hard. It just makes her miserable. I call her every week or so. Hi. How are you. I'm fine. How are you. That's good. Maybe I should, I dont know. I've never really told you about my life. I dont like to talk about sad things.

Has your life been sad?

No. It hasnt. But hurting people is sad. I suppose I handled it wrong. I should have broken the news to her gradually. Although I'm not sure how you would go about that. Maybe we could go in your Maserati. A road trip. I've never been to Wartburg. How long would it take?

Not long.

I had tried to tell her. Sort of. But of course she wouldnt listen. God. I pulled up to the house in a rental car and got out and walked around back and she was in the garden. I'd no idea what to wear. I just walked up to the fence and said hello. She couldnt even guess who it was of course. She looked up and she said: Yes? And I said: Mama, it's William. And she knelt there for a minute in the dirt and then she put her hand over her mouth and these big tears started to roll down her cheeks. She just knelt there. Shaking her head back and forth. As if she'd been told that someone had died. Well, I suppose someone had. Finally I told her I thought we should go in and she got up and we went in the kitchen and she made some instant coffee. Which I detest. And there we sat. Me trying to smile at her with these teeth that I'd spent four thousand dollars on. I was dressed pretty conservatively but I suppose the blouse I had on was somewhat revealing and anyway she just kept looking at me and finally she said: Can I ask you something? And I said sure. You can ask me anything. And she said: Are those real?

Well. She was taking it all so poorly that I thought I'd mess with her and I had on these gold earrings with a single pearl. Good pearls. Japanese. About nine millimeter with good luster and a nice pink overtone. So I tweaked one of them and I said: Yes, they are. They were a gift. Which they were. And she got even more flummoxed and she said no. She said: I mean your . . . And she sort of waved at my tits with the back of her hand.

So I just put my hands under them and pushed them up under my chin and I said: Oh. You mean these? And she was looking away and she nodded and I said: Yes, they are. As real as hormones and silicone can make them. And she started to bawl all over again and she wouldnt look at me and finally she said: You've got bosoms.

Bosoms, Darling. God. The only thing I could think of was this restaurant where we used to eat in Tijuana. It was about the only place in town where you could get a decent steak. Argentine beef. And the menu was in Spanish of course but they had these English translations on the facing page and there was a dish on the menu called pechuga de pollo and when you looked over at the English it said chicken bosoms. I guess someone had told them that breast was suggestive. So bosoms. Jesus. That just tore it. I dont know why. It just totally pissed me off. I looked at her and I said: Mama, try not to think of it as losing a son. Try to think of it as gaining a freak. And then she really went to bawling. So. There you are. I think I told you that she wouldnt go anywhere with me. Wouldnt be seen with me. I stayed two days. I had a purse full of—what is it that John calls them? Crisp caesars?

Crisp caesars.

Probably about three thousand dollars. My big homecoming. I'd fantasized about it a hundred times. I was going to take her to Knoxville and take her shopping at Miller's and have lunch at Regas. God. Such a fool. What was I thinking? She asked me if I used the ladies' room. I mean did she really think that I could walk into a men's room looking like this? So that was it. Total fucking fiasco. Sorry. I'm trying to quit cussing. My sister came home from school in about an hour and of course she had no notion who this creature was. Sitting in the kitchen with her mother. Until I spoke to her. She was twelve. And she just looked at me and she said: William? Is that you? You're beautiful. And then I busted out bawling. God I love that child.

I know you told me that your father was dead.

Yes. He died when I was fourteen. I was having an awful time. He loathed the sight of me. He used to pay the other kids to beat me up after school.

You're kidding.

Darling I dont kid. After a while even they got tired of it. They wouldnt take his money anymore. And they were a pack of the most despicable little shits you can imagine. He'd gotten tired of waling on me himself because he had these vertebrae . . . brae? Is that right?

Yes.

Vertebrae in his neck that were always giving him trouble and every time he beat me his neck would ache for days. I told him that it was probably a legacy from having been hanged in a previous incarnation but as you can imagine he failed to see the humor in that. Or anything else for that matter. So what happened was there was this dog that lived next door to us that used to terrify me. It would launch itself against the fence snarling and slobbering and it had these eyes that were just crazy and my father and this horrible animal both died on the same day. And the next morning I woke up and I just lay there in my bed and this extraordinary peace had come over me. It was transcendent. No other word for it. I knew that I was free and

I knew that freedom was just like it says in the speeches. It's worth whatever you have to pay to get it. And I knew that I would have the life I dreamed of. It was the first time in my life that I was ever happy and it made up for everything. Everything. It was just a gift. I was just transformed. And I had this strength. And I wasnt angry anymore. My heart was full of love. I think it always had been. I'm sorry. I'm going to be a mess.

She took a linen handkerchief from her purse and opened her compact and dabbed at her eyes. She closed the compact and put it away and looked at him and smiled. Are you sure you want to hear all this?

Yes. I do.

All right. A year later I was working in New York in this upscale restaurant and sharing a walk-up flat with a real girl. I was fifteen. I had a fake ID and I was making really good money and I was working on my English and I'd started my hormone treatments. This doctor I was going to told me that I was a gracile mesomorph. And I said yes and you're a nasty bugger. Because we were friends by then. But I asked him what that meant and he said it means that you're going to be a goodlooking girl. And I said that's not good enough. What about spectacular? And he smiled and he said: We'll see. And we did. I remember coming down one morning to go to the deli and I sort of trotted down the stairs. I just had on jeans and a T-shirt. And my titties jiggled. God. I was so excited. I ran back up the stairs and came trotting down again.

Of course by then I'd started drinking and that almost finished me off. I was a born alcoholic. Luckily I met someone. Sheer blind luck. He got me into AA. I had trouble with the God thing. A lot of people do. And then I woke up one night in the middle of the night and I was lying there and I thought: If there is no higher power then I'm it. And that just scared the shit out of me. There is no God and I am she. So I began to really work on that. I'm still working on it. Maybe that's the way it's supposed to be. But I've made some progress. I was mad at him for screwing me up the way he did but maybe he's not as perfect as people like to think. He's got a lot on his plate and he has to do it all himself. No help.

Do you believe in God?

The truth?

Sure.

I dont know who God is or what he is. But I dont believe all this stuff got here by itself. Including me. Maybe everything evolves just like they say it does. But if you sound it to its source you have to come ultimately to an intention.

Sound it to its source?

You like that? Pascal. About a year after this I woke up again and it was like I had heard this voice in my sleep and I could still hear the echo of it and it said: If something did not love you you would not be here. And I said okay. That's it. Plain enough. Maybe it doesnt sound like much. But it was to me. So I do like the program says, Bobby. One day at a time. I need to spend more time with women and it's difficult. They feel threatened. Or we get to be friends and then I tell them and you can feel the distance settle in. Rare exceptions. Very rare. I'm trying to get Clara to come down here. To go to school here. You can guess who's against that. I've been reading about the sexual dimorphism in the brain. It may be more adaptable than people think. It may be that you can change it. You know where this is going because we talked about it. I want to have a female soul. I want the female soul to contain me. That's what I want and that's all I want. I thought that it might be always out of my reach but now I've started to have faith. That's what I pray for when I pray. To be let in the door. To be a member of the feminine. It doesnt really have anything to do with sex. With having sex. And all the rest is just fluff.

She smiled. She raised one slender arm and looked at the thin whitegold Patek Philippe Calatrava she wore. What time is it? she said.

Two eighteen.

Very good.

Is that a pre-war?

It is. No complications.

The story of your life.

The story of my new life. My life as I wish it to be. I have to go. I have a three oclock call. You're a sweetheart Darling. Thank you. And thank you for listening to all my bloody travails. I havent asked a thing about you. I'll call you. Is that all right?

Yes.

He paid the check and they rose to go. The only thing that I dont like about sitting in front is that you dont get to walk through the restaurant.

You do enough damage.

I know. It's just something I have to live with.

On the sidewalk she kissed him on both cheeks. All the time I've known you, I've never once asked myself what it is that you want.

From you?

From me. Yes. That's very unusual for me. Thank you.

He watched her until she was lost among the tourists. Men and women alike turning to look after her. He thought that God's goodness appeared in strange places. Dont close your eyes.

III

The winter months deepened but the Kid seemed to have left. She was taking courses after school at the University and she seldom got home before dark. Then one evening she came in and threw her books on the bed and he was sitting at her desk. Come in, he said. Shut the door. Where've you been?

I've been at school.

Yeah? It's after seven oclock. You dont think that's a bit late? He hauled out his watch and checked the time. He tapped at the crystal and held the thing to his ear.

How do you know what time I'm supposed to be home?

Right. Sit your ass down. You're making the place untidy.

She pushed over the books and stretched out on the bed with her hands under her chin.

That's not sitting. That's lying down.

What's the difference?

You cant pay proper attention. The full vertical and upright position facilitates the flow of blood to the brain. The frontal lobes in particular. As mandatory with aircraft landings for example. Preparatory to impact and the ensuing dismemberment and subsequent incineration. I thought you were trained in anthropology?

That's not anthropology. It's gibberish.

Yeah yeah sure sure. Sit your nelly ass up. I dont have a lot of time to squabble.

Quibble.

That either.

She pushed herself up and sat and levered off her shoes and dropped them over the side. She crossed her legs and pulled the quilt up about her. The Kid had commenced his pacing. Jesus. The ups with which I put. All at the beck and call of some hickette from Hootersville. Up here under the eaves. Squirreled away with the nuts. Well fuck it.

Where are the others?

The other whats?

Your little friends.

Dont worry. They'll be here in their own good time. Where was I?

Squirreled away with the nuts.

Right. Maybe we should move on. Where's your report card?

What do you care where my report card is?

You got a B.

What business is that of yours?

That's a first, Florence.

It was in religion.

So? Religion's not a subject?

She doesnt know what she's talking about. Sister Aloysius. She doesnt even know what the argument is.

Yeah. But you started quoting Aquinas to her in Latin like the smug little bitch that you are. What did you expect?

I thought you only cared about the math.

It's still a B. And it's still on your record. I suppose you intend to count your way to Paradise.

Jesus. What are you talking about?

Talking about you flunking religion.

I didnt flunk. I made a B.

Yeah? It's the same thing.

I thought we were moving on.

Right.

Although I suppose I should ask to what.

Jesus. The winter months. Okay?

Sure. Why not? It's getting dark sooner. You may have noticed.

Yeah? Have to be wary with you. This could be one of your philosophical observations.

What are you writing?

I'm just checking some of these people off. What are we looking at here? Early retirement? Where the fuck are these people?

I dont want these people.

Yeah? How do you know? You need to take a break, Brenda. You may not be at the edge but you can see it from here. Dont we have anybody in the wings for Christ sake?

The lawndwarves in the shadow of her desk put forth woodenly. Jesus, said the Kid. Not you. Where the hell is Grogan?

He clapped his flippers and the bathless one appeared out of the closet and doffed his floppery billcap. There were three rolls of fat at the base of his skull. As if his head had been assembled in a press. He held his cap at his chest in both hands and lowered his eyes and bowed to the girl. God prosper your kind, Mum, he said. Then he put his cap back on and folded his hands at the small of his back and began to do the shake-a-leg of the Lollipop Guild, grimacing the while.

Why cant we ever get any music for Christ sake? Okay. Enough with the hoofing. What else you got for us?

Grogan took off his cap and clutched it before him and began to sing to the tune of "Molly Brannigan":

Them old cangrejos
Is a-leapin in me lederhose
Why I bedded with the bitch
Is somethin only Jesus knows
And it's off to the chemist
For a pot of ointment I suppose
Since Molly's gone and left me
Here alone with the . . .

Okay, said the Kid. Jesus. Whatever happened to ballads of love and patriotism? What are you doing?

She'd pulled the quilt over her head. I'm going away, she said, her voice muffled under the covers.

Grogan had begun to dance again. His Irish stomp. She could hear him clomping about in his clodhoppers. The Kid told him to cool it. She cant see the fucking acts with her head under the covers.

I dont want to see the acts. Tell them to go away.

She'll be all right in a minute. Probably had a rough day at school. Hey under there. You cant be going to bed. It's only seven thirty.

I have school tomorrow.

What? Knock it off, Grogan.

She pushed back the covers. I have school tomorrow.

I have school tomorrow, he mimed.

What happened to Grogan?

I think he left. You probably pissed him off.

What do I have to do to piss you off?

Just bear with me. Let me look through some of this stuff.

Oh great.

The Kid flipped through his book. Maybe we've just tried to get a little too upscale with you.

Upscale?

Yeah. Sometimes it's a mistake to try and tailor your acts.

Sure.

Anyway, I'm beginning to sniff out a hint of the prurient in that patrician demeanor of yours.

He pushed away some papers on her desk and sat back in the chair with his notes. Jesus, he said. Who takes these bloody pictures. Dog acts? Are you shitting me? You never know what you're going to find when you drain the swamp. And the names. The Supposables? How about The Disposables? Or The Suppositories? Christ. Got to be something here.

The only one I care about is Miss Vivian.

Yeah. But she aint an act. Let's stick with the program.

It's not a program. It's just stupid.

Sure. What the fuck is this? Jugglers? Wait a minute. Here we go. These two look good. Hailing from Snook-Cockery in the West Country. Okay.

He shoveled away his notes and clapped his flippers and leaned back in the chair. Places, he called. The closed door flew open and a pair of diminutive hoydens in pale taffeta sallied forth doing the shuffle-off-to-Buffalo and rolling their painted eyes. They began to sing inanely in a highpitched trill, their arms locked and their cheap patentleather shoes padding on the boards. The Kid moaned and clutched a flipper to his brow. Jesus, he whispered. He rose from the chair and clapped his flippers. That's it. Thank you. Jesus. What is this fucking business coming to? Get these septic titpigs out of here. Mother of God. What is that smell? Liederkranz? Out, goddamit. That's it. Break. Back here at eight.

He went down to the Seven Seas in the evening and sat at the barstool against the wall. Janice opened a bottle of beer and slid it to him. Your buddy's back there, she said.

He raised up to see over the heads of the bar drinkers. Oiler was sitting at a table by himself. He got up and took his beer and went back. Bobby boy, Oiler said.

What are you doing?

Waitin on my hamburger. Sit down. You want one? I'm buyin.

Sure.

Go tell him. I aint gettin up.

Western walked out to the grill on the patio. Make it two, he said.

Two what.

Hamburgers.

He's havin a cheeseburger.

Okay.

Cheeseburger?

Sure.

Everthing?

Yeah.

Fries?

Fries.

He went back in and kicked back the chair and sat. Where's all the crazies?

Oiler looked around the room. I dont know. Maybe they finally came and seined em up and hauled em off.

You been reading the papers?

I have. I just started.

You have any notion how a three million dollar jet aircraft can wind up in the Gulf of Mexico with nine people dead in it and it doesnt get reported in the paper?

I was fixin to ask you that.

I had some visitors the other evening.

At your place?

Yeah.

You had a break-in?

Why would you think that?

Just the way you said it.

No. Two guys in suits. They sort of looked like Mormon missionaries.

What did they want?

I dont know. They asked me about the plane. They said that one of the passengers was missing.

You're shittin me.

Western sipped his beer.

You aint shittin me.

No.

I got to suppose that they know who it is that's missing.

Yeah, I suppose they wouldnt know that without knowing who was present. Or would they?

They might. What? They think we know where this dude is?

I dont know. What I do know is that anytime some squirrelly crap such as this comes up it seldom travels alone.

Oiler leaned with his elbows on the table. All right. They know how many people were on the plane because we said how many.

I dont think so.

You're makin my fuckin head hurt. What did they say about the Jepp case?

They said it was missing.

And they know this how? You're not jerking my chain about any of this shit are you?

No. Why would I?

I dont know. You got a twisted mind.

Not that twisted.

Missionaries.

Yeah.

I'm beginning to get an ugly feeling about this.

I thought you already had one.

Uglier, then. More ugly?

Uglier.

Anyway, I got some advice for you. But then you probably already know what it is.

I do.

You go back out there to look around and these missionaries are going to be moving in with you.

I set some little traps for them. If they come back I'll know they've been there.

Sure. Then what?

I'll burn that bridge when I come to it.

You already have. When are you going down to Port Sulphur?

Monday. I think.

You dont mind diving the river.

I dont like it. But no. I can do it.

Why is that? It's as dark as anywhere else.

It's not just the dark. It's the deep.

How dark it is is what tells you how deep it is.

Maybe. I knew a guy who dove the Indian Ocean where he said the light was good to five hundred feet. He said you'd get vertigo when you looked down. But he still couldnt dive it. And it wasnt because he ran out of light.

Well. He ran out of something.

How did we get on my phobias?

Hell, Western. If it wasnt for your phobias I wouldnt fuck with you at all. Here we go.

The frycook set their plates on the table with the cheeseburgers and took a bottle of mustard and one of ketchup from either armpit and salt and pepper from the rear pockets of his rancid jeans. What else? he said.

I think we're covered.

Oiler looked at the plastic jar of mustard and then reached for it and opened his cheeseburger and squirted the mustard. In for a dollar, he said.

You cant get a decent cheeseburger in a clean restaurant. Once they start sweeping the floor and washing the dishes with soap it's pretty much over.

Oiler nodded and sat chewing. Well, these sumbitches are pretty damned good, so there you go.

Best cheeseburger I ever ate was at the lunchcounter at Comer's Pool Hall on Gay Street in Knoxville Tennessee. You couldnt get the grease off your fingers with gasoline. You still havent told me where you're going.

Yeah, I know. We're goin to Venezuela.

When.

Week and a half. He held up two fingers. After a while two more beers arrived. Western watched him. What's the job? he said.

We're goin down there to replace a run of old flange joints that're leaking. The Taylor barge left two days ago and I expect we'll be gone a while.

How long a while.

I dont know. Probably two months.

You cut out the joints and weld in a pup joint.

That's right. Then you got a completely welded pipe. No problems. Taylor developed all the technology. We did the first hyperbaric welded joints on a pipeline in the North Sea about sixty miles out of Peterhead. Not that long ago. You've never been there.

In Scotland.

Yeah.

No. I havent.

Love the name. Anyway, you can run pipe with a lay barge around the world if you want to. You just keep welding new lengths topside as you go and lower them into the sea behind you. But you cant join two pipes. And that's what we did. On the sea bottom.

Was that the first time it had ever been done?

We'd done test runs down here off Grande Isle a couple of years before that. That was the first time we'd used the spar units with the underwater habitat.

You're welding the pipes in the dry.

In the dry. Those things weigh a hundred and forty-six tons. The spar units. The lay barge drops it down with a derrick. We were welding the ends of two pretty good runs of pipe together. I think they were twenty-seven and thirty-five miles long. The first thing you have to do is cut off the cement and line up the pipes and then cut them to length with a hydraulic saw. They haul up the two sections of excess pipe together with the pull-ends and then they let down the spar unit with the underwater habitat. There's more to it, but basically you clamp the ends of the pipe into either end of the habitat where the waterproof clamps are built in and then you pump out the water and weld in your forty inch pup joint. Of course this is thirty-two inch pipe, so if nothing else it gets a bit crowded in there.

But you're basically in an air chamber.

Sure. You can eat your lunch in there.

How deep were you?

Three hundred and eighty-two feet. We had ten divers on the job, two of us in saturation.

You liked it.

I knew I was cut out for this before I even knew what it was. Plus the money.

Sure.

I always had a feelin the money didnt mean all that much to you. Maybe that's the problem.

I dont know. A lot of money would probably move me. I could do some things I wanted. But you'll never get rich selling your time. Not even doing hyperbaric welding.

Probably right. There's more brain surgeons than there are hyperbaric welders, but you're probably right. About getting rich. Still I can tell you that I've been poor and this is better. Even if it aint rich. You want to go?

To Venezuela.

Yeah.

You got that kind of pull at Taylor's?

I got a couple of favors out. What do you think?

I dont think so. How deep are we talking?

Five hundred and sixty feet.

Where do you fly into?

Caracas. We're at a place called Puerto Cabello. About two hours up the coast.

You've been there before.

Oh yes. What do you think?

I dont think so.

We could go to Caracas.

Yeah.

You could go as my tender.

That's just a fucking boondoggle.

What do you care? You could try a bellrun. Hell, Bobby. I wont let you drown.

I know.

Let me ask you this.

All right.

What do you think is down there?

That's not the problem.

I know. It's what's up here.

He touched his temple.

Yeah. Well.

You think too much. Not sure I know about what. I dont know what goes on in that head of yours anyway. But if I had what you've got up there I wouldnt be doing this shit in the first place.

I thought you loved it.

Yeah, well. I know this is probably as good as it's goin to get and I'm a pretty grateful motherfucker.

I cant answer your question, Oiler. I just know I'm not going. Saying that it's just in your head doesnt change anything.

Yeah, well. I think that there are things that you're afraid of that you just do it. You dont sit around and go over all the reasons not to. Suppose you're in the airbell and you've got these reasons for being afraid to back through the sump. Maybe that's one of your analogies. If you're afraid then you're stuck. You're not nowhere. You're always backing through the sump.

Western smiled.

You think that when there's somethin that's got you snakebit you can just walk off and forget it. The truth is it aint even following you. It's waitin for you. It always will be.

I dont know. I think that fear sometimes transcends the problem. What if it's about something else? Which means that solving it may or may not solve it.

You're saying that whatever you're afraid of may not really be what you're afraid of.

I suppose.

All right. Well. It's none of my business. Maybe that car wreck did a number on you. I guess you werent afraid of driving a racecar a hundred and eighty miles an hour.

Maybe I should have been.

He drained his beer and set the empty bottle on the table. Doesnt change anything though, does it?

You live a peculiar life, Bobby.

I've been told that.

I'm sure you have. Here's something else you've been told. That doesnt change anything.

Okay.

The dead cant love you back.

Western rose. I'll see you.

All right.

You take care.

You too Bobby.

When he got back to his apartment it had been gone over pretty thoroughly. His first thought was for the cat but the cat was under the bed again. It's me, he said, patting the floor, but the cat wasnt coming out. He walked around, putting things back. The gear from his divebag was strewn about the floor and he gathered it up and repacked the bag and zipped it closed and put it back in the closet. He scooped up his clothes from where they'd been dumped in the floor and piled them onto the bed. Then he stopped. He sat on the edge of the bed.

It's not the same guys. These are different guys.

He went to the closet and got his divebag out again and set it by the door. He swept up his shirts on their wire hangers from off the rod in the closet and piled them at the door and he got his grandfather's scuffed gladstone bag down from the closet shelf and packed his socks and T-shirts in it and snapped it shut.

He took a canvas bag into the kitchen and filled it with canned goods and coffee and tea. A few dishes and kitchen utensils. He packed up his books in a duffelbag and he set these by the door as well. The little stereo and a box of tapes. He pulled the phone jack out of the wall and he pulled the covers off the bed together with the pillows and he walked through the place a final time. He picked up the catbox. He didnt own a lot but it already looked like too much. He unplugged the tablelamp and carried it to the door and then began to take everything out to the truck and load it in the cab or wedge it in front of the boom. Five trips and he was done. He knelt and crawled up under the bed talking to the cat until he could reach it. Come on, Billy Ray. Nothing's forever.

It wasnt the sort of news that a cat likes to hear. He walked through the little apartment stroking the cat's fur and then he went out and shut the door and went through the gate to the street and got into the truck and with the cat in his lap he drove down St Philip Street to the Seven Seas.

It was one oclock in the morning. He went in carrying the cat. Janice was tending bar and she looked up and smiled. Who's your friend?

This is Billy Ray. Is there a room upstairs?

There's Lurch's room. I dont know how clean it is.

That's all right. Can I have it?

I should ask Josie.

I'll talk to her. Look, I've got everything I own in a truck outside.

I dont want to go around looking for a motel this hour of the night. If she's promised it to somebody I'll move out.

What happened? You get evicted?

Something like that. His stuff is all out isnt it?

Yeah. I think so. They boxed everything up and sent it to his sister in Shreveport. I hope you're not getting me in trouble.

You'll be fine. Where's the key?

She got the cigarbox from under the counter and took out the key and laid it on the bar. He picked it up and turned the brass fob in his palm. Number seven.

Lucky seven.

Wasnt so lucky was it?

Yeah. Well, you never know. It's been pretty gray around here. As for the luck part you'd have to ask Lurch. Anyway it's the last room down the hall on the left. I dont think there's a number on the door. You sure you want to move in up there?

Why?

I dont know. The four years I've been here three people have moved out. Including Lurch. And they all went the same way Lurch did. You might want to think about that.

I will.

He carried his stuff in from the truck and out through the patio doors and up the stairs. The room was stripped save for an iron bedstead and a small wooden table and chair. A sink and a small refrigerator. A hotplate. No mattress on the bed. The place smelled of mold and gas. He brought everything in and piled it on the table or in the corner and shut the door. The cat was investigating the room. He wasnt too happy about any of it.

He spread his blankets and clothes and sleepingbag over the bedsprings and made up a sort of bed and he put the cat's plastic box in the corner and filled it from the bag of chopped clay and then he went back downstairs and got a beer and stood at the far end of the bar.

You dont want to talk to me, Janice said.

He took the beer and walked up and sat on one of the stools.

How's the room?

It's okay. There's no mattress on the bed.

You're sleeping on the springs?

Yeah. Sort of.

I hate that. Especially if you're with someone.

I hadnt thought about that.

You just come out all waffled. So how come you're changing digs in the dead of the night?

I had a break-in. Among other things.

That's a bummer. What'd they get?

I dont know. Not much. I dont have much to get.

Oiler says you live like a monk.

I guess I do.

Why dont you ask Paula out?

What?

Ask Paula out.

I dont think so.

Why not?

I dont want to get involved with anybody.

You know she's got the hots for you.

No I dont.

Come on.

I dont think so.

Okay. What's the other things.

Other things?

You said a break-in among other things.

Western tilted his head. Why?

Who else am I going to hassle?

I dont know. I'm going to bed.

Good night.

When he came down in the morning it was ten oclock and there were people standing at the bar in their pajamas and slippers drinking Bloody Marys and reading the Sunday paper. Jimmy nodded to him from his table.

You've moved in.

You people dont have much of anything to talk about, do you?

It'll probably come as a relief to you. To just get it over with.

You're probably right.

We all saw it coming.

Western smiled and went out and walked up St Philip to where he'd parked the truck.

When he came back in the afternoon he had a mattress and a couple of bags of groceries. He parked in front of the bar and got out and carried the mattress in off the truck. Josie watched him from behind the bar. The mattress was something of a struggle but nobody was getting up to help. He stood it against the cigarette machine and turned. What am I going to owe you? he said.

Hell, Bobby. Get moved in. I aint worried about you.

All right.

Oiler was in here huntin you.

Did you tell him I was moving in?

No. He told me.

Jesus.

He shouldered his way through the patio doors and labored up the stairs with the mattress. When he'd carried everything in he went out and drove the truck down Decatur until he found a parking spot. Then he walked up St Philip to his little apartment and let himself in through the gate and put the key in the door and pushed it open. One more door to close forever. He stepped in and switched on the light. He stood looking at the clothes he'd left on the bed and then he walked into the kitchen. In the bathroom he turned on the light and bent and carefully pulled open the bottom drawer on the right. He'd left a round ballpoint pen in the center of the drawer with the cap off so that it would roll and when he eased the drawer open the pen was lying against the front edge of it. He shut the drawer and walked back into the front room and went out and locked the door and went back down to Decatur Street. He stopped at the corner and got a paper and walked down to Tujague's.

It was five oclock on a Sunday afternoon in November and he was the sole patron. A few people at the bar in the other room. A waiter came with a loaf of bread and a plate of butter. He poured water from the antique glass carafe on the table and went away.

There was no menu. You ate what they brought. He had shrimp remoulade and then a soup of seafood and rice. The broiled brisket served with a horseradish seafood sauce. He had a glass of white wine and a fillet of seabass and he drank coffee served in a glass. A group of tourists came in. The place seemed to have a calming effect on them. Western knew the feeling. They looked at the photographs on the walls. The hundreds of two-ounce bottles of liquor displayed. He ordered another coffee and a dish of vanilla ice cream. By the time he left it was almost seven oclock and he walked back to the Seven Seas. There was a note from Red and he put it in his pocket and climbed the stairs and fed the cat and went to bed.

In the morning when he drove down to Belle Chasse it was still gray early light. He parked the truck and walked across the yard. Past the training tank and the steel buildings. He unlocked the metal door and walked back to the operations room and turned on the lights and switched on the hotplate and got down the coffee and the filters.

Oiler came in around six thirty. I figured it was you, he said.

Yeah? How'd you figure that?

I just figured it would take you a while to get to where you could actually sleep in that looney bin. You get moved in okay?

Yeah. I'm all right.

What happened? You have more visitors?

Several more, probably. My dancecard is pretty full.

Oiler poured a cup of coffee and stood stirring it with a plastic spoon. So is that why you moved?

Yeah. It was probably time anyway. Jimmy said I was overdue.

Jimmy would know.

I hope not.

Did you know that he was an old hardhat diver?

No. I didnt know that.

It could be a look into the future. You might ought to think about that.

I hear that a lot. I'm surprised nobody's come calling on you.

Did I say that?

What, the missionaries?

The missionaries.

You didnt tell them where we hid the missing passenger did you?

No. They tried to beat it out of me but I kept mum. Finally they hooked up a one-twenty to my balls but I just gritted my teeth.

I hate it when they do that.

What time are you all leavin?

We're not going till tomorrow.

What happened?

Cant say.

Do you think that plane is still out there?

I dont know. It would take a goodsized crane to haul it up and a goodsized barge to load it onto.

I'm guessing they'd be doing this at night.

You still scanning the newspapers?

No. I gave it up.

Oiler reached and got the coffeepot and poured his cup and put the pot back. This whole thing could just go away you know.

Wouldnt that be nice.

But you dont think it's going to be nice.

Probably I dont.

In the morning they drove downriver in Red's old Ford Galaxie.

What have you got in this? A three-ninety?

No, it's got a four twenty-eight. I'm going to try to find some CJ heads for it. I've got a cam that I never put in. You dont fool with cars anymore.

No. I gave it up.

You still got the Maserati.

Yeah. I dont drive it enough. Which worries me. The headgaskets begin to go and you get water down in the piston liners and they start to rust. Among other things.

Why that car?

I dont know. It's not as fast as a Boxer. Or a Countach. But it's better built. Things dont fall off of it. Mangusta? Maybe. Goodlooking car. Nothing can outbrake it. There's a lot you could do with that 351 but you'd have to put a bigger transmission in it. And of course the 308 wont outrun a fat man. Plus they're hard to find. So, Bora. The suspension is soft? Not really. It only leans so far. And I suppose you get used to all that Peugeot nuttiness. The subject is really aesthetics. The Bora is the prettiest car. That's it. Over and out.

If I had that thing I'd drive the wheels off of it.

I dont doubt that for a minute.

How fast do those Formula cars go?

The Formula Ones will break two hundred miles an hour. Not many places to do it in. The Mulsanne Straight at Sarthe. I dont know what the Formula Twos will do. None of them have speedometers in them of course. After a few laps the only thing you know for sure is that you're not going fast enough.

What was the biggest problem you ran into?

Money. Of course. If you're just talking about the car itself there are always two kinds of failures. The kind that you couldnt fix and the kind that you didnt know needed fixing. If something just packs up in the middle of the race all you can do is shrug. But if you never get the suspension right and it's costing you a couple of seconds a lap . . . Well. We never did get the car sorted. You're finally reduced to jacking with the tire pressure. The stagger. You tell yourself that you can drive anything but it's no way to go racing.

You never drove dragsters?

No. You?

No. Those things scare the shit out of me.

Frank called me one morning and he said Let me swing by there and pick you up. I want to show you something. So we went over to see this rail job that these two brothers had built and we walked out behind the house and they threw back this tarp. Like they were unveiling a work of art. They'd gotten hold of a pair of 391 Chrysler Hemi engines and they'd yoked them together with this huge Spicer U-joint. Then they mounted a pair of 671 GMC superchargers on top of the engines. They'd never had this thing dyno'd but the numbers had to be huge. Frank said the first time they fired it up birds fell dead out of the trees two blocks away. It didnt even have a transmission. Just this big Eaton two-speed truck axle. And all of this is sitting in a chassis they'd welded up out of angle iron and plumbing pipe. Just an unbelievable thing to see. Frank and I stood there looking at it and I said What do you think?

And he said what do I think? And I said Yes. And he said I'll tell you what I think. I wouldnt get out of the electric chair to get in it.

They pulled into the parkinglot and walked over to the cafe to get coffee and wait for Russell. It was still dark out. A few gulls wheeled above the docklights. The cafe was pretty lively. Red got a paper and slid into the booth and looked out at the gray waterfront. This thing is supposed to be a real clunker. I dont know what they think it's a hazard to but I'll bet that guy would love to leave it where it's at.

I'll bet he would too. How long do you think we'll be down here?

Couple of days. Mostly it will depend on how long it takes to pump it out. You going to eat?

I dont think so. Just coffee.

Yeah. Where the hell's the waitress?

When they walked back out on the dock there were streaks of light on the far side of the river. Red flipped his cigarette into the water. You want to get the truck?

Let me have the keys.

We can stack our gear here and get it sorted. Russell ought to be here by now.

That should be him.

Russell had brought printouts of deck plans and elevations of some ancient tugs. These things tend to be one of a kind, he said. So I dont know how useful these will be. This little jewel was built at Bath Iron Works in 1938.

Red leaned and spat. I know those suckers are heavy, he said.

They are that. Taylor's leased a two hundred ton steamdriven crane mounted on a barge. I cant wait to see them fire that thing up. All right. Let's just take these with us.

He rolled the prints and slid them back into the tube and twisted on the cap. You all ready?

Let's do her.

Let's do her.

They motored out past the pilings, dark with pitch and trailing a green scurf in the claycolored water. The wake of the boat breaking up somewhere back in that dark forest of poles where things lived. They turned downriver, keeping to the western levees, the gray mist of the water breaking over the bow of the launch. You couldnt hear above the noise of the engine and they rode in silence, pointing out alligators where they slid into the river. By the time they reached the dive site they were pretty cold and they climbed out onto the deck of the barge and stomped and waved their arms and when the sun came up they stood with their faces to it like worshippers.

About three feet of the mast of the tug was sticking up out of the river at a slight angle. The Coast Guard had marked off the site with buoys. The crane barge was just upriver from the tug and it was huge and shaggy-looking. There was a light on in the deckhouse but there didnt seem to be anybody around.

Red nodded at it. What do you think that thing runs a day?

I dont know. But I'll bet it's paid for.

They sat on the deck while Russell went over the dive with them. Western laid back and stretched himself out on the deck and closed his eyes.

You gettin this, Bobby?

You have my undivided attention.

What's the answer to Gary's question?

The bollard pull on this thing is probably not over thirty tons. But that was in 1938 and it's got to be less now. There's no way you can pull this thing up by the H-bitts. You'd just pull them out of the deck. Better to run the aft cable first. The rudder may be too close to the hull to get the cable through and if it is we'll have to take a drill down there and make a hole to run it through. We need about two inches for the cable.

Red had stretched out on his back and was aiming an imaginary rifle at a high jet. How do you propose that we measure two inches? It's pitch black down there.

Just use your dick.

Which way is it pointed?

Your dick?

It's pointed upriver. You can tell by the mast.

What happened to it anyway? Anybody know?

It was bringing a freighter up and they decided to run a couple of extra lines—weather or something—and the tug got gurded and tipped over.

That sounds pretty dumb.

Anytime you lose a boat on the river the first word that comes up on your screen is dumb. Usually preceded by fucking. What else?

I think that's it. Questions?

Is there any likelihood of this thing breaking up in the sling?

No. Tugs dont break up. Tugs are forever.

All right.

Do I get an A?

I dont know. Red? Does he get an A?

What's the tug weigh, Bobby?

A lot.

Sounds like an A to me.

The tenders had brought down a pair of Viking commercial wetsuits and laid them out on the deck along with two late-model SuperLite 17 helmets. Red and Western stripped down to their shorts and T-shirts and the tenders helped them into their gear and talked to them about the new EFROM wireless underwater phones they were going to use. There was no visibility in the river even with a light and the divers would be connected by an eighteen foot nylon jumper rope. They sat on the edge of the barge and pulled on heavy steeltoed construction boots and the tenders stood the two pairs of Justus stainless steel tanks on the deck behind them and held the tanks while they slipped into the harness and buckled and adjusted the straps. They buckled on their weightbelts and the tenders sorted the umbilicals and snapped on the safety lines and they looked back and raised their thumbs and pushed off into the river.

The visibility was instantly zero and it went from mud to black in just a few feet. The Ikelights they would normally use in low light were useless. They only made a dim brown smudge in the river and held at arm's length looked to be fifty feet away. Burning mud, Oiler called it. The round plate of muddy light overhead closed slowly and they descended in darkness, the wall of the river carrying them downstream. Western tried the phone. You there? he said.

I'm here.

They wore balaclavas but Western could feel the cold in his head. A sharp pain. Like eating ice cream too fast. They descended in total blackness and the bottom of the river was suddenly there. Sooner than he would have thought. He almost lost his footing. He put one hand down. A sandy loam under his glove. Firmer than he would have thought. He stood and turned and faced upriver.

We're down a ways, Red said.

Yeah.

He leaned into the current. The heavy unending wall of it. He turned and put his shoulder forward and began to move up the river floor in the heavy boots.

He could feel the hull of the boat upriver to him by the change in the current. Like a shadow in the moving water. He put up his hands before him. An acoustic feedback. What he touched was the edge of the rudder. He ran his hand over the rough steel plate and knelt and followed it down into the sand.

All right. We've got it.

What have you got?

I think it's some kind of a goddamn boat.

He shaped out the deep castiron nacelles that housed the propellers. The rudder was enormous and he traced it forward and wedged his fingers in at the leading edge. Red pulled up alongside him. Western took the nylon lead rope loose from his belt and fed it through the gap between the forward edge of the rudder and the hull and ran it back and forth a couple of times and then hooked the loop end of it back through his belt.

I think we're good here.

All right. I'm going to cut you loose. I'll take my end up front.

This thing is what? Ninety feet?

That's what Russell has.

I'll see you topside.

Andale pues.

Western hauled a few yards of the rope loose and started upriver. He thumbed the button on his divephone. You there?

I'm here.

I think we're doing good.

There's always something.

Always something. Over and out.

He dragged the rope behind him, one hand on the hull of the tug. A ship was trudging past upriver and he stopped for a moment. The engines overhead made a clanky metallic sound in the sourceless dark. His first dive in the river was two years ago. The weight of it moving over him. Endlessly, endlessly. In a sense of the relentless passing of time like nothing else.

When he got to what he thought was half the length of the boat he called Red again. I'm going up, he said.

Roger that.

He took off his weightbelt and hooked it to one of his lines and let the line go in the dark. He unhooked the jumper and rose slowly up over the canted hull. Past the single chine and on up to the row of tires chained along the upper hull to where it canted back into the tumblehome. He pushed off the deck and rose and broke through the surface of the river and spread his hands and turned, drifting slowly. One of the tenders stepped to the edge of the barge and slung a heaving line out over the face of the river just below him. He reached and got hold of it and the tender gave him a thumbs-up and straightened the rope in the fairlead of the winch and threw the lever and Western swung downriver on his back and then the winch slowly towed him in.

The tenders helped him off with his tanks and his helmet and someone brought him a coffee. He set the cup on the deck and took off his gloves and watched the river until Red surfaced. You get it? he called.

We're good, Bobby.

They towed Red in and he handed over the lead rope and the tenders unsnapped his helmet and lifted it off. Piece of cake, he said.

You ever bump into anything down there that you didnt know what it was?

Not yet. I've thought about it. I saw an alligator snappingturtle in a zoo in California that the sign said it weighed two hundred and sixty pounds. Head the size of your fist. I kind of wish I hadnt seen it.

Yeah, said Western. I think they get bigger than that.

Yeah?

So do bullsharks.

Bullsharks.

Yeah.

Well, they wouldnt get this far up the river.

They've been caught as far north as Decatur Illinois.

They handed Red a coffee and he sat sipping it. He looked at Western. You're givin me the goddamn fidgets, Western. He turned and looked at Russell. When is he goin to fire that thing up?

They go up the Zambezi as far as the falls. They eat everything in the river.

What?

Bullsharks.

In Africa.

In Africa.

That's bullshit. They got crocodiles in that river twenty feet long. How they going to eat one of them?

They just gut em. They eat the guts first.

Bullshit.

Lions wont drink out of the Zambezi south of the falls.

That's bullshit.

I know. About the lions anyway. I made that up. Could be true though.

They ran the lead ropes through the winch and the cables came up and they yoked them and watched them slide off into the river. They yoked up the sling and by early afternoon a good part of the wheelhouse was out of the water. The crane pilot doubled down the gears and the barge shuddered and ground on. Red leaned and spat into the river. The cabins on these things are always tall, he said. You got to be able to see out over everything.

I think that's right.

How long are we looking at down here?

Why? You got a hot date?

You never know.

I take it he's going to run it all night.

Yeah.

What time do they want us out here in the morning?

Daylight.

All right.

You ready?

I'm a ready motherfucker.

They checked in at the motel out on the highway. You want to get a drink?

I dont think so. I'm pretty tired.

I'll see you in the morning.

Western closed the door and dropped his bag in the floor and went in and showered and came back and stretched out on the bed. He slept for eight minutes and woke again and lay staring at the ceiling. After a while he got up and got dressed and walked down to the bar. It was still early. He sat at a table in the corner and the waitress came over and wiped the table and put down a paper napkin and stood looking at him.

Are you married? he said.

Did you want to order or what?

Just bring me a Pearl.

She brought the beer and a glass. She stood looking at him. I'll bet you are though, aint you?

Married.

Yeah.

Yeah. I'm married forever. I always will be.

So how come you askin me if I'm married?

I just wanted to know what it's like. For normal people.

Are you sayin I aint normal?

No, Lord no. Me?

You aint normal.

No.

What's wrong with you?

I'm not sure.

Are you married sure enough? Cause I aint.

I shouldnt be bothering you.

You aint botherin me.

I'm not trying to pick you up.

I dont know if you are or not. I just know you aint doin a very good job of it.

In the morning they sat on the deck of the barge and drank coffee and ate sandwiches out of the lunchbox. They watched the tug and they watched the crane operator. He brought the railings up out of the river and the engine stalled down again and he downshifted the gearing again. White smoke belched from the pipe and the rigging creaked and the boom made a series of low ratcheting noises. The deck of the barge tilted slowly. Then it stopped. Western was watching the cables. He looked at Red. Red was holding his sandwich. After a while he began chewing again. Russell walked over and squatted.

How much water is in that thing, Western?

How quick an answer do you want?

I dont know. Something reasonable.

Cross section I would guess it's not over six hundred square feet mid deck. It goes to zero at the ends so just halve it lengthwise. Twenty-four thousand cubic feet. There's seven and a half gallons to the cubic foot. A hundred and eighty thousand gallons.

Russell took a pencil and a small notebook from his shirtpocket and crossed his legs in front of him.

It's fifteen hours, Western said. Except that it will take a bit longer than that. That's figuring the GPM that the pumps are rated at but they're not going to operate at maximum. And we're assuming that none of them quit on us.

Red bit into his sandwich again and shook his head. Russell put away his notebook.

But not before breakfast.

It's just a guess.

Sure. But you dont want those pumps sucking air.

When they pulled into the marina the lights were just coming on along the dock. Western pitched their divebags up onto the deck and Gary switched the motor off.

What time you want to see me in the morning?

Early.

Early it is.

They slung their bags over their shoulders and headed for the parkinglot. You get cold dont you? Red said.

Yeah. My head gets cold.

Yeah. There's a certain level of cold that after a while it's hard to get warm again.

Dry suits.

Yeah. They're a pain in the ass.

Bear suits. Thermal underwear.

I hear you.

When they pulled in at the salvage site the next morning there was a motorboat tethered off the end of the barge and two fairly decent-looking girls in jeans were sitting on the deck of the barge drinking beer.

Red stood and threw a line up onto the deck. He looked at Western. Did you order them?

No. But I'm looking at our crane operator with new eyes.

Women will fool you.

Yes they will.

I always heard they were attracted to heavy equipment.

They waved to the girls and the girls waved back. The tug was half way out of the water and the bilge pumps were slogging away.

You think he really believes he's going to put that thing back in service?

The tug.

Yeah.

Dont know.

You all want a beer? One of the girls was holding up a bottle.

No thanks. Where's our guy at?

He'll be back. We're fixin to boil up a bunch of shrimp.

Where are you all from?

Biloxi.

It's a wonderful world.

What?

I love Biloxi.

Biloxi?

Maybe he's resting up from his labors.

Maybe he's resting up for his labors.

I think there's something about the salvage business we aint come to grips with yet.

They motored upriver to Socola and drank beer at a little bar across the road from the docks. Red looked out the sandcrusted window.

You think the boat's all right?

I think so. They dont steal boats down here. They just steal everything else. It's a point of honor with them.

Not stealing boats?

No. Stealing everything else.

You think that was in his contract? Pussy for the crane operator?

Could be.

You ever think about some other line of work?

All the time.

Bullshit.

When they went back downriver the tugboat was hanging in the cables and music was coming from the wheelhouse of the barge. They pulled in and tied up. The crane pilot had fired up a gas grill and was frying up a bunch of shrimp in what looked like a garbage can lid.

When are you going to set this thing on the deck?

Whenever your fucked up crew gets here.

To set the chocks.

Yeah. You all want some shrimp?

Sure. You aim to take this thing down to Venice?

If it's goin I guess I am. Get a plate. There's some sauce over there.

What's your name?

Richard.

I'm Red.

How you doin Red.

I'm okay.

Dont call me Dick.

Why? Is your last name Head?

You're a funny motherfucker.

You got any beer in that cooler?

Sure. Help yourself.

What happened to the girls?

They aint nothin happened to the girls. They're just waiting on me to whistle.

Yeah, well. These shrimp are pretty good.

What about your buddy there?

Get a plate, Bobby. These are pretty good.

When he walked into the Seven Seas Janice waved him over. You had a call from Oiler. He said he'd call back tomorrow night around seven your time if he got a chance.

Where was he?

He was on a boat. The call was patched through on a radio-telephone.

Was that all he said?

It's all I could make out. The line was pretty bad.

Thanks, Janice. How's Mr Billy Ray?

I think he'll be happy to see you.

Thanks.

He went upstairs and fed the cat and stretched out on the bed with the cat on his stomach. You are the best cat, he said. I dont think I ever knew a finer cat.

He thought that he would go out and get something to eat. Then he thought he would see what was in the little refrigerator. Then he fell asleep.

He talked to Russell in the morning. The barge had pulled into Venice after dark and they offloaded the tug onto a lowboy and trucked it into the yard and unloaded it with the yard crane and set it up on blocks. He said there were dead fish in the bilge and a fairly large turtle.

He went down in the evening and waited in the bar until after ten oclock but Oiler never called. He went out and ate and came back and Janice handed him a slip of paper with a number on it. Debbie? she said.

Debbie.

He went to the payphone and called.

Darling.

Hi.

I had a dream about you and when I woke up I was worried.

What was the dream?

Are you all right?

I'm all right. What was the dream?

I know you dont believe in dreams.

Debbie.

Yes.

The dream.

Okay. It was very strange. This building was on fire and you had on this special suit. This special firesuit. It looked sort of like a spacesuit and you were going into the building to rescue these people. And you just walked into this enormous fire and disappeared and these firemen were standing there and one of them said: He's not going to make it. That suit is an R-210 and he would need at least an R-280 for this. Then I woke up.

He leaned with his elbow on the little shelf, the phone to his ear.

Bobby?

I'm here.

What do you think it means?

I dont know. It's your dream.

It's just that it was so very real. I almost called you.

I guess I should stay out of burning buildings.

Are you doing anything dangerous?

No more than usual.

That's not a no. I suppose you're not even aware that you have a death wish.

I have a death wish.

Yes.

I think I need to supervise your reading more closely. You do believe in dreams I take it.

I dont know, Bobby. You mean can they predict things?

Yes.

Sometimes. I suppose. I believe in a woman's intuition.

Are you working on that?

Always.

What is it that you think I should do?

I dont know, Baby. Just be careful.

All right. I will.

Western waited. This is a long silence, he said.

I know you, Bobby. You're not even a fatalist.

Not even.

I know you dont believe in God. But you dont even believe that there is a structure to the world. To a person's life.

It's just a dream.

It's not just that.

It's just what then? Are you crying?

I'm sorry. I'm being silly.

What else?

Why is there something else?

I dont know. Is there?

I dont know, Bobby. It's just that I've thought a lot about you lately. How many friends do you have who knew Alicia?

A few. You. John. People in Knoxville. Mostly you and John. The family of course. I dont want to talk about her.

All right.

You're just being morbid. I'll take you tomorrow if you like.

I dont have any time off.

I'll call you.

All right. I have to go. I'm not trying to worry you Bobby.

I know.

Okay.

The next morning when he walked into Lou's office Lou looked up and studied him. Then he sat back in his chair. Well. I can see you aint heard.

I guess not.

Red just left out of here. He's on his way up to the bar.

All right. Heard what?

Sorry, Bobby. Oiler's dead. No other way to say it.

Western went over and sat in one of the little metal chairs. Ah God, he said. You sorry sons of bitches.

I'm sorry, Bobby.

Have you called anybody?

Yes. I had his sister's number. She lives in Des Moines Iowa.

She's a schoolteacher.

I think that is right. Nobody's answered yet.

What happened?

I dont know. Hard to get straight answers out of those people. He was dead in the bell. They brought him up in the bell.

I thought he was in saturation.

I dont know. Who are the sons of bitches you're talkin about?

Dont pay any attention to me. They'll bury him at sea. You watch. He wont be coming home.

How do you know that?

You watch.

IV

It may have been a dog that woke her. Something on the road in the night. Then the quiet. A shadow. When she turned there was a thing on her windowsill. Crouching on the banquette with its hands clawed upon its knees, leering, its head swiveling slowly. Elf's ears and eyes cold as stone taws in the mercury yardlight raw upon the glass. It shifted and turned. A leather tail slithered over its lizard feet. The blind eyes searched her out. Swinging its head on its scrannel neck in the black iron collar it wore. She followed that lidless gaze. Something in the shadows beyond the dormer light. Breath of the void. A blackness without name or measure. She buried her face in her hands and whispered her brother's name.

They came a few days later. No special day. Spring of the year. The woods were white with dogwood blossoms even in the night. She sat at the dressingtable which had belonged to her greatgrandmother and which had been taken out of the house in Anderson County at night even as the waters were rising. She studied herself in the flecked and yellowed glass. The slight warp of it made of her perfect face a pre-raphaelite portrait, long and gently skewed. In the glass behind her a pale horde of ancient familiars. Clad in graveclothes and naught but bone beneath the moldering rags. Clamoring silently. She all but smiled at them and they faded in the glass until it gave back only her face. In the drawer of the dressingtable was a packet of letters tied with a blue silk ribbon. Antique stamps and a script in brown ink penned with a quill. Addressed to a house whose stones now lay in the silt at the bottom of a lake. A comb and brush of tortoiseshell. An eveningpurse of dulled orrice once carried to a dance where promises were made of which none survive. A small sachet of satin cloth faint yet with musty lavender. Of the woman who once sat here as a bride she remembers little. A lingering scent. A voice on the stairs that said have I burned a rose in a dish and forgot?

The Kid slipped a ring of keys from one flipper to the other and folded them away from sight and passed the flipper before him at his waist and opened it to show the keys were gone. Hi, Sweetcakes, he said. Dya miss me?

No, she said. She turned on the worn velvet settee. Where are your friends?

Thought I'd scope things out first. Make sure the coast was clear.

Clear of what?

The Kid ignored her. He paced up and back, his flippers clasped behind him. He went to the window and stood. Well, he said. You know how things are.

No. I dont. How are they?

But the Kid seemed lost in thought. Standing with his chinless face folded in one flipper. He shook his head. As if at some ill prospect.

You're just totally bogus, she said. Dont you think I can see that this is all just for my benefit?

What is?

The introspection. The consulting of some inner self.

Like there aint one I suppose.

Like.

Hmm.

You dont even concern me. You're just a pain in the ass. You and your entertainments. Your shopworn Chautauquas.

Jesus, Jessica. How about cutting me some slack? It's not like there's a playbook here. How about we start over? How about: Hi, come on in. Make yourself at home. Mi casa es su casa. That sort of thing.

You're not at home. I dont want you here.

Yeah, but that's not really the issue. If I wasnt here there wouldnt be this discussion about me being here and whether I'm welcome or not. I thought you were supposed to be this brainiac.

I wish you could listen to yourself.

Dont we all.

How long have you been here?

Not long. You?

I live here.

I sense the quality of the repartee declining. What sort of meds have they got you on, Luscious?

I'm not on any meds if it's any of your business. I didnt think you were coming back.

Yeah. Just in the nick as it turns out. We thought you might need some time to get acclimated. We had Mr Bones check you out on a twenty-eight day schedule. You were never far from our thoughts. The Bonesrody thought you might have been feeling a bit poorly back in the dog days but we didnt reckon it was anything to worry about. He suspected a bout of the vox populi attended by cramps. Which of course raises the old question of inner ailings and outer and where to draw the line. Always an issue. Not everything malodorous is a memory. Commodeodor in the corridors for instance such as might be found with the spring thaw in the colder latitudes. Farrago North Dakota or some such blighty sink where the mentally defective are wont to pool. Long away and far ago. As it says in the song.

He turned and studied her. Maybe best to not revisit those regimes. Or previsit. Let the cat out of the bag. Catfarts sure to follow, no doubt. Anyway, you shouldnt listen to everything you believe. You're liable to get hoisted on your own pilchard. How are the computations coming?

Now you expect me to chat gibberish with you I suppose.

I just wondered if you were finding numbers for everything, that's all.

She had put down her brush and she looked at the closet and she looked at the Kid again. I didnt think you were here by yourself.

Your trouble is you dont know when you're well off. Someone winds up under the bus and the driver comes to a stop and he stands up and you think he's going to send for help but then you see that he's scroll-

ing through the destinations on his roller trying to find some segue from geography to destiny. If you get my meaning.

I dont.

It's all right. We'll come back to it later.

Sure we will. I suppose you came on the bus again.

Jesus. Not the bus again. Not suitably dressed, I suppose. Improper bus attire. How did you get here?

I told you. I live here.

Yeah? You told Granny that you wanted to live in the woods with the raccoons and she hauled you off to see Doctor Hard-Dick to have your head examined except that's not all that got examined is it?

You dont know anything about it. And his name is Doctor Hardwick.

Yeah, whatever.

And you're here when I'm at school. Going through my papers.

You're never at school. You're always playing hooky. Anyway, have you thought about that question?

I know you've been reading my diary.

Yeah? I thought I was just some fearful delirium? What happened to that? I guess I should avoid repeating you back to yourself or you'll claim that I read it in your daybook but let's just say it was something about a small latterday autoarchon out of the high clavens of dingbatry flapping about in your prenubile boudoir. Well mysteries just abound dont they? Before we mire up too deep in the accusatory voice it might be well to remind ourselves that you cant misrepresent what has yet to occur.

I havent told my brother about you you know.

Yeah? I dont know what I'm supposed to make of that. You dont think he'll pack you off to Doctor Dickhead? Him and Granny? Word on the street is that your precious Bobby is at best a pudpuller and a wanker nonpareil.

You dont know anything about my brother.

Well, I suppose that's good. Loyalty. No need to get into the covenants. We can save that for another day.

Sure. You dont think they're getting restless in there? I hear snuffling.

They know where I am.

I suppose that sooner or later you'll exhaust your little bag of tricks. What happens then?

Time will tell.

Your shadow moving over the floor as you pass the lamp is a nice touch but I'm not buying it.

Just an elementary observation I suppose. Well, you cant say that we dont try.

Or the fact that you darken a mirror.

Yeah, but can he cloud one?

I dont know. I dont know and I dont care. It's not germane.

Or Lucy or Mabel. Maybe I should pinch myself.

That's to see if you're dreaming.

And that's not a reasonable inquiry I suppose. Well, we wont sweat it. There's thornier issues on the table. When are you going back to school? Your grandmother's not going to call in sick for you forever you know.

I know.

You keep odd hours.

I'm an odd girl.

Up all night scribbling calculations on your yellowpad. Maybe you should try counting sheep. Or in your case maybe logging sheep. For the numerically enhanced.

I'll keep it in mind.

Or you just sit staring into space. I guess that's part of the modus. How do you know it's not all gibberish?

You dont. That's what you're trying to find out.

When is Bobby Shafto coming?

My brother will be here in two weeks.

And then what?

What do you mean then what?

What are your intentions is what I mean by then what.

My intentions?

Yes.

He's my brother.

Like you havent set your cap for him. To phrase it chastely.

You dont know what you're talking about. Anyway, it's none of your business.

Well. You know me.

No I dont. I dont know you.

Yeah? The little weird one just yammers on and on, dont he? We seem to have a fly in the ointment here. Sweet sixteen and never been kissed and she's got an eye for her brother. Boy oh boy. You ever think you might try going out on a regular date?

With who? Or what? And I'm not sixteen.

Maybe just make an effort.

An effort.

At being normal. What was wrong with going out for cheerleader? As you were asked to do. Like your mom.

Would that have gotten rid of you?

You never know.

I think I know. Is that an animal of some sort?

Maybe. Things show up from time to time that appear to be one-offs. All the worse for the bio-folks. Anyway, we need to work on the lighting in here.

If you were talking in the next room could I hear you?

Jesus. What next room? You're in the attic.

Any next room. Some dankenroom of my choosing.

Where are we going with this?

Why cant you answer the question?

Okay. You can only hear what you're listening to. If you're listening to a conversation in a room and you stop and start listening to a different conversation you dont know how you do that you just do it. It's all in your head. It's not like moving your eyeballs. Your ears stay put.

So?

So what.

I'm thinking.

Yeah? Let me know when you're done.

I'm still having trouble with the bus business.

Weeping Jesus.

You sit in the seats.

The seat.

You sit in the seat.

Yeah. Unless they're all spoken for. Which can happen. I try to avoid that. As a straphanger my feet terminate about a foot shy of the floor.

Has anyone ever tried to sit on you?

Where is this going, Gretchen?

Have they?

Sure. You got to be on your toes. The shadow of some colossal fundament hoving. Blotting out the sun. You're sitting there reading your paper and the light dims. You cant take anything for granted. Of course I'm nothing if not nimble as you may have noticed.

So you're on the bus.

Can we get off the fucking bus?

You're on the bus. You and your fellow cohorts.

Mind your grammar, Sweetness. Co means fellow.

You and your cohorts. And you talk.

Sometimes. Maybe. Sure.

Can they hear you?

The copassengers.

Yes.

Dunno. See paragraph C above. It's all the same question. As in maybe they could if they listened. Whatever it is that they might be alerted to listen to. And by whom.

Can they hear you yes or no.

Like do they butt in with an opinion?

No. Not like. Let me ask you a different question.

Ask away.

Are you taking dictation?

Am I what?

Taking dictation. Are you listening to someone. Is someone advising you?

Holy shit. I only wish. You?

No. I dont know. I wouldnt know how to make sense of such a thing.

Yeah. Me either. What else?

What else?

Yeah.

I dont know what else.

Yeah, maybe. All right. So they wouldnt let you live in the woods so now you're up here in the attic.

Yes.

Why is that?

Because my uncle Royal who's half deaf watches the television half the night and yells at it.

He yells at it?

Yells.

What about you sawing on your fiddle till all hours?

Okay. That too.

So darlin Bobby Twoshoes on his Christmas vacation comes home and floors the place and runs a one-ten up from below to activate a lamp or two plus the stereo. Shutters on the windows. Never know when somebody might be passing through the yard in the dead of night on tenfoot stilts. Of course she still has to trip down a narrow stairwell to brush her teeth etcetera. And of course it's damnably drafty up here in spite of the bats of fiberglass insulation he's put in. The only heat is what seeps up from below. Maybe he could put some plastic over the windows what do you think?

I like it this way.

Yeah, well. It keeps the drinks cool on the windowsill I suppose. You could probably even hang a few hams from the rafters.

You forgot to mention the closet.

And of course he put in a closet. Where did he learn carpentry?

He taught it to himself. He can do anything.

Yeah? Well that remains to be seen.

What is that supposed to mean?

What do you think it's supposed to mean? I guess it's just a coincidence that Bobbyboy has got you sequestered away up here all by your lonesome.

Coincident to what?

You know coincident to what. Or do you want me to spell it out for you?

My personal life is none of your business.

Really? Well the small one is all but dumbstruck. What is it that you think I'm doing here, Hortense?

I've no idea.

Yeah, right. Jesus it's cold in this place.

So I can see your breath. Big deal. It's all just a big act. I'm not impressed.

Yeah, okay. So what else would you like to discuss?

Your departure?

I just got here.

What time is the first show? I think it's too late for a matinee.

Yeah? Well, who knows. I may do a few steps on the boards myself. You're not so easy to entertain, you know.

I cant really imagine you dancing.

Yeah, well. Sometimes it's hard to tell when a chap is dancing. Could be a number you're not familiar with.

The Kid had paused and was standing in the dormer window looking out over the darkening countryside. The wind sheared thinly along the tin eaves and the glass rattled in the sash and was still again. The girl watched him. My grandmother is going to be calling me to supper, she said. But the Kid seemed distracted. Yeah, he said. Okay. She turned to the mirror and for a moment she thought he was gone but he was there in the glass, his small figure framed in the last light. Watching her.

The purpose of all families in their lives and in their deaths is to create the traitor who will finally erase their history forever. Comments, anybody?

I had good reason. Anyway, I was twelve. Find anything else?

Genealogies are always interesting. You can trace the whole thing back to some stone tracks in a gorge if you like. You're about to doze off and then all hell breaks loose. When you peer into the glass these vergangenheitvolk are peering back. They at least didnt come on the bus. You'll be happy to hear. I think. Where does your stuff stand in these histories? Do reflections also travel at the speed of light? What does your buddy Albert think? When the light hits the glass and starts back in the opposite direction doesnt it have to come to a full stop first? And so everything is supposed to hang on the speed of light but nobody wants to talk about the speed of dark. What's in a shadow? Do they move along at the speed of the light that casts them? How deep do they get? How far down can you clamp your calipers? You scribbled somewhere in the margins that when you lose a dimension you've given up all claims to reality. Save for the mathematical. Is there a route here from the tangible to the numerical that hasnt been explored?

I dont know.

Me either.

Photons are quantum particles. They're not little tennisballs.

Yeah, said the Kid. He dredged up his watch and checked the time. Maybe you'd better go eat. You need to keep your strength up if you aim to wrest the secrets of creation from the gods. They're a testy lot by all accounts.

He closed the watch and put it away. He shook his head. Jesus, he said. Where do the days go?

In the evening he went down to the bar and got a hamburger and a beer. No one spoke to him. When he went out Josie tilted her chin at him. I'm sorry, Bobby, she said. He nodded. He walked up the street. The old paving stones wet with damp. New Orleans. November 29th 1980. He stood waiting to cross. The headlights of the car coming down the street doubled on the wet black stones. A ship's horn in the river. The measured trip of the piledriver. He was cold standing there in the fine rain and he crossed the street and went on. When he got to the cathedral he went up the stairs and went in.

Old women lighting candles. The dead remembered here who had no other being and who would soon have none at all. His father was on Campañia Hill with Oppenheimer at Trinity. Teller. Bethe. Lawrence. Feynman. Teller was passing around suntan lotion. They stood in goggles and gloves. Like welders. Oppenheimer was a chainsmoker with a chronic cough and bad teeth. His eyes were a striking blue. He had an accent of some kind. Almost Irish. He wore good clothes but they hung on him. He weighed nothing. Groves hired him because he had seen that he could not be intimidated. That was all. A lot of very smart people thought he was possibly the smartest man God ever made. Odd chap, that God.

There were people who escaped from Hiroshima and rushed to Nagasaki to see that their loved ones were safe. Arriving just in time to be incinerated. He went there after the war with a team of scientists. My father. He said that everything was rusty. Everything looked covered with rust. There were burnt-out shells of trolleycars standing in the streets. The glass melted out of the sashes and pooled on the bricks. Seated on the blackened springs the charred skeletons of the passengers with their clothes and hair gone and their bones hung with blackened strips of flesh. Their eyes boiled from their sockets. Lips and noses burned away. Sitting in their seats laughing. The living walked about but there was no place to go. They waded by the thousands into the river and died there. They were like insects in that no one direction was preferable to another. Burning people crawled among the corpses like some horror in a vast crematorium. They simply thought that the world had ended. It hardly even occurred to them that it had anything to do with the war. They carried their skin bundled up in their arms before them like wash that it not drag in the rubble and ash and they passed one another mindlessly on their mindless journeyings over the smoking afterground, the sighted no better served than the blind. The news of all this did not even leave the city for two days. Those who survived would often remember these horrors with a certain aesthetic to them. In that mycoidal phantom blooming in the dawn like an evil lotus and in the melting of solids not heretofore known to do so stood a truth that would silence poetry a thousand years. Like an immense bladder, they would say. Like some sea thing. Wobbling slightly on the near horizon. Then the unspeakable noise. They saw birds in the dawn sky ignite and explode soundlessly and fall in long arcs earthward like burning party favors.

He sat for a long time in the wooden pew, bent forward like any other penitent. The women moved softly down the aisle. You believe that the loss of those you loved has absolved you of all else. Let me tell you a story.

There were thirty-seven of her letters and although he knew them each by heart he read them over and over. All save the last. He had asked her if she believed in an afterlife and she said that she did not discount such a thing. That it could be. She just doubted that it could be for her. If there was a heaven, was it not founded upon the writhing bodies of the damned? Lastly she said that God was not interested in our theology but only in our silence.

When they left Mexico City the plane lifted up through the blue dusk into sunlight again and banked over the city and the moon dropped down the glass of the cabin like a coin falling through the sea. The summit of Popocatépetl broke through the clouds. Sunlight on the snow. The long blue shadows. The plane swung slowly north. Far below the shape of the city in its deep mauve grids like a vast motherboard. The lights had begun to come on. An edge to the dusk. Ixtaccihuatl. Dropping away. The coming darkness. The plane leveled off at twenty-seven thousand feet and headed north through the Mexican night with the stars milling in the sternway.

She was eighteen. It had rained all day on her birthday. They stayed in the hotel and read old Life magazines they'd found in a junkshop. She sat in the floor and turned the pages slowly and drank tea. Later when she went down the hallway to knock at his door the hall lights were on at mid day. At the end of the hall the curtains were lifting in the wind. She walked down and stood looking out. A gray and empty lot. The curtains were heavy from the rain and the windowsill was wet but the rain had stopped. There was a fire escape outside the window and the iron slats were a dark purple in the wet. In the yard below a shed made from roofing tin. A dog barking. Cool and troubling the air, the light. Voices in Spanish.

When he woke she was leaning against his shoulder. He thought she was asleep but she was looking out the plane window. We can do whatever we want, she said.

No, he said. We cant.

In the dying light a river like a frayed silver rope. Lakes deep in the stone coulees white with ice. The western mountains burning. The portside navigation lights came on. The starboard lights were green. As on a ship. The pilot would turn them off in the clouds because of the reflection. When he woke later far to the north a desert city was passing under the wing and sliding off into the darkness like the Crab Nebula. A cast of stones upon a jeweler's blackcloth. Her hair was like gossamer. He wasnt sure what gossamer was. Her hair was like gossamer.

It was cold in Chicago. Raggedy men standing around a steam grate in the dawn. She had nightmares as a child and she would crawl into bed with her grandmother and her grandmother would hold her and tell her that it was all right and that it was only a dream. And she said yes it was only a dream but it was not all right. The last time they went to Mexico City he had left her in the hotel while he went to the airline office to confirm their reservations. When he came back to the hotel he had to tell her that the airline office was closed and that the airline had gone out of business and that their tickets were worthless. They went to El Paso on the bus. Twenty-four hours. The smoke from the Mexican cigarettes like a burning landfill. She slept with her head in his lap. A woman two seats ahead kept turning and looking back at her. At the golden hair spilling over the armrest.

Mi hermana, he said.

She looked back again. De veras?

Sí. De veras. A dónde va?

A Juárez. Y ustedes?

No sé. Al fin del camino.

His father was born in Akron Ohio and his grandmother Western died there in 1968. His sister called from Akron. She wanted to know if he was coming to the funeral.

I dont know.

I think you should come.

All right.

He showed up late in jeans and a black coat. The whole family was long dead and the funeral consisted of him and his sister and eight or ten old women and one old man who wasnt sure where he was. He met his sister at the door and walked her out to the street.

Are you going to the cemetery?

I'm going where you're going.

Why dont we just leave. Do you have a car?

No.

Good. Come on.

They drove to a cafe out on Washington Street. You didnt bring that black dress with you.

I dont own a black dress. Well. I do now.

How long have you been here?

About ten days. She didnt have anybody, Bobby.

Provide, provide.

I'm supposed to tell you that there's a bunch of gold buried in the basement of the house.

Gold.

She was quite serious. She wouldnt let go of my hand.

And lucid?

Yes.

They've torn down the house. They're building the freeway through there.

I know. But they havent torn down the basement.

You're serious.

Can we get some tea?

He put her on a plane that evening and then drove back to the motel and the next day he drove to the house. The only thing left was the driveway. He sat studying the ruins of the old neighborhood. At least there was no one around. It was a Saturday and the roadgraders were parked in a mud cut about a mile to the south. He walked up the old ribbed concrete drive where he used to play with his toy trucks and he stood looking down into the basement. The walls were gray rubble limestone. The wooden stairs rose into the empty gray sky. The floor itself was concrete but it was badly cracked and it didnt look too solid. All right, he said. What the hell.

He came back two hours later with a rented metal detector. An eight pound maul and a mattock and shovel. He climbed down into the cellar and began to scan the floor. He got a number of readings and he blew away the dust and marked the floor with a black greasepencil. By evening he'd dug six holes in the floor, breaking up the sandy concrete and digging down through the clay. He found a large file, the head of a hammer, the blade of a plane. An antique iron gear. He found an iron casting with two machined faces that was marked Brown & Sharpe. No idea what it was.

He pitched the tools one at a time up out of the cellar and climbed up the shaky stairs with the metal detector and collected everything and put it in the trunk of the rental car and drove back to the motel and went to bed.

He'd intended to return the detector the next morning and try to get a flight out but he had a dream about his grandmother and it woke him and he lay staring at the shadow of the windowframe on the upper wall cast there by the groundlights in the shrubbery outside. After a while he got up and got a plastic cup off the dresser and still in his shorts he went out to the drink machines in the breezeway and got some ice and a can of orange juice and came back and sat on the bed in the dark.

She'd worked in the textile mills in Rhode Island as a child. She and her sister. They read to each other by candlelight at the end of those twelve-hour days in a room where you could see your breath. Whittier and Longfellow and Scott and later Milton and Shakespeare. She was thirty when she married and his father was her only child. The man she married was a chemist and an engineer and he held several patents in the vulcanization process of rubber and the basement was his home laboratory and workshop. It was a magic place and even as a child Western was given the run of it.

The dream was that his grandmother had called down the stairs to him where he sat at his grandfather's workbench and he went to the stairs and she said: You were so quiet. I just wanted to know you were still there.

He ate breakfast in the motel coffeeshop and drove back out to the house. He checked the dial on the metal detector and then passed the plate back and forth over the concrete behind the stairs. Twenty minutes later he was squatting on his knees grubbing in the musty clay at the bottom of the hole he'd dug. What he lifted out was an eighteen inch length of heavy lead waterpipe.

He twisted away the dirt and the remains of the old sacking in which the pipe had been wrapped. It was about an inch and a half in diameter and stopped at either end with a female cap. The threads were sealed with white lead. You could see the rim of it around the edge, yellow with age. He stood up and carried it over to the wall and found a space in the stonework to jam the cap into and he tried to twist the pipe but the cap wouldnt move. He shook it. It felt completely solid.

There were sixteen of them in all. Buried in three holes in the floor.

He stacked them against the wall and dug some more with the shovel but there was nothing else there. He ran the detector over a good bit of the space but he didnt pick up anything else. He'd lost all track of the time.

The pipes were a bit too heavy to throw up over the wall and he carried them one at a time up the ladder and down the driveway and piled them in front of the car. He left the maul and the shovel in the cellar and put the detector in the back seat of the car and opened the trunk lid and carried the pipes back and stacked them in the trunk. By the time he was done the rear of the car was visibly down on its springs.

When he got to the rental store it was closed and he drove back out to the hardware store and bought two sets of large visegrips and then drove back to the motel.

He backed the car as close to the door as he could get it and went in and laid the bag with the visegrips on the table and stretched out on the bed to wait for nightfall. He couldnt sleep and after a while he got up and got the visegrips and pried them off the display cards they were stapled to and put the cards and the bag in the trash and walked out to watch the darkness fall over Akron.

He carried the pipes in two at a time and stacked them just inside the door and then shut the trunk of the car and came back in and closed the door and locked it. He sat in the floor with the visegrips and backed off the jaws and fitted them to the caps at either end, adjusting the jaws with the knurled screw and clamping them shut at ninety degrees to each other. He laid the pipe on the carpet and stood on one visegrip and bent and took hold of the other with both hands and leaned into it. The pliers turned on the cap, raking up fresh metal bright under the teeth. He adjusted the jaws tighter and clamped them again and bore down on the pliers and this time the cap began slowly to turn. A coil of dried white lead spiraled up from the threads. He pushed the pliers to the floor and released the jaws with the toggle and clamped them again. A few turns and the cap felt pretty loose and he stood the pipe upright and turned the pliers by hand and lifted off the cap and laid the pliers in the floor and turned the pipe upside down and held it in both hands and shook it.

What tumbled out onto the carpet were about four double handfuls of US Mint double-eagle twenty dollar goldpieces bright as the day they were minted.

He sat there looking at them. He picked one up and turned it in his hand. He knew nothing about them. What they might be worth. If you could even sell them. He'd never heard of St-Gaudens. His strange saga as an artist. He stacked the coins like poker chips. There were two hundred of them. Thirty-two hundred in all? Face value sixty-four thousand dollars. They were worth what? Ten times that? He would find out that he wasnt even close.

He spent the next two hours turning the caps off the other lengths of pipe. When he was done the pipes and the caps were piled against the wall and there was what looked like at least half a washtubful of gold piled in the floor. He checked the dates and found none later than 1930 and he supposed that was the last year that any were buried. He scooped up a handful of the coins and hefted them and he looked at the pile. He thought that there must be well over a hundred pounds of gold piled up in the motel room floor. He got up and went to the closet and got down the extra blanket and spread it over the coins and went to bed.

He woke up at four twenty in the morning and switched on the light. He got up and went over and pulled away the blanket and sat in the floor looking at the coins. It surprised him. He already knew that he was going to buy a revolver.

In the morning he emptied his suitcase and carried the gold out to the car in the suitcase, four trips in all. He dumped the gold into the trunk and spread his clothes over it and shut the trunk and went back in. He threaded the caps back loosely onto the pipes and carried the pipes out and put them in the floor of the car on the passenger side. He put a half dozen of the coins in his pocket and got in the car and drove around to the coffeeshop and went in and ate breakfast.

He looked up coin dealers in the phone directory. There were two of them. He wrote down the addresses. Then he drove to the first store and parked and walked in.

The man was polite and helpful. He explained that there were two types of the coin. The St-Gaudens—or Standing Liberty—and the Liberty Head. The St-Gaudens was the more valuable.

How did you come by these? If I might ask.

They belonged to my grandfather.

They're very nice. You shouldnt carry them in your pocket.

No?

Gold is very soft. Two of these are close to mint. What we would call an MS-65. Uncirculated. Well, in the real world you never rate a coin higher than MS-63. MS stands for mint state.

He was looking at the coins through a loupe. Very nice, he said.

He wrote down figures on a pad as he examined them. Then he totaled them and turned the pad and slid it in front of Western. When Western walked out of the shop ten minutes later he had over three thousand dollars in his pocket. He sat in the car and ran the numbers through his head. Then he ran them again.

He took the metal detector back to the rental store and drove out to the hardware store where he bought four white canvas mason's bags with leather bottoms and leather straps and handles. He drove until he came to a vacant lot and he pulled over and got out and dumped the lengths of lead pipe in the weeds. He sold a dozen more coins at the other coin dealer's and that evening he bought for cash a black 1968 Dodge Charger with a 426 Hemi engine that had four thousand miles on the odometer. It had headers and twin four barrel Holleys on an Offenhauser intake. He had the dealer return the rental car and he bought a stainless steel Smith & Wesson .38 special revolver with a four inch barrel and for the next two weeks he drove through the midwest selling coins in batches of a few dozen. He had a lock for the steering wheel but he carried everything in at night and he slept with the .38. He had a coin collector's guide and he would sit in the motel at night and sort through the coins and slide them into small plastic envelopes and put them in the mason's bags. Every few days he'd take the coins and small bills to a bank and cash them in for hundred dollar bills. He swung down to Louisville and set out across country. By the time he got to Oklahoma he had nine hundred thousand dollars in a shoebox fastened with a rubber band and he still had one of the bags filled with coins. The Charger went like a scalded rat and he'd been stopped by the Highway Patrol once and now he drove more carefully. He'd no idea how he'd go about explaining the contents of the trunk to a police officer. He went to Dallas, San Antonio, Houston. By the time he got to Tucson he'd sold all but a double handful of the coins and he checked into the Arizona Inn and carried in all the money and stacked it on the dresser and then divided the stack by eye into two equal stacks and put the two stacks into two of the empty bags and fastened the straps. Then he called Jimmy Anderson's bar. She answered the phone. Heaven, she said.

Is God there?

He'll be in at seven. Can I help you? Bobby? Is that you?

Yes.

Where are you?

I'm at the Arizona Inn. I've got some money for you.

I dont need any money.

A lot of money. And I bought you a car.

It was quiet at the other end of the phone.

Are you there?

I'm here.

How did you know that I'd go look?

Because I asked you to.

V

The Kid was sitting at her desk in a frockcoat and frightwig. Rimless eyeglasses and a wispy goatee glued to his chin. She sat up in the bed and rubbed the sleep from her eyes. What are you supposed to be? she said.

He noted the time and laid his watch by on the desk. He adjusted his glasses and leafed through the pages of his notebook, sucking the while on a clay pipe. Very well, he said. Did he attempt liberties with your person?

What?

Did he attempt to remove your insteps?

Remove my what?

Your unspeakables. Did he attempt to pull them down.

Unmentionables. It's none of your business. And the good doctor smoked cigars, not a pipe.

Was there digital manipulation?

You look ridiculous in that get-up.

Were there attempts perhaps to slobber upon your clamlet?

You're disgusting. Did you know that?

Did you ask him to stop?

Would you ever mind leaving please?

The Kid peered at her over the tops of his glasses. The hour's not up. Any nightsweats?

They had put her on antipsychotics and she took them for a couple of days until she got a chance to read the literature. When she got to Tardive Dyskinesia she flushed everything down the toilet. The Kid was back the next day, pacing. She was already dressed to go out with her brother. Make yourself at home, she said.

Yeah right. What time can we expect you?

Late.

When they came in they would make tea and sit and talk mathematics and physics until their grandmother came down in her robe to fix breakfast. By the time he left for Caltech in the fall he'd changed his major from math to physics. The reasons he gave in his letter were the best he could come up with but they werent the reason. The reason was that in talking to her on those warm nights at his grandmother's kitchen table he had seen briefly into the deep heart of number and he knew that world would be forever closed to him.

The Kid stood at the window. Cold out there, he said. What are you writing?

I'm trying to ignore you.

Good luck with that. Where'd you get the snazzy fountain pen?

It belonged to my father. It was given to him by President Eisenhower.

Yeah? No defacto defectors in that lot, were there? You dont think that odd I suppose. What are you guys doing tomorrow? I dont know, you? I dont know. What do you say we blow up the world? Hey, there's an idea.

He left the window and began to pace again. He wrinkled his brow and shaped one flipper into the palm of the other. We might have very different notions about the nature of the oncoming night, he said. But as darkness descends does it matter?

I dont know.

An outlier such as yourself always raises again the question as to where this ship is headed and why. Is there a common denominator to existence? Core questions can make you look stupid. Are you with me?

Sure.

Good girl. Where was I?

Looking stupid.

Right. The question that comes to mind of course is who is the ideal guest.

Of the universe.

Yes. Coupled with the question of where it actually is in fact that we are. These are not static problems since there are no static things. Is the ideal guest the next such in a sequence of such? Is that what you'd have guessed? Or that maybe the game is rigged?

More tautologies.

So? What's wrong with that? At least they're not hard to spell. Can you really write and carry on a conversation at the same time?

It depends on the conversation.

Let me see.

She turned the pad and slid it over the bed and he bent to look. Jesus, he said. What the fuck is that?

It's shorthand. Gabelsberger.

It looks like worms crawled out of an inkbottle. This stuff goes in your file you know. Do you scribble when you're having your little chats with Doctor Hard-Dick? Why do I get the feeling that he at least gets a little respect?

What little he gets is because he's a doctor. Whereas you're a dwarf. And his name is Hardwick.

Jesus.

I'm sorry. I shouldnt have said that.

I've heard of looking a gift horse in the mouth but not of whacking him in the teeth with a shovel.

I am sorry.

Yeah, well. Probably comes from listening to him say nasty things about me. Anyway I really dont know how you deal with someone who regards you as the product of an unruly liver. He probably doesnt get it that if you scratch from the menu everything that's hard to swallow it's going to make for a pretty lean lunch.

I'm sorry I called you a dwarf. I wish I could take it back.

Yeah. It wouldnt make me any taller though, would it? Anyway, you need to give a bit more thought to your own recent history before wishing me out of it. You sure you're logging all this?

Dont worry. It's a coldstop file. Everything's retrievable.

Maybe. Of course there's always the likelihood of something getting reconfigured into another format by cybertrolls somewhere down in the circuitry.

I'm going to bed.

She switched off the bedside lamp and in the dark of the room where the mercury light framed the window she pulled off her jeans and her sweater and socks and crawled into bed and pulled the covers up and lay listening. She could feel him move closer. Listen, Ducklescence, he whispered. You will never know what the world is made of. The only thing that's certain is that it's not made of the world. As you close upon some mathematical description of reality you cant help but lose what is being described. Every inquiry displaces what is addressed. A moment in time is a fact, not a possibility. The world will take your life. But above all and lastly the world does not know that you are here. You think that you understand this. But you dont. Not in your heart you dont. If you did you would be terrified. And you're not. Not yet. And now, good night.

She shut the door behind her and leaned against it. Cigarette smoke was coiling in the lampshade at her desk. The Kid sat with his feet up. Wearing a jaunty snapbrim hat.

Dont get up, she said.

Dont worry. Nobody's getting up.

It's a joke.

Yeah sure. Your lipstick is smeared.

She crossed the room and sat on the bed. She was dressed in a silver lamé top and a tight blue silk miniskirt. Black stockings and three inch heels. She tossed her blonde hair and took a compact from her purse and opened it and sat wiping her mouth with a handkerchief.

Quite a picture, said the Kid. He took his cigarette from the dish on her desk and took a long draw and blew the smoke sideways. Quite a picture. Where you been?

Dancing.

Yeah?

Yes. I didnt know you smoked.

You've driven me to it. Where's Bobby Boy?

He's gone to bed.

The Kid hauled out his watch and opened it. A few faint notes of bellchime. I guess you went for a late snack after the clubs closed.

Maybe. If it's any of your business.

You could give me a little credit you know. All I've done for you.

All you've done?

Yeah.

You've endarkened my soul.

Jesus. You've got a pretty short memory. How can you say shit like that? Is that a serious comment? Wait a minute. Bobbsy's on his way up here. Isnt he?

No.

The object of your sordid affections. That's his tread on the staircase.

You're disgusting.

The wholly devoted. Well well. I guess I'd better skedaddle.

You're full of it. There's no one on the stairs. I'm going to bed.

Jesus. What are you doing?

I'm getting undressed.

You cant do that.

Watch me.

The Kid covered his face. Christ, he said. Now where are you going?

She crossed the room with her clothes over her arm. I'm going to hang up my things. Why? Is there someone in here?

She opened the closet door and put her shoes in the rack and hung up her skirt and blouse and closed the door and padded back across the floor in her underwear and climbed into bed and pulled up the covers and switched off the lamp on the table. Good night, she said.

She cowled herself in the quilt and lay listening. After a while she pushed back the covers. The Kid was still at her desk. How long are you going to sit there?

I dont know. It's quiet.

Dont you have other clients you could be seeing?

No.

I'm sorry I was mean to you.

Really?

Yes.

It's okay.

I'm going to sleep now.

Okay. Good night.

Good night.

When she'd filled out the forms she went back to the desk and the nurse took them and looked them over and then handed her another one.

Cant I just write: Do with me what you will. And sign it?

No. You cant.

They gave her a locker key and a gown and a pair of slippers and sent her down the hall. In the room she undressed and folded her clothes and put them in the locker and pulled on the gown and found the strings and tied them. Then she sat on the bench and thought about what she had decided to do. A woman came in and smiled briefly at her and opened a locker at the end of the row. Just like heaven, she said. You trade everything in for a robe.

Did you ever play heaven when you were a child? Dress up in sheets and sit around?

No, said the woman. She turned her back on the girl and began to undress. She put on the gown and tied it and stepped into the slippers and shut the locker door and locked it. She shuffled past with the key in her hand and the girl told her that she was supposed to pin the key to her gown so that she wouldnt lose it but the woman just went past and out into the hall.

After a while she got up and shut the locker door and locked it. Then she pinned the key to her gown and stepped into the slippers and went out.

In the examining room she sat on a gurney while a nurse took her temperature and her pulse and bloodpressure. You're a quiet one, she said.

I know. I've got a lot to be quiet about.

The nurse smiled. She tied off the girl's arm with a length of rubber tubing and pulled at the tubing and let it snap. Then she fitted her with an IV and taped it down and an orderly came and wheeled her down the hallway.

A cold white room. After a while a woman came in and looked at her chart. How are you? she said.

I'm okay. So far so good. Who are you?

I'm Doctor Sussman. Why are you by yourself?

I'm not by myself. I'm schizophrenic. Are you going to shave my head?

No. We're not.

Are you the one who's going to fry me?

No one's going to fry you. Do you have any questions?

Do you have a fire extinguisher handy?

The doctor tilted her head and studied her. I suppose. Why?

In case my hair catches fire.

Your hair's not going to catch fire.

Then what's the fire extinguisher for?

You're making a joke.

Yeah. Sort of.

You dont have any questions?

No.

Nothing that you'd like to know? You're not curious.

I cant answer that without being rude. Anyway I'm not here because of what I want to know. Quite the opposite.

What medications are you on? There's nothing here.

I know. I flushed em.

The doctor studied the sheet on the clipboard. She tapped her lower lip with her pen. The nurse had come in and stood fitting a syringe to the IV. She looked at the doctor.

I flushed em, she said again.

Yes. I heard you.

Does that mean you up the amps?

No.

The doctor had moved out of sight behind her. The nurse took a jar from the counter and opened it and began to smear electrolytic gel over her temples. The gel was cold.

Where's the doctor?

I'm here, said the doctor.

I'm going to pass out now.

Yes. It's all right.

When she woke in the recovery room she'd no sense that any time had passed. It was night. At first she thought she was in her bed at home. But she had a rubber biteguard in her mouth. She spat it out. There was a burnt smell in the darkness. Something rank and slightly sulphurous. She put her hand to the plastic nametag around her wrist. That's me. I can check and see.

The door was open. A light in the hall. After a while she pushed herself up. Her head hurt. The cauterized horts in their charred and blackened rags stood smoking at her bedfoot. Dusted with ash but faintly luminous for that. They looked dispirited, sullen, angry. The Kid was pacing up and back. His face was black with soot. The wispy hairs on his head were singed to a stubble and his cloak was smoking. She put one hand to her mouth.

Cute, he said. Really fucking cute.

I'm sorry.

You think this is funny?

No.

What the fuck were you thinking of?

I dont know.

Look at this shit. Is this your idea of a good time?

I'm really sorry.

We got people in the fucking burn unit for Christ sake. Not to mention the smell.

I didnt know.

You should have asked. Christ. He turned away and spat an ashy spittle and looked at her and shook his head. The clutch of blackened chimeras listed and seethed in the hallway light.

I'm sorry, she said. I really am.

Oh that's good. You get that, guys? She's sorry? Well shit. Sorry? Why didnt you say so? Well fuck it. What the hell.

John Sheddan hit the bricks on a cool Friday afternoon and made his way down to the old town of Knoxville to see if he could cadge a pilsner. In the ensuing hours he would borrow two hundred dollars and with it he would buy two hundred dollars' worth of prescription drugs off the street and take them to Morristown and resell them for three hundred. From there he would go to Bill Lee's poker game and win seven hundred dollars and have sex with a female minor in the back seat of a friend's car. From here he would make his way back to Knoxville and board a plane at McGhee Tyson Airport and be in New Orleans well before midnight. Western came upon him almost by chance. Passing the Absinthe House he saw his hat on a table at the window. He turned in and stood watching him until Sheddan lowered his paper and looked up. Lord Wartburg, he said.

Mossy Creek.

I thought I felt myself under observation. Come sit. You dont read the news.

No. What's happened?

Nothing. Just my ongoing work on your profile.

Western tipped back the other chair and sat at the small wooden table. When did you get here?

Sheddan folded the paper and looked at his watch. About ten hours ago. I just got up. I love this town. I just havent figured out how to make a living here.

Tough town.

Yes. You cant trust people, Squire. Honor among thieves is a thing of the past.

You're joshing me.

Not a bit of it. Where's the bloody waiter? Have you had your lunch? No, of course not. It's odd the people who show up in this place.

Me for instance.

No. Not you. Let me just settle up here. We'll go someplace congenial and have a bite of lunch.

They lunched at Arnaud's. Sheddan perused the winelist, shaking his head. Impressive. Who pays these prices, Squire? God. Well, should be something here of interest. An unpretentious Beaujolais. Stay clear of the Villages variety and you'll be well ahead of the game.

You're not having fish then.

I am having fish. It's what they have here. One is not therefore perforce required to drink something insipid. Lobster an exception of course. No reds there. I've always liked this place. It's like a fucking movie set. And it never changes. There are a couple of restaurants in Mexico City it would remind you of. Brat says it's like dining in a barbershop.

Sheddan had turned his waterglass upside down on the linen but the waiter came in a few minutes and righted it and poured it full and then poured Western's.

Excuse me, said John.

Yessir.

Would you take this away, please?

You wouldnt care for water?

I would not.

The waiter carried off the glass on his tray and John bent to the winelist again. Within minutes another waiter appeared and poured another glass of water and set it on the table. Sheddan looked up. Excuse me, he said.

Yessir.

I've no brief with any of the help here. You are all equally free to pour water endlessly. My problem is that I dont want any water. Is there some way that we could at least arrive at a moratorium? Perhaps negotiate? I'd be willing to come to the kitchen and meet with everyone.

Sir?

I dont want any water.

The waiter nodded and took the glass. Sheddan shook his head. God's piles, he said. What is it with the endless pouring of the waters in this country? If you actually needed something—such as a drink—you couldnt get them to the table with a naval flare. It used to drive Churchill crazy.

He folded the winebook away and looked about. Good to be here early. People forget that this town is a port. Overrun with tourists as it is. You get oddities of every stripe. Streets filled with disturbed persons. I saw in the Absinthe House a while back sitting at the bar in illfitting clothes what I feel fairly certain to have been a hairy-eared dwarf lemur from the Madagascar highlands. Tethered to a stool alongside a seaman and drinking beer from a bowl. And it occurred to me that this exotic creature enjoyed small advantage in its singularity when compared to the average tourist—who to my mind comes more and more to resemble something out of an infelicitous drug trip. There are elegant restaurants in this town—unchanged in a century or more—where waiters in formal livery serve an upscale cuisine to bloated oafs who've chosen to dine in their gymclothes if not in their actual undergarments. No one even seems to find this odd. What are you having? Did you want a cocktail?

I think just the wine.

Very good. Are we having fish?

I think the snapper.

Good choice. Maybe we should rethink the wine.

He opened the winebook again and leaned chin in hand. The point, Squire, is that where they used to be confined to State institutions or to the mudrooms and attics of remote country houses they are now abroad everywhere. The government pays them to travel. To procreate, for that matter. I've seen entire families here that can best be explained as hallucinations. Hordes of drooling dolts lurching through the streets. Their inane gibbering. And of course no folly so deranged or pernicious as to escape their advocacy.

He looked up. I know you dont share my animus, Squire, and I own it to be somewhat tempered when I reflect upon my own origins. We dont get far from our raising, as they say in the south. But have you in fact looked around you lately? I think you know how dumb a person is with an IQ of one hundred.

Western regarded him warily. I suppose, he said.

Well half the people are dumber than that. Where do you imagine all this is going?

I've no idea.

I think you've some idea. I know that you think we're very different, me and thee. My father was a country storekeeper and yours a fabricator of expensive devices that make a loud noise and vaporize people. But our common history transcends much. I know you. I know certain days of your childhood. All but weeping with loneliness. Coming upon a certain book in the library and clutching it to you. Carrying it home. Some perfect place to read it. Under a tree perhaps. Beside a stream. Flawed youths of course. To prefer a world of paper. Rejects. But we know another truth, dont we Squire? And of course it's true that any number of these books were penned in lieu of burning down the world—which was their author's true desire. But the real question is are we few the last of a lineage? Will children yet to come harbor a longing for a thing they cannot even name? The legacy of the word is a fragile thing for all its power, but I know where you stand, Squire. I know that there are words spoken by men ages dead that will never leave your heart. Ah, the waiter.

Western watched him eat with a certain admiration. The enthusiasm and the competence with which he addressed matters. They shared a bottle of Riesling for which Sheddan demanded an icebucket. He waved the waiter away and poured Western's glass. Important to establish the ground rules at the onset. Excuse me. Dont even think of pouring wine into our fucking glasses. I see your look. But the truth is I've few demands. Think about it. Stay slightly ahead of the curve. Try to keep the more common miseries at bay. Dont look luck in the eye. Cheers.

Cheers.

The German varieties tend to be a bit sweeter. Which I like. The French favor whites which can double as window cleaner.

It's very nice.

The last time I lunched here was with Seals. A few weeks ago. I thought we were going to be eighty-sixed.

Thrown out.

Yes.

What happened?

The place was crowded and someone unleashed a truly villainous fart. Absolutely horrible. I looked around at the adjoining tables and people were just sitting there with their eyes glazed over. So Seals throws down his napkin and pushes back his chair and rises and demands to know who did it. Christ. We're going to get to the bottom of this, he says. And then he began to point out possible culprits and to demand that they own up. It was you, wasnt it? Jesus. I tried to hiss him down. By now several large and unruly-looking chaps had gotten to their feet. The manager arrived just in the nick and we got Seals seated but he continued to mutter and they rose all over again. Do you know what I find particularly galling, he told them. It's having to share the women with you lot. To listen to you fuckwits holding forth and to see some lissome young thing leaning forward breathlessly with that barely contained frisson with which we are all familiar the better to inhale without stint an absolute plaguebreath of bilge and bullshit as if it were the word of the prophets. It's painful but still I suppose one has to extend a certain latitude to the little dears. They've so little time in which to parlay that pussy into something of substance. But it nettles. That you knucklewalkers should even be allowed to contemplate the sacred grotto as you drool and grunt and wank. Let alone actually reproduce. Well the hell with it. A pox upon you. You're a pack of mudheaded bigots who loathe excellence on principle and though one might cordially wish you all in hell still you wont go. You and your nauseating get. Granted, if everyone I wished in hell were actually there they'd have to send to Newcastle for supplementary fuel. I've made ten thousand concessions to your ratfuck culture and you've yet to make the first to mine. It only remains for you to hold your cups to my gaping throat and toast one another's health with my heart's blood.

Ah well, Squire, I tell you everything and you tell me nothing. It's all right. I know your history. A man broken on the wheel of devotion. You're a missing Greek tragedy, Squire. Of course your story could still come to light. A foxed and speckled manuscript in a vault in an ancient library in some city in Eastern Europe. Moldering but pieceable. I say that I know your history but of course I exaggerate. Little I'd like better than to have a peek into those intrafamilial sordidities concerning which you remain so circumspect. Hard money says it would make the Greeks look like Ozzie and Harriet.

Rave on.

I always thought you'd go back to your science.

I guess my heart wasnt in it.

Where was your heart?

Elsewhere.

I feel old, Squire. Every conversation is about the past. You told me once that you wished you'd never wakened after your accident.

I wish it yet.

When you're ninety you'll be weeping for love of a child. That could be unseemly. I'm hardly a stranger to grief and pain myself. It's just that the provenance of these discomforts is not always clear. I've long had the thought that to cook everything down to a single plight might make it more palatable. I sometimes wish that I had a dead sister to weep over. But I dont.

I never know how seriously to take you.

Couldnt be more in earnest.

Probably true. One more oddity to deal with.

Oddity is it? Mary's celestial knickers, Squire. Today I met a man named Robert Western whose father attempted to destroy the universe and whose supposed sister proved to be an extraterrestrial who died by her own hand and as I pondered his story I realized that all which I took to be true regarding the soul of man might well stand at naught. Yours, Sigmund.

You dont know anything about my sister.

True enough. Or any sister. I never had one. Or been in love. I dont think. Well. Maybe.

Where is Miss Tulsa?

Gone to Florida to visit relatives. You see me enjoying a brief stint of freedom. Not wholly unwelcome, as you may imagine. Here, Squire. Have some more wine. We'll change the subject.

Western put his hand over his glass. The long one smiled. You dont take me seriously. But I'll prattle on a while yet. Maybe you're just a hoarder of misery. Waiting for the market to rise.

I'm not miserable, John.

Well you're something. What? A study in regret? Classical, that. The ground of tragedy. The soul thereof. Whereas grief itself is only the subject matter.

I'm not sure I follow you.

I'll go slower. Grief is the stuff of life. A life without grief is no life at all. But regret is a prison. Some part of you which you deeply value lies forever impaled at a crossroads you can no longer find and never forget.

Do you have a license for this?

Let's have some coffee. You're beginning to look maudlin.

Well, I wont joust with you on your own ground. You're a man of words and I one of number. But I think we both know which will prevail.

Well said, Squire. We do indeed, more's the pity.

The waiter came. He returned with cups and carafe. Sheddan peeled the wrapper from a cigar and clipped the end with a device which he'd taken to carrying on his keychain. He lit the cigar and puffed at it and held it at arm's length to study it and then clamped it in his teeth. The other bonus of course is that it doesnt crowd one's nap time. The early lunch. I saw Pharaoh the other day. She was asking after you.

You saw who?

Bianca. She's an interesting girl. You should take her out. I think she's fairly spoiling for a fuck.

I dont think so.

Really.

Really.

You'd get fucked to a faretheewell. I can warrant it.

I'm sure.

I asked her once what it was she would like to do that she had not.

And?

She gave it some thought. I dont know, she said. Fuck in the mud? And I said no. Aside from that. Maybe something of a nonsexual nature. Well. She said that was a tough one. She didnt see how it would be interesting. She said, and I quote: People's fantasies are usually not all that interesting. Unless it's something truly sick and twisted and depraved. Then of course you get interested. You care.

You care?

Her words. She liked the cut of your jib. I warned her that you were a difficult case. To put it mildly. Well. I'm not without sympathy for your plight, Squire. And of course the world of amorous adventure these days is hardly for the fainthearted. The very names of the diseases evoke dread. What the hell is chlamydia? And who named it that? Your love is not so likely to resemble a red red rose as a red red rash. You find yourself yearning for a nice oldfashioned girl with the clap. Shouldnt these lovelies be required to fly their pestilential knickers from a flagpole? Like the ensign of a plagueship? I cant of course but be curious what an analytic sort such as yourself makes of the fair sex in the first place. The slurred murmurings. The silken paw in your shorts. Beguiling eyes. Creatures soft of touch and sanguinivorous of habit. What runs so contrary to received wisdom is that it really is the male who is the aesthete while the woman is drawn to abstractions. Wealth. Power. What a man seeks is beauty, plain and simple. No other way to put it. The rustle of her clothes, her scent. The sweep of her hair across his naked stomach. Categories all but meaningless to a woman. Lost in her calculations. That the man knows not how to even name that which enslaves him hardly lightens his burden. I know what you're thinking.

What am I thinking?

Something along the lines of the old chestnut about the lothario who in his heart despises women.

I'm not thinking that.

No?

I'm thinking in a rather vague and unstructured way about the bizarre concatenation of events that must have conspired to bring about you.

Really.

Really.

Well. I suppose we're somewhat of a piece. Again, I've encountered no greater mystery in life than myself. In a just society I'd be warehoused somewhere. But of course what really threatens the scofflaw is not the just society but the decaying one. It is here that he finds himself becoming slowly indistinguishable from the citizenry. He finds himself co-opted. Difficult these days to be a rake or a bounder. A roué. A deviant? A pervert? Surely you're joking. The new dispensations have all but erased these categories from the language. You can no longer be a loose woman. For instance. A trollop. The whole concept is meaningless. You cant even be a drug addict. At best you're just a user. A user? What the fuck is that? We've gone from dope fiends to drug users in just a few short years. It doesnt take Nostradamus to see where this is headed. The most heinous of criminals clamoring for standing. Serialkillers and cannibals claiming a right to their lifestyle. Like anyone else I try to sort out where I fit into this menagerie. Without malefactors the world of the righteous is robbed of all meaning. As for myself again if I cant be decorum's sworn enemy while savoring its fruits I simply see no place for me at all. What would you recommend, Squire? Go home and draw a warm bath and climb in and open a vein? Never mind. I see you weighing the merits of it. I enjoy my life, Squire. Against all odds. Anyway, Hoffer has it right. Real trouble doesnt begin in a society until boredom has become its most general feature. Boredom will drive even quietminded people down paths they'd never imagined.

Boredom.

Squire, I'm a scoundrel very nearly without peer. But in our time decent people actually attract comment. We dont know what to make of them. They have few friends, while I have more friends than I know what to do with. Why is that?

I dont know.

I think it's because people are bored out of their fucking minds. I cant come up with anything else. And there may even be something contagious about it. Certainly there are mornings when I wake and see a grayness to the world I think was not in evidence before. A conversation we've had. I know. The horrors of the past lose their edge, and in the doing they blind us to a world careening toward a darkness beyond the bitterest speculation. It's sure to be interesting. When the onset of universal night is finally acknowledged as irreversible even the coldest cynic will be astonished at the celerity with which every rule and stricture shoring up this creaking edifice is abandoned and every aberrancy embraced. It should be quite a spectacle. However brief.

Is this your new preoccupation?

It's forced upon one. Time and the perception of time. Very different things I suppose. You said once that a moment in time was a contradiction since there could be no moveless thing. That time could not be constricted into a brevity that contradicts its own definition.

I said that.

Yes. You also suggested that time might be incremental rather than linear. That the notion of the endlessly divisible in the world was attended by certain problems. While a discrete world on the other hand must raise the question as to what it is that connects it. Something to reflect upon. A bird trapped in a barn that moves through the slats of light bird by bird. Whose sum is one bird. We should go.

Do you think I'm bored?

No. Bright people often have a good load to carry. But boredom is seldom a part of it. It's all right. I'm always pleased to see just that small bit deeper. You deny our brotherhood. Insisting as you do in your sly way that our genealogies and our socioeconomic standings have set us apart at birth in a manner not to be contravened. But I will tell you Squire that having read even a few dozen books in common is a force more binding than blood.

What else?

What else. I dont think it's schadenfreude to take a certain pleasure in that odd bit of envy that I occasionally see in you. Just a flicker. Soon to pass.

You think that I envy you?

It's irritating, isnt it?

God help us.

Sheddan smiled. He pulled on the cigar and held it at length and studied it. He blew softly at the ash. It's not that common a thing for people to appreciate what they have. Especially perhaps something so strange and rare as a noble wretchedness. If one has to be unhappy—and one does—then it's better to be admired than pitied. However loath we may be to so encloak ourselves in the first place.

We should probably go. I need to get some sleep.

Of course. And I.

Thank you for lunch.

You are more than welcome. Nice to have several benefactors to choose among.

He sorted through a pack of credit cards and laid one on the table. I tip so well the waiters are often startled. The tourists as you can well imagine are a niggling bunch. You told me of a dream once that you may or may not remember. Rather curious. We were moving along a stone wall in a slurry of ash. A scene of ruin. There were dark flowers hanging over the wall. Carnivorous flowers, you thought them. Black and leathery in appearance. Like a dog's cunt, you said. We sat in the rubble waiting. Finally a phone rang. Do you remember?

Yes.

I answered and listened and then I said no and then I hung up the phone. And in the dream you asked me what they had said and I told you that they wanted to know if we knew anything about them. And I said no. And they said: We didnt think so. And then they hung up. You were the dreamer. Yet if I'd not told you what they said would you have known?

I dont know.

Nor I. Why do you think your inner life is something of a hobby with me?

I've no idea.

No doubt you see in it something sinister. It's not.

The waiter came and took the check. When he returned the long one bent and signed the bill with a name unknown to him and closed the leather folder. He smiled. I'm going to say that I'll die before you. And that you may well envy me in the going. There's something in life which you've forsworn, Squire. And while it may be true that I in turn envy you your classic stance, I dont envy it much. Trimalchio is wiser than Hamlet. All right. Shall we?

•

When Western came through the patio doors in the morning Asher was sitting at the corner table with his satchel stashed in the chair beside him. He didnt look up from the paper he was studying. Western went on to the bar and got two beers and came back.

Bobby.

Is the fateful tale unfolding?

Yeah right.

Where are you?

What do you know about Rotblat?

Not much.

Did your father know him?

Sure. I dont remember him ever coming to the house though. They had different views about things. Why?

I just wondered if your father ever said anything about him. I guess even more specifically about his wife. Why she went to the gas chamber while he stayed home.

You think he should have gone back to Poland and died with her.

Yes. Dont you?

Yes. What else?

Would you have?

I didnt.

Your father thought that Russell was an idiot.

No. He thought he was a lunatic.

Your father never went to Pugwash.

No. Some people called it Pigwash. A slightly lesser form of hogwash.

Asher crossed his boots in the empty chair. He was thin and rawboned and had sandy red hair. In his scuffed leather jacket and boots Western always thought he looked more like an oilfield geologist. He thumbed through some pages in his notebook. He tapped his chin with his pencil and looked at Western. How are you doing, Bobby?

Not so good. I've got pancreatic cancer. I've got maybe six months.

Asher sat upright. Jesus, he said. What?

I'm just jacking with you.

Christ, Western. That's not funny.

I guess not.

You've got a fucked up sense of humor. Did you know that?

I've been told that. Maybe I just wanted to see if you were listening.

I listen.

Maybe we should just move it along.

Christ. All right. Let's get back to Chew.

All right.

He was at Chicago.

Yes. Then Berkeley.

You said that he was the pied piper that your father followed. Into oblivion? Do I have that right?

I dont know. Probably a bit strong. My father was a free agent. A lot of people thought that S-Matrix theory was a reasonable theory. Promising, even. It was just superseded by chromodynamics. Ultimately by string theory. Supposedly.

We're still in the early sixties.

Yes.

String theory is beginning to look like endless mathematics.

That's the principal complaint I suppose. One of the first things that showed up in the equations was a particle of zero mass, zero charge, and spin two. Pretty promising.

A graviton.

Yes. A creature imagined but never seen. I dont know that much about string theory but it's a physical theory, not a mathematical one. It keeps getting assigned a different number of dimensions. It's enjoyed a good deal of support but not from everybody. If the subject comes up in Glashow's presence he's likely to leave the room. Witten says that we'll know something in twenty years.

That's Glashow's poem? The last word is not Witten?

Yes. Or I think so. Are the mini-biographies still a part of the project?

They are. I'm just not all that sure where to put them. Did Russell know any physics?

No.

Is that why your father was dismissive of him?

No.

It's all right to say that the reason we cant fully grasp the quantum world is because we didnt evolve in that world. But the real mystery is the one that plagued Darwin. How we can come to know difficult things that have no survival value. The founders of quantum mechanics—Dirac, Pauli, Heisenberg—had nothing to guide them but an intuition about how the world should be. Beginning at a scale hardly known to even exist. Some spectral anomalies. What is that? Oh, that's an anomaly. An anomaly. Yes. Well. The fuck you say. Did Einstein work with Boltzmann?

I dont know. What he got from Boltzmann was a common suspicion that the laws of thermodynamics at some scale might not be fixed. Ehrenfest had the same idea. A very destructive idea.

Did Ehrenfest work with Boltzmann?

I would say no.

What did they share?

They both committed suicide?

Jesus, Western.

It wasnt just the quantum dice that disturbed Einstein. It was the whole underlying notion. The indeterminacy of reality itself. He'd read Schopenhauer when he was young but he felt that he'd outgrown him. Now here he was back—or so some would say—in the form of an inarguable physical theory.

Didnt keep him from arguing, though. Did it?

No.

What else?

The road to infinity may well unravel fresh rules as it goes.

Do you have your father's papers?

No.

They're not at Princeton?

Not all of them.

Where are they?

There were some at my grandmother's house in Tennessee. Mostly the papers from Lake Tahoe.

There were.

Yes. They were stolen.

They were stolen?

Yes.

From your grandmother's house.

Yes.

Who would steal them?

No idea. They didnt leave a note.

Had you read them?

Some. I looked through them. They were in a tin breadbox. When he left Teller's program and went back to particle physics he found that things had moved along a bit.

S-Matrix theory.

Western shrugged.

Asher recrossed his legs and tapped his chin with the eraser again. A breakthrough.

Dangerous word. Witten said that string theory could be a half century ahead of itself.

I suppose the hope is that it will turn out to be some sort of theory of everything.

Who knows? Feynman once said that we were now discovering the fundamental laws of nature and that day will never come again. Feynman is a bright guy but I think that's a somewhat questionable thing to say. Should science by some miracle forge on into the future it will uncover not only new laws of nature but new natures to have laws about. The last lines of Dirac's book are: "It seems that some essentially new physical ideas are here needed." Well. There always will be.

What happened to Kaluza-Klein?

It's still around. It's reappeared in modern unification theories. The question of course is whether these in turn have any value. The original theory was a pretty elegant edifice. Einstein was taken with it. He wrote a rather neat paper on the subject. It had drawings and everything. But he came to see most of the problems and eventually he dropped the whole thing. I know that my father dug up Kaluza's 1921 paper. There was a five dimensional field theory that went with it and it was quite a piece of work. It included a general relativistic theory of gravitation. It was what got Klein interested and when the Kaluza-Klein version came out it incorporated quantum mechanics. De Broglie was interested. These were interesting times in physics.

As in the Chinese curse?

Something like that I suppose. The reason for point particles is that if you stick something ugly in there—such as physical reality—the equations dont work. A point devoid of physical being leaves you with location. And a location without reference to some other location cant be expressed. Some of the difficulty with quantum mechanics has to reside in the problem of coming to terms with the simple fact that there is no such thing as information in and of itself independent of the apparatus necessary to its perception. There were no starry skies prior to the first sentient and ocular being to behold them. Before that all was blackness and silence.

And yet it moved.

And yet. Anyway, the whole idea of point particles is contrary to common sense. Something is there. The truth is we have no good definition of a particle. In what sense is a hadron "composed" of quarks? Is this making reductionism put its money where its mouth is? I dont know. Kant's view of quantum mechanics—and I quote—is "that which is not adapted to our powers of cognition."

Kant's view of quantum mechanics.

Sure.

Jesus, Western.

You dont think that he was talking about the supernatural do you?

Probably not.

To the skeptic all arguments are circular. I guess that means even this one. Anyway, I dont want to get into some aimless flap about the meaning of quantum mechanics. It's the most successful physical theory we've ever had. If there's anything wrong with Copenhagen it's that Bohr had read a lot of bad philosophy. Perhaps we should move along.

All right. Chew.

Well. Maybe not that far along.

You're joking.

Yes.

Chew thought that S-Matrix theory was the theory that would take high energy physics forward.

Yes.

Did it?

It was the theory of the week. For about a year.

No pun intended, I suppose.

Two, actually. Sorry. It actually originated with Heisenberg in the early forties. With Wheeler even earlier.

But now we're in the sixties.

Yes. The particle zoo. Quantum field theory was in their sights for a while but they should have known better. S-Matrix theory was a very ambitious theory. Bootstrap theory, Chew liked to call it. His version, anyway. It got ahead of itself and Geoffrey Chew was at the helm.

And your father was fully aboard.

Yes.

Did your father know David Bohm?

Yes. He liked him very much.

I would think they might have had very different political views.

They did. David went to see Einstein one day to try to explain to him why his—Einstein's—objections to quantum mechanics were wrong. They spent two hours in Einstein's office at IAS and when Bohm came out he had—as Murray put it—lost his faith. He wrote a really good book on quantum mechanics trying to get it all down but it didnt help and he spent the rest of his life trying —in effect—to find a classical description that fit the theory. A quantum equivalent of squaring the circle. In the meantime he was hounded out of the country by the State Department.

Hidden variables.

Yes. Very well hidden. The problem is the reverse of Feynman's path-integrals. You cant visualize Feynman's theory but the mathematics is sound. You can visualize hidden variables. That is, you can visualize how they might work. Sort of. You can draw a picture. But they dont work.

Western stopped. Asher was writing in his notebook. He didnt look up.

The bootstrap theory was eclipsed by the arrival of the quark.

Earlier, actually. Murray and Feynman shared a secretary at Caltech and they were pretty jealous of each other's work. But it was mostly on Murray's part. Still, on the day that Murray delivered his paper on the eight-fold way George Zweig encountered Feynman coming up the hallway bent over and shaking his head and as he passed in the hallway George heard him mutter to himself: He's right. The son of a bitch is right. A short time later when George was at CERN he woke up one night with the suspicion that nucleons were not basic particles.

It just came to him.

Not exactly. Still, it's a simple enough idea. That nucleons are composed—as it were—of a small companionship of lesser particles. Groups of three. For the hadrons. All but identical. He called them aces. He told me he didnt think anyone else could figure this out and that he had all the time in the world to formalize it. He didnt know that Murray was on his trail and that he had less than a year. In the end Murray called the particles quarks—after a line in Joyce's *Finnegans Wake,* referring to cottage cheese. Three quarks for Muster Mark. And he swept the field and won the Nobel Prize and George went into therapy. But George came out the better for it.

This is a true story.

You can look it up. Well, actually you probably cant. Not all of it. But it's also true that Murray originally presented the theory as speculative. As a mathematical model. He always denied this later but I've read the papers. George on the other hand knew that it was a hard physical theory. Which of course it was.

Feynman was George's Faculty Advisor.

Yes.

Bootstrap theory would have self-destructed eventually.

Murray says that it morphed into string theory. Eventually. But it was made irrelevant by the success of gauge field theory anyway.

What happened to Chew?

He's still at Berkeley. He's had a good career. But nothing like what he once envisioned. And string theory is still a mathematical morass.

Did anybody else's papers get stolen? Other than your father's.

Not to my knowledge. But I really dont know.

You'd looked through them. The breadbox papers.

Yes. They were mostly on the weak force. People thought that the weak theory would end up looking like quantum electrodynamics but that wasnt his view. He thought the fact that this approach worked for QED didnt mean anything. Yang-Mills had been around for a few years but nobody knew what to do with the bosons that came with the theory.

They were thought to have no mass.

At the time they were thought to have no mass. Yes.

Like the photon.

Like the photon. Yes. The mediation was in these particles. The particles that came to be called the W and Z bosons.

The Yang-Mills vector bosons.

Yes. Glashow came up with a gauge theory that included the W particles and what he was now calling the Z particle. Still no real explanation for the masses. They were hand-fed in. Then in '64 Higgs came up with his mechanism and Weinberg understood that if you could use the Higgs mechanism as a way to break the symmetry you could use it as a way to actually arrive at masses for the vector bosons. Or you could put it the other way around. The W particle initially got assigned a mass of forty GeVs and the Z particle eighty. They eventually turned out to be I think something like eighty and ninety-one. Weinberg published what is now a famous paper on this problem in 1967 and nobody read it. But my father read it. The theory still spun off these infinities that nobody could get rid of. I think the paper had five citations in five years. There didnt seem to be any way to square renormalization with Yang-Mills. 't Hooft finally figured it out in 1971 but in the meantime my father already saw his edifice cracking and he sat down and attacked the Higgs problem but he couldnt get it to work. I think the word he used was incoherent.

He seemed to have been putting a lot of faith in an unproven theory.

The Higgs.

Yes.

He was a bit like Dirac. Or Chandrasekhar. He had an abiding faith in the aesthetic. He thought the Higgs paper too elegant to be wrong. For instance. You can add Glashow's SU(5) theory to the list. Lovely theory. And wrong.

Is the Higgs wrong?

Dont know. In the meantime what was happening in the real world was Weinberg had figured out that Glashow's Z particle had to be right. Everybody else hated it. The problem was that it was too massive. Just fucking enormous. The Z boson is heavier than some actual atoms. But even if you could get it up to speed in an accelerator you still had the problem that it had no charge. Still he figured that if you had these neutrino-nucleon collisions that spun off the W particle and gave you a lepton with the opposite charge you'd have to get a Z particle every once in a while. And since the Z carried no charge this meant that the neutrino coming in would stay a neutrino. Charge is conserved in the weak interaction the same as in any other interaction. You wouldnt see a lepton with the opposite charge to the W particle because it wouldnt be a W particle. It would be a Z particle. He figured that you wouldnt see anything, and that was what you had to look for. Or all you would see would be a burst of hadrons and that would be the signature of the Z that people said would never be found.

Asher sat with his pencil between his teeth. Neat, he said.

In any case, neutral current events were finally found at both CERN and Fermilab. Z particles. Some confusion about it but it went away. Weinberg and Glashow and Abdus Salam just won the Nobel Prize for the new electroweak theory.

The first step in Grand Unification.

Well. Maybe.

What happened to your father?

He died.

I know.

He left Berkeley and went up to a cabin in the Sierras. When I first went up there he was already sick. I went with him to the hospital at La Jolla. Why La Jolla I dont know. Then he went back to the Sierras. I think maybe he went back to La Jolla one more time. He had no reason to be hopeful about anything. The last time I saw him I just drove up there and spent the day. He'd papered the walls of the cabin with printouts of old particle collisions from the Bevatron. He'd lost a lot of weight. He didnt have much to say. The prints were stuff from the fifties. I suppose there must have been something like a sequence to them. Maybe I should have paid more attention. He didnt seem eager to talk about it and I didnt pursue it. It was beautiful up there. There were golden trout in the lakes. That's a species, not just a color. But that was the last time I saw him. A few months later he was dead.

In Juarez Mexico.

Yes.

What happened to the cabin?

It burned down.

Was there anyone living in it?

No.

How did it happen to burn down?

I dont know. Maybe it was struck by lightning.

Struck by lightning.

One might suppose.

You left school after that.

Yes.

Why?

The history of physics is full of people who gave it up and went on to do something else. With few exceptions they have one thing in common.

Which is?

They werent good enough.

And you?

I was okay. I could do it. Just not at the level where it really mattered.

And your father?

Most physicists have neither the talent nor the balls to take on the really hard problems. But even sorting out the significant problem from among the thousands is a talent not thick on the ground.

What led him back to the Bevatron plates?

I dont know. I think he spent time just mulling over the laws of the universe. Are they immutable? Things that once seemed to have been resolved. Are there in fact completely massless particles? Gauge invariance aside. Are you sure? If you had leptons with a mass of ten to the minus whatever how close could they get to the speed of light? Is it measurable?

What else?

I dont know. Wouldnt the values of the constants have to somehow know what was coming?

That sounds like Penrose.

Well. Maybe.

What else?

I dont know. Stückelberg.

Stückelberg.

Yes.

Who's that?

Who indeed.

Well?

Stückelberg was a Swiss mathematician and physicist who showed up at Sommerfeld's lab a couple of years too late. But he'd figured out most of the exchange particle model of fundamental forces, worked out a good bit of the S-Matrix theory and the renormalization group. The list goes on. A covariant perturbation theory for quantum fields. The vector boson exchange model—which he dropped and which later won the Nobel Prize for Hideki Yukawa. No acknowledgment. I mean, what would you say? I stole the whole thing from some guy named Stückelberg? The Abelian Higgs mechanism. Even the interpretation of the positron as an electron traveling backward in time. Possibly unprovable but an insight that could take its place in the rare pantheon of world-shaping theories. Theory later attributed to several others. No recognition. Groundbreaking work in renormalization. Ditto. You might want to mention him. Nobody else did.

How do you spell it?

Just like it sounds.

Right.

Western spelled it.

All right. Back to the constants.

Back.

What would an explanation for the constants look like?

I dont know.

Yeah. I know. Why didnt Dirac just come out and say that the particle he'd turned up was an anti-electron? He must have pretty well known it by 1931.

Murray asked him that. Some years later.

What did he say?

He said: Pure cowardice.

Asher shook his head. Western almost smiled.

Being wrong is the worst thing a physicist can be. It's up there with being dead.

Yeah.

You wonder about people who rarely publish anything. Wittgenstein for instance. What is that about? A good part of my father's papers are gone. So a good deal of who he was is something I'll never know.

Is that painful to you?

Everything is painful to me. I think. Maybe I'm just a painful person.

They sat in silence.

Sorry, said Western. I've got to go.

Do you really believe in physics?

I dont know what that means. Physics tries to draw a numerical picture of the world. I dont know that it actually explains anything. You cant illustrate the unknown. Whatever that might mean.

If I could do physics, I would. No matter what.

Western nodded. He pushed back the chair and rose. Well. In my experience people who say no matter what seldom know what what might turn out to be. They dont know how bad what might get. I'll see you.

He got Janice to look after the cat and he packed a few things in two small soft bags and in the evening he took a cab out to Airline to the locker where he kept his car. Chuck was in the office and he came out and stood in the doorway and nodded at Western's bags. You takin that thing on a road trip?

Yep.

Where you goin?

Wartburg Tennessee.

How far is that from Roosterpoot Arkansas?

It's a real place.

What's there?

My grandmother.

That's a pretty good drive, aint it? What, is she fixin to kick off and leave you some scratch?

Not that I know of.

How long a drive is it?

I dont know. Six hundred and some odd miles.

How long will that take you?

Maybe six hours.

Bullshit.

Five and a half?

Get your ass out of here.

He dropped his bags at the locker and unfastened the padlock and rolled up the overhead door on its tracks and switched on the single overhead lightbulb. The car had a cloth cover over it and he made his way along the wall to the front and undid the tie-straps and folded the cloth back across the hood and the stainless steel roof and carried it outside and shook it out. Then he folded it up and carried it back in and put it on the shelf at the front of the locker alongside the trickle-charger. He lifted the scuttle and disconnected the clips from the charger and the timer and pulled the wire out through the wheel-well and he checked the oil and the water. Then he dropped the scuttle and came around and wedged himself through the door and put the key in the ignition and pushed the starter button.

He hadnt driven the car in six months but it cranked and started with no problem. He blipped the throttle and checked the gauges and put the shifter in reverse and backed slowly out of the locker onto the asphalt. He got out and switched off the light and closed the door and fastened the padlock and he opened the hood of the car and wedged his bags in and dropped the hood and got in and ran the engine up a couple of times. White smoke drifted across the storage area. The engine smoothed out and the car sat there burbling throatily. The trident that identified the Maserati he liked to think of as Schrödinger's wavefunction. Of course it could also be the sign for Davy Jones's locker. He smiled and eased the shifter into first and pulled the car around and drove out through the gate.

It was dark by the time he reached Hattiesburg. He had turned on the lights at dusk and he drove to the Alabama State line just east of Meridian in one hour flat. One hundred and ten miles. It was seventy miles to Tuscaloosa and the highway was straight and empty except for an occasional semi and he opened the Maserati up and drove the forty miles to Clinton Alabama in eighteen minutes redlining the engine twice at what the speedometer logged as a hundred and sixty-five miles an hour. By then he thought he'd probably used up most of his luck with the State police and the small town speedtraps he'd blown through and he motored leisurely through Tuscaloosa and Birmingham and crossed the Tennessee State line just south of Chattanooga five hours and forty minutes after leaving New Orleans.

It was one ten in the morning when he pulled off the highway and drove down the deserted main street of Wartburg. Everything was closed. He turned around at Bonifacius and came back and turned up Kingston Street and drove past the courthouse and on into the country. Just the sound of the cobbly tires on the two-lane blacktop road and the moon low over the dark hills to the west. He crossed the old bridge and turned up the farm road and drove on. When he pulled up opposite the house he switched off the headlamps and sat there in the dark with the motor idling. There was a mercury vapor lamp at the back of the house but the house itself was dark and quiet. He sat there for a while. Then he switched the lights on again and turned the car around in the road and drove back to town.

A sheriff's patrol car picked him up and followed him out to the edge of town and then turned and went back. He drove down Highway 27 south towards Harriman and pulled into a motel just outside of town. It was two thirty in the morning. He stood at the office door and pushed the buzzer and waited. Pretty cold out. He could see his breath. He pushed the button again and after a while the man came and let him in.

He filled out the card and turned it around and pushed it back across the counter. The man picked it up and held it at arm's length to study it. He was small and graylooking. He didnt look like he got out much.

I had a brother lived in Monroe Louisiana. Died there, in fact.

He bent and squinted out at the driveway where the Maserati sat in the soft red glare of the vacancy sign. Jap car, he said. My niece drives one. Well, it's a free country I reckon.

It's not a Jap car.

Well what is it if it aint?

It's Italian.

Yeah? Well we fought them sumbitches too. That'll be fifteen seventy-one with the tax.

He paid the man and got the key and drove down to the room and went to bed.

In the morning he drove back into Wartburg and ate a late breakfast at the little restaurant and read the Wartburg paper. Out in the parkinglot two teenage boys were looking at the car. The patrons in the cafe glanced at him from time to time as he ate and after a while the younger of the two waitresses came over to freshen up his coffee.

I'll bet that car out yonder belongs to you.

Western looked up. She had fresh stitches in her head. She poured the coffee and set the pot on the table and pulled the pad of checks from the pocket of her apron. Did you want anything else?

I might. I'm pretty hungry.

He studied the menu. Do you get a lot of calls for the wartburger?

Yeah. It's pretty popular.

He folded the menu shut. I think I'll quit while I'm ahead. He looked up at her.

You're not from around here, are you?

Shoot no. I hate this place.

I heard this was a party town.

Wartburg? Where'd you hear that at? You're funnin, aint you?

You've got a boyfriend in Petros.

Husband. How'd you know that?

I dont know. You're not wearing a ring.

I wear it. Just not when I'm workin.

How often do you get to see him?

Twice a week.

Has he seen those stitches yet?

Not yet.

What are you going to tell him?

How do you know he didnt put em there?

Is he a doctor?

You know what I mean.

Did he?

No. I told you. He aint even seen em yet.

So what are you going to tell him.

You're awful nosey, aint you? I'm goin to tell him I slipped and fell if it's any of your business.

I just wondered if you had a good story.

What makes you think I need a story? You dont know what happened.

Do you need a story?

Maybe. Why would I tell you?

Why not?

Where are you from?

Right here.

No you aint.

New Orleans?

I dont know. Are you?

If that's all right.

She looked back toward the counter and then looked at him again. You're kindly a smartass, aint you.

Yes.

If you are kind of cute.

You're not so bad yourself. Do you want to go out?

She looked toward the counter again and back. I dont know, she whispered. You make me kindly nervous.

That's part of my strategy. It's good for the libido.

It's good for the *what*?

What's he in for? Manslaughter?

How did you know that? Were you talkin to Margie?

Who's Margie?

That's her standin over yonder. What did she say about me?

She said I should ask you out.

I'm goin to kick her butt.

I'm just teasing. She didnt say that.

She better not of. Did you want anything else?

No thanks.

She tore off the ticket from the pad and laid it face down on the table. Are you from New Orleans sure enough?

Yes.

I aint never been there. Are you a gambler?

No. I'm a deep sea diver.

You're full of it. I got to wait on these customers.

All right.

Are you serious about what you said?

About what.

You know. About goin out.

Maybe. I dont know. You make me kind of nervous.

Well that might be good for whatever that thing was you said. If you have one.

How much tip do you want me to leave?

Well I dont know, Darlin. Whatever your heart tells you.

All right. You want to flip for double or nothing?

How would I know how much I was flippin for?

What difference would it make? It will either be twice that or nothing.

All right.

You do it.

Why?

I might have a two-headed coin.

Yeah, she said. Knowin you you might.

She took a quarter from the pocket of her apron and flipped it and caught it and slapped it down on her forearm and looked at him.

Heads, he said.

She lifted her hand away. It was tails.

You want to go again?

All right.

She flipped the coin again and he called heads again and it was tails.

One more time?

How much do I have now?

Four times what you had to start with.

I know that. I can do the math. You just want to keep doublin till I lose.

That's right.

Well I think I'll quit.

Smart girl.

I got to wait on them people. How much do I get?

He took a fold of bills from his pocket. I was going to leave two dollars. So you get six.

No I dont. I get eight.

Just checking that math of yours.

I was good at math in school. English was what I hated.

He handed her a twenty dollar bill and she reached in her apron to make change.

That's all right, he said. Keep it.

Well thank you.

You're welcome.

I didnt know if you was some sort of smart-aleck or somethin.

But you do now.

Sort of. I got to go.

What's your name?

Ella. What's yours?

Robert.

I'm off tonight.

Your husband will shoot me.

My husband's in the penitentiary.

You never did say how you got those stitches.

Maybe I'll tell you when I know you better.

He slid out of the booth and stood. I'll see you Miss Ella.

Bye.

He walked across the parkinglot and got in the car and started it. When he pulled out into the street she was watching him from the window and she held up her pencil to say goodbye.

He pulled up into the driveway under the old walnut trees and shut off the engine. His grandmother's car was gone. He sat there looking at the place. Tall white clapboard farmhouse. In need of paint. He thought he saw the curtains move in the bay window. He got out and stood there looking out across the fields. The winter woods along the ridge behind the house were dark and bare and everything was strangely quiet. He could smell the cows. The rich odor of the boxwoods. When he shut the car door three crows lifted silently out of the trees on the far side of the creek and hooked themselves away over the gray winter bottomlands.

He opened the screen door and tapped at the glass and closed the door again and stood waiting. The cows had come out into the barnlot and stood watching him. So little changed. Nothing the same. The door opened and a young girl stood looking up at him. Yes? she said.

Hi. Is Mrs Brown in?

No, she's not.

What time do you expect her?

She said she'd be back around twelve oclock. She's went into town to get her hair done.

Western looked out across the lot toward the barn. He looked at the girl. I'll come back, he said.

Did you want me to give her a message?

No, that's all right. She'll know who it is. I'm going to leave my car here and just go for a walk. I'm her grandson.

Oh. You're Bobby.

Yes.

Did you want to come in?

No, that's okay. I'll be back in a little bit.

All right. I'll tell her.

Thanks.

He got one of the soft leather bags out of the floor of the car and with the door open he sat on the broad carpeted sill and changed his shoes. Then he shut the car door and set out.

When he got to the creek he followed it up into the woods and crossed on the flat stones below the old wooden spillway. The spillway boards were cupped and black with age and the water that ran over them looked dark and heavy. Of the gristmill itself nothing was left save the stones of the foundation together with the rusted iron axle that had once carried the millwheel and the rusted iron collars in which it once had turned. He walked out the path and sat under the cottonwoods and watched the pond. He'd gone to the finals of the State Science Fair when he was sixteen. His project was a study of the pond. He'd drawn life size every visible creature in that habitat from gnats and hellgrammites through the arachnids and crustaceans and arthropods and nine species of fish to the mammals, muskrat and mink and raccoon, and the birds, kingfisher and wood duck and grebes and herons and songbirds and hawks. Like Audubon he'd had to draw the great blue heron leaning over the water because it was too big for the paper. Two hundred and seventy-three creatures with their Latin names on three forty foot rolls of construction paper. It had taken him two years to do and it didnt win. Later he'd gotten scholarship offers in biology but by then he was deep into mathematics and pond ecosystems were little more than a childhood enthusiasm.

He sat there for a long time. A muskrat had put out from shore at the deep end down near the dam and it swam up the pond toward him. Just its nose and a widening V of water. *Ondatra zibethicus.* One winter they'd built in the pond a house of woven sticks and reeds that was a perfect miniature of a beaver house and he'd asked his biology teacher if this meant that the muskrat's knowledge and the beaver's descended from a common source but the teacher didnt seem to understand what he was talking about. He'd paddled out to the house in his duckboat and cut a small hole in the dome of the roof with a keyhole saw and peered in with a flashlight. A nest of grass on a platform of sticks just above the waterline and a warm sweet smell that flooded up and stopped him where he sat astraddle the board seat in the little boat. A memory long forgotten swept over him and he was a child four years of age standing in the front seat of the 1936 Studebaker his father drove all through the war and his mother was sitting beside him in her best dress and coat and she had wet her handkerchief with her tongue and wiped his chin and his mouth and adjusted his cap while his father backed up the car and the wartime plywood house in which they lived receded before them. It was the smell of her perfume on that day that had flooded his nostrils. The muskrats would repair the roof faultlessly. But they never built another house in the millpond.

Clouds had moved over the sun and it grew colder. The muskrat was gone and a wind stirred the water. He got up and swiped at the seat of his trousers and went on up along the west side of the creek. When he got to the fence he took the trail up the mountain, climbing among ilex and laurel here on the north slope. A few old standing chestnut trunks dead and gray these fifty years or more. He reached the crest of the ridge in less than an hour and sat in the broken sun on a fallen log and looked out over the countryside below. He could see his grandmother's house and the barn and the road and the adjoining small farms beyond, the pieced fields and the fencelines and woodlots. The rolling hills and ridges to the east. Somewhere beyond that the installation at Oak Ridge for enriching uranium that had led his father here from Princeton in 1943 and where he'd met the beauty queen he would marry. Western fully understood that he owed his existence to Adolf Hitler. That the forces of history which had ushered his troubled life into the tapestry were those of Auschwitz and Hiroshima, the sister events that sealed forever the fate of the West.

A hawk appeared out of the woods below and rose effortlessly and came about and drifted quarterwise down the wind and turned and rose again and hovered. Broadwing. *Buteo platypterus.* It passed so close he could see its eye. Eleven millimeters. The great horned owl's were twenty-two. The same as the whitetailed deer. But rich in rods. Nighthunter. The hawk turned and dipped and skated off down the slope and then rose again, standing into the wind. Motionless. You should have migrated by now. The hawk turned once more and then it was gone. He looked again for his grandmother's house. The green metal roof. The red brick chimney in need of tuckpointing. Her car in the driveway. How far is that? Two miles? He rose and hiked out along the crest of the ridge. A cold wind in the sun. Fox scat in the pathway. A twelvebore shotshell case trodden into the dirt. The small bent hardwood trees rooted in rock and pointing out the way the wind had gone.

He came down the mountain by a different route and crossed the creek and came out into the road a half mile below the house. When he walked up the driveway his grandmother was coming from the barn. She was dressed in coveralls and wore her gardening hat and a denim barncoat and she carried a stainless steel milkpail with a cloth over it. When she saw him she smiled and smiled.

He met her at the gate and took the pail from her and she put her arms around him and held him. Oh Bobby, she said. I'm so happy to see you.

How are you, Granellen.

Dont ask.

All right.

Well you can ask a little.

Are you okay?

I'm not braggin, Bobby. I'm still above ground.

He had turned to deal with the gate behind her. Here, she said. Let me have that.

He handed her the pail while he latched the gate. I just hate to see people set a milkpail on the ground.

He smiled and turned and took the pail again and they went on toward the house.

How's Royal?

She shook her head. He's not doin much good, Bobby. I dont know what all I'm goin to do with him if he gets much crazier. I went down to Clinton to look at that place they've got down there and I thought, well, I wouldnt want for somebody to stick me in here. There's a place over in Nashville he could go to that I hear is pretty good but that's a long ways. And I dont know how much longer I'm going to be drivin, neither. Is the problem. I dont know, Bobby. We may wind up down there together. Mostly I'm just in prayer mode about it.

She wiped the bottom of the pail with a cloth and set the milk in the galvanized cooler on the back porch and stepped out of the green rubber kneeboots she was wearing. These are Royal's. But I wear em cause they're easy to get off and on and I aint goin that far anyways.

They went into the kitchen. I hate to ask anybody how long they're stayin cause it sounds like you dont want em to. But you aint fixin to do me like you done last time and just drink a cup of coffee are you?

No. I can stay a few days.

She took off her hat and shook out her hair and took off the coat and hung it on a rack of coats by the door. Set down, she said. I'm goin to go up and get out of these here coveralls. I hate to milk in the middle of the day but sometimes you dont have a choice about it. Take off your coat and set down, Bobby.

All right.

He pulled out a chair and hung his leather jacket over the back of it and sat. The chairs had come out of the mountains and were made of ash, the spindles and rails turned on a treadle lathe in a world no longer even imaginable. The seats were of woven rush much worn and mended back in places with heavy rough twine. When she came back down she went to the refrigerator. I know you've not eat, she said. Let me fix you somethin.

You dont have to fix me anything.

I know it. What would you like?

I'd like a garden tomato sandwich on lightbread with mayonnaise and salt and pepper and a sliced hardboiled egg on top.

We had the last tomato here about six weeks ago. I have to say that sounds pretty good though. I've got some store tomatoes.

I'm not hungry, Granellen. I'll keep till supper.

Well I've put some beans on. Bart's girl brought over some country ham they cut and I was fixin to make biscuits and gravy.

That sounds good.

Did you want some iced tea?

Okay.

They sat at the table and drank the tea from tall green fairground glasses.

How do you get parts for that thing? he said.

What thing?

The refrigerator.

It dont need parts. It just runs.

Amazing.

I never could understand why they call it a refrigerator. Instead of just a frigerator. It dont do it twice. That I know of.

Good question.

Royal still calls it the icebox.

Well at least he doesnt call it the piano.

His grandmother laughed and then put her hand over her mouth.

Well, she said. Not yet, anyways. I'd better hush. Where all did you get to this mornin?

I went up to the pond.

Lord. The time you spent at that pond. You used to have that refrigerator so full of bottles and jars. The things you had in there, I got to where I was afraid to open the door.

You were awfully good about it.

I always thought you'd make a doctor.

Sorry.

I didnt mean it like that, Honey.

I know.

You dont have anything to be sorry about.

Western wiped the beaded water from the glass with the back of his forefinger. Yes, well.

What?

Nothing.

No, what?

Nothing. It's just that you dont really think that.

Dont really think what?

That I dont have anything to be sorry about.

She didnt answer. Then she said: Bobby, what is done is done. It cant be helped.

It's not much consolation, though. Is it? He pushed away the glass and rose from the chair. She reached to put her hand on his arm. Bobby, she said.

It's all right.

Can I say something?

Yes. Sure.

I dont think that the good Lord meant for anybody to grieve that way.

What way is that, Granellen?

This way.

Well. I dont think he did either.

You know I worry about you.

He stopped and turned. He stood with his hands on the back of the chair and looked at her. You think she's in hell, dont you?

That's a hateful thing to say, Bobby. A hateful thing. You know I dont think that.

I'm sorry. That's who I am. Or what.

I dont believe that.

It's all right.

Please dont go, Honey.

I'm all right. I'll be back.

He walked out down the driveway and set off along the blacktop road. He'd not gone far before a car stopped and a man looked at him over the top of the partly lowered glass.

You need a ride?

No Sir. I appreciate you stopping.

The man looked out down the road. As if to assess Western's chances upon it. You sure?

I'm sure. I'm just taking a walk.

A walk?

Yessir.

The car pulled ahead and then slowed again. When Western came alongside the man bent to see him better. I know who you are, he said. As if he'd identified a Nazi war criminal hiking the roads round Wartburg Tennessee. Then he drove on.

When he got back to the house an hour later he got his bags out of the car and closed the front decklid and closed the car door and went in. He got his coat off the back of the chair. The sun hadnt come back and he was chilled. His grandmother was in the livingroom. You've not rented out my room, have you? he said.

Not yet.

Who was that girl who was here?

Her name's Lu Ann. She comes about twice a week.

Where's Royal?

He's layin up in the bed. Me and him keeps different hours.

Western turned down the hall and went up the narrow wooden staircase.

His room was at the back of the house, hardly larger than a closet. He dropped his bags in the floor and stood looking out the window. A flicker was moving along one of the walnut tree limbs that hung over the roof. A yellowhammer, in this part of the country. He turned and sat on the small metal bed. Rough gray blanket. In the alcove in the wall opposite were some of his books. Three large silver cups won stock-car racing. A statue of the Sacred Heart. There was a model of a 1954 Ferrari Barchetta built from factory drawings. The body was made of sixteen gauge aluminum hammered out over bucks he'd carved from an oak six by eight. On the wall over the bed was a large square of lacquered linen fabric cut from the fuselage of an airplane. It was pale yellow and had the number 22 painted on it in blue.

He stood up and reached down Dirac's *Principles of Quantum Mechanics*, fourth edition. He thumbed through it. The margins filled with notes, equations. Checking Dirac's work, God help us. He closed the book and laid it aside and sat with his elbows on his knees and lowered his head into his hands.

When she called him for supper he was lying on the bed with one foot on the floor. The room was dark save for the light from the hallway. He picked Dirac's book up off the floor and got his shavingkit out of his bag and went down the hallway to the bathroom.

When he came downstairs Royal was sitting at the head of the table in the diningroom with a dinnernapkin tucked at his chin. He waited till Bobby had passed along the table into view before speaking in order not to have to turn his head. Hello Bobby, he said.

How are you doing, Royal?

I'm okay. How are you makin it?

I'm all right.

Are you still livin over across the waters?

No. I live in New Orleans.

I was there one time. Years ago.

How did you like it?

I caint say as I did all that much. I got in jail down there.

What did you get in jail for?

Bein dumb. They had rats in there the size of lapdogs. We'd shoot em with paper clips with a rubber band and they wouldnt even look at you. They was always in a hurry. Goin somewheres. I dont know where.

His grandmother came in carrying bowls of mashed potatoes and beans. Western got up and followed her back into the kitchen.

What can I take?

Here, she said. Take these.

She handed him a platter of sliced ham and a bowl of biscuits with a cloth over it and she followed him out with the gravy and a bowl of corn. She brought out the coffee and poured it and they sat, he and his grandmother across from each other and Royal at the head of the table. They bowed their heads and his grandmother said grace and then said thank you for sending Bobby to us. Western had sneaked a look at his uncle. He had his eyes closed. When Granellen got to the part about thanking the Lord for Bobby he nodded. Yeah, he said. We appreciate that. Then they passed the bowls and began to eat.

Where'd you get the sweetcorn at, Ellen?

Out of the freezer, Royal. Where would you expect?

I dont understand why you caint freeze tomatoes.

I dont either, I just know you cant.

Why caint you freeze tomatoes, Bobby?

I dont know. You can freeze most fruit. Berries.

You think a tomato's a fruit?

Pretty much. You could call it a berry too I suppose.

A berry.

Yes.

Well I've heard that fruit business before. Which you couldnt prove it by me. Or the berry thing for that matter. You believe that?

It's a member of the nightshade family. Which includes belladonna. The Spanish brought it back from Mexico.

From Mexico.

Yes.

Royal stopped chewing and sat looking at his plate. What you're sayin is that they wasnt no tomatoes till Columbus come over here and got em.

Yes. Or potatoes or corn or about half the other things we eat.

Potatoes.

Yes.

Let me ask you this.

All right.

What do you think the Italians made sauce out of if they wasnt no tomatoes?

I dont know.

What do you think the Irish ate if they didnt have no potatoes? You know what it is you're thinkin of?

What is it that I'm thinking of?

Tobacco.

Could be.

Walter Raleigh brought tobacco back with him. That's why they used to have Walter Raleigh cigarettes. I knew people that smoked em. Had his picture on the pack. You got coupons with em that you could send off and get stuff.

What kind of stuff?

I dont know. Toasters maybe.

Western buttered a biscuit and spooned some of the rich red gravy over it. This is delicious, Granellen.

Well thank you.

What about corn?

What?

What about corn?

Royal chewed. Yeah, he said. He might could of brought back corn. They call it Indian corn.

Or beans.

Beans.

Beans.

Royal nodded. Well as far as I know people been eatin beans since the first day of creation. I think Adam et em. Him and Eve. They'd eat a big bait and set around and toot at one another.

Royal.

Bobby smiled. Royal speared a piece of ham off the platter and set about cutting away the thin rind of fat. He shook his head. You got to watch what you say around here. You'll see. He looked up. I'm a prisoner here, Bobby. Plain truth of the matter. I dont never go nowheres. Dont never see nobody. Nobody to talk to. He shook his head, chewing.

I told you I'd take you down to the Eagles. Anytime you wanted to go.

I dont want to set around and talk to them old farts.

His grandmother looked at Western.

Well I dont. What time is it?

Almost six.

Royal stood and tore the napkin from around his neck.

Royal you have hardly eat anything.

I'll take it in there with me.

He disappeared into the livingroom with his plate and fork. In a few minutes they could hear the television.

He sets in there and argues with it. You'll hear him here directly.

He seemed okay.

You've not heard the half of it yet. Sometimes he thinks we're back in Anderson County. We've only been gone from there for thirty-eight years.

In the livingroom they could hear Royal muttering.

I guess he wishes he was back in Anderson County.

Well. I do too. For all the good it might do me.

I know you miss the house.

She nodded. My grandfather and my uncle built that house with two hands in eighteen and seventy-two. Of course they'd commenced to cuttin the timber for it before that. Ever stick of it come off the property. It was framed up out of beams and joists and they cut lumber for the better part of a year, walnut and poplar, and they hauled the logs on skids with a six mule team. Some of them logs was twenty foot long and two people couldnt reach around em. They was pictures of them in the old press in the livinroom. They built a sashmill back in the woods about a mile from the house that was powered by a steam engine and they hauled the logs in and hauled the lumber out, just stacks and stacks of it. And they put it on the stick, as they called it, and it set there in a pole barn for I dont know how long before they cut into the first board of it. I dont know how they knew to do what they done, Bobby. I want to say that they could of done anything. They didnt even own a book. Other than the Bible of course. I dont reckon they hardly even had a sheet of paper. I always thought it was a good thing that God dont let us see the future. That house was the most beautiful house I ever saw. Ever floor in it was solid walnut and some of them boards was close to three foot wide. All of it hand planed. All of it at the bottom of a lake. I dont know, Bobby. You have to believe that there is good in the world. I'm goin to say that you have to believe that the work of your hands will bring it into your life. You may be wrong, but if you dont believe that then you will not have a life. You may call it one. But it wont be one. Well. Listen at me. I just get sillier and sillier.

That's not silly, Granellen.

Anyway. It was wartime. I know they was lots of people would of been glad to trade a riverbottom farm to get back a son they'd never see again. That and more. Still, we tried to hold on to it. But they just took it. They had what they called these negotiators? But they wasnt nothin to negotiate. They just tried to get you to sign and not give them no trouble. Take the first payment. The stipulation, they called it. If you held out it went to condemnation court and I think some people did get more than what the government wanted to give em but by the time they got it land prices had went up double so they wound up with less anyway. You had two weeks' notice. Then you had to be gone. You wasnt even supposed to take the furniture but most did. They'd leave out in the middle of the night. Like thieves. We lived in a rented house in Clinton till March of nineteen and forty-four. It was hard. I know they was families got thowed off their farms back in the thirties by the TVA and come to Anderson County and got thowed off all over again. They was even families had been removed from their homesteads in the Great Smoky Mountains National Park in the thirties, TVA in the thirties again, and the atom bomb in the forties. By that time they didnt have nothin.

Sure you will, yelled Royal. You lyin son of a bitch.

Granellen shook her head. The ones I felt sorry for was the tenants. They never had nothin to start with. They just lived in shacks on some of them farms. There wasnt no provisions for them, they just had to go. And of course there wasnt no place for them to go to. Some of them families was colored. They was some of em wound up just livin in the woods like animals. And that was a cold winter, too. People would see em crossin the road at night in the carlights. Whole families. Carryin blankets. Pots and pans. People tried to find em. Take em some flour and meal. Coffee. Maybe a little sidemeat. I think about those children. I do yet.

If you aint a lyin sack of shit then Jesus never drew a breath.

Excuse me, said Granellen.

She pushed back her chair and rose and went to the livingroom door. Royal, she said, you can curse if you have got to, but dont you blaspheme in my house. I wont tolerate it.

Royal didnt answer.

She came back and sat down. I wont set in there with him. I watch the news up in my room. I go up usually right after I get done with the dishes and he sets down here half the night. Hollerin.

He lay in the little room listening to the wind outside the house. He'd shut the door to the hallway and there was no heat in the room and it got pretty cold. His mother was nineteen when she went to work at Y-12, the electromagnetic separation plant. One of the three processes for the separation of the uranium 235 isotope. The workers were driven out to the compound in buses, bumping over the rough graded road, through dust or mud given the weather. Talking was not allowed. The barbed wire fencing ran for miles and the buildings were of solid concrete, massive things, monolithic and for the most part windowless. They sat in a great selvage of raw mud beyond which lay a perimeter of the wrecked and twisted trees that had been bulldozed from the site. She said it looked as if they had just somehow emerged out of the ground. The buildings. There was no accounting for them. She looked at the other women on the bus but they seemed to have abandoned themselves and she thought that she might be the only one of them that while she did not know what this was about knew all too well that it was Godless and that while it had poisoned back to elemental mud all living things upon that ground yet it was far from being done. It was just beginning.

The buildings held over one thousand miles of pipe and a quarter million valves. The women sat on stools and monitored the dials in front of them while uranium atoms raced the tracks in the calutrons.

Measuring them a hundred thousand times each second. The magnets that propelled them were seven feet in diameter and the windings were of solid silver fabricated from fifteen thousand tons of it borrowed from the US Treasury because all the copper had already gone into the war effort. An older woman told her that the first day with the women all at their stations and having no least notion what any of this was about the engineers had thrown the consecutive switches and an enormous dynamo hum filled the hall and hairpins in their hundreds shot from the women's heads and crossed the room like hornets.

She entered a guardhouse with the others and was given a badge with her photograph in a small black metal frame and two black pens. She had already passed her security and health inspections. In the women's locker room she was assigned a locker and given a pair of white coveralls and white cloth bootees that fitted over her shoes. Later they would work in their street clothes. No one was told what it was that they were doing. They were given simple instructions and they sat for eight hours a day at their stations under the glare of the fluorescent lights, watching a dial and turning a knob. If you spoke to anyone you could be terminated. You could even be jailed. The pens were radiation dosimeters.

She sat there for six months and then one day a group of physicists stopped behind her station. They were speaking in a language she did not understand. Then one of them spoke to her in English.

I cant speak to you, she whispered.

I know you cant. I want you to call me.

He leaned and put a slip of paper with a phone number penciled on it on the console.

Will you? he said.

She didnt answer.

I hope you will, he said. She tore her eyes away from the dials for just a moment but he had moved on with the others. That was the first time she ever saw his father. Both of them would die of cancer. They lived at Los Alamos. Then Tennessee. His father had been married before but he never told her because she was an Orthodox Jew. Western found out that this woman was still alive and living in Riverside

California and years later Alicia would go to see her. She agreed to meet her at a coffeeshop in town. This is going to be brief, she said. And it was.

His grandmother told him that the first time she ever saw his father she knew that nothing would ever be the same again. The first time that she brought him to the house. I didnt know what was goin to happen. I tried to pray about it but I didnt know what it was I was prayin about. I shouldnt have told you that.

You didnt say anything bad.

No. But I thought it.

He slept. He woke again. You shouldnt have come, he said.

He got up and got his jacket and put it on over his T-shirt and stood looking out the window. His breath fogged the glass. The light from the vapor lamp cast the falling shapes of house and tree across the field toward the road. He turned and went out and down the hall. The lights were still on and he went down the stairs in his socks and shorts and jacket. Royal was asleep in the livingroom in his armchair. The gray screen of the television had numbers across the bottom and it gave off a low steady hum. He went into the kitchen and opened the refrigerator and stood there. In the basket at the bottom were some carrots and he took one and closed the refrigerator door. He stood at the sink looking out the window and eating the carrot. It tasted earthy. Something was crossing the field beyond the barn. Possibly a fox. Or a cat. A few more years and his grandmother would be gone and the property would be sold and he would never come here again. The time would come when all memory of this place and these people would be stricken from the register of the world.

The night was cold. So still. He'd eaten the carrot save for the stalk. Then he ate that. Earthy and bitter. So bitter. He went upstairs and went to bed.

He went for long walks in the woods. He saw no one. A man walking in the woods in the fall of the year in that part of the world was an object of suspicion if he'd no gun with him and he'd have taken a gun but that the thieves who broke into the house two years earlier had taken them all. They'd taken his Gibson mandolin. His grandmother's costume jewelry. They'd also emptied all the papers out of the old

Jackson press in the livingroom and carried them off and when he asked his grandmother about that she only shook her head.

He went through the things in his closet. Mementoes of his youth. Fossils, shells, arrowheads in a jar. A sharpshinned hawk he'd mounted, much motheaten. He supposed he should have understood the nature of the robbery when he first learned of it but he did not.

Royal was every bit as strange as his grandmother had said. He'd rear up in his chair and demand the opinions of those long dead. He looked out the window at Granellen's green Dodge and asked her when she'd traded cars although she'd had the Dodge for eleven years.

He drove into Knoxville. A gray and rainy day. It was hard to keep the glass clear inside the car and he'd taken with him a small towel to wipe the windshield. The Maserati was a strange car, full of French hydraulics. The brake pedal had zero travel and that took getting used to. He drove down Gay Street and out Cumberland Avenue. He knew almost no one in this town. Everything had a gray and abandoned look to it. He drove out the Alcoa Highway and pushed the car to a hundred and fifty trailing a thin roostertail of watervapor in his wake.

In the morning he left the house at dawn and walked up the road to the bridge and crossed the fields to the old quarry, following the faint ruts of the quarry road into the woods. Some crows dropped down out of the trees on the ridge above him and flew away in silence. Great square blocks of stone stood in the woods beyond. The stone was the same color as the treetrunks and the quarry formed an amphitheatre in the woods. A flat stone floor and two stepped levels and a reflecting pool still and deep and black. The walls rose up on three sides, the blocks ribbed with flutings where featherdrills had been used to bore them for the dynamite.

He crossed along a low wall of sawn blocks opposite the pool and sat as he had sat that summer evening years ago and watched his sister perform the role of Medea alone on the quarry floor. She was dressed in a gown she'd made from sheeting and she wore a crown of woodbine in her hair. The footlights were fruitcans packed with rags and filled with kerosene. The reflectors were foil and the black smoke rose into the summer leaves above her and set them trembling while she strode the swept stone floor in her sandals. She was thirteen. He was in his second year of graduate school at Caltech and watching her that summer evening he knew that he was lost. His heart in his throat. His life no longer his.

When it was over he stood and clapped. The flat dead echo halting off the quarry walls. She curtseyed twice and then she was gone, striding off into the dark, the shadows of the trees bowing to her in the light from her lantern where it swung by the bail. He sat on the cold stones with his face in his hands. I'm sorry, Baby. I'm sorry. It's all just darkness. I'm sorry.

The last night of his visit they sat at dinner and ate quietly. His grandmother had fixed fried chicken and biscuits with white gravy. Royal sat poking at his food and then he put down his fork and looked up at the wall, his napkin at his throat. It's one void after another is what it is, he said. It aint just the one. Like it says in the good book. You think the void is just the void but it aint. It goes on.

Eat somethin, Royal, his grandmother said. You need to eat. Instead of secondsaying the Bible.

They ate. Western looked at his grandmother.

Do you think there might be any of her papers here?

Bobby, to the best of my knowledge there is not.

I just wondered if you'd come across anything.

She shook her head. They went through ever room. You're welcome to look. You know that.

All right.

What papers? said Royal.

Alice's papers.

Alice is dead.

We know she's dead, Royal. She's been dead ten years.

Ten years, said Royal. Dont seem possible. Cold and dead.

Suddenly he began to cry. Western looked at his grandmother. She got up from the table and went into the kitchen.

Later when Royal had gone into the livingroom Western and his grandmother sat at the kitchen table drinking coffee. I'm glad you came, Bobby, she said. I just wish you'd stay longer.

I know. But I have to go.

Do you think this family has a curse on it?

Western looked up. A curse?

Yes.

Do you?

Sometimes.

What, like the sins of the fathers?

She smiled sadly. I dont know. Do you believe in God, Bobby?

I dont know, Granellen. You asked me that before. I told you. I dont know anything. The best I can say is that I think he and I have pretty much the same opinions. On my better days anyway.

Well. I hope that's true. I guess that's the other thing I'd blame your father for. And I know it's not up to me to go around placing blame.

What is? The other thing.

Just his effect on Eleanor. Trying to confuse her. He'd make her cry. Making her doubt her faith I guess you'd say.

Is that what they divorced over?

I dont know. Indirectly, I suppose.

What would directly be?

I think you know.

He had trouble staying home.

Well.

You think they were poorly matched.

I do. Of course she was awfully smart herself.

Why do you think they got married?

I dont know, Bobby. It was wartime. I think a lot of young people got married that might of waited otherwise. He liked pretty women. And she was the prettiest.

It didnt serve her well though, did it?

It seldom does.

Do you think that's true?

I do. Beauty makes promises that beauty cant keep. I've seen it too many times. Twice in this house.

She poured more coffee.

I miss the stove, Western said.

I know. You couldnt get nobody to cut wood for it.

Can I ask you something?

Of course you can, Bobby.

What is it that you regret?

Well. I think you know what I regret.

I mean things you might have done differently. Or not done. That kind of regret.

His grandmother turned and looked out the window across the darkening fields, her hand to her mouth. I dont know, Honey. Not all that much. I think people regret what they didnt do more than what they did. I think everbody has things they failed to do. You cant see what is coming, Bobby. And if you could it is no guarantee you'd make the right choice even then. I believe in God's design. I've had dark hours and I've had dark doubts in those hours. But that was never one of them.

She'd finished her coffee and she pushed the cup away. She folded her hands and looked at Western.

I didnt mean to make you feel bad, he said.

You didnt, Bobby.

Do you want to look at some pictures?

Oh Bobby.

What?

I thought I told you.

Told me what?

They took them.

They took the photo albums?

Yes. I thought I told you.

No.

I'm sorry, Honey.

It's all right.

I'm sorry.

They took everything in the press?

Yes. They emptied out the drawers and left the drawers settin in the floor.

So they took Grandaddy's hogrifle and the shotguns. My mandolin. The kinds of things that thieves might take and pawn. And then they took all the family documents. You didnt think that was peculiar?

I did think so. Nothin ever showed up in the pawnshops. They checked all the ones over in Knoxville.

They werent thieves, Granellen. That stuff wasnt going to the pawnshop. It's at the bottom of the lake. Probably off the Highway 33 bridge along with God knows what else.

What are you saying, Bobby?

Nothing. It's all right.

No, what are you saying?

Nothing.

It has to do with your father. Doesnt it?

I dont know. I really dont. I shouldnt have said anything.

His grandmother put the flat of her palm on the table as if she were about to get up but she didnt. She looked more than tired.

Are you all right?

I'm all right, Bobby. Dont pay no attention to me. I get lonely sometimes is all. She turned and looked at him. Do you ever?

He wanted to tell her that he knew no other state of being. Sometimes, he said.

His grandmother was born in eighteen ninety-seven. McKinley was president and the country was at war with Spain. There was no electricity, no telephone, no radio, no television, no cars, no planes. No heat, no airconditioning. In most of the world no running water and no toilets. Life had changed little since the middle ages. He watched her. She had turned away. She shook her head, he didnt know what it meant. But she turned and looked at him again. Do we have cause to be afraid, Bobby?

No. You dont.

Do you?

He left at daybreak without saying goodbye. Standing briefly at the window looking out at the gray dawn over the countryside. The creek shrouded in mist, the pale shapes of the cottonwoods. Frost on the fields. Nothing moving. He slung one bag over his shoulder and picked up the other and went down the steps.

He put the bags in the car and went back into the kitchen and filled two saucepans with hot water from the tap and went out and poured them over the glass front and rear to melt away the frost. Then he set the pans on the porch steps and got in and started the car and turned on the wipers and backed the car down the drive into the road and turned and headed toward the highway.

He took I-40 west up onto the Cumberland Plateau and he was in Crossville in forty minutes. A sandcolored crust of snow lay along the edge of the road and it was very cold. He ate breakfast at a truckstop. Eggs and grits. Sausage and biscuits and coffee. He paid and left. Outside in the parkinglot a man was standing with his arm across the stainless steel roof of the Maserati while his girlfriend took his picture.

He pulled into the Quarter at four oclock in the afternoon and parked the Maserati in front of the bar and got his bags and walked in. Harold Harbenger was sitting at the end of the bar and he raised one hand in huge greeting. As if he'd been sitting there all this time waiting. Bobby boy, he called.

Where you been? said Josie.

I went to see my grandmother.

You went to Knoxville?

I did.

Josie shook her head. Knoxville, she said.

Has there been anybody in here looking for me?

I dont think so. You can check with Janice. Was there anybody looking for me in Knoxville?

Western smiled. I'm guessing you hope not. What time does the bank close?

Down on Decatur?

Yeah.

Four oclock. She looked at her watch. It's ten after.

I know. So what time do they open?

Probably ten.

In the evening he drove the car back out to the storage locker and covered it and hooked it up to the tricklecharger and took a cab back to the Quarter and ate at the Vieux Carré. Then he went back to the bar and climbed the stairs and went to bed with the cat humming against his ribs.

In his dreams of her she wore at times a smile he tried to remember and she would say to him almost in a chant words he could scarcely follow. He knew that her lovely face would soon exist nowhere save in his memories and in his dreams and soon after that nowhere at all. She came in half nude trailing sarsenet or perhaps just her Grecian sheeting crossing a stone stage in the smoking footlamps or she would push back the cowl of her robe and her blonde hair would fall about her face as she bent to him where he lay in the damp and clammy sheets and whisper to him I'd have been your shadowlane, the keeper of that house alone wherein your soul is safe. And all the while a clangor like the labor of a foundry and dark figures in silhouette about the alchemic fires, the ash and the smoke. The floor lay littered with the stillborn forms of their efforts and still they labored on, the raw half-sentient mud quivering red in the autoclave. In that dusky penetralium they press about the crucible shoving and gibbering while the deep heresiarch dark in his folded cloak urges them on in their efforts. And then what thing unspeakable is this raised dripping up through crust and calyx from what hellish marinade. He woke sweating and switched on the bedlamp and swung his feet to the floor and sat with his face in his hands. Dont be afraid for me, she had written. When has death ever harmed anyone?

In the morning he went down to the Du Monde and drank coffee and read the papers. At ten oclock he walked across the street to the bank. An old white stone classic revival building that sorted oddly with the Quarter architecture. Legacy of Latrobe. He went to the desk at the rear of the lobby and signed the register and gave his key to the clerk and followed him down to the vault where the clerk unlocked the gate and offered him through with an outheld hand. They passed along a row of small engineturned steel doors until they came to his number and the clerk fitted the keys and opened the door and slid out the gray enameled steel tray and placed it on the table behind them. He opened one of the locks and handed back the keys and turned and left the room.

Western fitted the key and turned it and raised the lid. Inside was a fat brown manila envelope. He lifted it out and undid the string clasp and opened it and took out the letters. Her journal for the year 1972. He looked inside and then put everything back in the envelope and rewound the string on the clasp and put the envelope on the table and closed and locked the lid of the tray and slid it back and closed the small steel door and locked it. He turned and left with the envelope and he signed out on the register in the lobby and thanked the clerk and walked out into the street.

He stretched out on the little bunk and took a letter from the envelope at random and opened it and read it. He knew them all by heart yet he read with care. The cat walked purring up and back along the edge of the bed.

He didnt know where his own letters were. Maybe he didnt want to know. He folded the letter and put it back in the envelope and took another from the bottom of the stack. At age twelve she had a picture of Frank Ramsey in a dimestore frame standing on her bedside table. She wanted to know if you could be in love with someone who was dead. She said that in fourteen years they would be the same age. He didnt read anymore. The later ones were hard for him to read. The letters in which she told him that she was in love with him. He put them away in the manila envelope and closed it and put it under the mattress and went out and down to the bar.

Josie motioned him over with a jut of her chin.

You had a call. Here.

She handed him a scrap of paper with a number on it. He turned it and looked at it.

Male or female?

It was a guy.

Thanks.

He called the number but there was no answer.

He fed the cat and went out and down the hall to the bathroom. He went in and closed and latched the door and opened the ancient tin medicine cabinet and stood looking at it. There were old bottles and jars and a couple of twisted empty tubes of toothpaste. He went back to the room and got the empty grocery bag and came back and raked everything out of the cabinet into the bag and folded the bag and put it in the wastebasket. The cabinet was fastened to the wall with four screws. The heads of the screws were flanged boltheads. He reached into the trashbasket and tore a small piece of paper off of the bag and reached and pressed it hard with his thumb over the head of one of the fasteners and came away with a good impression of it and he put the strip of paper in his shirtpocket and closed the cabinet door and left.

When he came back he'd been to the hardware store on Canal Street and he had a cheap imported set of three-eighths-inch drive sockets. They were in a little tin tray and there was even a small ratchet with an extension. He got the packet of letters from under the mattress and went back down the hall to the bathroom. He shut the door and latched it and opened the medicine cabinet and found the right socket and fitted it over the extension and fitted the ratchet and backed off the two bottom screws. He'd put the rubber stopper in the sink in case the screws fell in and he backed off the top two screws while holding the cabinet by the mirror and then he set the cabinet in the floor. The wallboard had been cut away to get to the studs. The crosspieces that the medicine cabinet was screwed to were stepped forward the thickness of the wallboard and it was easy to wedge the pack of letters between the two-by-fours. The holes in the back of the cabinet were keyhole in shape and he left the screws slightly loose so that he could just hang the cabinet over the screwheads and he wouldnt need a screwdriver to lift it off again. He got a few of the jars and bottles out of the trash and put them back in the cabinet and shut the cabinet door.

He went up to the A&P and bought a dozen cans of catfood and came back and went up to the room. He set the bag of tins on the table and lifted the cat by its armpits and looked into its eyes. The cat hung bonelessly in his hands. It blinked peacefully and looked away.

Vigilance, Billy Ray. Vigilance. And catfood.

When he'd fed the cat he went down and called Lou but he was gone for the day. He went out and walked through the Quarter. The rich dank smell. The smell of oil and the river and ships. Whitman had once lived in the house at the corner. Windowlights coming on in the dusk. The old lamps down Chartres Street like burning gauze in the fog. The Shelby ran for twenty-six laps and then it didnt show up. It was too dark to see smoke but he scanned the far side of the track for signs of fire. He walked down to the pits where Frank was waiting for the cars to come around again. No flag on the track. So far so good. I know you're hoping that it aint the engine.

I'm hoping that it's not the car.

It wasnt. The teeth had begun to strip off of the cluster gear until the box seized up and then the rear U-joint came uncoupled and the driveshaft went clanking off across the concourse and Adams pulled the car off onto the grass and unbuckled the threeway and got out and walked off across the fields carrying his helmet. He told Frank that the car had come apart like a cardboard suitcase in a California rainstorm. They went into town to a bar, Adams still in his Nomex, and sat in a booth. Adams raised his hand. Let me have a double scotch with water back. Or just make that three. He turned to the others. What are you guys having? he said.

The race was on television but they couldnt really see it from where they were sitting. Later Western walked out down to the chicane and sat in the grass and watched the cars come down, downshifting on a trailing throttle and braking with the headlamps moving from side to side as they approached and the front discs lighting up until they were sun-red with bits of fire coming off the edges and then fading to black again as the calipers came unclamped and the cars accelerated out of the turn in third gear and upshifted and howled away down the straight.

VI

From the day she'd stood in the vestibule of St Mary's with her classmates all in white like dead children in a dream. Their white patentleather shoes. Their chaplets and veils and the white prayer-books with the gilded buckles they clasped between their palms in prayer. From that day the God of her innocence had slowly ebbed from her life. In a dream she'd seen him weeping over the cold clay of her childsbody in a nameless crossroads, kneeling to touch his dead handiwork. Until finally the Kid showed up with his companions. On the nature of that which God might flee or God abandon there was only silence, but she thought that she and the visitors to her attic might well be candidates. The Kid and his shadowkind had come trekking across a vast waste. A landscape bleak and interminable. She thought it to be alive and she saw little merit in it. She spoke her virgin sins through the wicket. Once. Again. And then no more. Hell hung on longer. She saw the resurrect vomited up from the pit to wander vacanteyed and smoking through the streets. Blinking in the unaccustomed light. She woke from dreams of struggle. Of leaden flight. Some sat and she listened for the sound of rain on the seamed metal roof but the rain had stopped in the night and there was only the drip of water from the eaves. Something on the road. Something coming. Some sweatsoaked beast, some hooded and wheezing abhorrence atrundle upon the footpath. Just the faintest movement of the air like a gradient of ill come unshelved and drifting toward her lonely outpost.

When her aunt Helen came to visit she asked the girl what she wanted to be when she grew up and she said dead.

I'm being serious.

So am I.

No you're not. You're being flippant and morbid. Now. What would you like to be?

Terminally ill?

Her aunt got up and left the room.

When she woke again the Kid was in the room pacing and there was a thin man in rolled shirtsleeves tinkering with what looked to be an antique film projector mounted on a wooden tripod. The Kid waved a flipper at it. These bloody things, he said. Pain in the ass. What do you think Walter? Maybe this week sometime?

The projectionist didnt answer. He tugged at his billcap and bent to see about the trouble. The white smoke from his cigarette coiled in the beam of light. She sat clutching her pillow. The Kid glanced her way. No rush, he said. We got lights and chimeras but of course the action is always another question altogether.

What are you doing?

Trying to get the bloody projector up and running. Snooze some more if you like. This may take a while.

The projector set up a ratcheting and chattering and the yellow frame of light on the attic wall began to flicker. The number eight appeared briefly, then seven, then six, then all went black. Jesus, said the Kid. Somebody get the houselights.

She turned on the bedside lamp. What are you doing? she said.

The Kid tilted an old wooden cigarbox out on her desk and rummaged through it. He sorted through the reels of film and unspooled a length and held it to the light. No telling what's in here. Old eight millimeter. This stuff hasnt seen the light of day in donkey's years.

What stuff?

Pretty good shape for the most part. All things considered. Jesus. Look at this little group. It's all genetics, isnt it? Wait till you see some of these citizens.

I'm all genetics you mean.

Dunno. That's pretty much why we're here, isnt it? Crikey. Look at this one would you? Anyway, if we intend to wage high war upon their asses we're going to need more than bloodtypes. What do you think Walter? Any news?

The projectionist thumbed back his cap and damped the sweat from his forehead with a rolling motion of his shoulder and took a screwdriver from his rear pocket.

The Kid unscrolled the film. It dangled in a lolling helix. He shook his head. Go back a little further and you got people sitting around the fire in leopardskin leotards. Whoops. What was that?

The light on the wall flickered and died again.

False alarm, said the Kid. He respooled the film and sorted out another reel. Patience. Never my strong suite. Probably be my comeuppance before this thing is over. Doggedness on the other hand. Jesus. How did the chickens manage to shit in here?

What thing?

What?

What thing? You said this thing.

This thing?

You said before this thing is over. What thing?

Maybe I mis-spoke.

No you didnt. What thing?

Christ. I should have known. Okay. Shut it down Walter. Just unplug the fucker. All right. Fuck it. He turned to the girl. Look. What's wrong with a little history? You should count yourself lucky we even came up with this stuff. Dawn raid on the poultryhouse. Everything covered with dust. Chicken droppings. In spite of everything that you've read some things really dont have a number. But it's worse than that. Some things dont have a designation at all. Of any stripe. Well how can that be she asks. Well simple enough says the small gowned person of unflappable demeanor. The name is what you add on afterwards. Afterwards of what? Afterwards of it appears on the screen. Your screen my screen we all screen. We got some herky jerky images of dudes and dudesses but they got no name. They used to have names but they dont anymore. The last witness who could have put a name to the faces is boxed up in the ground alongside them and if not nameless as well will soon be so. So. Who are they?

The fact that they once walked about in the nomenclative mode is small comfort. Small comfort to whom? Well shit. You just throw up your hands. You dont have to have a name you say. Okay. Dont have to have a name in order to what?

He paced. He appeared to be thinking.

More of the same, she said. I suppose you're musing.

Maybe. I guess if you had a muse you wouldnt need me.

I dont need you. You're just a liability. You're not even amusing.

Yeah. You said.

Why dont I have a muse?

Where would you get one? You're a one-off. You're lucky you didnt come with an extra head.

Thanks. What thing?

What?

What thing? The thing in before this thing is over.

Christ. Not to be derailed, is she? Speaking of doggedness. Why cant we just move it along? Do it my way for a change.

We always do it your way.

I'm trying to look after you, Your Weirdness. You think this is easy? Walter gets the time machine up and running and we're going to view some history, that's all. Maybe a brief philosophical digression stressing the importance of a neutral stance. Start with the nameless and unknown and you might be less likely to say I told you so. Numeration and denomination are two sides of the same coin. Each one speaks the other's language. Like space and time. Ultimately we got to come to grips with this math thing of course. Which is not going to go away.

Why am I a one-off?

The Kid paused and held his flippers out and looked up in a gesture of invocation and then went to pacing again.

Nobody is totally unique.

Nope. Just you.

I'm the only one.

Yup.

But you cant say what it is that I'm the only one of.

Well, you could say the only one of a kind, I suppose. But of course you're right. There's no kind. Which leads us to the paradox that where there's no kind there cant be one.

One as a number or one as a being?

Either. You cant have anything till another thing shows up. That's the problem. If there's just one thing you cant say where it is or what it is. You cant say how big it is or how small or what color it is or how much it weighs. You cant say if *it is. Nothing is anything unless there's another thing. So we have you. Well. Do we?*

No one is that unique.

Yeah?

You cant compare me to some entity floating alone in the void.

Why not? Look. Let's show some movies. Okay? Picture worth a thousand words. That sort of thing. Twenty-four per second. Or are these eighteen? We actually found an old keywind Kodak in one of the boxes.

Movies.

Yeah.

Of what?

Remains to be seen. As the sign said down at the undertakers. Why dont we just roll it?

I thought the projector wasnt working.

What, you got no faith in Walter?

Why is he dressed like that?

I dont know. He hangs with an older crowd. You can ask him if you like but he's not real chatty. Hold it. We got action. Douse the lights, will you?

She turned off the lamp. On the wall the frame of grainy yellow light flickered and numbers appeared each in a circle. Eight, seven, six. A clock hand turned in the circle and swept them away.

Why is the six written out?

Shh. Jesus.

If the projector was upside down you'd know it.

Quiet.

And besides there's no nine anyway.

Will you cork it for Christ's sake?

The numbers ran to two. A shadow loomed on the screen. Down in front, hissed the Kid. The projector ratcheted on. Pale figures began to jerk forward. Homemade clothes. They smiled thinly. A few made mows at the camera. Or waved across the years.

Who are they? she said.

Can we have quiet in the house? Jesus.

Why are they waving?

What do you want them to do? Send a postcard? Just pipe down, will you?

The film clattered on. Burns and blisters appeared and vanished. Men and women in summer clothing. Straw hats and bonnets. A child's funeral. A small coffin carried from the bed of a wagon by men in bib overalls. She saw a man dropped to his death through the floor of a raw wood scaffold while a minister held his book to his chest and stood with one hand aloft and a sheriff in a rumpled suit took his watch from his vest pocket. She saw a gathering of men in their shirtsleeves with their coats across their forearms, their hats in their hands. Their heads looked like they had strings tied around them.

Who are they? she whispered.

Just hang on, okay?

Two women standing and smiling on the lawn of her grandmother's house in Akron. I think I know them, she said. The car in the driveway. She'd seen it in old photographs. It was tall and black. Classic that, said the Kid. Desmodromic valves.

Can you stop it? Can you rewind it?

You cant rewind it. Jesus. Maybe you should pay more attention the first time around.

Can you slow it down?

How are you going to slow it down?

She didnt answer. She tried to think when the movie camera was invented. She saw people standing in a lake with their arms outstretched. Their ancient black wool bathing costumes. She saw a child who may have been her father. Walking toward the camera. Shadowed by the sun. Creature of light. Her mother in front of their house at Los Alamos. There was snow on the ground and furrows of mud curving away in the road and snow on the mountains beyond.

Frozen clothes hanging stiff as corpses from the washline in the yard. Her mother turned from the camera and waved it away. Pulling her coat about her to hide her condition.

That's me inside her.

Yeah. Nameless as yet I would suppose.

If Bobby was Bobby I was Alice.

That sounds really dumb.

It was really dumb.

Finally she herself. Turning on pointe in her costume at a ballet recital in a church basement in Clinton Tennessee in October of 1961.

Just stop it, she said. Can you stop it?

Well, sure, said the Kid. You can always stop it. You sure that's what you want to do?

Yes. Please.

Okay. Fuck it. Shut it down. That's it. Jesus. The thanks I get.

The projector flapped to a halt, the light flickered out. She turned on the lamp. The Kid swiveled in his chair and shook his head. You really break me up, he said.

I'm glad I amuse you.

Yeah. I dont need amusing. It's all a murky business anyway. Take a bunch of stills and run them tandem at a certain speed and what is this that looks like life? Well, it's an illusion. Oh? What is that? Well who cares if you can bring back the dead. Of course they dont have much to say. What can I tell you? Call before digging. You might think the trick is to pick the track of some collateral reality. If you fail to see the fallacy. The relevant malevolence. You can dial in some fresh vectors but that's no sign they'll commute. Is that a good idea? What if folks want to come back?

They cant.

Good girl. The point is that you're never going to have a blank screen. And of course it's not what's on the screen but who put it there. If you do look up and there's nothing on the screen you'll put something there yourself why not.

That's me I suppose.

Sure. Whatever moldy sinistralium you might've cooked it up out of. We wont even attempt to rescind your notions about what it is you get to pick and choose among from what is and what aint. We'll try to couch things in your terms. It's in our interest. Keep the warpage to a minimum. You want to write the little bastard off as just whomever-the-fuck that's your prerogative. Here by happenstance? Sure. Maybe a change of diet would do the trick. Cut back on the saturated fats and no snacks before sacktime. We can work on that. Maybe ID a few of the current menacements traipsing through the nightwoods.

I dont want to ID them. I just want them to go away.

Look. Why dont we let the thing cool. We got a few more reels.

How do I know it's not just stuff out of a junkstore? Or something you've cobbled up? Some of those people look older than Edison.

Do they now.

And they're not entertaining. They're sad. The dead are not loved long, you said. You may have noticed it in your travels, you said.

You could open your heart a little.

I did open my heart. And this is what I got. And anyway some things cant be fixed. And history is not for everybody.

Jesus. Where's my pencil? Get this stuff down.

And why do you make fun of me?

Who said it's fun?

Surely you must know who it is that cuts the ludicrous figure here.

Do I? Who you gonna ask? And dont call me Shirley.

I've no reason to believe that those are really my people.

Yeah, well. It's a wise child.

And I dont pretend to know what I dont. I'm not devious.

Which I am I suppose.

I never said you were devious. I said you were a fucking liar.

Jesus. Are you done?

You tell me.

You dont think there could have been somebody around with a little handcranked Kodak sequestered away in their coat? Was that you tripping on the boards or wasnt it?

How would I know?

How many people were in the audience?

What?

How many people were in the audience? It's a fair question.

I dont know.

Sure you do. Not that long ago. Break out the aspergillum.

Eighty-six.

Isnt that code for shitcan? Anyway, probably right. And anyway even if you wanted to see more I dont know what the point would be if you think it's all a fake.

That is the point. And I dont want to see more.

I thought we were all friends here.

No you didnt. And what dawn raid on the chickenhouse?

What?

You said that the filmcans had chicken droppings on them.

Yeah?

You said dawn raid.

In a manner of speaking. What, you think it was a secret mission?

Who would raid a chickenhouse?

Good question. Fight fire with fire. Poultryhouse operative. Hardly unheard of.

He wandered to the window and peered out.

She looked up. There was a trunk in the chickenhouse. It was falling apart. The chickenhouse was. Bobby used some of the lumber out of it. There was a bunch of stuff there. Some crates of masonjars. Old furniture. There was a horsehair sofa that Bobby had cut pieces of leather out of to make Indian moccasins when he was a kid. The trunk was an old steamer trunk and it had a lot of old papers in it. My father's college papers. Some letters. From the house in Akron. I suppose he intended going through them. But he died. And the papers were all stolen.

Oh rueful day.

It was a rueful day. Most rueful day.

Yeah, well. I thought you didnt like to dwell on the family misfortunes. Bib overalls to Time magazine in two generations. One more to oblivion. Over and out. Well, what the hell. If we knew where everybody was going we might know what to pack for the trip. Still, you dont want to lose faith.

Lose faith in what?

Something can always turn up.

Nothing's going to turn up. How much more?

How much more what?

Film.

I dont know. A few reels.

Go ahead.

Really?

The projector should be cool by now.

Yeah. I saw Walter fanning it with his cap. I dont know why I get miffed. It's not like I wasnt warned.

Warned about what?

About you, Tuliptits.

What do you get out of calling me names?

Names are important. They set the parameters for the rules of engagement. The origin of language is in the single sound that designates the other person. Before you do something to them.

You can have a conversation without being rude.

Yeah? Well, we need to get your attention. You seem to think that listening is optional and we have to try and scotch that.

We?

Me and my staff.

Your staff*?*

What's wrong with that?

Why dont you ever call me by my right name?

I dont know. I think I liked it better when you were Alice. I thought you were a more down-to-earth girl. With Alice we just had the malice. With Alicia we got to call out the Militia. What's in a name? A lot, as it turns out. You want to see some more of this or what?

I take it the cohorts are not coming.

Nope. Today it's film. You ready?

Yeah. Okay. Sure.

Attagirl. Douse the lights, will you?

She reached and switched off the lamp. All right, called the Kid. Roll em.

He arrived in Paris in the fall of 1969, coming on the boat train from London. The last thing Chapman said to him was the old saw about racing. Fast chaps, rich chaps, and idiots. Sometimes you can find all three in a single Nomex suit.

Would that be me?

You're too late, Bobby. The day of the gentleman racer is over. I've seen a lot of blokes who were rich and dumb become poor and smart. Everything in racing is a tradeoff. Except big brakes. The only edge you might have is that in Formula racing there actually is a substitute for cubic inches. It's called engineering.

He walked out of the Gare du Nord carrying his two leather bags and stood in the Paris night. He stood there a long time. Just getting his shit together. Finally he got a cab and gave the driver the address of the Mont Jolí in the rue Fromentin near Pigalle. The hotel was favored by traveling entertainers and any morning there would be jugglers and hypnotists and exotic dancers and trained dogs in the lobby coffeeshop. He rented a garage in the ninth arrondissement and began to collect tools. The car arrived on a transporter a week later and Armand arrived a day after that. Every day he'd take the bus out through the bleak suburbs and unlock the door and take down his coveralls and pull them on. The Lotus stood on jacks and he and Armand would roll around the concrete floor on mechanics' dollies setting the caster and camber and toe-in on the car. Adjusting the sway bars. Then recalibrating the injection and the timing on the tiny screaming engine.

They would tow the car out to the track with Armand's truck and trailer and take turns driving it with the new settings and then tow it back, sometimes in the dark.

In those first evenings he sat by himself at the bench rebuilding the spare engine. Chapman had done the machine work and sleeved the cylinders. Everything was aluminum and the clearances were enormous. He tightened the connecting-rod bolts and measured the boltstretch with a dial indicator. He checked the book and measured again. There was a paraffin heater in the shop but he was always cold. He and Armand would eat lunch at a tabac two blocks from the garage. The regulars were astonished to see an American in greasy coveralls sitting among them.

She left school and came to Paris and in the evening he would take her to dinner at Boutin's down the street from the hotel. Miller used to eat here back in the thirties. Wonderful veal dish with a cream sauce that cost seven francs. The prostitutes couldnt take their eyes off her. The first race was at Spa-Francorchamps and the Lotus ran like a train for twenty-seven laps and then quit cold when the petrol pump packed up.

He took her down to IHES and they found a room for her and said goodbye. Chapman sent the other car over in March. He and Armand would travel all over Europe in a thirdhand transporter living in the transporter or in cheap hotels and eating well. They ran okay but they never won a race. At the end of the season he sold the car and in November of that year he had a letter from John Aldrich. For the following year he was invited to drive Formula Two cars for the March team. He wasnt sure why. He met her for dinner in Paris and she talked to him feverishly about mathematical ideas that to him threatened to abandon reality of any kind he'd a stake in.

When they walked into the operations room Lou was on the phone. He nodded and rang off and looked up at Western. The prodigal son. Are you back?

I'm back. You got anything for me?

No.

Why cant I go to Houston?

Because you werent here when we made up the crew. Maybe you can get Red here to explain it to you.

I had to go see my grandmother.

You said that. And we had to go to Houston.

When are they leaving?

They left this morning. For the most part.

You dont have anything.

Nothing I'd recommend.

What have you got that you wouldnt recommend?

Lou pushed back in his chair and studied Western. There's an outfit out of Pensacola that's looking for a diver. I dont know anything about them. You might not even get paid.

What's the job?

You'll have to ask them. They want somebody to meet their crew on a jack-up rig. They'll fly you out in a chopper.

For how long?

A week. Maybe. I'd take extra socks.

How do I get to Pensacola?

That would be on you. Nobody's picking up the tab for that.

All right.

All right? That's it?

That's it.

Lou shook his head. He copied out a phone number onto his pad and tore off the sheet and handed it to Western. Be my guest, he said.

Western looked at the phone number. If you thought this was so questionable how come you took their number?

I love this job. Look. I'm sure you know that company policy here is to run this shop for the convenience and entertainment of the employees. Taylor just wants you to be happy. If they can make a couple of bucks on the side, well, that's all right too.

Red nodded at the piece of paper. You want some good advice, Dear Heart?

Sure.

Ball that thing up and pitch it in the trash over yonder.

How deep are they going to be working?

I dont know. It's a jack-up rig so it cant be all that deep. My guess is they're going to unstack some rigs.

Coldstacked.

Yeah.

What do you think?

I might go if somebody had a gun to my head. Maybe you should listen to Red. The first rule in hazardous duty work is to know who it is you're working for.

Red nodded. Amen on that, he said.

The chopper dropped through the partial overcast almost directly over the derrick. The rig with its lights looked like a refinery standing in the black of the sea. The landing lights of the helicopter picked up the letter H on the landing pad and above it the name of the rig. Caliban Beta II. The pilot settled onto the deck and killed the lift on the rotor and looked across at Western. All right, he said. You understand that this is supposed to be a pretty good blow coming.

I'm all right.

You been on one of these before?

Yeah, once. Why?

Because if you get any serious seas you cant get aboard them.

You dont think anybody is coming out here.

I'd be surprised.

Western reached in the back for his divebag and climbed out. The light aluminum door hummed in the wind. The wind moaned in the steel rigging overhead and in the light-towers and it moaned in the big Link-Belt cranes.

I'll take you back if you want, the pilot said. It's no skin off my ass.

Thanks. I'm all right.

He shut the door and the pilot leaned over and secured the latch and pulled pitch on the collective and the helicopter lifted off the pad. Western stood there with his clothes thrashing about him in the wash of the rotor, watching through squinted eyes as the chopper rose up into the lights and then banked away toward the Florida coast with the navigation lamps dimming and finally vanishing in the darkness.

He shouldered his bag and made his way along the steel catwalk toward the cabin and opened the steel door and stepped over the sea transom into the companionway. He closed the door and secured it with a turn of the wheel and leaned on the table there and took off his steeltoed construction boots and left them in the floor. The operations room was just off to the left. He shouldered his bag and went down the stairs in his sockfeet to the quarters below.

Everything had the look of a ship. The narrow corridors and the gray steel bulkheads. The iron handrails and the lights in their wire cages overhead. But it wasnt a ship and except for the low steady throb of the prime mover deep in the bowels of the rig there was no sound and there was no movement.

He found the mess and the galley and he opened the reefer and got out some sliced corned beef and a loaf of bread. He made himself a sandwich and spread some mustard over it and he poured a glass of milk. He left his bag on the wooden picnic table in the mess and wandered through the quarters. The rooms were small and fitted with bunkbeds. The legs set in holes in the floor. Small bathrooms with steel showers and stainless steel commodes of the type used in prisons. He stood in the companionway with the milk and the sandwich. Hello? he called.

He wasnt sure how to get back to the galley. He made his way along the corridors and up and down the steel companionways and finally he came to an outside door. He'd eaten most of the sandwich and he'd drunk the milk and he set the empty glass in a corner and finished the sandwich and then turned the big iron wheel to back off the latch on the sea door.

The wind snatched the door and slammed it against the bulkhead. He stepped out and wheeled the door shut behind him and made his way along the catwalk and down the steel stairs. Below him was the drillingfloor. The tower rose into the windy night and in the overhead lights birds circled mutely and stood against the wind and then turned to be sucked away instantly into the blackness. He leaned against the bulkhead with his jacket popping. There were stinging bits of salt in the air and the whole rig seemed to be adrift and careening through the night sea.

He turned up his jacket collar and went along the deck. He looked in through one of the heavy glass windows bolted into its painted steel frame. He was already very cold and his teeth had begun to chatter. He continued along the bulkhead until the helicopter pad came in sight and then he made his way to the doorway he'd first entered and went in and shut the door and went down to the galley and got his bag off the mess table.

He went along the gangway and took the bunkroom closest to the mess and set his bag on the little desk and switched on the lamp. He sat on the bunk and leaned back against the cool metal wall. A slight electric tremor. He thought he could doze off to it. He sat up and unzipped his bag and got out his fleecelined nylon jacket and laid it out on the bunk. Then he got up and went down to the galley again. He looked through the reefer and the walk-in hoping to find a beer but there was no beer on the rigs. He got out a can of apricots and he looked for a canopener but he couldnt find one. Finally he took a meatcleaver and stoved in the can with the heel of the blade and got a spoon and went back to the bunkroom and sat on the bunk eating the apricots. They were pretty good. He ate some more and then took the can back to the galley and put it in the reefer again. He wandered the lower deck looking into the rooms. He stood listening. Hello? he called.

He went back to his bunk and got out a paperback copy of Hobbes's *Leviathan*. He'd never read it. He pulled down the pillow from the upper bunk and fluffed the pillows and lay back and opened the book.

He read the first twenty pages or so and then put the open book on his chest and closed his eyes.

When he woke Hobbes was still on his chest. He lay listening. The sound of the outer storm muted in the structure. Something else. He sat up and closed the book and swung his feet to the floor. It was two twenty in the morning. He put his hand against the cold steel of the bulkhead. The deep heartbeat in the bowels of the rig. Some two thousand horsepower. He got up and went out in his sockfeet and down to the dayroom. He turned on the television. Static and white snow. He tried several channels and then turned it off.

He went back up the companionway and opened the outside door. The wind was in full gale. A high shriek. The sea below the airgap was a black cauldron and the birds were gone. He pulled the door shut and cranked the wheel. He went back to the galley and got the can of apricots and went up the hall to his room and sat on the bunk and ate some more of the apricots and then set the tin with the spoon standing in it on the desk.

The first time that he saw her at the hospital she came shuffling up the hallway in the paper slippers they'd issued her and she smiled thinly and took his hand. When he came the next day he handed her a package but she wouldnt take it.

Why? he said.

I know what's in it.

What's in it?

Slippers.

Okay.

I like these. I'm sorry, Bobby. You're sweet to bring them. But I dont want them. I dont want to be different.

But you are different.

No. I'm not. In any case if I wanted to be who I am I wouldnt be some person wearing special slippers.

Maybe we should talk about something else.

He lay back on the cot with his arm over his eyes. I shall not die for thee oh woman of body like a swan. I was nurtured by a cunning man. Oh thin palm, oh white bosom. I shall not die for thee.

He fell asleep turned to the cold steel wall, his face in his hands.

He slept and woke again and lay listening. The thrumming in the walls. He thought that what he was hearing now was the storm. He got up and went up to the jackhouse and looked out the window. A wild salt spray blowing across the catwalks and through the superstructure. The sodium lights were steaming. He turned the iron wheel and put his shoulder to the door and leaned against it. Out in the torrential night a continual highpitched scream and blinding rain. He pulled the door shut and turned the wheel. Good God, he said.

He went down and wandered through the crew's quarters on the third deck below. At one point the lights flickered and he stopped and stood still. Dont do this, he said.

The lights steadied. He turned and went back to the cabin and rummaged a flashlight out of his bag and shoved it in his back pocket and went out again. When he came back he had a bowl of ice cream and he sat in the bunk and crossed his legs and took up Hobbes again. He went to sleep with the lights on and when he woke it was day.

He went topside and stood looking out at the storm. Whole sheets of spray were passing over the decks. The entire rig was shuddering and seas were lapping at the bridge rails from forty feet below and falling back again. He went down and sat on the bunk and dug out his shavingkit and his toothbrush. Then he just sat there. He had an uneasy feeling and it wasnt the storm. More than uneasy. He tried to go over what the helicopter pilot had said to him. It wasnt much.

After a while he went down to the galley and found some eggs and fixed breakfast and made a cup of tea and sat down at the table to eat. Then he stopped. There was an empty coffeecup over on the counter. He didnt remember seeing it there before. Would he have noticed it? It must have been there. He got up and went over and took hold of it but of course it was cold. He sat back down and ate the eggs.

He put the cup and plate and the silver in the sink and went up to the dayroom. He tried the television again. Nothing. He racked the balls on the pooltable and broke and ran a game of eightball. Padding around the table in his socks. The table had a list to it at one corner and the rails were pretty dead to bank off. He ran the table and stood his cue in the rack and went back down and stretched out on the bunk. He got up and went to the door and shut it. There was no way to lock or latch it. He put his toothbrush back in his shavingkit and got a towel out of his bag and went down to the bathroom and showered in one of the steel stalls and shaved and brushed his teeth and came back and put on a fresh shirt. He padded down to the galley and got some hamburger patties out of the freezer and put them on the counter to thaw. Then he went up to the operations room and sat and watched the storm. Someone was on the rig with him.

He went back and slept in the bunk with the desk pushed against the door and when he woke in the late afternoon the desk was backed away a good foot. The vibration of the rig was slowly walking it across the floor. He looked around the room. What else had walked? He got up and pulled the desk away and went down to the galley and got the meatcleaver and came back and sat on the bunk and hefted the thing in his hands. He pushed the desk back against the door again and tried to read. He went back up to the operations room. The storm continued almost unabated and dark was moving over the gulf from the west. A number of lights were out in the rigging. He sat watching the distant sea darken to black.

He wandered through the quarters below with the meatcleaver in his hand. Later he went up to the galley and fried two hamburgers and put them between slices of bread with mustard and sat at the table and ate them and drank a glass of milk. The milk in the glass shirred in endless circles. He looked at the meatcleaver lying on the table beside his plate. Henckels. Solingen. Could you bury that in someone's skull? Sure. Why not?

He tried to think of who had known that he was going to Florida. What if the rig went down in the storm? Rigs do. Who would know he was even on it? The airline put him in Pensacola. After that nothing. The helicopter? Gulfways? Did it even say Gulfways?

The rig isnt going down in the storm. What do they want? What does who want? Would you just get on a helicopter with anybody? You did. One more day. Two max.

He went back to the room with the meatcleaver in hand and pushed the desk against the door and stretched out on the bunk and closed his eyes. This is really stupid, he said.

When he woke it was close to midnight. The bunk was shaking and he thought that that was what had awakened him. The desk was half way across the room. He wondered would the lights go out. No reason for it. Everything on the rig was selfcontained.

He sat up. He was cold and he thought maybe it was the cold that woke him. If there was someone on the rig they would have come by now. What sort of seas could take down a jack-up rig?

He went up the corridor and opened the metal door and looked out into the howling. He shut the door again and went back and sat on the bunk. A long time till daylight.

They could just walk down the hall with a cheap infrared detector. Stop at the room that contained a warm body.

Make you walk to the shower? To minimize the clean-up?

Make you take your clothes off?

He sat listening. Watching the thin strip of light under the door.

Would he knock?

For what?

Would he wait for the light to go off?

You could bring in food and water and then barricade the door.

Two more days? Maybe.

He knew he would do nothing.

The crew came back midmorning of the following day. Coming down the companionway in their socks headed for the galley. By the time he got the bunks squared away the corridor was empty. He went up to the jackhouse and pushed open the door and stepped out onto the deck. The wind was still blowing and the dark seas lapped heavily but the storm had mostly passed. Down on the drillingfloor dead seabirds lay everywhere.

He ate lunch with the crew. They were a good bunch, unsurprised to see him there. He went back to his room and waited for the diveboat to come but the diveboat didnt come. He went up to the drilling office but the driller didnt know anything about unstacking any rigs. Someone had collected the dead birds and thrown them overboard and he watched the rig slowly swing into action. The big yellow traveling block rocked in the rigging and the drill was back on line by midafternoon and the drilling began again which would continue on into the night and every day and every night. He lay in his bunk listening to the voice of the driller over the squawkbox. The voice of the mudlogger. He'd left the light on over the desk. Men passed up and back outside the door going to and from the mess. The voices were like a balm to him. To be a part of some enterprise. A community of men. A thing all but unknown to him for the greater part of his life. He drifted in and out of sleep. The voices went on all night. We're running at a hundred rpm's. Two mp's are up to seven hundred.

You want to run up there about a hundred and twenty. You get around there too fast it's wobblin and all it's goin to do is just hang up on the wall. I dont give a fuck what you do in the hole.

Well what can we put in there?

More iron I guess.

You there?

Yeah.

Three to four. Maybe five.

I think it's goin to be eighty-two. Eighty-two. Keep drillin though.

Yeah. Pick up a single.

How many stands is that out?

Thirty. Thirty-one now.

About five stands of drillpipe left.

What joint is that you got hangin?

Ninety-nine.

Ninety-nine. What's that mud weight?

Ten-five.

Need to be certified.

He slept and woke. Four o four. Quiet outside. The speaker squawked softly. We got a little formation change. We're gettin into some dolomite. About four o seven. Eleven ninety-seven. It's close to bein limestone. Not much difference in it anyway. Sort of changed color a little bit. Just a little more crystalline than limestone. But you pick up one piece and you can see right through the middle of it. Half of it dolomite and half of it limestone. I thought it was shale to start with.

Seems to be drillin better. Bigger pieces. You can see teethmarks on it where that bit's been gettin hold of it. I guarantee you it's got a good appetite.

At five he got up and went down to the mess and ate a dish of ice cream and talked to two of the roughnecks sitting there drinking coffee. Where's your guys at? they said.

Coming tomorrow. I hope.

They nodded. You get paid for however long you're out here though. Right?

Right.

Good on you.

He went back to his bunk and lay in the sweet darkness. The storm had passed. The deep throb of the prime mover walked the bowl slowly across the table. Below them the drillbit turning a mile deep in the unimaginable blackness of the earth.

Bit man says his bit's quit.

Let's hold up on makin a bit up. We may change bits on it.

Pick up Mudlogger.

Mudlogger here.

Pick up on the drill floor. Where you at?

We're back here at the kellystand. I'll be right out there.

He lay with the rough blanket over him. News from another world.

Different formation. Shale one, maybe. I rezeroed the stroke counter. That's midway shale. Selma chalk.

What was that last survey depth?

Sixty-seven seventy-one. One degree.

What's the next kelly down to it?

Seventy-four thirty-three.

Is that one and two more? Or three more?

Three more.

When he woke again it was almost morning. The squawkbox was quiet. Then the driller came on. It's not drillin all that damn good. Forty, fifty feet a hour? Let's circulate there about fifteen minutes. Shut down and watch it. Make sure it aint flowin or nothin. It's all good we'll go ahead and put our slug in it.

He dozed.

Crane operator? What's them seas look like out there?

Five or six.

No fill on the bottom, said the mudlogger.

Make me some hole.

When he walked into the bar Janice looked up and waved one finger in a circle and motioned toward the end of the bar. He followed her down and set his bag in the floor.

What's going on?

You're not going to be happy.

What's happened?

Somebody got into your room.

Where's Billy Ray.

I dont know. I've been all over the neighborhood.

Western looked away.

I'm sorry Bobby. He could still turn up.

Did you see them?

No. Harold saw that the door was partly open and he knocked. I went up and it looked to me like somebody might have been through your stuff. We went all over looking for him. I been walking around the neighborhood every evening calling Billy Ray, Billy Ray. I know people think I'm nuts. I'm really sorry, Bobby.

Well. Let me go up.

It's those guys that come in here, isnt it?

Yeah. I suppose.

She searched his face. He picked up his bag. I dont really know. I dont know what they want. I dont even know who they are.

You're going to book, arent you?

I dont know, Janice. I really dont.

He wandered the streets tapping at Billy Ray's bowl with a spoon. Like some wandering mendicant. He never saw him again.

When he came down to the bar two days later there were two men waiting at a table against the far wall. They wore white shirts and black knit ties and the sleeves of their shirts were rolled to the elbows. They appeared to be drinking water. They both saw him at the same time and turned and looked at each other. Western went to the bar and got a beer from Janice and crossed the room to where they sat and kicked back a chair and set his beer on the table. Good morning, he said.

They nodded. They waited for him to say something else but he didnt. He took a swig from the beer.

Do you want to go someplace else?

To do what?

We just want to ask you a few things. Did you want to see some identification?

No. Do you?

We're just here to do our job, Mr Western.

All right.

You dont know who we are.

I dont care who you are.

And why is that?

Good guys, bad guys. You're all the same guys.

Are we now.

You are now.

I think we should go someplace else.

I'm not going anywhere with you. I think you know that.

Are you some sort of fanatic, Mr Western?

Yes. I suppose you could say that. I actually believe that my person belongs to me. I doubt that sits well with chaps such as yourselves.

It doesnt sit one way or the other. We just want to ask you a few questions in connection with this case we've been assigned to. We wonder if you might look at a few photographs.

Western sipped his beer. All right. Friends of mine?

We'd be inclined to doubt it. But we dont know.

And while I look at the photographs you'll be watching me look.

Is that all right with you?

Sure.

The first man took a brown envelope from his coat pocket and scrolled a rubber band off of it and placed the envelope on the table and slid out a packet of photographs and handed them to Western.

You want me to just look at these.

If you would.

Western began to thumb through the pack. The photos were prints. All the same stock and mat. He looked at the backs of them. Each had a four digit number in the upper left corner. He shuffled through them slowly. Young white males, mostly dressed in suits. Mostly they looked European. A few wore hats.

Are they in some particular order?

No.

The next one he turned up was his father. He held it out to one side. I guess we know who this is.

We do.

How many of them do you guys recognize?

We'd rather not say.

Me either.

You're not going to look at the rest of them.

I'm just fucking with you.

Because we could always subpoena you.

Could but wont.

And why is that?

We're big boys Walter. I dont know what this is about but I do know you dont want it in the papers.

My name's not Walter.

Sorry I meant to say Fred.

It's not Fred either. How about the photographs.

He went through the rest of them. There was one other face that was familiar to him but he couldnt put a name to it. He laid it on the table. This guy is familiar. He worked at the lab. Young guy. I dont know his name. If I ever did.

But that's it.

Yes.

Western slid the photos together and squared them on the tabletop and split them and fanned and shuffled them and handed them across.

You're a card player, Mr Western?

At one time. Not now.

Why is that?

I met some card players.

Good reason.

Who's the guy?

What guy?

The missing guy. Forty-two twenty-six.

The man turned the cards over and he sorted through them until he came to the number. Missing guy, he said.

Yeah.

How did you happen to remember that number?

I dont happen to remember things.

We dont know that he's anybody.

Yeah, right. Would you tell me if he was?

No.

Fair enough.

All right. Thank you for your time Mr Western.

You're welcome. Will I be seeing you again?

Probably not.

Do you know who all those people are?

We're not at liberty to say.

He squared the deck of photos and put them in the envelope and picked the rubber band off the table and slid it over the envelope and tapped the envelope on the table and looked at Western. Do you believe in aliens, Mr Western? he said.

Aliens.

Yes.

Odd question. I didnt this morning.

The man smiled and rose and the other man rose with him and stood. He'd yet to speak at all.

Thank you, Mr Western.

Western nodded. You're just welcome all to hell.

Kline's office was on the second floor and Western climbed the stairs and knocked at the door. The name in gold and black on the pebbled glass. He waited and knocked again. He tried the door and it was unlocked and he pushed it open. The outer office was empty but Kline was sitting at his desk in a glassed-in office to the rear and he was on the phone. He nodded to Western and made a cupping motion with his hand. Western shut the door behind him. There was a parrot in a cage in the corner of the room. Newspapers on the floor. The parrot crouched and studied him and then raised one foot and scratched the back of its head. Kline hung up the phone and stood. Western, he said.

Yes.

Come in.

He crossed the office and they shook hands and Kline gestured at the chair. Sit down. Sit down.

Western pulled the chair back and sat. He nodded at the bird. Does he talk?

As far as I know he is now a deaf mute.

Now.

I inherited him from my grandfather. My family had a carnival. He was one of the acts. My grandfather died and the parrot hasnt spoken since. Sort of like my grandfather's clock.

Is that a true story?

Yes.

What did the parrot do? In the carnival.

He rode a bicycle. On a wire.

Can he still ride one?

I havent asked him. Although supposedly it's something you never forget.

He didnt seem to like me.

He doesnt like anybody.

I should ask what you charge.

I get forty bucks an hour. Including phone conversations.

Are we on the clock?

Not yet. I need to know what you're up to.

Do you get a certain number of nut cases?

Yes. Are you one?

I dont think so. What do you do with them? The nut cases.

I just string them along and take their money.

You're kidding.

Yes.

You said on the phone that you dont do divorces. What else dont you do?

Kline swiveled his chair slightly and swiveled back. This is going to be something weird, isnt it? Isnt that where we're headed?

I dont know.

Why dont you just lay it out. With whatever economy you can muster.

Okay.

Western started with the airplane and he finished with the oil rig and with the two men in shirtsleeves at the Seven Seas. Kline sat with his fingertips pressed each to each. He was a close listener. When Western finished they sat.

That's it, Western said.

Is that what you do? You're a salvage diver?

Yes.

You're a refugee from the university system.

I suppose.

Are you seeing a shrink?

No. You think I should be?

It's sort of a standard question. A psychology major?

Physics.

What's a gluon?

It's the exchange particle in quark interactions.

Okay.

You knew the answer.

I didnt, actually. I just thought it was a weird name. Do you know what I did before I got into this business?

No. I dont think you were a cop.

No. I was a fortuneteller.

Is that true?

Everything's true.

Was this in the carnival?

Yes. It was a family enterprise. They were a colorful lot. Bavarian immigrants. Steuben. Possibly gypsies in the old world, I'm not sure. They settled in Canada. I was actually born in Montreal. In later years kids would sometimes come up to me and say that they wanted to join the circus and I would say no you dont. Go away.

You hated it.

I loved it. Are you on the run?

I dont know. I dont think so. Not yet.

What is it that you're not telling me?

A lot of things. What do you want to know?

What happened to you.

Something happened to me?

I think so.

What if I'd rather not tell you?

Then you'd rather not tell me.

I had a sister who died.

That you were close to.

Yes.

How long ago was this?

Ten years ago.

But you dont want to talk about it.

No.

All right.

Am I on the clock yet?

You're getting close.

Do you usually interview your clients this way?

What way is that?

I dont know. In a sort of personal way I suppose.

Maybe not.

Why me?

You're kind of interesting.

But there's something about me that's not forthcoming.

Kline looked at his watch. Maybe we should start. It's surprising what people will tell you about themselves when they're paying for it.

All right. Did you really tell people's fortunes?

Yes.

Did you have a gift for it?

I dont know as it's a gift. It's mostly common sense. Observation. Insight.

What is it that I'm not telling you?

I dont know. What is it that you've never told anyone?

Probably lots of things.

Other than things you might be ashamed of.

Still lots.

I think there may be things we keep to ourselves for reasons pretty much unknown to us.

When I was thirteen I found a wrecked airplane in the woods.

Okay. And you never told anyone.

No.

Was there anyone in the plane?

Yes. The pilot.

He was dead.

Yes.

You were by yourself.

Yes. Well, I had my dog with me.

Why didnt you tell anyone?

I dont know. I was scared.

You'd never seen a dead man before.

No.

How long had he been dead?

I dont know. A few days. A week. It was cold. Winter. There was snow on the ground. He was slumped over in the cockpit. The plane was jammed up against a tree.

Were they looking for the plane?

Yes. It was in a National Forest in East Tennessee. It had snowed and it wasnt that easy to see it.

How long was it before they found it?

A week maybe. I think it was about a week later. That they found it.

That's a strange tale.

I suppose.

There's something else.

I guess what was strange was that I knew the plane. I knew what it was.

You knew the plane.

Yes. I'd never made a model of it but I knew the plane.

You built model airplanes.

Yes. This was a fairly exotic plane. A Laird-Turner Meteor. An antique closed cockpit racing plane.

What was it doing in such a remote area?

He was on his way to a meet at Tullahoma Tennessee.

How did you get my name?

I'm sorry?

How did you get my name?

I got it out of the phone book.

Why me?

Why not?

You just closed your eyes and there I was.

I thought you were probably Jewish.

Really.

Yes.

In spite of the spelling.

Yes. Are you Jewish?

Yes. Do you know how many Jews there are in private investigation?

No.

Me.

That cant be true.

No. But close.

Why is that?

I think it lacks panache.

But not for you.

Apparently not. Do you think that you're in danger?

I dont know. I dont know what I would do about it if I were.

The underwater plane. You went back out to look for it.

Yes. I'm pretty sure the buoy was gone. I dont know. I could have missed it. The water was pretty rough.

Do you really think that there was somebody on the oil rig?

I did. Now I'm not so sure.

The racing plane in the woods in the snow. You went back to see it too.

Yes.

The next day?

Two days later.

Did you take your dog?

No.

Why not?

Because it seemed to make him nervous.

Do you think he knew there was a dead man in the plane?

I think he did. Yes.

How would he know that?

I dont know.

You took something.

I took something?

From the plane.

Yes.

Okay.

I cut a piece of linen out of the fuselage. With the number 22 on it. A big square. Like a flag.

This was a pretty exotic airplane.

Yes. It was a beautiful thing. Very fast. It had a Pratt & Whitney fourteen cylinder radial engine that put out a thousand horsepower. This was 1937. Ford automobiles at that time put out eighty-five horsepower. The top of the line V-8s. The downscale version put out sixty. You just wanted to talk to the guys who designed it.

The plane.

Yes. These were twentieth century Leonardos. If not Martians.

So what did you think when you saw it lying in the woods?

I thought it was about as strange a thing as I'd ever seen.

Coming upon airplanes with bodies in them I'm going to say is a fairly unusual experience. But for you it seems to be commonplace.

Commonplace.

Statistically speaking. Multiple millions of times more than the average citizen might experience.

Am I supposed to be superstitious?

Deep sea diving. Car racing. What. A love of hazard?

I dont know.

What do you want me to do for you?

Tell me what I should do to stay alive I suppose.

Some guy out of the telephone directory.

Yes.

I guess I would say just in general that the more seriously you take all this the longer you're likely to be around.

All right.

Do you carry a gun?

No. I own one. You think I should carry it?

Statistically it will shorten your life, not lengthen it. The unpleasant truth is that if someone is trying to kill you there is not a whole lot you can do about it. Your only real safety would be in disappearing. And even with that there are no guarantees.

I've thought about that. It seems like something of a last resort.

It is. The last resort save one.

Yes.

The wicked flee when none pursue. It's Bobby, right?

Yes.

What is it that you've done?

I wish I knew. Do you get a lot of clients who are fearful for their lives?

Some.

What sorts of clients.

Women sorts of clients. For the most part.

Women with husbands.

Or boyfriends.

Have you ever lost one?

Yes. One.

What happened?

They let him out of jail. Didnt bother to tell anyone. She was dead in two hours. Your sister was something of a beauty.

Yes. How would you know that?

Because beauty has power to call forth a grief that is beyond the reach of other tragedies. The loss of a great beauty can bring an entire nation to its knees. Nothing else can do that.

Helen.

Or Marilyn.

Well, I dont want to talk about her.

I know.

Where are we with this.

Even if you didnt want to flee the country a new identity would solve some of your immediate problems. But you'd probably have to move somewhere. Since you dont know what they want with you it's hard to know what sort of effort they might put into looking for you.

But if they want to find you they will.

Oh yes.

I think the idea that the government of the United States of America routinely assassinates its citizens is something of a paranoid fantasy among certain political groups.

I would agree with that. Unless you're one of those selected for assassination.

My problem is I dont have enough information.

Your problem is that you dont have any information. I wouldnt start any investigation with no more to go on than what you've given me. It would be an investment with no guarantee of getting anywhere at all. No one can tell you how to deal with an enemy that is completely unknown to you. The best advice would probably be to make a run for it. A strategy fairly effective against all adversaries, domestic and foreign.

Yes. As a friend of mine once said: I would rather make a good run than a bad stand. We're talking about a new identity. Right?

Yes. If you want me to set it up for you I'd do it with no charge on my own part. You'd get a passport, a driver's license, and a social security card. Fully backstopped, as they say in the trade. It will set you back eighteen hundred dollars. In this case a bit less.

Is this something that you do?

No.

Would I get to choose my name?

No. You would not. The phone's about to ring.

I'm sorry?

The phone's about to ring.

The phone rang.

I'm guessing that's just a cheap trick.

Yes.

Eighteen hundred.

Yes. It's pricey. A bit. But it's also the best. You can actually become another person for next to nothing. Then you can just go away. Just dont get fingerprinted anywhere.

You're not going to get that?

No.

Kline rose and stood looking out the window. The racing plane, he said.

Yes.

You knew something that no one else in the world knew.

Yes. I guess that's so.

Kline nodded. He could see across the rooftops to the river. The warehouses and the docks and sections of the ships between the buildings. He turned and looked at Western. What was the number on the vertical stabilizer?

On the Laird.

Yes.

Do you fly?

I used to.

It was NS 262 Y.

These people think that you know something that in fact you dont.

Is that how you see it?

Is there some other way to see it?

He and Red sat at a small table at the rear of the bar. Red took a sip of his beer and set the bottle on the table beside his keys.

His mother says she's going to call the police. But if the police find him they're liable to throw his dumb ass in jail.

For what?

Damn, Bobby. How far do you think they'd have to look?

Yeah. You've got a point. Why dont you go?

I'm afraid of what I might find.

That he's dead somewhere.

No. That he's alive somewhere. Lafayette. Apparently he's livin in a housetrailer maybe eight or ten miles out of town.

That's all you've got.

It's a small town. Somebody there knows him.

I'm sure that's true. All right.

All right? Really?

Yeah.

You're a good fucker. The old lady said she wanted a picture of him holdin up a newspaper like they do in the movies but I told her I didnt have a camera. Which I dont. I told her I'd get him to sign a piece of paper. Maybe sign the newspaper. That would work wouldnt it?

What if I find out that he's dead?

I dont know. I aint tellin this woman that her darlin boy is dead over the phone. I'm just not.

Well. Get the key off of there.

Two days later driving through the swamps east of Lafayette on little more than a Caterpillar track through the black dirt—liveoak parklands and stillwater bayous with cypress knees standing out of the green muck—he came to a fork in the road and sat there with the engine idling. When you come to a fork in the road, take it. He took the righthand track. No reason. He went on, lurching and sliding through the boggy places in the road. Potholes of black mud. Gray-looking cormorants standing on logs out in the swamp. Turtles.

Two miles on and the road ended in a cleared lot where a house-trailer sat pitched and leaning in the mud. The wheels half buried and the tires rotting. A pickup truck. He switched off the engine and sat there. Then he got out and shut the door and hallooed the house.

Some birds flew. He stood leaning against the fender of the truck taking in the scene. A rope hammock slung between a pair of trees with shreds of the hammock hanging underneath where someone had fallen through it. A coiled plastic hose. A galvanized washtub. There was an alligator hide nailed to a tree with the feet sticking out. After a while he called again.

The door banged open against the side of the trailer and a deranged-looking man in a beard stood spraddlelegged in the doorway with a shotgun leveled at his waist. Who are you? he croaked.

Jesus, said Western. Dont shoot me.

Western?

Yeah.

What the fuck. Where did you come from?

I've been sent on an errand of mercy.

Did you bring whiskey?

I did.

Get in this house you son of a bitch. You're goodern ary angel. Where's the hooch?

Western opened the truck door and got the bottle of liquor from behind the seat. He made as if to bobble it and caught at it wildly with his hands.

Dont fuck around, Western. Get your ass up here.

How are you doing?

Not worth a shit. Get in here.

He sat in a moldgrown springshot sofa in the front room of the trailer. The place just smelled generally of rot. He looked around. Jesus, he said.

Borman stood the shotgun in the corner and sat in a brokendown lounger opposite and propped his feet on a plastic ottoman and took the bottle and twisted off the cap and spun the cap across the room. He took a pull and squinted one eye and stiff-armed the bottle across to Western. Whoo, he said.

I dont suppose you have any glasses.

They're in the kitchen.

Western started to get up.

I dont think you want to go back there.

He sat back down again.

It aint a pretty sight. Sink's so full of dishes you got to go outside to take a leak.

Okay.

I used to just set the dishes out in the yard. Somethin would always come along and clean them up. Then somethin started carrying them off. Maybe a bear, I dont know.

Western took a drink and passed the bottle back. Borman drank. The brown liquor boiled in the bottle. When he lowered it the bottle was a third gone and his eyes were watering. He wiped his mouth and held the bottle out. Hell, Western. I've drunk worse liquor than that. Here.

I'm done.

You goin to leave me to drink by myself like a common drunk?

You are a common drunk.

What are you doin out here?

Your family's been calling about you. Red didnt know what to tell them. Whether you were alive or not. For instance.

He wouldnt come out though, would he?

He said the last time he went looking for you it was somewhere in California and you got him drunk and got him in a fight and got him in jail and when he finally got home six days later he was missing two teeth and had the clap.

You tell him when you see him that I said he's just a big dripping pussy.

I'll be sure to tell him.

You know what he told me one time?

No. What did he tell you one time?

He said he seen a dude in India drink a glass of milk with his dick. Do you believe that?

Jesus.

Borman drank. Western pointed at the wall. What is that? he said.

What is what?

On the wall there. What is that?

I dont know. Looks like dried puke. You sure you dont want another hit on this?

No thanks. This place looks awful.

It's the maid's day off. Hold it. Dont move.

What?

Dont move.

Jesus, Borman. Put that damned thing down.

Borman had put the bottle between his knees and fetched a pistol up from somewhere in the depths of the lounger and was aiming it at Western's head.

Good God, Borman.

Dont move.

The explosion in the trailer was deafening. Western dove to the floor. He put his hands on top of his head. His ears were ringing and he'd hit his head on the table. He felt to see if there was any blood.

You crazy bastard. What the hell is wrong with you?

Got you you son of a bitch. Hell, Western. Get up from there.

Are you crazy?

It's just ratshot.

Western raised up and looked at the wall behind him. The walls of the trailer were perforated all over with tiny holes in clusters and here and there small brown stains or blotches among the perforations. He looked at Borman. Borman was lowering the hammer on a Walther P38. Roaches, he said. It's war, Bobby. I take no prisoners. Get your ass up. Hell. You aint hurt.

My goddamned ears are ringing like a snaredrum.

Yeah? I guess I've got used to it.

You dont get used to it. You get deaf.

I wish you'd of brought me out a can of SR 4756 and some caps. I've got an old Lee Loader around here somewhere. You could reload these things with river sand. Seal em with wax. When these sons of bitches find out I'm out of ammo they'll take the place over. It'll just be Katy bar the door.

When they find out you're out of ammo.

Yeah.

Borman?

I only got one box left. Of the ratshot.

Borman?

Yeah?

They're going to come and take you away. Do you understand that?

You think I'm losing it.

What else is there to think?

You're a smart guy, Western. Do you really think they're not coming anyway? You say we cant see into the future? We dont have to. It's here. I still got five boxes of the hundred and eighty grain longnose for the rifle and maybe eight boxes of shotgun shells. There's a fifty-five gallon drum of water under the house and enough staples for a pretty decent siege. Dried fruit. C-rations. A couple of crates of MREs. There's a trapdoor in the floor in there. I got a barrel sunk in the ground under the trailer. It's sort of like a duckblind. Rocks piled around it. Loopholes in the key positions.

He drank. He looked at Western. Burst of glory, Bobby. The final option. That's all there is.

Western had gotten up off the floor and was waggling a finger in his ear. You're as nutty as a goddamned fruitcake.

Borman smiled. He drank. He leaned suddenly forward and whipped out the pistol again. Dont move, he hissed.

Western dove into the couch with his hands over his ears. After a while he looked up. Borman had fallen over in the lounger laughing soundlessly, his shoulders shaking.

You're a sick fuck. Did you know that?

Oh man, said Borman, wheezing.

Let me ask you something.

Sure.

When was the last time you saw anybody out here?

Define anybody.

Anybody. A human being.

Define human being.

I'm serious.

So am I.

How long have you been out here?

I dont know. Six, eight months.

Is that true? All that stuff?

All what stuff?

The guns and the pit and everything.

Nah. I'm just fuckin with you, Bobby. Well. Partly.

Is that your truck out there?

Yeah.

It looks like it's been sitting there a hell of a long time.

The swamp is not kind to machinery.

I dont think it's been too kind to you.

I'm doin all right.

You're doing all right.

Yeah.

Borman I dont think you get it. You've slipped a cog somewhere. This is not all right. This is a hell of a long way from being all right.

Borman thought about that, reclining in the lounger, looking at the ceiling. At the dried corpses of the slain palmetto bugs. He took a drink of the whiskey. Why dont we just sit here and drink a little whiskey and relax. Shoot the shit.

Have you got any money?

Borman straightened one leg so as to reach in his pocket. I got a little, Bobby. What do you need?

Hell, Richard. I dont need anything. I just wanted to know if you were all right.

I'm all right.

How do you get out to get your groceries?

There's an old fool lives about two miles up the road. He's got a car. We go in and he gets drunkern shit and I drive his ass back.

He offered the whiskey again but Western shook his head.

Hell, Bobby. Take a little drink. You need to loosen up some. Everthing'll be all right.

Western took the bottle and drank and passed it back. Are you sure you havent gone completely dipshit out here?

I aint sure of anything. Are you?

Probably not.

You want to know when was the last time I saw anybody. I could ask you when was the last time you didnt see anybody. When was the last time you just sat by yourself. Watched it get dark. Watched it get light. Thought about your life. Where you'd been and where you were goin. Was there a reason for any of it.

Is there?

I think that if there was a reason then that would just be one more thing to inquire about. My notion is you probably make up reasons after you've decided what it is you're goin to do. Or not do.

He looked at Western.

Go ahead, said Western.

Ahh, said Borman. He tossed something invisible over his shoulder and raised the bottle and drank. He sat. When were you in Knoxville last?

Not that long ago.

Knoxville, Borman said. Did Red send you out here sure enough?

Yeah.

Good fucker. We go back a ways.

Do you want to go back with me?

Borman studied the label on the whiskey bottle. I dont think so, he said.

All right.

I'll tell you who did come out here.

Who.

Oiler.

Oiler?

Oiler.

When?

A while back. We went into town and got drunk.

Oiler's dead, Richard.

Borman sat. He leaned and set the bottle on the floor and turned and looked out the small dirty window. Shit, he said.

I'm sorry.

That really sucks.

I know.

What happened?

Diving accident. Down in Venezuela.

How long ago?

A couple of months.

Borman shook his head. That really sucks.

Yeah.

Damn I hate that.

He leaned forward and handed the bottle across. Western hesitated but Borman looked ready to hold it there forever. He took it and drank and passed it back. What a good son of a bitch, Borman said.

Yes.

Borman pushed the heel of his hand against his eyes. How many people do you know who are not pretty much assholes?

I dont know. I know a few.

Yeah? Oiler's about the only one I can think of. Just offhand.

Well, there's you and me.

Borman drank and set the bottle on his knee and held it by the neck. Hell, Western. You aint *even* an asshole.

I havent progressed that far.

No.

Just a garden variety turd.

I dont know.

But not a son of a bitch.

No.

Or a prick.

Borman smiled. No. You aint a prick.

What about a fuck of some description?

I dont know. Fuck has got to have an adjective in front of it.

Like sick fuck.

Yeah. Like sick fuck. Poor fuck, dumb fuck.

You think I'm a dumb fuck?

I dont know what kind of a fuck you are.

But some kind.

Yeah.

Are you a sick fuck?

Probably. Yeah.

What's the worst thing you can be?

Borman thought about that. A piece of shit. There aint no reprieve from that.

Total contempt.

Total.

No such thing as an apology.

Not for that.

Are you a son of a bitch?

Me? Absolutely.

No question.

No question. Goldplated with a warranty.

Is that why you're out here?

You mean did God send me out here to waste away in the swamps because I was a son of a bitch?

Yeah.

Probably.

Do you believe in God?

Hell, Bobby. Who knows.

If somebody calls somebody just a plain fuck it just means they left off the adjective?

Plain is an adjective.

Is Long John a son of a bitch?

No. He's too pathetic.

Is he a sick fuck?

Let me put it this way. If you look up sick fuck in the dictionary you'll find his picture. Damn I hate that about Oiler.

You want to go into town? Get something to eat?

I guess. Sure.

He drained the last of the whiskey and reached under the lounger and pulled out a pair of red and blue bowling shoes with the number 9 on the back of the heel.

What are those?

Shoes.

Is that all the shoes you've got?

Is that all right?

I guess. What happened to your regular shoes?

Boots. Pretty nice pair of Tony Lamas. I've got to guess they're in a bowling alley somewhere.

I didnt know you bowled.

I dont. Are you ready?

They walked out in the yard and stood looking at Borman's truck. Borman seemed little the worse for wear for a man who'd just drunk the better part of a quart of whiskey.

The fuel pump was goin out and I kept crankin it and it finally backfired through the carburetor and when it done that it broke about half the teeth off the starter gear.

Not the flywheel.

No, thank God. I pulled the starter. It's layin in the floor yonder.

We could take it in and get a rebuilt. It wouldnt cost much.

Yeah. What are you goin to do about the tires?

Western looked at the tires. Yeah, he said.

Fuck it, Bobby. Let the son of a bitch set there. I'll get it up and runnin one of these days.

All right. You ready?

Yeah. You're liable to try and shanghai me.

I'll bring you back. Hell, Borman. I dont care if you lay out here and die.

Spoke like a gentleman. All right. Let me lock up.

Lock up?

Yeah.

All right.

Borman looked around. Somewhere out here the last ivorybill died. Thirty years ago probably. I still listen for them. What sense does that make? They're gone forever.

I didnt know you were a bird watcher.

I'm not. I'm a forever watcher.

Forever is a long time.

Tell me about it. I have weird dreams, man. I dream about animals sometimes and they'll be dressed up in robes like judges and they'll be trying to decide what to do with my ass. In the dream I dont know what it is that I've done. Just that I've done it. You may be right. Maybe I need to get out of here.

They went to a cafe on Fourth Street and ate porterhouse steaks with baked potatoes and hot apple cobbler with vanilla ice cream. Borman went to the counter and came back with two cigars and sat and handed one to Western. Western smiled and shook his head.

Fuck you, said Borman. More for the rest of us. What are you? Turning into some kind of an aesthetic?

Ascetic.

Whatever.

I never did smoke cigars. You're thinking of Long John.

Yeah. I get you two mixed up all the time.

He bit off the end of the cigar and spat and lit the cigar and shook out the match and laid the mate in the ashtray. He leaned back, blowing smoke. I hate this goddamned town.

Go somewhere else.

Sure. I could go back to fucking McMinnville.

Go somewhere else. The world is wide.

Yeah. It's wide and then you fall off. I read somewhere that on Jupiter or someplace if you had a powerful enough telescope you could look and see the back of your own head. Is that true?

I dont know. Maybe. The gravity's pretty strong so maybe it bends the light around like that. Theoretically I suppose it could be true. Of course you wouldnt be able to hold up the telescope because it would weigh five hundred pounds. And you wouldnt be able to stand up or breathe or anything like that. Probably if you looked down your eyeballs would fall out of their sockets and break on the ground like eggs.

You like all that shit, dont you?

Western shrugged. It's interesting. I used to be pretty good at it.

Yeah? I was a pretty good ballplayer. Middlin good. I went to the minors. One year. I knew I wasnt ever goin to the show so that was that. Did you know that Oiler used to play the clarinet?

I did know that.

That's some weird shit.

I guess it's not something you would have expected.

People are a fucking puzzle. Did you know that?

Western sipped his coffee. It may be the only thing I do know.

You still play music?

No.

I'd expect it from you.

Playing music?

Yeah.

Because?

I just would.

You think it's not a guy sort of thing.

You know I dont think that. I saw you in action at the Wayside Inn one night.

Western smiled. I dont remember that I did all that much damage.

Maybe not. But I remember you gettin back up off the floor when a lot of guys might not have.

Sheer ignorance.

Anyway, mostly it's just that you're a fucking puzzle.

I am.

Yeah. You.

That's what Sheddan says.

Well. Probably Sheddan would know.

And you're not.

Hell, Bobby. I provide more entertainment than ten of you. Straight as you are I dont see how you even *know* half the crazy motherfuckers you hang with. You want a beer?

Sure.

You ought to smoke this cigar.

Let me have it.

Borman handed him the cigar and then held up one hand for the waitress.

It's not education. Sheddan's got a pretty good education. Damn good, for that matter. But there's things about you that are not true for him or me. Or Red.

For instance.

Maybe it's just that people will say things about you that they wont say to you.

Bad things?

No. Just things that might be true about you. Do you think you can learn all there is to know about yourself from yourself?

No. I dont think that.

The waitress brought the beers. Western took the book of matches from the ashtray and lit the cigar. He shook out the match. You dont think there are things about Long John that people say behind his back?

Not really. I think for the most part they cant wait to get the news to him.

So give me an example.

Of what.

Of something that somebody has said about me. You dont have to spare my feelings.

Hell, Bobby. I dont give a fuck about your feelings.

How did we get on this subject?

I dont know.

Is it because you dont think we'll see each other again?

I dont think that. All right. Here's one. That you'd get out of the shower to take a leak.

Is that so bad?

I didnt say it was bad.

Who said it?

I did.

Why wont you call your mother?

I aint got a telephone.

There's a payphone on the wall back there by the restroom.

I'll call her, Bobby.

I wish I could call mine.

I'm an end of the roader, Bobby. I always was. Maybe I just didnt know it.

What do you think is out there?

Borman shook his head.

Well?

Have you looked around lately, Son? What do you think is coming? Christmas? You cant even hire mourners anymore. After a while they'll figure out a way to just dissolve you. Your brain shuts down and the next thing you know there's only a pair of shoes and some laundry piled up on the sidewalk.

You surprise me. This is your last port of call?

Probably. Maybe not. Too soon old and too late smart. You dont know anything till it gets here. You told me once that maybe the end of the road has nothing to do with the road. Maybe it doesnt even know there's been a road. You ready?

Western drained his beer and put the burning cigar in the ashtray. He picked up the change and left a tip and stood.

They walked out and stood at the curb. You go ahead, said Borman. I'm not goin back.

You want me to come and get you later?

Nah. I'm all right. I'm goin to go see my widow woman.

Is this something serious?

Not really. She's what you might call an older woman. But she's a cheerful soul. Always up for a good old roughhouse fuck.

How old is she?

Seventy-three.

Damn, Borman.

Borman grinned. I'm just fucking with you, Bobby. I dont know how old she is. Forty, maybe. Redhead. Meanern a snake.

He gripped the cigar in his teeth and looked off down the street. He scratched at his beard. I appreciate you comin out, Bobby. Tell Dogdick I'm still alive and still crazy.

Let me ask you something.

Sure.

Suppose you were in trouble and you just had two quarters. Would you call me or would you call Sheddan?

Yeah. You got a point.

How are you going to get back out to the trailer?

She's got a car.

And then what?

And then nothing.

What are you going to do for groceries?

She'll get me some stuff.

I can let you have a few bucks.

You sure?

Sure.

All right. I aint proud.

Western peeled off two hundred dollars and handed it to him.

Thanks Bobby.

What are you going to do?

I dont know. Wait.

For what?

I dont know.

When will you know?

When it gets here.

You know, I dont believe I could live like you're living.

Yeah. Well, wait till you have to.

Sheddan said that he saw you in New Orleans about a year ago with a really big girl. Is this her?

No. That was Jackie.

What happened to her?

The hot weather came and I had to let her go. She was a full axe-handle across the ass. Besides which when the mood came over her she could have the disposition of a pitbull on angeldust.

So what was the attraction.

She was an interesting woman. It didnt hurt that she gave the best head of any woman I ever knew. But she was interesting. You couldnt tell what she was goin to do. I like that in a woman. She gave me a blowjob in a phonebooth on Bourbon Street one night. One of them that's only glass from about the waist up? I had to pretend like I was talkin on the phone. People walking by. Then I thought what the fuck. So I called John Sheddan and told him I was getting a blowjob in a phonebooth.

You're not going to introduce me.

To my widow woman? No.

She is seventy-three?

Nah. I dont think she's even forty. I'm just tryin to throw you off the scent. You've got me confused with Jerry Merchant. If they werent on social security he wasnt even interested. I walked in on him one time when he was staying with me up over the Napoleon and he had somebody's grandmother in the bed. She tried to pull the sheets up but he just pulled em off in the floor and stood there grinnin. She looked like a goddamned bog person. She put her hands over her face. Like that was goin to help. I didnt even want to think about him puttin her through the kind of sexual indignities he was partial to. Of course the more I tried not to think about it the more I thought about it. You take care, Bobby.

And you.

He watched him as he walked down the street. Striding along in his bowling shoes. Dirty and disreputable and jaunty. When he got to the corner Western thought that he would look back and wave or something but he didnt. He turned up a street named Rue Principale Quest and was gone. Western walked back down to the truck and got in and headed back to New Orleans.

VII

She'd fallen asleep with her book open on the quilt beside her but she must have wakened in the night and turned off the lamp. When she woke again it was paling day at the window and the Kid was sitting at her desk reading. She sat up and pushed her hair back. What are you reading? she said.

New data. Fix your robe will you? Jesus.

She pulled her robe closed.

Glad you're awake. Something's come up. We picked up a signal. Band four. This thing has just come in. Odd history to it.

What thing?

The Kid gestured into the room. She turned to look. Under the eaves stood two men in sou'westers. On the floor between them a brassbound steamer trunk.

Who are they?

Pretty interesting. We dont know how far back we're looking. It was pretty deep in the hold and God knows where it's even been. Okay guys.

They set about unstrapping the trunk. The heavy brass clasps. Everything thick with verdigris. The trunk was standing on its end and they opened it sideways, bookfashion. A small man stepped out and stretched and shook himself and put one hand to the back of his neck and ratcheted his head slowly to one side and then the other. He stepped back and assumed a boxer's stance and threw a quick series of jabs. Then he stepped forward and stood, his mouth clacking woodenly. As if he were chewing gum.

The inside of the trunk was lined in a sort of paisley material and the occupant himself was turned out in a little suit of the same stuff, coat and trousers, matching vest and cap. He wore a yellow cravat and a silver watch chain from which hung a collection of small medallions—holy medals, school awards, milagros of coinsilver. A small seal that bore the name of a milk company. She tucked her robe about her and leaned forward in the bed the better to see him. He seemed to be a dummy. Made of wood. His mouth opened and closed with a clapping sound and his eyes were bright and glassy. He crouched and put up his fists again and then stood back and smiled his wooden smile.

We dont have the program, the Kid said. There's some jacks in the back of his coat. An access panel. We dont know what's missing. Thought you might like to take a gander. He's got a sort of handmade look to him.

What do you want me to do?

I dont know. Ask him some questions. I'll sit here and take a few notes.

What sort of questions?

Ask him his name.

The mannequin was leaning against the open trunk with one foot crossed over the other. He looked cocky and slightly dangerous.

What's your name? she said.

Puddentain. Ask me again and I'll tell you the same.

What's your name?

Puddentain. Ask me again . . .

Okay, said the Kid. I think we got it.

What are those things on his watch chain?

Woodsmen of the World. Immaculate Conception. There's a Phi Beta Kappa key. Probably from a pawnshop.

He keeps staring at me.

He keeps staring at you?

Yes.

He's a dummy.

I know. He looks familiar.

She'd climbed out of the bed and was sitting crosslegged on the floor. Might be a good idea not to get too close, said the Kid.

I dont think he likes me.

So? I thought you were going to ask him some questions.

Where do you come from? she said.

The dummy cocked his head. He looked at the Kid. Who's this dishy bitch?

The Kid whispered to her from behind his flipper. It could be a Personal Advisor program. Lots of opinions. It doesnt mean he's got a brain.

Up yours, said the dummy.

He's very rude.

Why dont you address your remarks to me, Blondie?

Who are the Woodsmen of the World?

Who knows? said the Kid. Something to do with trees.

It's a brotherhood, said the dummy. You spasticlooking fuck.

He's got screws in his head. He looks sort of screwed together. Like maybe he's had an accident of some sort.

Probably some kid had him.

Maybe he gets in fights.

Bingo, said the dummy. He bobbed and weaved and fetched up an uppercut and then fell to chewing again. Clack clack clack.

He seems to be waiting for something.

Waiting for you, Dollytits.

Does his hat come off?

Dont know. It's probably nailed on. I dont think you want to get too close.

I'm not.

Bet your ass, said the dummy.

Do you travel a lot?

Sure.

What sorts of places do you visit?

Sure.

Maybe he's been dropped on his head, said the Kid.

What else is in the trunk?

I dont know. Could be a battery pack. Transformer. Maybe even something cute like a ballastdriven generator.

What do you do in there? she asked.

What do I do? I dont do a goddamn thing. What do you think I do? It's a traveling wankery and that's about the size of it. What time do you get off?

Do you think he's anatomically correct?

Sure, said the dummy. Birchwood balls and a clockwork cock.

She looked at the Kid. I dont know what to do with him.

Maybe we should be taping this stuff.

You dont know anything about him?

Well aside from not knowing who he is or where he's from or what he's up to I think we've pretty much got it covered. There's waterstains in the trunk suggestive of misadventure at sea. Dont know if Walnuthead here might have suffered immersion on his travels. Could be a corroded circuit or two. Ask him something else.

You do that, said the dummy.

He has sort of a southern accent. How old are you?

Dont know. Papers lost in transit.

Do you speak any other languages?

Sure. Doubledutch and piglatin. I play the twelvestring psaltery and the pathological lyre and I can fart in four octaves. What about yourself, Deweydrawers?

Do you know any math?

I can count forward without repeating myself and backward without starting over. Try it some time.

Can you solve problems?

Sure I can. What about you, Peachfuzz?

She turned to the Kid. What does it say on the trunk?

What does what say?

There's a sticker on the trunk.

Yeah. It says progeny of Western Union.

Progeny?

Property. Property of Western Union.

The two chaps in their slickers stood waiting. Puddles of water pooled about their seaboots.

Where did you get the suit? she said.

It's my suit. Whaddaya mean where did I get it? I came with it.

That's it, said the Kid. He folded shut his notebook. Fuck it. You cant win em all. Load his weird ass up.

They stepped forward and tilted the trunk and one of them picked up the dummy.

Crandall? she said.

They stopped. They looked at her and they looked at the Kid.

Load his ass up.

Crandall is that you?

What is it with this broad?

Crandall it's me. It's Alice. I'm a lot bigger now.

And Bob's your ruddy fucking uncle. Get me out of here. Christ.

I'm sorry, Crandall. I was only six. Dont go. Please.

The stevedores waited. They looked at the Kid.

My grandmother made that suit. Out of the old curtains in the upstairs bathroom. She even made the hat.

Will somebody please tell me what this silly bitch is going on about?

Please dont go.

Travel the seven fucking seas for this? Jesus.

That's it, said the Kid. Bloody hell. Stick to the program. Didnt I say that? Stick to the program? Is that so goddamned difficult? Fuck it. Get his ass out of here.

He came upon the long one at his customary wateringhole leaning back in one chair with his feet crossed in another a good distance away. His hat tilted over one eye. A Macanudo Prince Philip in his teeth. He hardly even looked up. Sit down, he said. And no cute chat. I'm in a vile mood.

Again?

I suppose you sense a trend. Dont answer that.

Nice boots.

John studied them. Looks are deceiving. A poor fit, as it turns out. Hand made by Scarpine and Sons of Fort Worth. They have my lasts on file. What are you drinking?

Nothing, thank you.

A coffee.

No.

Suit yourself.

I will. Where are you staying?

You'll find me at the Burke and Hare. Hostelry for impecunious gentlemen.

I saw an old friend a day or two ago who was asking after you.

Sheddan took the cigar from his teeth and studied it. Cant be too old or he'd be among the deceased.

Borman.

I thought he was in fact among the deceased. Is he still with Dame Jaquelyn?

No. He's ditched her for a new companion he refers to simply as his widow woman.

Well. She has shoes to fill. Not to mention drawers. The last time I saw Lady Jaquelyn she had moved out of clothes altogether and into tarpaulins. Awnings. The whole affair calls up images you'd rather not entertain. Her great hummocky fundament wobbling away down the street like a sack of cats headed for the river. You just dont want to think about it. Flailing about in that tentlike lingerie. Like an actor struggling to find his way back through the curtain. Snufflings. Cries of discovery. Just the boldness of it takes your breath. Sit down, Squire, for God's sake.

Western sat. Is that why the brown study?

No. Tulsa's left.

Sorry.

Decamped. Flown the coop. It's hard to keep them entertained, Squire. They keep upping the ante. You think you've done a workmanlike job of fucking them but that's just the beginning. God. The hoops a man will put himself through. At some age you fancy you might rise above these sorts of things and at some age you dont. What is it that we're looking for? It's not grace or salvation and it is droll beyond words to imagine that it's love. The ancients claim that there is truth in the grape. God knows I've looked. I suppose that when a man is sick of pussy he's sick of life but I do think the bitches may have finally done me in. God but we're fools. For something that should be delivered with the morning milk. As Crowley would have it. Jesus. Why am I asking you?

I dont know.

Sheddan pulled at his cigar. He shook his head. Not even all that sexy a woman. Goodlooking but in an odd way. Incisors like a Jurassic cat. A man shouldnt ignore a thing like that.

Pleistocene.

What?

Pleistocene. Cat.

Yes, well. Find me something that alliterates.

He held up the bottom of his glass in his fingers and rotated it slowly. The icecubes held true north. The sweeter the more lethal, Squire. Oh you do occasionally find one who flies her true colors. It's even refreshing in a way. A bitch to the teeth, fair field and no favor. Dried scrotums strung on a cord hanging from the footboard. But these other ones. The shy smile and the downturned eyes. Jesus. Spare me.

What has happened to our cavalier, John? This is a grim portrait.

I told you. I'm not in a good mood. Still at heart I know there's more wisdom in sorrow than in joy. Maybe you can see why I resent being called a cynic.

Tell me.

It doesnt fit the case. What's the adjective most commonly attached to cynicism?

I dont know. Cheap?

Yes. And it's not. It's not even cynicism and it damned sure isnt cheap. Well, piss on it. Anyway, you can complain bitterly about the fair sex and still maintain a grudging admiration. I'd even make the claim that if you've never contemplated killing a woman you've probably never been in love. What are you doing for the rest of the evening?

I dont know. Why?

I thought we might dismember a brace of crustaceans. Wash them down with a chilled Montrachet.

While discussing the verities.

While.

I think I'll take a pass.

I've some fresh plastic to cover the tab.

Kind of you. But I'm tired and you're out of sorts.

As you like, Squire. Although a good meal does do wonders for a man's disposition.

I'm amazed at your freedom of movement. Arent you supposed to report to a parole officer from time to time?

I'm working on that.

Is Judy helping you?

No. I had to let her go.

You had to let her go?

Yes.

You fired her?

Yes.

But she was working for you pro bono.

God, Squire. Is that supposed to provide some sort of warranty against dismissal? I've had to take matters into my own hands.

What, you're going to defend yourself?

I suppose you could put it like that. I'm paying off the judge. Interesting thing is that they're letting me do it on the installment plan. Courtesy of the bagman, of course. His Honor gets his up front. I like the simplicity of it. I've never understood why justice wasnt supposed to be for sale. Perhaps including a reasonable credit plan. What's so special about justice?

Now you are being cynical.

Not a bit of it.

You think I'm naive.

I dont think you're naive. You are naive. My understanding of it is not what makes it so. Why dont you have a coffee?

All right.

Sheddan ordered a coffee and a fresh gin and tonic. The waiter nodded and moved away.

You think she's flown the coop for good?

Tulsa.

Yes.

Probably more good than ill. Quién sabe. I asked a woman to marry me one time. In a restaurant.

And?

And she picked up her purse and left.

That was it?

That was it.

That's a strange story.

I thought so. An evening like that will unstructure you.

Unstructure?

Yes.

Were you serious?

About the proposal?

Yes.

Yes. Of course.

How long had you known her?

I dont know. Two. Three days.

You're joking.

I dont know, Squire. Maybe a year.

Did you think she would say yes?

I did. More fool.

Did I know her?

No. This was in California. You were in Europe.

I suppose you suddenly saw in her a wisdom you had not heretofore suspected.

Cruel, Squire. But a certain truth there. I realized that while she found me entertaining she had other plans for life.

Did you ever hear what became of her?

Yes. She's a cardiac surgeon at Johns Hopkins.

You're serious.

Completely.

Interesting.

The waiter came with their drinks. Here we are, said John. Your health.

And yours.

We dont move through the days, Squire. They move through us. Until the last cruel crank of the ratchet.

I'm not sure I see the distinction.

It's just that the passing of time is irrevocably the passing of you. And then nothing. I suppose it should be a comfort to understand that one cannot be dead forever where there's no forever to be dead in. Well. I see your look. I know that you see me enfettered in some cognitive morass and I'm sure that you would contend it to be the ultimate solipsism to believe that the world ceases when you do. But I've no other way to look at it.

It's just that I'm not sure how it would change anything.

I know. But I can hear the dice clattering as well as the next chap.

Ultimately there is nothing to know and no one to know it.

Ultimately. Yes.

Are you slipping away from us, John?

Sheddan smiled. He sipped his drink. I dont think so. Even if all news of the world was a lie it would not then follow that there is some counterfactual truth for it to be a lie about.

I suppose I would agree. If it does have a somewhat lampish smell to it. The Greeks, I suppose.

I suppose. Possibly of course of humbler origins.

Such as Mossy Creek.

Such as. Do you ever think what it would be like to meet a person you've known for a long time for the first time in these later years? To meet them anew.

You're thinking they would be a much different person to you if you didnt know their history.

Yes.

How would it differ from when you first met them?

That's not it. We're talking about them as they are now. Only with a past unknown to us.

I dont get it.

Skip it. How about another coffee?

I have to go.

Then with my blessing, Viejo. It's an odd place, the world. I was in Knoxville a while back and there was this wino got hit by a bus. He was lying on the sidewalk where he'd been carried and people were just sort of standing around. Gay Street. In front of the S & W. Someone had gone to call. And I bent down and asked him if he was all right. I mean he damn sure wasnt all right. He'd just been run over by a bus. And he opened his eyes and looked up at me and he said: My sands are run. Jesus. My sands are run? The ambulance came and they took him away and I scoured the papers for several days but I couldnt find anything about the incident.

Maybe he was sent to carry a message to you.

Maybe. Life is brief. Carpe diem.

Or maybe just watch out for buses.

Sheddan sipped his drink and set it back on the table. Buses, he said.

I've got to go.

Friends are always telling you to watch out. To take care. But it could be that the more you do so the more exposed you become. Maybe you just have to turn yourself over to your angel. I may even start praying, Squire. I'm not sure who to. But it might lift a bit of weight from the shoulders, what do you think?

I think you should follow your heart.

He drank the last of his coffee and stood. The lamps had come on down Bourbon Street. It had rained earlier and the moon lay in the wet street like a platinum manhole cover. Take care, John.

And you, Squire. Or did I just recommend against that?

He couldnt sleep. He'd taken to walking the Quarter at all hours in what was to be the last of the years in which you could do that before the muggers took over the streets. He didnt know what to do with her letters. He didnt see Kline about the carry permit. He doubted it would help anything. Lou left messages at the bar but he didnt go back to work. Janice watched him come and go. Red was in Argentina. Rio Gallegos. Where the winds blew lawn furniture and dead cats over the lightwires. He saw Valovski in the bar once or twice. In a cafe on the edge of the Quarter one morning he saw someone he thought he knew.

Webb, he said. Is that you?

Webb turned and looked at him.

It's Bobby Western.

Hell, Bobby. I know you. How you makin it?

I'm okay.

What are you doin now?

Not much of anything. What are you?

Same here.

You still on the trucks?

Nah. I quit about a year ago. I fucked up my foot. Stepped off a curb and twisted it or somethin. It aint been right since. I finally quit. I was slowin everbody down. Fair's fair. I get a little money from the city.

Those were good jobs.

Like we always said. A hundred dollars a week and all you can eat.

Western ordered coffee and the counterman turned to get it.

You aint got a smoke on you have you Bobby?

No. I dont smoke.

That's all right.

Let me get you a pack.

Hell, Bobby. It's all right.

What do you smoke?

Camels. No filter.

Western walked down to the cigarette machine at the end of the counter and put in three quarters and pulled the handle. The pack slid into the tray along with his change. He got a paper and walked back and laid the cigarettes on the counter. Webb nodded and picked up the pack. Thanks, Bobby. That's white of you.

You're welcome.

I've tried to quit these things. I aint sure it can be done. You never smoked?

Nope.

I did quit drinkin. Just flat give it up. But these things I believe have got heroin in em.

Was drinking a problem?

I dont know. I guess I'd have to say it was. I'd wake up in strange places. I woke up one time in somebody's parked car and I thought, well, what if you woke up dead? That kind of got to me. I mean, do you think if you died drunk you'd sober up before you met Jesus?

Good question. I dont know.

I thought about that. Standin in front of him drunk. What would he say. Hell, what would *you* say?

I guess I dont think your soul gets drunk.

Webb thought about that. Well, he said. Maybe yours dont.

He lit the cigarette and blew out the match with the smoke. Western unfolded his paper and looked at it. He looked at Webb. Do you ever feel like somebody is after you?

Webb dropped the match in the ashtray. It smoked gently. I dont know, he said. I was married one time. Does that count?

I dont think so.

Why? You think somebody's after you?

I dont know. I just wonder if maybe lots of people dont feel that way.

For no reason.

Yeah.

Webb smoked. Like most people he liked being consulted. I had a uncle one time was a certified character. He'd steal a hot stove. He wouldnt even talk to you unless the subject was larceny. Anyway, they were after his ass all the time but I couldnt see as it bothered him all that much.

Did he ever do time?

Sure he did time. I couldnt see as that bothered him either. I been in jail one time in my life. One time. Drunk and disorderly. And I'm goin to tell you, Bobby, I dont want no second servings.

What finally happened to him?

The sugar got him. He lost a leg over it. Wound up a security guard in Houston Texas. Been on the job about three weeks when some Mexicans come through the skylight and shot him between the eyes. I dont know what that says.

Life is strange.

Tell me about it. But I'm goin to say it's stranger for some than for others.

Maybe it just says that you pay for what you do.

I believe that to be a true statement. I surely do.

Still I think some people might pay more than what they owe.

You speakin for yourself, Bobby?

I dont know. But I would like to know who keeps the books.

Amen.

Western finished his coffee. Good to see you, Webb. You take care.

And you, Bobby.

He walked out in the street. He wished he'd given him some money but he didnt know how to go about it.

On Friday he walked into the bank and wrote out a check on the marble counter for two hundred dollars and presented it at the cage. The teller put the check in the slot in the machine and punched up the numbers. He sat there for a minute. Then he looked at Western.

I'm sorry, he said. This account has a lien on it.

A lien?

Yes.

What sort of lien?

It's been attached by the IRS.

As of when?

He looked at the machine again. As of the third of March. I'm sorry.

He slid the check back across the till. Western looked at the numbers.

I cant withdraw any money.

I'm afraid not. I'm sorry.

He walked out down the lobby toward the street. When he got to the door he stopped. Then he turned and came back.

He signed in on the safe deposit log and went down to the vault with the security officer. The officer took Western's keys but when he got to the number there was a strip of tape across it with some writing and some numbers. He turned back to Western. I'm sorry, he said. The contents of your box have been seized by the Internal Revenue.

How often does this happen?

Not very often.

They dont need a court order?

I dont believe they do, Sir.

They have to have something.

I dont think so. If you'd like to talk to one of the bank officers.

That's all right.

He went back up St Philip Street to the bar and sat and drank a Coke. The bar was almost empty. Rosie watched him.

I like to watch you think, she said.

Western smiled and shook his head. Not from here you dont.

She stacked glasses on the backbar. Dont let the bastards grind you down.

I may have to move to Cosby.

Well. They wont go to Cosby.

No. They wont go to Cosby. You can bet your ass on that.

Not even the Feds will go to Cosby.

Interpol wont go to Cosby Tennessee. The NKVD wont.

Maybe you should keep that in mind.

He smiled and pushed off the barstool and raised one hand and went out. He walked down to Decatur and flagged a cab. He'd had an even grimmer thought sitting at the bar.

Walking up the alley he could already see the big shiny padlock on his locker. Chuck was coming out of the office picking his teeth. Come on in, he said.

He sat at his desk and looked at Western. I tried to call you. I got a disconnect.

Yeah. I moved.

There wasnt anything I could do about it.

I know. What time do you close the gates?

Chuck tapped his fingers on the desk. Did you look at that notice? he said.

No.

You might want to. Impounded by the US Government. You might want to read it.

All right. Let's say I've read it.

That car is the property of the US Government, Bobby. If you attempt to appropriate it your ass will go to jail. That's why it's sitting there. I dont know what their problem is with you, but I've had dealings with them. They dont care about the car. What they want is you. You might want to think about that.

Western looked out the door. Chuck swiveled gently in the chair. Then he swiveled back. How much do you owe them?

I dont owe them anything.

Well. Again. I've been to the mat with those sons of bitches. If it's just nonpayment or even failure to file there's not a whole lot they can do. But you commit a felony and they have got you by the balls. Your ass is goin to jail.

I'm sure you're right.

What's the car worth?

I dont know. Fifteen thousand.

Walk away, Bobby. It's not a car anymore. It's a big chunk of cheese. Why do you think it's still here? Just walk off and leave it.

Walk off and leave it.

You'll thank me. If they had some easier way to nail your ass they'd have done it by now.

Western stood in the doorway looking out up the row of buildings to where his car was locked away. What if I got a lawyer?

You can get a lawyer if you want. You still wont get your car back.

You're just fucked.

Yes.

Western nodded.

These are not people that you want to have a conversation with, Bobby.

Yeah. Well. It's a little late now.

You get in their files you dont get out again.

Ever.

Ever.

And I'm in their files.

What do you think?

All right.

You take care Bobby.

When he got back to the bar he went to his room and sat on the cot and stared at the floor. He thought about his own stupidity. He'd had some eight thousand dollars in the bank and now he had thirty dollars in his pocket. When are you going to take this seriously? When are you going to take steps to save yourself?

In the morning he showered and went out and got breakfast and walked uptown. The IRS was in the post office. He climbed the stairs and stood at the receptionist's desk until she looked up and asked him what it was he wanted. He told her that his bank account had been attached and he'd like to talk to somebody about it.

What's your name.

Robert Western.

She got up and went into another office. After a few minutes she came back. Have a seat, she said. Someone will be with you shortly.

He waited almost an hour. Finally he was sent to an office at the rear. A small room looking out over the parkinglot. The agent was dressed in a tan summer suit. Sit down, he said.

He was looking through Western's file. He didnt look at Western. Our problem with you, Mr Western, he said, is that you seem not to have been employed for a number of years.

I work as a salvage diver. Before that I was a city employee.

And before that.

I was in school. Is that a problem?

No. The problem is failing to disclose your income to the Internal Revenue Service.

I didnt have any income.

You understand that if you give false information to a federal agent even orally you can be charged with a criminal offense. With a felony, in fact.

So?

So that brings us to question number two. During this period you apparently traveled a great deal and whiled away the hours driving expensive racecars and staying at nice hotels.

They werent all that nice.

The agent was looking out the window over the parkinglot. He turned and looked at Western. So, how did you finance all this?

My grandmother left me some money. It was not enough to qualify for inheritance tax.

You have some sort of documents to support this.

No.

No. How were you paid the money?

In cash.

In cash.

Yes.

The agent leaned back and studied Western. Well, he said. You have a problem, dont you?

Wouldnt it be up to you to prove that I received the money?

No. It wouldnt.

It wouldnt.

No.

How can I get my bank account released? And my car.

You cant. You're under investigation for tax fraud. Since you seem to move rather freely in international circles we've also taken the precaution of revoking your passport.

You've revoked my passport?

Yes.

I work overseas. I need my passport in order to work.

You need your passport in order to flee.

Western leaned back in the chair and studied him. Who do you imagine that I am?

We know who you are, Mr Western. What we dont know is what you've been up to. But we'll find out. We always do.

Western looked at the nameplate on his desk.

Is that you? Robert Simpson?

Yes.

You dont go by Bob I suppose.

I go by Robert.

My friends call me Bobby.

The agent gave a slight nod of his head. They sat. After a while the agent said: I'm not your friend, Mr Western.

I know. You're my employee.

The agent seemed almost amused.

You dont know anything about me.

Really? said the agent. He reached and turned the file folder slightly on the desk and then folded his hands in his lap. I think you'd be surprised.

Western studied him. I'm not under investigation for tax fraud.

No?

No.

What do you think you're under investigation for?

I dont know.

Western rose from the chair. I'm not sure that you do either. Thanks for your time.

He walked back through the Quarter. He went down to the end of Toulouse Street and stood looking out at the river. A fresh breeze. Smell of oil. He sat on a bench with his hands folded and thought of nothing at all. Someone was watching him. How do you know? You can feel it. What does it feel like? It feels like someone is watching you. He turned his head. It was a young girl sitting on a bench across the walk. She smiled. Then she looked away. Shaking her hair. Her face to the wind off the river. What do they think they see? Her back straight.

Feet together. She was blonde, pretty. Young. If someone said to you that you had thrown your life away over a woman what would you say? Well thrown.

For all his dedication there were times he thought the fine sweet edge of his grief was thinning. Each memory but a memory of the one before until . . . What? Host and sorrow to waste as one without distinction until the wretched coagulant is shoveled into the ground at last and the rain primes the stones for fresh tragedies.

When he went back to Stella Maris in the spring after her death the people there looked at him curiously. They knew little what to make of him. Perhaps he'd come to be committed himself. On the registration form he had to enter the name of the patient he'd come to see. He looked up at the nurse.

Is Helen still here?

Helen Vanderwall.

I think so, yes. An older woman.

Is that who you've come to visit?

Yes. It is.

He bent and wrote her name in the ledger. A woman came and walked with him down the hall.

She was sitting in a chair by the window dressed in a flowered smock. She smiled at him and he told her who he was and the smile did not change. She reached and took his hand and she wouldnt give it up again. He pulled up the other chair and sat. I knew who you were, she said. Directly I saw you at the door. She's been so much on my mind. I've sat here so many times and I tried to think how to touch her in some way. I didnt know what it was that I wanted her to do. But here you are.

How did she know? To send me.

I dont know. I always thought that there must have been something that told her things but I never asked her. I didnt think it would be something I should ask her. But it didnt make any difference. You always knew that you could depend on her.

They went down to the cafeteria and had coffee and pie. They sat at a table by the window. Outside a few people were walking the grounds.

The first warm days. The trees still bare. Her skin was like paper. Eyes so pale. She sat at his left and ate with her left hand. Her right hand still holding his. Her forearm drawn and thin and blue.

You're not supposed to feed them but of course we do. There was one that was just coal black that I had a particular fondness for. He bit me one day. Just a nip on the finger. I didnt tell anybody. I told Alicia because I wanted her to keep a lookout for him and tell me how he was doing. I wasnt mad at him. But she never could find him. I used to watch for him down here when I came down but I never did see him again. I think maybe a cat got him.

Squirrels.

Squirrels. Yes. You dont mind do you?

No.

That's good. I've got to where I pretty much dont worry about what people mind or what they dont. Alicia was always good about it. She'd hold my hand forever.

She was good about a lot of things.

I was happy for her when she left but I didnt know I would miss her so much. I should have. When she came back I thought that maybe she wouldnt be leaving again anymore and I felt bad about that. I guess I felt guilty about that.

You felt guilty?

You know. Because I was glad she was here. And I knew I shouldnt be glad about that.

Why did you think she wouldnt be leaving?

I just knew.

She told you?

Sort of.

She could have been wrong.

The old woman turned and smiled at him and then looked out the window again. The first time I ever saw her was one morning and she was in the dayroom. She was just sitting there by herself so I went over and sat next to her and I wanted to talk to her but she was so young and I didnt know what to say so I asked her if she was through with the paper. She had the paper in her lap and I was trying to make her acquaintance. So I asked her if she was going to do the crossword puzzle and she said that she'd already done it. Well of course there it was. The way the paper was folded. I could see it. And I sort of smiled but I didnt say anything. Later on of course I found out that she really had done it. Just in her head. You could ask her what something was and she would know what it was. She'd know the number and everything. She'd say that's seven down or whatever and she'd tell you what the word was. She knew what it was because she'd already worked it. It was just everyday to her.

Western looked across the cafeteria. The empty tables. The quiet midafternoon. A few teadrinkers and their charges.

Did she have any other special friends here?

I wasnt a special friend. She didnt really have any special friends. Everybody was the same to her. Even if they were mean she was still their friend.

She put their joined hands on the table and looked at them. She looked at Western.

I guess you knew that Louie died.

No, I didnt. I'm sorry.

He used to get so mad. He'd jump up and throw his wig across the room. He threw it one time and it landed at James's feet. James was reading a magazine and it just sort of slid up under his feet and he jumped up and went to stomping it. He didnt know what it was. Or maybe he was just pretending. Alicia was very fond of him too.

Of James.

Of James. Yes. He was very concerned about the bomb. I guess I shouldnt say anything about that.

It's all right.

He used to ask her about it. He'd sit there and take notes in his notebook. She knew all about it, of course. He'd come up with these ways to attack the bomb and she would show him why it wouldnt work and he'd go off and after a while he'd come back with something else. He had these big magnets that were supposed to keep everybody safe. Do you see that woman there?

Western looked across the room.

The one in the blue dress.

Yes.

Do you think she looks like me?

Western thought about the question. No, he said. I dont.

Well that's a relief.

You dont like her.

Well, I just dont think she's very nice.

I see.

Some people thought that she was my sister.

Are there any sisters in here?

There havent been in the time I've been here. Maybe it's a policy, I dont know. Do you think your father was off his rocker?

Was he off his rocker?

You know. To make bombs to blow everybody up.

Well. I guess that's a reasonable question.

He looked at the woman in the blue dress. She looked a great deal like Helen. I dont know, he said.

He looked toward the bench across the walk. The girl was gone. It was noon. In a minute he would hear the bells from the church. Shortly after her birthday that year she had signed herself out and gone to her grandmother's and stopped all medication and in a week's time they were all back. The Thalidomide Kid and the old lady with the roadkill stole and Bathless Grogan and the dwarves and the Minstrel Show. All of them gathered at the foot of her bed. When she turned on the tablelamp it set them to blinking.

The bells tolled. He rose and walked up St Peter Street to the cafe and put a quarter in the payphone and dialed Kline's number.

It's Bobby Western.

Where are you?

I'm at a payphone in the Quarter.

Let's not talk on the phone. Do you want to meet me?

Have you got some time?

Yes. Where are you? Are you near the Seven Seas?

I can be.

Why dont I swing by and pick you up in about thirty minutes.

All right. Thanks.

He hung up the phone and walked back up Decatur to St Philip and up St Philip to the bar.

Kline pulled up at the curb facing the wrong way and leaning to see in the door. Western walked out and got in the car and they pulled away.

Do you like Italian?

I like Italian.

Do you know Mosca's?

Sure. I have to tell you that I'm broke.

Dont sweat it. I'll put you on the cuff.

All right.

He started to say something else but Kline raised one hand and smiled. They drove in silence out Airline Highway and pulled into the parkinglot behind the restaurant and got out. Kline shut the door and looked at Western over the top of the car. I sweep this thing from time to time. For whatever it's worth. It's a pain in the ass but there you are.

Do you ever find anything?

Oh yes.

And your office?

Same thing. Most of it is just industrial surveillance. The tech gets better every year. It's amazing what you can pick up. It's really pretty much a game. Except of course that sometimes people get hurt.

They walked across the parkinglot. What about in here?

Not a problem. Mosca's is a haven. They have to be.

The maitre'd nodded to Kline. The place was full. They sat at a small table near the door and Kline flipped open the wine menu and began to look through it. Do you know this place?

I think not as well as you.

Everything's good.

What are you having?

Probably the fettuccine with clams.

Is that what you usually have?

No.

Kline studied the winelist. Still, I do tend to be a creature of habit. And in my business that's probably not a good idea.

Western smiled. Are they after you?

Mostly they're after my data. As I am after theirs. How about a St Emilion?

Sounds good.

He folded the wine menu shut. He folded and put away his glasses.

I'll tell you how good it gets. A few years ago the CIA was bugging the typewriters at the Soviet Embassy and running the tapes through a computer. The program decoded the clicks. Length of travel of the key. Frequency, the small changes in the timbre of the strike dictated by the angle of the keyhead. Anything that could be parsed out and computed and assigned a probability. The space bar of course gave you the word break. The program came up with a rough approximation of the written Russian. Their Russian-speaking crypto people would go through it and then they'd send it down to a translator and get a clean copy back in English.

How did you hear about it?

A brother in the trade. What are you having?

Western folded the menu. I'll have the same as you.

Good choice.

I was serious about not having any money.

I know. It's all right.

The waiter came and poured water into their glasses. He nodded to Kline and he looked at Western. Would the gentleman care for a drink?

No thanks.

They ordered. The waiter thanked them and took the menus.

They know who you are, said Western, but they dont say.

That's because they dont know who you are.

Is that the normal procedure?

I think I'd just call it good manners.

Is this place connected?

No. Sort of. Mostly they just look after their customers.

Does Carlos Marcello come here?

Carlos Marcello owns the place. Or he owns the building. But it's the best Italian food between LA and Providence. I think you said you had family in Providence.

Yes.

He was in here a few weeks ago with Raymond Patriarca.

Marcello was.

Yes.

Did you know who Patriarca was?

No. I had to ask. It would be interesting to speculate about that conversation.

I'm sure. Are these people clients of yours?

No. They have their own people.

Of course.

What happened to your money?

What makes you think something happened to it?

Just a wild and reckless guess.

The IRS seized my bank account.

When was this?

A few days ago.

Kline shook his head.

Is there anything I can do about it?

No.

Nothing?

No.

They can just take it.

You could get a lawyer. But it wont help. How much did you have in the account?

About eight thousand dollars.

You surprise me.

You didnt think I'd be that dumb.

No.

I didnt either.

What else do you own?

I did own a car.

They got that.

Yes.

What else?

I dont own anything else. I did own a cat. If you can own a cat.

They took your cat?

They just left the door open. I'm still trying to find him.

You owe back taxes.

They say I do.

Based on what?

Apparently on my lifestyle. My grandmother left me some money. I split it with my sister. It was the money I went racing on.

You dont think it's odd that they would know that? That you went racing in Europe.

I guess I dont know what's odd anymore. They pulled my passport too.

They pulled your passport?

Yes.

Kline spread one hand on the tablecloth and looked at it.

That's bad isnt it? said Western.

Well, it means they think you'd leave the country if you had to.

The waiter brought the wine and uncorked it and placed the cork on the table and poured a bit of wine into Kline's glass. Kline swirled it and smelled and tasted it and nodded and the waiter poured their glasses and set the bottle on the table. Kline tilted his glass toward Western. He couldnt seem to think of anything to toast.

You let him pour.

Yes. He knows me. Did you tell them where the money came from?

Yes.

What else did you tell them?

As in I hope to God you didnt tell them anything else.

Pretty much. You've been paying your income tax otherwise though.

Yes.

Here's the problem. If you just ignore them then it's only a misdemeanor. But if you file and pay your taxes but neglect to mention a sum of money inherited from your grandmother—for instance—then that is not a misdemeanor. That's a false tax report and that's a felony. It will put you in a federal penitentiary for a reckonable part of your definable future.

I think I heard that before somewhere. If I failed to pay any taxes I'd be okay. But if I paid part of my taxes I'm going to jail.

Something like that.

Why havent they arrested me?

They will. They're still working on it. No federal agent assumes that a perp has only committed one crime.

What else do they think I've done?

I'd say that you would be more likely to know that than I would.

Wouldnt seizing my assets put me on the alert?

In order to get the State Department to revoke your passport they would have to make a move against you. They did.

I'm beginning to lose my appetite.

We could talk about something else.

Yeah.

Was it an expensive car?

It was a Maserati. Not a new one. A 73 Bora.

I dont really know anything about cars.

It's probably worth about as much as a new Cadillac. Maybe a bit more.

Sorry.

I'm really on the run, arent I? Whether I know it or not.

I cant answer a question like that, Bobby. But you might want to try and protect yourself.

You dont think it's too late for that.

I dont know. I just know that it's not as late today as it will be tomorrow.

What would you do?

You know what kind of a question that is. If I were you I'd be teaching somewhere or building bombs or whatever it is that you people do.

Sure. What's your own background? Other than the circus.

The circus is my background. I never even finished grammar school.

Really?

Really. Been married once. No children. Amicably divorced. I dont have any tragedies in my life to give it a form and destination outside of my control. I like what I'm doing. But I could be doing something else. I've been blessed. I'm not even sure I'd change the bad things. Here comes the food.

They ate mostly in silence. Like Debussy Kline took his food seriously. When he'd finished he leaned back and drained the last of the wine from his glass and sat turning the stem in his fingers and studying it. Then he set it on the tablecloth. Pretty damned good, he said.

Western smiled. Yes, he said. Thank you.

Kline bunched his napkin and laid it by. I cook at home, he said. But there are some things you just cant get quite right. I think it's the stock. That's where they have the edge.

The stock?

Yes. Unless you have an old rancid stockpot that you can just sort of throw every horrible thing into—rotten turnips, dead cats, whatever—and let it simmer for about a month—you're at a real disadvantage. Do you want to look at the dessert menu?

No thanks.

Right. He picked up the wineglass again and turned it. A small drop had collected in the bottom. He tilted the glass and let the drop run to the rim. Bright as blood. He raised it and let it onto his tongue and set the glass back. Whatcha gone do? he said.

I dont have much choice. Go back to work. Try and get a little money ahead.

When was the last time you worked?

I havent worked since I came back from Florida.

Have you talked to them lately?

Taylor's?

Yes.

I still have a job, if that's what you mean.

That's not exactly what I mean.

You think it's likely they would attach my paycheck.

Oh I think it's more than likely.

And this would go on for?

Ever.

Western drank the last of his wine. I dont have anywhere to go, do I?

Do you want some coffee?

All right.

The waiter appeared. In a few minutes he brought the coffee. Kline drank his black. Do you have any assets at all?

No.

What did your sister do with her share of the money?

She bought a violin.

A violin?

Yes.

How much money did you give her?

Something over half a million dollars.

Damn. How old was she?

Sixteen.

Can you give that kind of money to a sixteen year old?

I dont know. There's probably a State law. Like marriage. I gave it to her in cash.

How much was the violin?

A lot. It wasnt a Stradivarius but something pretty close.

Where is it?

I dont know.

But it could solve a good deal of your immediate cash problems.

I know.

What else.

What else.

What has occurred recently in your life that you dont have an explanation for.

I lost a good friend on a commercial dive in Venezuela.

Yes. You told me. The company is supposed to be looking into it.

Taylor's.

Taylor's. Yes. But you havent heard anything.

No.

What else.

Two years ago they broke into our house in Tennessee and carried off a bunch of my father's papers and my sister's papers and all the family letters going back almost a hundred years. They took the family photo albums. They took all the guns in the house and some other things apparently to make it look like a burglary but of course it wasnt a burglary.

They did.

Yes.

It's always a they, isnt it?

I dont know.

But it didnt occur to you to empty out your checking account.

Western didnt answer.

Kline raised two fingers for the bill. You havent thought about this very much, have you?

I guess not.

I know what you do think.

What do I think?

You think that you're smarter than they are.

So?

So it wont help you. They're not any smarter than they have to be and they're just as smart as they need to be.

Goldilocks operatives.

Yes. They're just right. And you're not.

What else. About them.

Their dedication. It's really remarkable. And everyone's guilty. They dont have to even think about it. They are never in pursuit of the guiltless. It wouldnt even occur to them. They would think the entire notion comical.

The waiter brought the bill. Kline paid in cash. Are you ready?

They walked out through the parkinglot. I cant advise you what to do, Bobby. But I get the sense that you're just waiting. The problem with that is that when what you're waiting for gets here it will be too late to do anything about it. If you want to do the ID package let me know.

Thanks. I appreciate it.

All right.

You think I'm not being straight with you.

I dont know.

I dont know what else to tell you.

It's all right.

There's a letter from her that I've never opened.

Why not?

I just didnt.

It would be too sad.

Western didnt answer.

Let me try again. It's because then you would know everything that you will ever know. As long as you havent read the last letter the story's not over.

Something like that.

It might tell you where the violin is.

It might. She had some money too. I just have a hard time with this.

Well. Her things are going to go somewhere.

Western nodded.

It was a cool day. Overcast. A threat of rain. When they got to the car Kline stood leaning on the roof. He looked at Western.

When smart people do dumb things it's usually due to one of two things. The two things are greed and fear. They want something they're not supposed to have or they've done something they werent supposed to do. In either case they've usually fastened on to a set of beliefs that are supportive of their state of mind but at odds with reality. It has become more important to them to believe than to know. Does that make sense to you?

Yes.

What is it that you want to believe?

I dont know.

Why dont you get back to me.

All right. What else.

That's all.

You still think there's something I'm not telling you.

I'm not worried.

You mean I'll get around to it.

People will tell a stranger on a bus what they wont tell their spouse.

It's pretty bleak, isnt it?

He didnt answer. They got in the car. Kline started the engine. I'm not sure you even get it, he said.

Get what?

That you're under arrest.

I'm under arrest.

Yes. You're not charged with anything. You're just under arrest.

He moved to a shack out on the dunes just south of Bay St Louis. In the evenings he'd walk the beach and look out over the gray water where skeins of pelicans came laboring down the coast in their slow tandem flights above the offshore swells. Improbable birds. At night he could see the lights come up along the causeway. Lights along the horizon, the slow passing of ships or the distant lights of the drilling rigs. There was cold water from a cistern at the house but no electricity. A small castiron railroad stove in which he burned driftwood. He'd no money to buy bottled gas for the cookstove so he cooked on the woodstove as well. Rice and fish. Dried apricots. The days cooled and he sat on the beach in the raw wind off the gulf wrapped in an army blanket and read physics. Old poetry. He tried to write letters to her.

Where he walked the tideline at dusk the last red reaches of the sun flared slowly out along the sky to the west and the tidepools stood like spills of blood. He stopped to look back at his bare footprints. Filling with water one by one. The reefs seemed to move slowly in the last hours and the late colors of the sun drained away and then the sudden darkness fell like a foundry shutting down for the night.

At daybreak he hiked out through the dunes and up the sandy road to the highway and trudged along the edge of the blacktop looking for dead animals. He skinned them out with a single-edge razorblade and carried the raw unstretched hides to the little grocery store two miles down the road. Raccoon and muskrat. Once or twice a mink. Nutria tails for the bounty. He bought tea and canned milk with the money. Cooking oil. Hotsauce and tinned fruit. He carried home dead rabbits from the road that had not been there the day before and cooked and ate them.

He washed his clothes in the dishpan and hung them to dry over the porch railing. Sometimes they'd blow away down the dunes. On sunny days he'd walk the beach naked. Solitary, silent. Lost. Nights he built fires on the beach and sat there wrapped in his blanket. The moon rose over the gulf and the moon's path dished and tilted on the water. Birds flew down the beach in the dark. He didnt know what kind they were. He thought about the passenger but he never went back out to the islands. The fire leaned in the wind and seawater hissed in the burning wood. He watched it burn to coals. The embers glowed and faded and glowed and bits of fire hobbled away down the beach into the darkness. He knew that he should wonder what was to become of him.

He'd found an old rod and reel in the shack and he sharpened some rusty number six hooks and baited them with pieces of muskrat and cast them with their half ounce dropper leads far out into the surf.

Raw cold weather. Rain. The old shake roof leaked badly and he had buckets and pans set about the floor everywhere. One night the lightning woke him. A lurid glare in the windowglass and a crack like a rifleshot. He sat up cautiously. The fire in the stove was all but out and it was cold in the room. He sat quietly in the dark waiting for the windows to light up again. There was someone sitting in the chair in the corner.

He lifted the glass chimney from the lamp and took a wooden match from the drawer and struck it along the edge of the table and lit the wick and replaced the chimney and ratcheted down the flame with the little brass wheel. Then he held the lamp up and looked again.

He was much as she'd described him. The hairless skull corraded with the scars perhaps come by at his unimaginable creation. The funny oarlike shoes he wore. His seal's flippers splayed on the arms of the chair.

Are you alone? said Western.

Jesus, Jonathan. Yeah. I'm alone. Cant stay long. I'm just sort of playing hooky, actually.

You werent sent here to see me.

Nope. Come on me own hook. I was going through my calendar and the date caught my eye.

It's come and gone before.

True enough.

Why are you here?

Just thought I'd see how you were doing.

How did you know where to find me?

The Kid rolled his eyes. Christ, he said. Is that your question?

I dont know.

We go back a bit. One way or another. Me and thee.

By hearsay. How do I know what to trust?

You dont have a choice. All you can believe is what is. Unless you'd prefer to believe what aint. I'd have thought we might be past all that by now.

I'm not past anything.

Yeah, well. Probably cant help you there. Anyway, I was in the neighborhood. You're a little different from what I expected.

How is that?

I dont know. A bit down at the heel. How long you been out here?

A while.

Yeah? Not the most luxurious of digs.

He looked around the room. He covered a yawn with one flipper. Been a long day. Not easy dealing with these rimrunners. Dementia in absentia. Well, best not to open that kettle of fish.

Can of worms.

That either. Anyway, I suppose we all bear some responsibility for Sis. Some more than others of course. Still it's hard to think of her as just some sort of experiment. Watcha think?

What do you think?

Cool under pressure. I like that. So where do we go from here? Oh boy oh joy.

Lightning lit the room again. Christ, said the Kid. Does it storm like this all the time out here? I just thought you might have the odd query or two. You can jump in anytime. I'm working off the books.

What makes you think I would trust you?

I wish you could hear yourself.

Western didnt answer. The Kid sat studying his nonexistent nails. Yeah, well. Now his feelings are hurt. He thinks he's bright. You think you're bright, Kurtz?

No. I did once. I dont anymore.

Good. You just got brighter. We may have a chat after all.

What makes you think I want to chat?

Cut the crap. Like I said, we dont have a lot of time. How did you wind up out here anyway?

The place belongs to a friend.

Some friend. You got no electricity?

No.

Toilet?

No.

The lightning flared again. The Kid was sitting slightly sideways in the chair. Well, he said. Could be worse. Some folks are surprised that you're still around at all.

Yeah. Me too. At times.

I suppose even if you're off the board you might still get to sit around and see how the game turns out.

I think I know how it turns out.

Yeah. Just a pure analytical proposition I suppose. Requires no knowledge, just definitions. You get a sea view here do you?

A distant one.

The Kid rose and stretched. I would think this place would give you the morbids. Why dont we go for a stroll on the beach? Stretch the legs. You might even feel up to unburdening yourself a bit.

A stroll on the beach.

Sure. Get your jacket. We're losing the light.

They walked on the beach, but the Kid looked thoughtful. Bent forward with his flippers clasped behind his back. Out at sea the ragged wire filaments of lightning stood briefly and then again along the darkening rim of the world. You're something of a fucking puzzle, the Kid said. What, you got no questions? I thought it would be fun to have a guy inquiring about his sister's sanity from the sister's own hallucinations.

Do you really know anything about her?

Why not? I'm a split-off piece of her psyche aint I?

I dont know. Are you a piece of mine?

Dont know. It's just a plague of fucking mysteries aint it?

She said that you always got everything wrong.

It was mostly just a way of taking her mind off things. Throw her a bone why not.

I'm not sure I believe you.

Boy. That's rich.

Why is that?

Why is that? Because you're talking about something of which there is no nothing is why is that.

I thought you were here to answer my questions.

Okay. Sure. Why not?

Where are we going?

Going for a walk on the beach. Get some air.

He sniffed deeply.

I thought I saw you once before.

Yeah?

On a bus going up Canal Street.

Well, you get a lot of people look like me.

They trekked out through the sand. The slow combers rolled in from off shore, pale in the dark. The storm was moving in and the lightning flared again. The hot chains of ignition falling broken into the sea. The Kid was bent over, preoccupied. In the glare Western could see his small eggshaped skull and the visible commissures of the plates through the papery skin. The chewed-looking ears.

So where's your questions?

Okay. How old are you?

The Kid stopped and stood. Then he went on, shaking his head.

All right. How about: How did you find me?

You asked me that.

How did you?

I asked around.

You asked around.

Sure. I been on the street for years. Wouldnt have it any other way.

What's the strangest thing you ever beheld? In your travels.

The Kid shook his head. That's not what we're here to discuss. In any case, you wouldnt believe me. There's a lot of wreckage out there. Lot of sparclingers. But they cant cling forever. You got people who think it would be a good idea to discover the true nature of darkness. The hive of darkness and the lair thereof. You can see them out there with their lanterns. What is wrong with this picture?

A thin crack of thunder rolled down the black sky.

Storm's coming in, said the Kid. We need to truck it along.

I was hoping to see some of the horts.

Yeah, well. Probably not. What was it that woke you?

I dont know. The lightning.

You sure you werent dreaming?

I'm not sure now.

Let me rephrase the question: You sure you werent dreaming?

Western slowed. The Kid trudged on. He had been dreaming. At some last reckoning a child's name had been called but the child did not answer and the ship of heaven plowed on all alight into eternity leaving her alone on the darkening shore forever lost. He hurried to catch up.

Can I ask you a question?

That is a question. You got another one?

Where do you go when you leave here?

Elsewhere.

Elsewhere.

Absolutely. Look. I'm here on my own dime. I dont think you get it. Here we are. Not a soul in sight. You need to think about that.

I dont know what you want.

What *I* want? Jesus. I told you. It's my day off. How long do you think I'm going to be here? You wont even act on your own beliefs.

What beliefs?

There you go.

The Kid strode on. Boy, he said. I didnt expect to find such a goddamned boob. You're walking along the beach with this entity you think is some part of your dead sister's geist and you want to chat about the fucking weather.

I never mentioned the weather.

Or whatever. He gestured at the black and lapping sea. Suppose the floor gave way and the whole fucking thing drained off into some unguessed world of caverns deep in the earth? Vasty and black. You could walk down to the bottom and have a look around. Just a huge great chowder flailing around in the muck. Whales and squids. Your plate-eyed krakens with their eighty foot long testicles. Then a big smell and then nothing. Whoops. Where'd everybody go?

I really dont know what to ask you.

Of course you dont. You're a fucking imbecile.

He hauled out his watch and tried to see the time in the darkness. He waited for lightning. What a dumb fucking idea this was.

What would have happened if you and your little friends had simply left her alone?

Hey. A question. Kind of a dumbassed question but what the fuck. I think she'd be just as bloody dead except—I flatter myself—sooner. You wouldnt believe the fucking Chautauquas we had to come up with. And damned little thanks into the bargain. I think half the time she thought I was there just to pick her brain. Well fuck it. Maybe I was. Half the time. Some evil little shit from some heretofore unknown hinterworld to ferry data back to Base One to gear up for the big one.

Is the big one coming?

What do you think?

Probably.

Yeah. Probably. Like probably the sun rose this morning. Jesus. I could be home in bed you know.

What is Base One?

Forget it. I'm not going into organizational structure with you. You wouldnt know what to do with it anyway. You're a nosey guy I can tell already and you'll think you can ferret out data about automorphics and replicates plus all the noncommutational stuff you get into when you start looking at four-dimensional lattices and then we're back to the same dreary bullshit about what's real and what aint and who gets to say. Some of this stuff is its own log by definition and pretty much the whole shebang is running at twenty-four seven culpability. So why dont we just move it along.

Okay.

Jesus. That was easy. Anyway, it's just a way of speaking. Base One could be a paytoilet in the subway station at Twelfth and Broadway. Who gives a shit?

A phone rang.

Good, said the Kid. Saved by the bell. He dealt about him in his flapping clothes and dredged up a telephone and clapped it to his ear. Yeah, he said. Okay. Christ and his dripping disciples is there a full moon or what? Where does all this dingbatry hail from? Yeah sure. I dont give a solitary rhapsodic fart what he said. Tell fuckface I'm on sabbatical and I'll be back when the winds change.

He stopped the better to listen. The wind wrapped his clothes about him. Western waited.

All right. Fine. He thinks the whole thing cant go up in flames? Good. He's welcome to his incinerated opinions. Yeah. We downloaded all that. It's been checked and rechecked. No. We're in a thunderstorm here. Out on the beach. I'd send you the coordinates but I cant see my watch. It's dark as the inside of a cow. Yeah. The guy's sister. She offed herself a few years back. No. He doesnt have a fucking clue. Okay. Roger and out. Yeah yeah sure sure. They're a pack of clamorous and gaping assholes and you can tell em I said so.

He rang off and shoved the phone into his clothes and set off down the beach again shaking his head. Never a respite from this bullshit. Well fuck it. One more passenger. Off to where? You yourself were seen boarding the last flight out with your canvas carrion bag and a sandwich. Or was that still to come? Probably getting ahead of myself. Still it's odd how little folks benefit from learning what's ahead. Dont they look at the ticket? Curious. Those shadows are actually shorebirds going downcoast in this crap. Where the fuck do they think they're going?

What if I ask you a peculiar question?

Jesus, said the Kid. This'll be rich. He's strolling on the beach at midnight in a thunderstorm with his dead sister's psyche and he wants to know if he can ask a peculiar question. You're nothing if not fucking droll, are you? Sure. Fire away. I can hardly wait.

What do you know about me?

Well shit. I didnt think it would be *that* peculiar. What do you care? And why is this about you?

How about just a fact or two?

Sure. Fact one: He's five feet eleven. Fact two: He weighs a hundred and fifty-two pounds.

You sure about that? I used to weigh more.

You used to eat more.

They trudged on. The wind was picking up. The Kid turned his shoulder to the blowing spume. Sand went seething down the beach in the dark.

I guess I'm not going to get to see any of your dog and pony shows.

No? What is this then?

I cant say it's been all that entertaining. Could we stop for a minute?

Sure.

The Kid turned and faced him.

What you want me to believe, said Western, is that you came here to help her in some way.

Help her in what way? She's dead.

When she was alive.

Jesus. How do I know? You see a figure drifting off the screen and you pick up the phone. How do you know that the call of the coletit from the bracken is not really the lamentations of the damned? The world's a deceptive place. A lot of things that you see are not really there anymore. Just the after-image in the eye. So to speak.

What did she know?

She knew that in the end you really cant know. You cant get hold of the world. You can only draw a picture. Whether it's a bull on the wall of a cave or a partial differential equation it's all the same thing. Jesus. It's come a fucking gale. Can we walk?

Okay. If you took a test what sort of test would it be?

You mean like the Minnesota Multiphasic to see if you are ker-aazy? He waggled his flippers and rolled his head about.

Is that the kind it would be?

There aint no test so there aint no kind it would be.

Did she have a specific name? As a project?

No. We never found a place to put her. We just tried to keep her alive. She wouldnt profile. The diodes would light up No Entry and you could try again but that was really pretty much it. There's just a blank in the schema. Like an anomaly in a spectrograph. You could sort out a new template, but there's nothing you can do with it. Things dont work out? Yeah, well. First trials prone to failure and all that. You make some corrections. Run the program again. A few home truths in the mix. Life is life. You share half your genes with a cantaloupe.

What about you?

What about me what?

Do you share half your genes with a cantaloupe?

No. I am a fucking cantaloupe. Can we move it along a bit?

Why didnt she fit any of the templates?

Because none of the templates fit.

Yes, but why?

The Kid stopped again. Look, he said. We're not going into the techs. I know you see it like some sort of spatiochemicalbiological misfit or something but most of our guys dont see it that way at all. They see it as a matter of belief.

Belief?

Yeah. As in nonbeliever. No matter the magnitude of your doubts about the nature of the world you cant come up with another world without coming up with another you. It may even be that everybody starts out fairly unique only most people get over it. Come on. I felt a raindrop.

But *why* do they get over it?

Christ on a bicycle, Bobbykins. How the fuck do I know? We dont make the people, we just make the templates. It's a file, that's all.

Are you saying that the only difference between her and everybody else is that you dont have a template for her?

No, *you* are.

Western looked out over the dark sea. He could taste the salt on his lips.

It's some sort of electronic template.

No. It's hydraulic. Jesus.

That maps the mental terrain.

Plus the gallbladder dont forget.

The gallbladder?

It's a joke. Weeping Mother Mary.

Sorry.

Yeah, right.

You think I'm a dork.

You are a dork. What I think has got nothing to do with it. Can we move it along here? We're going to get wet. Christ. Are nightbreezes off the sound supposed to howl like this?

They trudged on, the Kid's robes flapping. You dont always get what you want. But then you dont always want what you get so it's probably pretty much of a wash. Anyway, you dont really want to talk. You just want somebody to tell you that it's not your fault.

It is my fault.

Let me try putting it another way. You just want somebody to tell you that it's not your fault.

Maybe I dont know what it is that you want.

Yeah. Well, that's my fault. I just never imagined that you'd be this thick.

They plodded on through the sand. They seemed to have some destination in mind. Western stopped again and then hurried to catch up.

Are you an emissary?

Of what?

I dont know.

Sure you do. Or you wouldnt be asking the question. Anyway, maybe I'm not the little dude we've all come to know and love. Harbinger of hope and suppository of dreams. Maybe I'm the evil twin. Who do you even get to talk to about her?

My grandmother. My uncle Royal.

Yeah? That's a big help. Uncle Royal in the boobyhatch kitted out in nappies and bib. And I'm an agent? Who aint? You dont have to agree with everything but when you get assigned you go. Jesus, it's freezing. Hell of a front for this time of year.

Do you think there's some sort of shelter up ahead?

Not for you. Anyway, your problem is that you dont really believe that she's dead.

I dont believe that she's dead?

I dont think so.

You think I believe in an afterlife?

How would I know?

The first spits of rain fell.

Do you mind terribly if we dont loiter? How come you never got another cat?

I just didnt want to lose anything else. I'm all lost out.

Why is the lamp of wrong always sheltered from the wind? Anyway, you still got yourself to go.

I know.

What's your thoughts on that? The sooner the better?

Sometimes.

A sharp crack of lightning lit up the empty beach before them. The rain began to pelt down.

Who knows? said the Kid. Maybe you and Sis can rendezvous in the sweet by-and-by. Jesus. Look at this shit. Pain and corruption. The times she went behind my back. Sometimes she'd just douse the lights and go to sleep. Midsentence. She'd of been a piece of work no matter what. Mary and Joseph, did you see that? Can we step it along? Dont you just love the taste of ozone? Like a fucking zinc milkshake. You dont say a lot do you? I've heard of rafts of nicely poached fish washing ashore after one of these electrical storms. You think that could be true?

Western slowed. He palmed the water from his face. The Kid was becoming obscured in the slashing gusts. Slapping along in his outlandish attire.

He was wet and chilled. Finally he stopped. What do you know of grief? he called. You know nothing. There is no other loss. Do you understand? The world is ashes. Ashes. For her to be in pain? The least insult? The least humiliation? Do you understand? For her to die alone? Her? There is no other loss. Do you understand? No other loss. None.

He'd fallen to his knees in the wet sand. The salt rain blew in off the sea. He seized his skull and called out after that small and shambling figure receding down the beach in the gusts. Lightning flared over the dark water and over the beach and the liveoaks and the sea oats and the wall of pines dim in the rain. But the djinn was gone.

When he woke in the small hours the storm had passed. He lay there a long time. Watching the gray light come up in the room. He got up and went to the window and looked out. Gray day. His wet clothes were piled in the floor and he picked them up and draped them over the kitchen chairs. Later he went down to the beach but the rain had washed everything away. He sat on a driftwood log with his face in his hands.

You dont know what you're asking.

Fateful words.

She touched his cheek. I dont have to.

You dont know how it will end.

I dont care how it will end. I only care about now.

In the spring of the year birds began to arrive on the beach from across the gulf. Weary passerines. Vireos. Kingbirds and grosbeaks. Too exhausted to move. You could pick them up out of the sand and hold them trembling in your palm. Their small hearts beating and their eyes shuttering. He walked the beach with his flashlight the whole of the night to fend away predators and toward the dawn he slept with them in the sand. That none disturb these passengers.

When he got back to the city he called Kline.

You're back.

Sort of.

You want to meet me for a drink?

Sure.

Tujague's?

What time?

Six.

I'll see you then.

They sat at one of the small wooden tables in the bar and ordered gin and tonics. Kline clouded the lenses of his glasses with a quick breath each and wiped them with his handkerchief. He put them on and looked at Western.

What do you see? said Western.

Did you know that there's a system that can scan your eye electronically with the same accuracy as a fingerprint and you dont even know it's being done?

Is that supposed to comfort me?

Kline looked out at the street. Identity is everything.

All right.

You might think that fingerprints and numbers give you a distinct identity. But soon there will be no identity so distinct as simply to have none. The truth is that everyone is under arrest. Or soon will be. They dont have to restrict your movements. They just have to know where you are.

It sounds like paranoia to me.

It is paranoia.

The waiter brought the drinks. Kline raised his glass. Cheers, he said.

Happy days. What else have you got in the way of good news?

You shouldnt despond. Information and survival will ultimately be the same thing. Sooner than you think.

What else?

Difficult to say. Electronic money. Sooner rather than later.

Okay.

There wont be any actual money. Just transactions. And every transaction will be a matter of record. Forever.

You dont think people will object to this?

They'll get used to it. The government will explain that it will help to defeat crime. Drugs. The sort of large scale international arbitrage that threatens the stability of currencies. You can make up your own list.

But anything that you buy or sell will be a matter of record.

Yes.

A stick of gum.

Yes. What the government hasnt figured on yet is that this scheme will be followed by the advent of private currencies. And shutting these down will mean the rescinding of certain parts of the Constitution.

Well. Again, I'm sure you know what this conversation sounds like.

Of course. Let's get back to you.

All right.

Do you think they've seized your father's papers at Princeton?

Probably.

You're past all that.

I dont know what they're up to and I never will. And now I dont care. I just want them to leave me alone.

They wont. You didnt get along. You and your father.

I didnt have a problem with my father. And I didnt have a problem with the bomb. The bomb was always coming. Now it's here. It's lying doggo for the present. But it wont stay that way. My father died alone in Mexico. I have to live with that. I have to live with a lot of things. I went to see him a few months before he died. He wasnt doing well. There was nothing that I could do for him. But that didnt excuse doing nothing.

How good a physicist was he?

He was smart. But smart is not enough. You have to have the balls to dismantle the existing structure. He made some wrong choices. A lot of his friends had Nobel Prizes but he wasnt going to get one.

Is that such a big deal?

In physics it is.

How good a mathematician was your sister?

We come back to that from time to time. There's no answer to it. Mathematics is not physics. The physical sciences can be weighed against each other. And against what we suppose to be the world. Mathematics cant be weighed against anything.

How smart was she?

Who knows? She saw everything differently. She would figure something out and then half the time she couldnt explain to you how she'd done it. It was hard for her to understand what it was that you didnt understand. That smart.

He looked at Kline. I think that up to the age of eight or so she was pretty much like any other precocious kid. Questioning everything. Always waving her hand in class. Then something happened to her. She just got quiet. Strangely polite. She seemed to understand that she had to be careful how she treated people.

He sat staring at his glass. He ran his finger down the side of it. We're married to Greek geometry. But she wasnt. She didnt draw pictures. She hardly even did calculations.

He looked up at Kline. I cant answer your questions. She had a good heart. I think it occurred to her fairly early that she was going to have to be good to people.

Why did she kill herself?

Western looked away. At the next table a woman was watching him.

She was leaning slightly forward. Ignoring the two men sitting at the table with her. He looked at Kline.

And then you'll shut up.

I think so.

Because she wanted to. She didnt like it here. She told me from the time she was about fourteen that she was probably going to kill herself. We had long conversations about it. They must have sounded pretty strange. She always won. She was smarter than me. A lot smarter.

I'm sorry, said Kline.

Western didnt answer. The woman sat watching him. The lights were coming up along the street.

We were in love with each other. Innocently at first. For me anyway. I was in over my head. I always was. The answer to your question is no.

That wasnt my question.

Sure it was.

Kline spooned away the water from the table with the back of his hand where his glass had wept. He put the glass back down. Did your father know that she was bright?

Of course.

Kline nodded. He turned and looked at the woman. The two men had stopped talking. Kline smiled. Would you care to join us? he said.

She put her hand to her mouth. Oh, she said. I'm sorry.

Western looked at Kline. Kline drained his glass. Are you ready? he said.

I think so.

Kline put a five on the table. He's going to say something, isnt he?

Yes.

Excuse me, the man said.

Kline smiled and rose. Western thought that the man would get up but he didnt. He and the other man watched warily as they passed.

Where are you parked?

I'm just down the street here. You need a ride?

No. I'm okay. What would you have done if the guy got up?

He wasnt getting up.

What if he did?

It's a hypothetical question. It's meaningless.

Interesting. What do you get out of this?

Out of what?

Jacking with me and my problems.

I should send you a bill.

Probably.

Maybe it's not exactly you that's interesting to me.

Yeah?

Or maybe I think that when your ship comes in you might hire me.

Dont hold your breath.

About you hiring me?

No. About the ship.

They walked past Jackson Square. The carriages in the street and the mules standing foot to foot. A windy day in the Quarter. A paper cup followed them down the street.

You dont think you're coming unglued.

No. Maybe. Sometimes.

What are you going to do?

I dont know.

I wouldnt hang out at the bar.

I'm not. Dont worry.

They had reached Kline's car. Western looked down Decatur Street. Maybe I could live a life of crime.

You said that.

However you imagine that your life is going to turn out you're not likely to get it right. Are you?

I dont know. Probably not.

It's not just that I dont know what to do. I dont even know what not to.

You sure you dont want a lift?

Western looked at him across the top of the car. I have to do something. I think I get that.

Kline didnt answer.

I thought more than once that if she wasnt schizophrenic then the rest of us were. Or we must be something.

Some things get better. I doubt this is one of them.

I know.

People want to be reimbursed for their pain. They seldom are.

On that cheery note.

On that cheery note.

He walked down the street and crossed the railroad tracks. The redness of the evening in the glass of the buildings. Very high a small and trembling flight of geese. Fording the last of the day in the thin air. Following the shape of the river below. He stood above the bank of riprap. Rock and broken paving. The slow coil of the passing water. In the coming night he thought that men would band together in the hills. Feeding their small fires with the deeds and the covenants and the poetry of their fathers. Documents they'd no gift to read in a cold to loot men of their souls.

VIII

The city was cold and gray. Gray stooks of snow along the curb. The date for registration at the university came and went. She'd not been out in days. Then weeks. Her brother sent her a television set and she sat looking at it still in the box. It sat there all day. Finally she set about unpacking it. She put on her robe and opened the door and got the television up in her arms and went down the hallway with it and knocked at the last door with the back of her hand. Mrs Grimley, she called. She waited. Finally the old woman cracked the door and peered out.

Let me in. This thing's heavy.

What is it?

It's a color television. Let me in.

The old woman swung the door open. A color television? she said.

Yes. She pushed her way past. Where do you want it?

Mercy, child. Where did it come from?

I think you won it. Where do you want me to put it? It's getting heavy.

In the bedroom. My Lord. A color television? Come on back here. I cant believe it. What did they do? Deliver it to the wrong door?

Something like that. Where?

Right here, Darling. Right here. She patted the top of the dresser and scooped everything to one side. You are just a angel.

She hefted the thing up onto the dresser and stood back. Mrs Grimley had already undone the cord and was on the floor with it. Her rolled stockingtops under the hem of her housedress, the knobbly blue veins at the back of her knees. Color television, she called. You just do not know what the day will bring. She backed out wheezing and held up one hand to be assisted. All right, she said. Turn that thing on. Here. Let me do it. This calls for a drink.

I have to go.

Dont go, Darling. We'll watch Johnny Carson. I've got a bottle of wine.

I have to. You enjoy.

The old woman followed her to the door, pulling at the sleeve of her robe. Dont go, she said. Just stay a little bit.

She stood at the bathroom sink and studied herself in the mirror. Gaunt and haunted. Her clavicle bones all but through the skin. She'd set out her bottles of pills on the counter. Valium. Amitriptyline. She unscrewed the caps and poured all the pills into an empty waterglass and dropped the bottles and the caps into the wastebasket. Then she filled the other glass with water and set the two glasses side by side and stood looking at them. She stood there for some time. She got her robe off the floor and went into the bedroom and sat at the little desk and took a folded paper out of a white envelope and opened it and sat reading it. She folded the paper and pushed it and the envelope across the desk and sat looking out the small window at the bleak winter trees. So perilously footed in the city. In the end she pushed back the chair and rose and went into the bathroom and flushed the pills down the toilet and drank the glass of water and went to bed.

Three days later the Kid was back.

You missed my birthday, she said.

Yeah. Too bad. Have you looked in the mirror lately?

No.

You look like shit.

Nice.

You and Bobbykins have split the blanket I take it.

We havent split anything.

He paced. Odd the way the world is. How you can have just about anything except what you want.

It's none of your business.

Of course one can only conjecture. Not sure what might have transpired at Christmas down there in the kingdom of coital cattle or whatever the fuck they call it.

It's none of your business.

You said that.

And where are the dear chimericals? They've yet to materialize. To coin a phrase. Should I look in the closet?

Do you know what you weigh?

No. Do you?

Yeah. Benchmark territory. You hit ninety-nine pounds yesterday.

He paused to study her. Then he began to pace again. He threw one flipper up. Dont say anything. I dont want to hear it.

I wasnt going to say anything.

You just did. When did you eat last?

I dont know. I didnt write it down.

You've what? Abandoned your shrinks to their contemplative world of self-abuse?

She shrugged.

Yeah. Right.

You never liked any of them anyway.

I dont know. They seemed a harmless lot. Except possibly for the groping. I was never sure what it was that everybody was supposed to get out of it. Not sure what it was they saw standing there. Young girl with an edge to her. Nightbites and a nervous cough. Cute though. Possibly bangable. This last one had scary teeth I think you said if I remember right.

You do. He did.

Yeah, well. We worry about pretty much everything you undertake on your own hook. It's our job. It all comes down to who you decide to listen to. We dont go around telling you that they *dont exist. A pretty liberalhearted lot by all accounts. I dont see a lot of structure there. They probably dont understand that a good bit of bad news has its origins in people not eating their vegetables. Which while we're on the subject what sort of country girl wont eat grits? When did that start?*

I never liked grits.

You broke your grandmother's heart.

I broke my grandmother's heart because I wouldnt eat grits.

Yes.

That's ridiculous.

That and insisting on calling dinner lunch and supper dinner. You and your brother. What are you smiling about?

Nothing. It's just that sometimes I think I would have found my life pretty funny if I hadnt had to live it.

Funny.

Yeah.

The Kid paused, his chin in one flipper. She knelt in her nightshift at the feet of the Logos itself, he said. And begged for light or darkness but not this endless nothing.

I dont care that you read my diary you know. My letters. And I never wrote about myself in the third person.

Yeah well. We're friends. We can correct each other's grammar.

I'm going to bed.

Are you going to brush your teeth and say your prayers?

Not tonight.

I'm putting together some new acts. I would do the auditions here but I know how you love surprises. Should have something on the boards in a couple of weeks.

I cant wait.

He went to pacing again. Emaciation's really not your best look, you know. Besides which we seem to be looking at a level of dishevelment I'm not sure we've seen before.

I'm going to bed now.

You said that. I'm worried you might be fixin to cut and run.

Where to?

Dunno. What can we do for you? You never ask.

You never listen.

You dont know what might be on the table. Rare gifts. Gilded feathers from an ancient bird. A calculus from the inward parts of a beast long extinct or a small figure crafted from an unknown metal.

I wont hold my breath.

Yeah.

Unreal artifacts in warrant of an unreal world.

Yeah well. Still it's a lovely thought. Dont you think?

No I dont. Good night.

She took the train to O'Hare and boarded a plane at eight twenty at night and flew to Dallas and checked into a hotel at the airport. In the morning she got a flight to Tucson where two hours later she had a job at a bar called Someplace Else. She rented a room at the rear of a house on Mabel Street and then drove the rental car north out of the city and went hiking in the mountains. The day was cool and sunny. Lying in the shale she watched two ravens in a china sky. Touching softly in midflight a thousand feet above the side of the mountain. Tipping and wheeling on the updraft. The slow shadows of clouds crossed the desert floor below. She chucked the heels of her boots into the loose scree and lay back in the winter sun. When she looked up the ravens were gone. She spread her arms. Wind in the sparse grass among the rocks. Silence.

The Kid arrived in about a week. He was waiting for her when she came in from work at two in the morning. He didnt even look up. Sitting in the worn leather chair in the corner of the room reading her notebook. I guess, he said, that the plan all along was to get down here as soon as possible so that you could discuss topology with Jimmy Anderson.

How did you know his name?

It's on the check. I cant say much for the pay scale.

We get tips. It's a bar.

Someplace Else.

Yes.

That's perfect. It's not in the Absolute Elsewhere I take it.

Nope. Well. Sort of.

Is this where the mathematicians hang out?

Yes. Church is coming next week.

What happened to school?

I decided not to go.

You're taking a sabbatical.

If you like.

The Kid was thumbing through the spiralbound ledgerbook. Not much here in the way of numbers. What's with the poetry?

I've always written poetry.

Yeah. I dont think you're here for the poetry, Duchess.

I dont think I've heard you take a position on career choices before. Does this mean that we're at naughts and crosses?

Maybe. What's cross and naughty is you splitting like you did. You shouldnt leave your friends twisting in the wind.

You're not my friend.

I love it when you hurt me. I thought we were further along than that.

Further along what? And why dont you let me see your *notebook?*

Part of it of course is just coming down off the drugs. Abandoning her doctors. The sense of loss and despair typical in the recently shrinkrapt. When did you eat last?

I ate.

Yeah? When did you sleep?

I dont know. Probably Wednesday.

How long ago is that?

This is Friday.

Yeah? So how many days?

She crossed the room and sat on the bed and started taking off her shoes. You dont know how far it is from Wednesday to Friday, do you?

You dont have to know everything.

What else dont you know?

What else dont you know, mimed the Kid. He sounded uncannily like her. I suppose you think you've found something out. But I might be leading you down the garden path. Or maybe if you dont get to start out in life counting on your fingers you're already at something of a disadvantage. Ever think of that?

No. I hadnt. Sorry.

Forget it. We need to move along. Some of the stuff we got from you needs going over. I got a few notes here.

Stuff you got from me.

Yeah.

He was dredging up papers from his clothes. He wet his flipper with his tongue and began to sort through them. We're starting to see these shifts. We checked everything and it's not the stylus so it must be the graph. Yeah? How's that work? All right. Maybe it's in the transmission. You cook off the overprint. Nope. Reversed polarities. That's got a familiar smell to it but we dont think it's the problem. And what you thought was a graph may be sequestering a dimension such that closer study reveals a lattice that no matter how you turn it it's always right side up which brings into play certain problems with boundary conditions and you've got an ugly feeling the whole system could be out of true or it's drifting and where to define your mean deviants who for the nonce shall remain nameless. It's nicely aisled and crossaisled and the long and the short of it is we'll know it when it gets here but is that good enough?

When what gets here?

The day of the locus.

The day of the locus.

Yeah.

This is what you came out here for?

Is that okay?

If they could get their hands on you they'd put you in the booby-hatch. Are you aware of that?

Yeah? Well it takes one to know one.

So did your little friends come with you?

You dont have to worry about them. Where was I?

Even if I knew I wouldnt say.

Not important. It's a new year. Time for everybody to buckle down. Did you make any resolutions?

No.

What did you do New Year's Eve?

We went to dinner.

We?

My brother and I.

Any dancing?

No dancing.

Maybe he's weaned himself off of that. The scented hair and the breath in his ear. Hard on a lad. To coin a phrase.

You're disgusting.

Still I suppose this was before you dipped down into the double digits avoirdupoiswise. Bones coming through the skin. Not the hallmark of the erotic. Even if hunger is rumored to hone the senses. Maybe you should get back to your calculations.

I work all the time. I just dont write that much of it down.

So what do you do? Just loll around and mull over the problems?

Yeah. Loll and mull. That's me.

Dreaming of equations to come. So why dont you write it down?

You really want to talk about this?

Sure.

All right. It's not just that I dont have to write things down. There's more to it than that. What you write down becomes fixed. It takes on the constraints of any tangible entity. It collapses into a reality estranged from the realm of its creation. It's a marker. A roadsign. You have stopped to get your bearings, but at a price. You'll never know where it might have gone if you'd left it alone to go there. In any conjecture you're always looking for weaknesses. But sometimes you have the sense that you should hold off. Be patient. Have a little faith. You really want to see what the conjecture itself is going to drag up out of the murk. I dont know how one does mathematics. I dont know that there is a way. The idea is always struggling against its own realization. Ideas come with an innate skepticism, they dont just go barreling ahead. And these doubts have their origin in the same world as the idea itself. And that's not something you really have access to. So the reservations that you yourself in your world of struggle bring to the table may actually be alien to the path of these emerging structures. Their own intrinsic doubts are steering-mechanisms while yours are more like brakes. Of course the idea is going to come to an end anyway. Once a mathematical conjecture is formalized into a theory it may have a certain luster to it but with rare exceptions you can no longer entertain the illusion that it holds some deep insight into the core of reality. It has in fact begun to look like a tool.

Jesus.

Yeah, well.

You talk about your arithmetic exercises as if they had minds of their own.

I know.

Is that what you think?

No. It's just hard not to.

Why arent you going back to school?

I told you. I dont have time to. I've got too much to do. I've applied for a fellowship in France. I'm waiting to hear.

Crikey. For real?

I dont know what's going to happen. I'm not sure that I want to. Know. If I could plan my life I wouldnt want to live it. I probably dont want to live it anyway. I know that the characters in the story can be either real or imaginary and that after they are all dead it wont make any difference. If imaginary beings die an imaginary death they will be dead nonetheless. You think that you can create a history of what has been. Present artifacts. A clutch of letters. A sachet in a dressingtable drawer. But that's not what's at the heart of the tale. The problem is that what drives the tale will not survive the tale. As the room dims and the sound of voices fades you understand that the world and all in it will soon cease to be. You believe that it will begin again. You point to other lives. But their world was never yours.

When he came past the Napoleon Long John and Brat were on the sidewalk at one of the tables drinking gibsons from large stemmed glasses. God's blood, said the long one. An apparition.

Juan Largo. Como estás?

Mejor que nunca. Sit down. What would you like? The highballs are on me. As the giraffe said to the bartender.

Western pulled back one of the little bentwood chairs. Brat. How are you doing?

I'm all right.

Are you in law school?

I've been admitted.

Where?

Emory.

Good school.

I think so.

Expensive school.

Yes.

You've come into some bucks.

I have. We thought you'd been carried off to Davy Jones.

Not yet.

He ordered a beer and sat with his feet crossed in the fourth chair. You're looking well, John. Color. Weight. Have you been taking the waters somewhere?

Not exactly. The truth is I've suffered something of a misadventure. You see me in the throes of recovery.

What happened?

A stint at Eastern State Hospital.

The criminally insane ward?

Mossy Creek smiled. He was unwrapping a Churchillian and addressing himself to the procedure of preparing it for smoking. He'd been at a party in Knoxville and as was his wont was using his host's bedroom phone to place a few fairly expensive longdistance calls. He was on the line with a girlfriend in San Francisco when the conversation degenerated into acrimony such that he finally slammed down the receiver and strode back out through the livingroom. On the coffeetable was a glass punchbowl filled with prescription pills. A multicolored pharmacopoeia of drugs of every provenance and purpose representing the then state of the art in the chemical reconfiguration of the human soul. He reached in and seized a great handful and crammed them in his mouth and washed them down with someone's gin and tonic and stalked out the door.

The waiter brought Western's beer. Western tilted the bottle toward his friends.

I woke up, said John, on a dentist's lawn. Forest Avenue. Some sort of security person was jostling my foot. I asked him what he wanted and he told me I couldnt lie there. And why is that? I wondered aloud.

This is a dentist's office. People are going to be coming here in a couple of hours to get their teeth fixed. They cant have you lying here. I asked him if it would be all right if I just moved over a bit so that I wouldnt be blocking the walkway but he said no. He said that it looked unprofessional. Which I suppose it did.

He clipped the tip from the cigar. Explaining how he'd struggled on hands and knees up the hill as far as Fort Sanders Hospital and crawled into the lobby to lie on the cool tiles.

Help me, he called.

Margaret did you hear somebody?

Hear somebody?

Help me.

There it is again.

They looked over the counter.

What's wrong with you?

Help me.

Two black men came with a gurney and took him to the emergency room. The resident came out and looked at him. What's wrong with you? he said.

Help me.

What do you want us to do for you?

Sheddan thought about that. Well. You could get me one of those half-grain tablets of morphine. You know, the blue ones?

The resident stood studying him. Finally he took some quarters from his pocket and handed them to one of the orderlies. They're going to wheel you down the hall to that payphone. I want you to call someone to come and get you. If you cant get someone to come and get you I'm going to call someone. To come and get you.

Yessir.

The orderlies wheeled him down the hall and they dialed Richard Hardin's number and handed him the phone. It rang for a long time. Finally Pat answered. Where are you? she said.

I'm in the emergency room at Fort Sanders. They want to put me in jail.

All right. I'll be there in twenty minutes.

He handed up the phone. She'll be here in twenty minutes.

She came swinging through the doors wearing a black silk trench-coat and dark glasses with a large black leather handbag slung over her shoulder.

What's wrong with you? Can you walk?

I dont know. Just get me out of here. This is not a favorable environment.

They walked him out to the parkinglot and the orderlies helped him into the car and shut the door. She sat looking at him. Do you want to come home with us?

I want to go to Eastern State.

John, you dont want to go to Eastern State. What time does your mother get up?

I want to go to Eastern State.

Why do you want to go to Eastern State?

He told her why he wanted to go to Eastern State. She sat quietly and listened. When he was done she turned and started the engine.

Where are we going? he said.

To Eastern State.

When they pulled up in front of the gatehouse it was graying light. The guard nodded and touched the bill of his cap. Morning, Mam. Can I help you?

He wants to commit himself.

The guard bent to look across to where John sat staring out over the hood of the car. He studied him for a minute, then he nodded. You all go right ahead, Mam.

She checked him in and filled out the forms and kissed him on the cheek and they led him away down the hall. He was fitted out in State pajamas and put to bed in an iron cot in one of the cubicles. When he woke again one of the orderlies was shaking him by the shoulder.

What is it?

John, your father is on the phone.

By now the long one had lit the cigar and he sat holding it between his thumb and forefinger studying it. He looked at Western. As you know, my father died when I was in high school. But I thought, well, he *could* be on the phone. They helped me down the hallway and handed me the phone. Which I took somewhat tentatively—as you might imagine—and I said: Hello? And it's that fucking Bill Seals calling me from California. Hi, he says. How are you?

Hi? How am I? I got a good grip on the phone and I said: Listen to me you fat, evil, depraved son of a bitch. What are you doing calling me here? What the fuck is wrong with you? And the orderly grabs the phone out of my hand and he says: Here, you cant talk to your father like that. I mean really, Squire. If I married an heiress and moved to the South of France I'd never hear from that bastard. But put me in the looney bin and he's on the phone before the ink can dry on the admission forms.

How long were you in there?

Six weeks. Their standard detox program. On Sundays the visitors would arrive and I'd be out on the grounds waiting for them as they came up the walkway with their lunch hampers. I'd come galumphing across the greensward and fling myself against the palings of the fence howling and slobbering like a rabid gibbon. Holding out a twisted claw. God wouldnt they shriek and flee. One woman ran into the street and almost got hit by a bus. It was pretty jolly. But it was something of a revelation. The families of the inmates. You've no idea what lurks in the hinterlands, Squire. Entire families of inbreds come to see the prize exhibit of their lineage. Some exotic species of microcephalic. A taperheaded dwarf. Something out of a Lewis Hine photograph. I dont think they should necessarily be gassed but is neutering so out of the question?

You're asking me.

Never mind. God. I'd probably be dragged before the board myself.

Western sipped his beer. John, he said. You are a bloody wonder.

Yes well. What puzzles me is the apparent need to fabricate evil gossip about one whose actual history is already so appalling.

What else?

Actually I do have a couple of pieces of news. One good, one bad, of course.

What's the good one?

Tulsa's back.

Okay. What's the bad news?

The bad news is that that's the good news. I dont really know what to do with her. I feel that I might be emplaned upon a new vector in my life, Squire. A turning in the road. I smell good fortune afoot. A little luck and I could see myself ensconced in a modest country retreat. A velvet smokingjacket for the evenings and a pair of mastiffs at the hearth. A good library of course. Wellstocked winecellar. Perhaps even a vintage black enameled Minerva in the porte cochere. I dont see her there. She's fun and sexy but she is distinctly not low maintenance and I am growing weary, Squire, and unlikely to become less so as we lurch forward. I just dont know. I told Brat here that I wanted to do the right thing and he almost choked laughing. But I'm serious.

Where is she?

She's still asleep.

Does she know about your feelings? Or the lack thereof?

I dont know. She's a pretty astute girl. Who knows? You're always on thin ice. Of course anytime a woman shows up after a long absence there is one thing you know for certain and that is that things have not gone well. This makes them subdued. For a while. I puzzle my own self, Squire, to fall back upon a Mossy Creek locution. I dont want to become a misogynist. You're smiling. What?

Nothing. Continue.

They're just a piece of work. I should have taken a page from your book. Die young for love and be done with it.

I'm not dead.

We wont quibble. She's a strange girl. She likes it here because they have good restaurants. But they also have a couple of good costume shops.

Costume shops.

Yes. She brings back these costumes and you have to wear them. Most recently we were dressed as rabbits. The odd thing is that she would really get into it. We'd have sex in these rabbit suits and she would squeal and stamp her feet.

Jesus, John.

I know. The things a man will do for love. Still, almost anything is welcome. It takes forever to get her off. It's like laboring over a drowning victim. For all my ragging there are times when I see with a cold clarity the wisdom of the path you've chosen. Hovering as you do out there at the edge of the intactile dark. A thing wholly beyond my talents. Broken upon the wheel of devotion. Sniffing tentatively at the cool air of the evening lands. No more questions. Who am I what am I where am I. Of what stuff is the moon stamped. What's the plural of woodwose. Where can I find good barbeque. I look for flaws in your stance. Aside from the obvious ones of the nonparticipant. As Jimmy Anderson says, the only thing worse than losing is not playing. I have to say that most horrors are at least instructive, but with women you learn nothing. Why is that? I know I'm not alone in this. Isnt the purpose of pain to instruct? Well piss upon it. I'm just in a funk. In the end you can escape everything but yourself. We two are different creatures, Squire. Which I've said to exhaustion. But what we share—aside from intelligence and a low grade generalized contempt for the world and all in it—is an airy and mindless egotism. If I told you that I was concerned for your soul you would fall out of your chair laughing. But salvation like many another prize may be simply a matter of daring. You would give up your dreams in order to escape your nightmares and I would not. I think it's a bad bargain.

Western sipped his beer.

Our friend is silent, Brat. What are your thoughts?

Brat shook his head. None. I enjoy these exchanges too much. Please proceed.

Sheddan took a draw on the cigar and studied the light gray and perfect ash. I'll take that back if you like.

Western smiled. No no. Fair is fair.

You concur then.

No. Of course not.

No it is then. But in contemplating your situation I keep arriving at new puzzles.

Such as?

I dont know. Such as why is your best friend a moral imbecile. For instance.

Maybe he's not my best friend.

No? What's this, Squire? You surprise me.

I'm disencumbering myself, John. My plans are to travel light.

Where are you traveling to?

Dont know.

You're scaring me. Are you leaving the country?

Probably.

Abandoning the deep?

Maybe.

You're nothing if not circumspect. What do you propose to use for funds? If I might inquire.

I'm working on it.

I can only assume that fresh demons have materialized out of your troubled karma.

Western smiled. He drained the last of his beer.

Otra cerveza, Squire.

No thank you John. I have to go.

We're dining at Arnaud's. You should join us.

Another time.

You look a bit preoccupied, truth be told.

I'm all right.

You know you might consider a brief stint in the laughing academy yourself. In my own case I found it salutary. Take a break. It seems to be the case as well that if you check yourself in—as opposed to being committed—you enjoy certain privileges. Such as checking yourself out again.

I'll keep that in mind.

It's improved my outlook, Squire. No question. What I found that surprised me was that the unbalanced enjoy a certain largesse of personal freedom increasingly abridged in the workaday world.

Western rose. Thanks John. I'll give it my deepest consideration. Brat. Good to see you.

And you, Bobby.

Sheddan watched him out of sight down Bourbon Street. He took a pull at his cigar. What do you think, Brat? Do you think he took me seriously?

No. Do you?

I dont know. But he should have.

He worked in a dive shop in Tucson that was run by a friend of Jimmy Anderson's where they paid him off the books. He lived in a rented room and cooked over a hotplate and when he left he had a secondhand pickup truck and a few thousand dollars. In New Orleans he went to see Kline.

What if I did just disappear?

I thought we'd been over that.

How likely is it they would find me?

Kline tapped the eraser of his pencil against his teeth. He looked at Western. That would depend on who they is. We still dont know what this is about. Is your car still sitting in the locker?

No. When the rent came due they hauled it off.

If you had some serious scratch salted away you could just head out for the territories. You dont.

Even with a new identity I suppose you cant use credit cards. Or bank accounts.

It can be done.

You told me one time that it was almost impossible to fake a death.

That's been my experience. Of course you only hear from the failures. And they're usually defrauding insurance companies for fairly good sums of money so there's a lot riding on it.

If I went to Mexico City could I fly out of the country?

Do you still have your passport?

Yes.

Is it current?

Yes. Just not with the State Department.

I think you'd be okay. But I'll tell you right now. Being broke and friendless in a foreign country is no picnic. And that passport is going to expire eventually.

True.

Anyway, if you think this is just about some delinquent taxes then I would have to say that if they only wanted some money from you they'd probably just send out a couple of chaps to turn you upside down and shake you and see what falls out. It's five oclock.

I know. I'll let you go.

Why dont we go have a drink.

All right.

They sat at the bar at Tujague's. Western turned his glass slowly on the antique wood. Kline watched him.

You're just fucking around, Western. Probably not a good plan.

I know. I was just thinking that I dont even know what a country is.

Not an easy question.

It seems to be mostly an idea.

Kline shrugged.

You would really have to become someone else, wouldnt you?

Yes.

You just have to make up your mind.

Not so easily done.

No.

Some people cling to the wreckage forever.

I might surprise you.

You might. But I think the ability to evaluate danger in the face of it is largely genetic. If you have it it's been a long time coming and if you dont have it it's not likely to get here anytime soon. It's fairly common among athletes. And psychopaths. Any number of wanted felons have been taken into custody at their mother's funeral. What they all have in common is that they love their mother. What the other chaps have in common is that they dont want to go to jail.

You dont think I'd make a good fugitive.

No. But as you say, you might surprise me.

Western smiled. He picked up his glass. Salud.

Salud.

You havent put me off.

Understood. I've seen people pushed to the wall by adversity come away very different people.

Some better some worse I assume.

Maybe just wiser.

What else would you like to talk about?

Kline smiled. He rocked the ice in his glass. You see yourself as a tragic figure.

No I dont. Not even close. A tragic figure is a person of consequence.

Which you are not.

A person of ill consequence. Maybe. I know that sounds stupid. But the truth is I've failed everyone who ever came to me for help. Ever sought my friendship.

Would this include your friend? The one who died in Venezuela?

You're just trying to see how weird I am. But the truth is that in all probability Oiler would still be alive if he'd never met me.

You know what that sounds like.

I know what it sounds like. You said that I should get on with my life. Well, I'm not getting on with anything.

I believe you. Sadly.

The hell with it. Dont listen to me. I'm just being morbid. I miss my friends. And of course she was right. People will go to strange lengths to avoid the suffering they have coming. The world is full of people who should have been more willing to weep.

I'm not sure I follow you.

It's all right.

No. Go ahead.

Western drained his glass and set it on the bar and held up two fingers to the barman and turned to Kline. Let me put it this way. The only thing that was ever asked of me was to care for her. And I let her die. Is there anything that you'd like to add to that Mr Western? No, Your Honor. I should have killed myself years ago.

Why didnt you?

Because I'm a coward. Because I have no sense of honor.

Kline looked out at the street. The cold hard light of the city in winter.

What else has slipped through your fingers?

We'll never know, will we?

What do you intend to do?

I think I'm going to go to Idaho.

Idaho.

I think so.

What for?

I dont know. It seems to be a popular place with people on the lam.

I would think that might make it a good place to steer clear of.

I'll let you know.

The first night he spent in a motel outside of Midland Texas. Pulling in off the highway at some hour past midnight. The cool air that blew in the windows of the truck bearing the smell of crude oil from the wells. The lights of a distant refinery burning out there on the desert like the rigging of a ship. He lay a long time in the cheap bed listening to the rap of the diesel trucks running up through the gears as they came out onto the highway from the truckstop a mile down the access road. He couldnt sleep and after a while he got up and pulled on his shirt and jeans and his boots and walked down the breezeway and out across the fields. Quiet. Cold. The fires from the pipes at the wells burning like enormous candles and the lights of the town washing out the stars to the east. He stood there a long time. You think that there are things which God will not permit, she had said. But he didnt think that at all. His shadow from the motel lights fell away over the raw stubble. The trucks grew fewer. No wind. Silence. The little carpetcolored vipers coiled out there in the dark. The abyss of the past into which the world is falling. Everything vanishing as if it had never been. We would hardly wish to know ourselves again as once we were and yet we mourn the days. He'd thought of his father little in recent years. He thought of him now.

•

On a two lane blacktop in southern Colorado late the following day he began to come upon cars stopped along the side of the road. Up ahead a State trooper was pulling them over. The sky was a deep red and smoke was moving away to the south. He pulled over and got out. People were standing in the beds of their pickups watching the fire. He walked on up the road. After a while he could feel the heat. The fire had passed over the road and the country was burning far away to the south. Three javelinas came trotting out of the ash and walked along the road with him. He dropped to one knee and put the flat of his hand against the tarmac. The javelinas watched him. After a while he went back. He slept the night in his truck by the side of the road.

In the morning he sat with his feet crossed under him and watched the sun rise. It sat swagged and red in the smoke like a matrix of molten iron swung wobbling up out of a furnace. Most of the other cars and trucks were gone and he sat drinking a can of tomato juice. After a while he started the truck and turned on the wipers to clear the ash from the windshield.

Driving up the road he could feel the heat blowing off the burned land. He came to a stretch of blacktop that held tire tracks in the tar. He passed a dead doe at the side of the road and pulled the truck over and stopped. He got out and walked back with his knife and stood over the animal and made a cut down the charred hide of her back and laid open the tenderloin. The backstraps, the old hunters called them. He sat on the tailgate and ate the meat with salt and pepper out of small paper packets from a drive-in. It was still warm. Tender and red in the center and lightly smoked. He sliced it and ate it off a paper plate with his knife and surveyed the country where it lay in ashes about him. Birds of prey circling. Kites and hawks. Their heads cocked to study the ground below.

He drove north. Small harriers stood along the powerlines. They lifted and circled and returned to the wire behind him. In the evening he sat on the roof of the truck and finished the tenderloin and studied the country. He pulled up the collar of his coat and watched the way the wind ransacked the grasses. Sudden furrows that ran and stopped. As if something unseen had bolted and lay crouching. He sipped the warm tea from his thermos and then stoppered it and unfolded his legs and jumped to the ground. But his foot had fallen asleep and when he landed he collapsed and fell into the ditch and lay there laughing.

He bathed in a creek that ran beneath the road. An old concrete bridge. The rebar showing through the rails. He stood naked and shivering on a gravelbar downstream and toweled himself off. The water was cold and clear in the pool below the bridge. Good smallmouth water. He slept that night again in the truck and woke in a milky light where the glass was sifted over with a thin skift of snow. He sat with his sockfeet in the sleepingbag and started the engine and turned on the wipers. Gray daylight and a distant circling of birds rising up out of the river basin a mile away. The thin cranking of their calls. A lone truck was coming up the highway. Droning on the grade. He leaned and opened the glovebox and took out a package of crackers and tore it open with his teeth and sat eating the crackers and waiting for the engine to warm.

He crossed the Platte River at Scottsbluff and parked the truck along the edge of a broad gravel flat and walked out and stood looking at the river. The low hills a deep violet in the twilight and the Platte like a frayed silver rope where it ran downcountry over the braided flats, threading the sandbars in the deep burgundy dusk. He sat in the gravel and carved with his pocketknife a small wooden boat from a piece of driftwood and sent it away downriver into the darkness.

He rolled across Montana in the low winter sun. Fields of turned earth. Tall grain elevators. Pheasants crossed the road with their heads bowed like wrongdoers. On the dead straights of the highway in the evening he could see the lights of trucks miles away. The dark of distant mountains. Nothing on the radio but static.

He slept in a motel just across the Idaho State line. A varnished wooden bed and wool blankets. It was cold in the room and he turned on the gas heater in the wall. He went into the bathroom and switched on the light. Green tile from the 1940s. A floral print in a dimestore frame hanging on the wall over the toilet.

When he woke it was 4:02 by the red clock on the night-table. He lay listening. The periodic lights from off the highway moving along the slats of the blinds and over the pine board walls. Then slowly drawing back again. He got up and pulled the blanket from the bed and wrapped it around his shoulders and walked out into the parkinglot in his socks. Immense spread of stars overhead in the cold. In a few minutes he was shivering and he realized he was going to need warmer clothes. He turned and went back in.

He spent the winter in an old farmhouse in Idaho that belonged to a friend of his father's. A two story frame house with a woodstove in the kitchen and neither electricity nor water. He walked through the empty upstairs rooms. A scattering of yellowed newsprint, some broken glass. Lace curtains at the windows that had all but gone to vapor.

He had some blankets and he found more in a chest and he piled them all up in the kitchen. In a few days he would drive into town and buy an insulated winter coat and a pair of gumboots. He drove the truck up to the barn and loaded it with haybales and brought them down to the house and hauled them in to line the walls of the kitchen, windows and all. Before the winter was out he would drag more bales up the stairs and cover the floor of the bedroom above the kitchen with them.

There was a bed in one of the downstairs rooms and he pulled the mattress off and dragged it into the kitchen and he set an old Eagle oil lamp on the linoleum floor and filled it with kerosene from a can of it he'd found in the mudroom and he lit the lamp and set the glass chimney back and turned down the wick and sat.

In the mudroom there were jars of fruit and tomatoes and okra but he'd no idea how long they'd been there. Some iron harrowteeth in a wooden box. The bones of a mouse in the floor of a stainless steel milkcan. He found an axe in the woodshed but he'd no way to sharpen it and when he came back from town again he had a chainsaw and two boxes of paperback books. Victorian novels that he hadnt read and wouldnt but also a good collection of poetry and a Shakespeare and a Homer and a Bible. He got a fire going in the stove and carried a bucket down to the creek where it crossed under the road in a culvert below the house and he came back and made coffee and put some beans to soak. He fed more wood into the stove and pretty soon the kitchen was almost warm.

When he woke in the morning mice were watching him. Deermice with enormous liquid eyes. When he looked out the glass of the kitchen door it was snowing.

Sometimes at night he'd be wakened by something moving in the rooms overhead. A few times he went up the narrow wooden stairway wrapped in a blanket and swept the rooms with the beam of his flashlight but there was nothing there. Tracks in the dust of the floor. Possibly raccoons. In the morning he fitted pieces of cardboard into the sash where glass was missing. A few nights later he heard them again and he went up and stood in the darkened room listening. The window flooded with moonlight. The black winter tree limbs stenciled over the floor. Then he heard something moving in the room downstairs. He thought he heard a door close. He went down quickly but there was nothing there and he went back to his nest in the hay by the stove and he learned to live with whatever things there were in the house and they with him.

In late winter an unexpected thaw. He walked the slushfilled roads in his boots. His diet was largely beans and rice and dried fruit and his clothes were falling off of him. He stood on the old wooden bridge below the house and watched the waters where they ferried darkly past the shelves of ice. There were cutthroat trout in the river but he'd lost all heart to kill things. One day he saw a mink loping humpbacked along a stretch of gravel. He whistled at it and it stopped and looked back at him and then continued on.

Once or twice he saw tire tracks in the muddy snow. The white plates of ice broken in the ruts. Bootprints on the planks of the bridge. He never saw anyone. Water from the snow that had melted off the metal roof stood in pools on the cupped boards of the upstairs bedroom floors and water dripped into the rooms below. Then a norther blew in with two feet of snow and the needle on the cheap plastic thermometer outside the kitchen door dropped to twenty-four below zero.

He kept the chainsaw with him in the kitchen so that it would start and he trudged through the drifts of snow looking for standing dead trees. The trunks a pale gray in the whiteness. He'd made a balm out of the blacking from the inside of the stove door mixed with cooking oil that he smeared under his eyes. One day he started an owl from an evergreen and watched it fly long and straight and silent out through the woods until it was lost to sight. In the morning he went with a broom and cleared enough snow from the door of the truck that he could open it and he got in and fitted the key into the ignition and turned it. Nothing.

A few days later there was a knocking at the front door. He froze, listening. He blew out the lamp and pulled himself into the corner where he could just see the glass of the kitchen door. He waited. A shadow. A figure in a hooded parka trying to see in. Gloved hands against the glass. After a while it went away.

A recluse in an old house. Growing stranger by the day. He'd half a mind to go to the door and call after the visitor but he didnt and the visitor never returned. He went to bed and woke sweating in the cold. He sat up. Clear winter starlight at the window and the dark trees hooded in snow. He pulled the quilt about his shoulders. Certain dreams gave him no peace. A nurse waiting to take the thing away. The doctor watching him.

What do you want to do?

I dont know. I dont know what to do.

The doctor wore a surgical mask. A white cap. His glasses were steamed.

What do you want to do?

Has she seen it?

No.

Tell me what to do.

You'll have to tell us. We cant advise you.

There were bloodstains on his frock. The mask he wore sucked in and out with his breathing.

Wont she have to see it?

I think that will have to be your decision. Bearing in mind of course that a thing once seen cannot be unseen.

Does it have a brain?
Rudimentary.
Does it have a soul?

He ran out of coffee first and then finally out of food altogether. He went hungry for two days and then he suited up and set out upon the road for the village eleven miles distant. It was very cold. The snow in the ruts frozen. He walked with his gloved hands over his ears, his elbows swinging from side to side. When he reached the first house two dogs came down the driveway barking but he bent over as if to pick up a rock and they turned and ran. No one about. A thin plume from the brick chimney. The smell of woodsmoke.

He'd not been on the streets long before he noticed people looking at him. Of late he'd seen himself only vaguely in the windowglass of the kitchen and now he stopped at a store in front of a mirror and studied himself. A disheveled bum with long hair and a reddish beard. Jesus, he said.

Dark caught him on the way back. He was towing his bags of groceries behind him in a child's wagon with one wonky wheel that he'd found in a junkstore. Great sheets of chloral green and purple light flaring over the sky to the north. A deer crossed the road ahead of him. Then another.

It was close to midnight by the time he reached the house and towed the wagon up the drive through the drifts to the kitchen door. He pushed the door open and kicked his boots against the sill. Hello the house, he called.

He'd bought a comb and scissors and a small handmirror at the drugstore and in the morning he took a screwdriver and unscrewed the mirror in its frame from the dresser in the upstairs bedroom and carried it down and propped it up on the cupboard shelf in the kitchen by the door where the light was good and he scissored off his beard and shaved with a basin of hot water. Then he set about cutting his hair. He'd done it before and it came out all right. He swept up the cuttings from the linoleum and put them in a grocery bag and stuffed the bag into the firebox of the stove and shut the stove door. He put on more water to heat and washed his hair and bathed with a sponge, standing in a galvanized washtub he'd found under the back of the house. The tub was rusty and leaked and the water ran across the linoleum to the wall and slowly disappeared. He had clean clothes in a denim drawstring bag and he dried himself and got dressed and combed his hair and looked at himself in the mirror.

He'd brought a couple of mousetraps back with him and he set them baited with cheese. The mice had pretty much taken over the kitchen. He turned down the lampwick until the flame was all but out and then lay back in the silence. The first trap clicked. Then the second. He turned up the wick and got up and emptied the little warm bodies into the trash and set the traps again and lay down. Click. Click.

When he went to the second trap the little whitefooted mouse had both its front paws on the bail of the trap and was trying to push it up off its head. He lifted the bail and watched the little thing wobble off across the floor and then dropped both traps into the trash and went back to bed.

Then one day the mice vanished. He lay listening for them in the dark. He turned on the flashlight and played it over the room. Nothing. The next night he heard a rustling in the hay and sat up and turned on the flashlight and in the beam sat a slender ermine with a black tipped tail. It looked into the light and then vanished and reappeared in the far corner of the room with such incredible speed that he thought there must be two of them. Then it vanished and did not reappear. A week later the mice were back.

He'd bought some school tablets and a small packet of ballpoint pens at the drugstore and at night he'd sit propped against the haybales and write letters to her by the light of the oil lamp. How to begin. Dearest Alicia. Once he wrote: My beloved wife. Then he balled the paper and got up and put it in the stove.

There were owls in the barn gable even before the snow was gone. He stood in the bay and played the light up into the loft. Two heartshaped faces peered down. Pale as applehalves in the light. They blinked and shifted their heads from side to side. Some wisps of straw fell.

He woke a few nights later and lay listening to the silence. He got up and lit the lamp and carried it into the front room and held it overhead. A bat was lofting itself silently through the rooms. He went to the front door and opened it and left it open to the cold and went back to bed and in the morning the bat was gone.

He went through the drawers of the press in the front room. A tiny teacup. A woman's glove. I dont know what to tell you, he wrote. Much has changed and yet everything is the same. I am the same. I always will be. I'm writing because there are things that I think you would like to know. I am writing because there are things I dont want to forget. Everything is gone from my life except you. I dont even know what that means. There are times when I cant stop crying. I'm sorry. I'll try again tomorrow. All my love. Your brother, Bobby.

He had gotten out of the habit of talking to her when he was in New Orleans because he'd find himself talking in restaurants or on the streets. Now he was talking to her again. Asking her opinion. Sometimes at night when he would try to tell her about his day he had the feeling that she already knew.

Then slowly it began to fade. He knew what the truth was. The truth was that he was losing her.

He remembered her in the winter twilight at the lake standing in the cold. Holding her elbows. Looking at him. Until finally she turned and walked back to the cabin.

He sat in his blankets with the lamp at his elbow. Sheddan said once that having read a few dozen books in common was more binding than blood. The books I gave you you devoured in hours. Remembering them almost to the word.

The weather is warmer. There is an owl behind the house. I can hear him at night. I dont know what to tell you. I'm going to stop now. All my love.

He got up and pulled on his boots and his coat and walked the road. A cold halflidded moon moving through the trees. Faint in the distance the boards of the bridge trundling under the wheels of a car. The lights moving along the ridge and then gone and the blowing cold and the snow blowing off the fields and then settling again. When she came to the door of her room in Chicago he knew that she hadnt been out in weeks. In later years that would be the day he would remember. When all her concerns seemed to be for him. He took her to dinner at the German restaurant in Old Town and her hand on his arm at the table drained everything away and it was only later that he understood that this was the day when she was telling him what he could not understand. That she had begun to say goodbye to him.

He woke and lit the lamp and leaned back in the haybales with the blankets wrapped about him. In the lamplight the water standing in the pail in the floor shirred up in thin rings and then went still again. Something on the road. Something deep in the earth. His face was wet and he realized he'd been crying in his sleep.

He swept the snow off of the truck with a broom and got the battery loose with a pair of pliers and hauled it into town in the little wagon and hauled it back. Seven hours on the road. Two days later he was gone.

He spent the night in an old railroad hotel in a small town in southern Idaho and he lay awake listening to the long shunt and clatter of the railcars and the clang and echo of them like news of ancient war. He stood at the window. It had begun to snow.

He drove south to Logan Utah and took Highway 80 across Wyoming. Green River. Black Springs. Cheyenne. He slept in the truck and drove on. Crossing the central plains. The big tandem trucks plying the highway in the blowing snow. Ogallala. North Platte. In the red dusk flights of cranes crossing the highway. Circling and descending onto the flats where they landed walking and folded their wings and stepped and stood.

He took the secondary roads north. A few cars passed and then none. A squat ricepaper moon rode the lightwires. On the road out of Norfolk he came upon a pair of lights shining down the roadside ditch. He slowed the truck. The lights were mounted one above the other and it took him a minute to figure out what they were.

He pulled over and parked. It was a car in the ditch on its side with the lights on and the engine running. White smoke drifted across the road. He switched off the truck engine and took his flashlight from the glovebox and got out and shut the door and crossed the road. He shone the light down into the windows but he couldnt see anything. He stood on the driveshaft and pulled himself up and looked down into the car. On the door below a man was curled up blinking in the light.

Western tapped at the glass. Are you all right? The man shifted slightly but he didnt answer. Western could see the man's breath. Strands of dead grass and mud and gravel pressed against the underside of the windowglass. Western climbed onto the rear quarter panel and got hold of the door handle and tried to lift the door but it was locked. He aimed the light down into the car again. Turn off the engine, he called. The man put his elbows over his face. Western switched off the flashlight and sat there. A dog barked in the distance. The lights of a farmhouse beyond through the dark of the woods. He climbed down and walked around to the rear of the car and pulled off one boot and leaned against the bumper and held the leather sole of the boot flat against the chugging exhaust pipe. The motor stumbled and died and he pulled his boot back on and climbed out of the ditch and crossed the road and climbed into the truck. He thought that the man crouching in the car was not the driver and he started the engine and pulled out down the road thinking he might see the driver come up in the lights hiking along the road but he didnt.

It was a cold Friday evening when he pulled into Black River Falls. He stayed at a cheap motel out on the highway and in the morning he was at Stella Maris by ten oclock.

The nurse took his name and looked up at him. Are you a relative?

No Mam. I'm just a friend.

I'm really sorry to have to tell you this, she said. But Helen passed away. About a year ago.

He looked off down the hallway. That's all right. Is there someone else I could see?

That's all right?

I'm sorry. I didnt mean it like that. What about Jeffrey?

She put down the pen and looked up at him. You're her brother.

Yes.

She studied him. In his logging clothes and his homemade haircut. Then she pushed back the chair and got up.

You're not going to have me thrown out are you?

No. Of course not.

Did you know my sister?

No. But I know who she was.

When she came back she led him down the hall to the dayroom. The same faint smell of urine and disinfectant. She held the door for him.

You can sit over there by the window. I'll just be a minute.

When she came back she was holding the door for Jeffrey. He was in a wheelchair. Western stood up. He wasnt sure why. Jeffrey wheeled his way across the linoleum and turned the chair slightly and looked up at him. Western held his hand out but Jeffrey only put his elbow in his palm and cranked it up and down a couple of times and looked over his shoulder at the nurse. She turned to go and Jeffrey looked at Western. Take your seat, he said.

He did so. They waited. It was only when the nurse had cleared the room that Jeffrey turned the chair and studied Western more closely. You dont look all that well, he said.

I've been better.

I thought you might be dead.

No. It hasnt come to that. How are you?

I just thought that if you werent dead you should have said so.

I'm sorry.

Maybe yes maybe no. I suppose you've come to talk about Alicia.

I just wanted to see the place. A last time.

You're dying.

No. But I'm going away.

How far?

Pretty far.

All right. That's understandable. I'm not going anywhere anytime soon.

What happened to you?

I got run over by a car. Okay?

I'm sorry.

Yeah. Me too. Hit and run.

Did they find the driver?

Did who find the driver?

Anybody.

You'll have to be more specific. I'm bipolar. Among other things. Me and Amundsen.

I dont think he reached the North Pole.

No. But he flew over it. You seem to have trouble getting to the point.

I just knew you were friends, that's all.

Me and Amundsen.

Well. No. Actually I know. Well, she had a lot of friends.

Still, in the end she didnt get what she wanted, did she. Pretty much like the rest of us.

What was it she wanted?

Come on.

No. I dont know.

She wanted to disappear. Well, that's not quite right. She wanted not to have ever been here in the first place. She wanted to not have been. Period.

Did she tell you that?

Yes.

You believed her.

I believed pretty much everything she said. Didnt you?

Do you believe in an afterlife?

And she said I dont believe in this one. Right?

Jeffrey dug a small pair of binoculars out from somewhere in his robe and leaned and scanned the lawn.

The world must be composed at least half of darkness, he said. We talked about that.

Do you miss her?

What, are you nuts?

What do you see over there?

Some green polka-dot lizards. Quite a few in the woods over there. Big fuckers.

Really.

Maybe not like you of course. But sure I miss her. Who wouldnt? I thought she'd be safe here. She wasnt. She should have told me. I'd have gone with her.

Would you really?

In a heartbeat.

But she didnt tell you.

No. Not that it was a forbidden subject or anything.

Do you remember anything that she said about it?

I dont know. I never thought that it was all that big a deal with her. She said one time that just because the world was spinning didnt mean that you couldnt get off. There's an owl in those trees over there.

What kind?

I dont know. I cant see it. Just the crows. I thought that she was a perfect person. Pretty much a perfect person.

I didnt like it that she swore.

Yeah? I did. You know what I liked?

No. What?

To see her meet someone for the first time—preferably some smartass—and they would be looking at this blonde child standing there and literally within minutes they'd be swimming for their lives. That was fun.

Did she ever talk to you about the little friends that used to visit her?

Sure. I asked her how come she could believe in them but she couldnt believe in Jesus.

What did she say?

She said that she'd never seen Jesus.

But you have. If I remember.

Yes.

What did he look like?

He doesnt look like something. What would he look like? There's not something for him to look like.

Then how did you know it was Jesus?

Are you jacking with me? Do you really think that you could see Jesus and not know who the hell it was?

Did he say anything?

No. He didnt say anything.

Did you ever see him again?

No.

But you never lost faith in him.

No. The Israelite heals. That's all you need to know. Let me quote Thomas Barefoot to you. His truth is not going to come back to him void. It's going to do what he wants it to do. You might want to think about that.

Who is Thomas Barefoot?

A convicted murderer. Waiting to be executed by the State of Texas. Anyway, when you have seen Jesus once you have seen him forever. Case closed.

Forever.

Yeah. He's a forever kind of guy.

You dont see any disjunct between what you know about the world and what you believe about God?

I dont believe anything about God. I just believe in God. Kant had it right about the stars above and the truth within. The last light the nonbeliever will see will not be the dimming of the sun. It will be the dimming of God. Everyone is born with the faculty to see the miraculous. You have to choose not to. You think his patience is infinite? I think we're probably almost there. I think the odds are on that we'll still be here to see him wet his thumb and lean over and unscrew the sun.

How long have you been here?

Eighteen years.

He turned and looked at Western and then turned back and studied the grounds again. Yeah, I think the same thing myself. What if they throw my ass out of here? Standing at a bus stop with a suitcase and twenty dollars in your pocket. So you dont want to attract too much attention. But still you got to pass for crazy. You cant malinger.

Do you feel that your medications are helping you?

Hell, Bobby. Helping me with what? You walk a fine line. You know they want to get rid of your ass. You're making the place look bad. New clients show up with their kith and they sequester you away. Plus you got no money. Have you got anything to smoke?

I didnt know you could smoke in here.

You cant. Not in the building. That wasnt the question.

I dont. Have anything. Sorry.

Okay.

He pulled his robe about him and watched out the window.

I'm starting to get on your nerves.

Not yet. I'll let you know, dont worry.

All right.

You could check yourself in here too you know. I could use the company. I think. You dont have anything else to do.

Friends have suggested it. I'll think about it.

You're not going to think about it. Even if you did it wouldnt help. Here's a little tale from the wards. There was a woman here named Mary Spurgeon. Twenty-eight years old. On her birthday. Her last, as it would eventuate. So they had this little party with a cake and everything and somebody had a Polaroid camera and they took some pictures and they took a picture of Mary and Alicia. And when Alicia saw the picture there was this white spot in Mary's eye and she looked at it closely and then she turned and left.

She went to the clinic and told the doctor that Mary had a retinal blastoma and needed to have her eye removed and she showed him the picture. The doctor looked at the picture and they went back to the ward and he looked at Mary's eye and called an ambulance and they took Mary away and she came back a week later with one eye gone and this big bandage.

She'd have died.

Yes. But of course the loonies didnt see it that way. They sent a deputation to ask why she did that to Mary Spurgeon. They wanted to know why she'd turned her in. Their words. Look what you've done, they said.

What did Mary herself have to say about it?

Mary herself was mute on the subject. But now Mary had cut her wrists and died in the hall bathroom in the wee hours after writing an obscure poem on the wall in her own blood.

This must have been very hard for her. She never told me.

Alicia.

Yes.

Yeah, well. There's a lot of stuff goes on in the ward that doesnt make the papers.

I suppose that's why she killed herself.

Mary.

Yes.

Who knows? She'd been on the edge for years. She should have been on suicide watch but she wasnt. Your sister left a week later.

Why do you think she didnt tell me?

Some part of her may have thought the loonies were right.

He lowered the glasses and studied the kept grounds. Do you think most people want to die?

No. Most is a lot. Do you?

I dont know. I think there are times when you'd just like to get it over with. I think a lot of people would elect to be dead if they didnt have to die.

Would you?

In a heartbeat.

I'm not sure I understand the difference.

Yeah you do.

What else?

Why? Is there something else?

There's always something else.

All right.

All right?

Sure.

He scanned the landscape. Here's a dream. This man was a forger of antiquities. He traveled in documentation. In the instruments for their preparation. An old world figure. A dark suit, somewhat traveled in. A down at the heels formality to which yet clung an odor of the exotic. His portfolio it was rumored had been fashioned from the hide of a heathen and in it he carried the makings of every kind of document. Parchment and French vellum and period paper with the apposite watermarks. Vintage seals and ribbons and signatures of State and pen nibs of every provenance together with inks organic in nature which hung in thin bottles from his belt by thongs. Perhaps you can imagine him.

I'm not so sure.

It's all right. He makes me smile, actually. It's not important. What the world would look like without his practice. Our choices would be limited. What is more of interest is his clientele.

Who are his clientele?

History is his clientele.

History is not a thing.

Well said. If problematic. History is a collection of paper. A few fading recollections. After a while what is not written never happened.

And a good part of what is?

Well. That's the subject at hand.

Who pays for it?

You do.

I do.

Yes. And every revision of history is a revision of wealth. And unless you're living in a dumpster you get to contribute.

I am living in a dumpster.

If you say so.

All this in a dream.

Why not?

Did you ever tell her this dream?

Didnt have to.

Why not?

It was her dream.

But you understood it.

Come on.

Is history about money?

Until you had money you didnt have history. How's that?

I dont know. Suspect. At best.

Rumor, hearsay. Lies. If you think that the dignity of your life cannot be cancelled with the stroke of a pen then I think you should think again.

Were those her thoughts?

No. Those are mine.

She must have said something about him. The peddler.

You know what it was like.

No. I dont.

All physical history eventually turns out to be a chimera. She said that even if you place your hands on the stones of ancient buildings you'll never really believe that the world which they've survived had at one time the same reality as the one you're standing in. History is belief.

I'm not sure I see the point of the story. What other dreams?

Dreams dreams. What sort of despair would drive a person to the looney bin to query the mad as to their views?

Good question.

Do you know the Wisconsin Card-Sorting Test?

I know of it.

Schizos are notoriously poor at it. It's an analytical tool. She was a whiz at it.

What did the doctors make of that?

They gave her more tests.

More tests.

Sure.

That's what they do.

That's what they do. She once scored an eight on the Stanford-Binet.

An eight?

Yes.

Okay.

They gave her the test again and she scored a five. Roughly the IQ of a loaf of bread. But she quit.

Sure. She wouldnt take any more of their tests. I think she said that she'd take the Coonsfeldt if they'd change the name. They wanted to know if she was anti-Semitic.

Or anti-Black?

Or.

He lowered the binoculars and looked at Western. They were doing a paper. Who the fuck knows what they were up to.

If you could leave here where would you go?

I dont know. I certainly dont know as I would want to leave here. It's far from perfect. But it's what there is. Why? You want to go on the road?

I am on the road.

Yeah. Well, you wouldnt want me along. I attract the wrong kind of attention.

Are you wanted by the authorities?

I dont know. Yeah. Maybe. But they cant fuck with me as long as I'm in the nuthouse. So there you go.

Or dont.

Or dont. It might be fun though. I dont have anybody to talk to.

You said that. Anyway, I know the feeling.

You said that.

She told me once when I was in a suicidal snit that there are certain dispensations for those who survive their own reviling. I think I know what she meant. But if she didnt follow her own counsel how seriously should you take it?

I dont know.

What if the purpose of human charity wasnt to protect the weak—which seems pretty anti-Darwinian anyway—but to preserve the mad? Dont they get special treatment in most primitive societies?

Supposedly.

What does your buddy Frazer say?

I think so. Anecdotally.

You have to be careful about who you do away with. It could be that some part of our understanding comes in vessels incapable of sustaining themselves. What do you think? Maybe you'd have to be crazy to think that.

What else.

She said that femininity encoded mandates that were far less forgiving than anything men were familiar with.

Do you think that's true?

I dont know. She said it, so it's got to give you pause. You say something.

About her.

Yeah.

When she was sixteen I gave her a car. This was in Tucson. After a few weeks she packed up her stuff and drove from Tucson to Chicago. Nonstop. It was a fast car and that's the way she drove it. She drove all distances nonstop. She'd wind her hair up in the window so that if she fell asleep it would jerk her awake.

That's typical of schizos.

Winding up their hair?

No. Traveling nonstop. What kind of car?

Do you know about cars?

No.

It was a Dodge. A souped up Hemi. Very fast. It would pass everything but a fillingstation.

Did you want her to kill herself?

No. I wanted her to be free.

Do you think that's freedom?

Maybe not. But a fast car and an open road can give you a sensation that's hard to duplicate elsewhere or otherwise.

Let me ask you something.

Ask.

Could you have guessed your life?

Hardly a day of it.

You're not going to ask me though, are you?

All right. Could you?

No. Of course not. Do you think we have any say in it?

There's no way to answer that question. My friend John maintains that if things are going reasonably well it's all your own doing and if not then it's all bad luck.

Yes. In my experience when you reach for something there's a good chance that it's not going to be there.

I have to go.

Okay. Are you all right?

No. Are you?

No. But we're on reduced expectations. That helps.

Do you think I'll see you again.

You might. You never know.

I think you do.

Take care, Bobby.

You too.

He thanked the woman at the desk and had turned to go when she spoke to him.

Mr Western?

Yes.

There are some things here. Your sister's things. I had them brought down. Did you want to take them?

He stood looking down the hall towards the door.

Mr Western?

I dont know. Her things?

The woman had picked up a box from the floor and set it on the desk. I think it's just her clothes. Some papers. You dont have to take them if you dont want to. We can send them to the Goodwill. But there's a check here for you too.

A check.

Yes. It's the balance of her account. And there's another envelope that was left here for you.

Left for me.

Yes.

By who?

I dont know. A woman left it.

He took the two envelopes and looked at them. One was addressed to him at his apartment on St Philip Street.

What's in this one?

It's a chain and I think a ring. Maybe a wedding ring. Apparently they belonged to your sister. It was sent to you in New Orleans but it came back. It's been here a while.

And some woman left it here.

Yes.

How did she know it belonged to my sister?

I dont know. She said that her husband found it. She didnt leave her name. Did you want to open the box?

That's all right.

Did you want to take it?

Yes. Okay.

She handed him the box and he put the envelopes in his back pocket and took it.

Thank you.

I'm sorry, the woman said. I'm sorry that I didnt know her.

Western didnt know what to say. He nodded and put the box under his arm and went down the hallway and out the door.

He sat in the truck and put the box in the seat beside him. It was fastened with tape and it had her name written across it in black marker. He had the envelopes in his hand. He looked at them. The envelope with the ring inside was marked Robert Weston. He opened the other one and looked at the check. Twenty-three thousand dollars.

He looked out the window. Well, he said.

He put the check back in the envelope and sat looking out at the trees beyond the parkinglot. He thought of her walking out through the woods in the snow and then he couldnt stop thinking about her and he pressed his fist against his forehead and closed his eyes. After a while he reached and opened the glovebox and put the envelope inside and shut the glovebox door. He sat looking at the other envelope. There was a ringshaped impression in the paper where someone had pressed their thumb against the ring inside. He tore the corner in his teeth and opened the envelope and tipped it up. The ring and the chain slid into his palm. He sat looking at them and then he slowly closed them in his hand. Oh baby, he whispered.

When he got to New Orleans he checked into the YMCA and called Kline from the phone in the hall.

Where are you?

I'm at the Y.

Why dont I swing by and pick you up out front in about an hour.

Around five.

Yes.

I'll see you then.

They sat at Kline's table and ordered Sazeracs. The waiter called Western Mr Western. Cheers, said Kline.

Cheers.

It was five thirty on a Thursday evening and the restaurant was all but empty. That's Marcello, said Kline, lifting his chin. He likes to eat early.

Who's that he's with?

Dont know. You dont drink water.

Not much. Probably not a good idea.

Probably. What was your sister doing up in Wisconsin?

She was in a sanitarium.

Why Wisconsin?

She tried to get into the place where they'd confined Rosemary Kennedy.

Did she think that they'd just let her in?

Yes. They didnt, of course. She wound up in a place that had once been run by some order of sisters.

Is the State a hotbed of looneybins?

Probably not enough to accommodate everybody.

You didnt have some connection with the Kennedys.

No.

I worked with Bobby in Chicago in the early sixties. Briefly. We were working with a guy named Ed Hicks who was trying to get free elections for the Chicago cabdrivers. Basically Kennedy was a moralist. Before long he was to have an amazing roster of enemies and he prided himself on knowing who they were and what they were up to. Which he didnt, of course. By the time his brother was shot a couple of years later they were mired up in a concatenation of plots and schemes that will never be sorted out. At the head of the list was killing Castro and if that failed actually invading Cuba. In the end I dont think that would have happened but it's a sort of bellwether for all the trouble they were in. I always wondered if there might not have been a moment there when Kennedy realized he was dying that he didnt smile with relief. After old man Kennedy had his stroke the Kennedys for some reason felt that it would be all right to go after the Mafia. Ignoring the longstanding deal the old man had cut with them. No idea what they were thinking. All the time Jack is schtupping Sam Giancana's girlfriend—a lady named Judith Campbell. Although in all fairness—quaint term—I think that Jack saw her first. Or one of his pimps did. Some guy named Sinatra. What are you going to say about the Kennedys? There's no one like them. A friend of mine was at a houseparty out on Martha's Vineyard one evening and when he got to the house Ted Kennedy was greeting people at the door. He was dressed in a bright yellow jumpsuit and he was drunk. My friend said: That's quite an outfit you've got on there, Senator. And Kennedy said yes, but I can get away with it. My friend—who's a Washington lawyer—told me that he had never understood the Kennedys. He found them baffling. But he said that when he heard those words the scales fell from his eyes. He thought that they were probably engraved on the family crest. However you say it in Latin. Anyway, I've never understood why there is no monument anywhere to Mary Jo Kopechne. The girl Ted left to drown in his car after he drove it off a bridge. If it were not for her sacrifice that lunatic would have been President of the United States. My guess is that with the exception of Bobby they were just a pack of psychopaths. I suppose it was Bobby's hope that he could somehow justify his family. Even though he must have known that was impossible. There wasnt a copper cent in the coffers that funded the whole enterprise that wasnt tainted. And then they all died. Murdered, for the most part. Maybe not Shakespeare. But not bad Dostoevsky.

Castro was no part of this.

No. In the end as it turned out he wasnt. When he took over the island he threw Santo Trafficante in jail and told him that he was going to be shot as an enemy of the people. So of course Trafficante just said: How much? You hear different figures. Forty million. Twenty million. It was probably closer to ten. But Trafficante wasnt happy about it. The Mafia had a long history of running the casinos for Batista. Castro should have treated them better. The Mafia. He's lucky to be alive. The odd thing is that Santo ran three casinos in Cuba for another eight or ten years after that. Language is important. People forget that Trafficante's first language is Spanish. Anyway, he and Marcello have run the Southeast from Miami to Dallas for years. And the net worth of this enterprise is staggering. At its height over two billion a year. Bobby Kennedy wouldnt have deported Marcello without Jack's okay, but by now the whole business was beyond disentanglement. The CIA hated the Kennedys and were working at cutting themselves loose from the administration altogether, but the notion that they killed Kennedy is stupid. And if Kennedy was going to take the CIA apart piece by piece as he promised to do he'd have had to start about two administrations sooner. By his time it was way too late. The CIA hated Hoover too and Hoover in turn hated the Kennedys and people just assumed that Hoover was in bed with the Mafia but the truth was the Mafia had endless files of Hoover as a transvestite—dressed in ladies' underwear—so that was a Mexican standoff that had been in play for years. There's more to it of course. But if you said that Bobby had gotten his brother—whom he adored—killed, I would have to say that was pretty much right. The CIA hauled Carlos off to the jungles of Guatemala and flew away waving back at him. Hard to imagine what they were thinking. They left him there—where he held a counterfeit passport—and his lawyer finally showed up and then the two of them were frogmarched off into the jungles of El Salvador and left to fashion new lives for themselves. Standing there in the heat and the mud and the mosquitoes. Dressed in wool suits. They hiked some twenty miles until they came to a village. And, God be praised, a telephone. When he got back to New Orleans he called a meeting at Churchill Farms—his country place—and he was foaming at the mouth over Bobby Kennedy. He looked at the people in the room—I think there were eight of them—and he said: I'm going to whack the little bastard. And it got very quiet. Everybody knew it was a serious meeting. There was nothing on the table to drink but water. And finally somebody said: Why dont we whack the big bastard? And that was that.

I'm not sure I understand.

If you killed Bobby then you had a really pissed off JFK to deal with. But if you killed JFK then his brother went pretty quickly from being the Attorney General of the United States to being an unemployed lawyer.

How do you know all this?

Right. The thing about the Kennedys was that they had no way to grasp the inappeasable war-ethic of the Sicilians. The Kennedys were Irish and they thought that you won by talking. They didnt really even understand that this other thing existed. They used abstractions to make political speeches. The people. Poverty. Ask not what your country blah blah blah. They didnt understand that there were still people alive who actually believed in things like honor. They'd never heard Joe Bonanno on the subject. That's what makes Kennedy's book so preposterous. Although in all fairness there's some question as to whether or not he ever even read it. I'm having the chicken grande.

All right.

You want to pick the wine?

Sure.

Western tipped open the wine menu. I have to say that this is a pretty engaging story. But I suppose what I'd like to know is what does it have to do with my problem?

This country is your problem.

It is?

It's not?

I'd have to think about it.

Well. That's probably a problem too. You've already outstayed your welcome. But still you cant come to a decision.

You think I'm in danger.

You really shouldnt be looking over there you know.

Sorry. I have to say that he's not all that prepossessing in appearance.

No. Five feet five and overweight. No telling how many people have died because that's all that they beheld.

Beheld.

Yes.

Western ordered a bottle of Montepulciano. Kline nodded. Good choice. I was sitting at this table with a friend of mine a while back and Carlos was at his table there with two other men. Not his bodyguards. They always sit out front where they can see everybody. But there were three women at that table right over there and I noticed that the waiters were being old world deferential. Particularly to the older of the women. When Marcello and his friends left they stopped at the table and Carlos bent down and took the duenna's hand and said something to her in Italian and then the other two men did the same. They paid no attention at all to the other two women. But Marcello's friends when they made their little bow put their left hand over their heart, and after they left my friend wanted to know if that was a Sicilian thing. The hand over the heart. And I said that it was. In fact, a very Sicilian thing. It was to keep their .38s from sliding out into the woman's soup.

What does he order?

I think usually some pasta dish. Puttanesca. He likes lobster. Things not necessarily on the menu.

Is he going to jail?

Barring divine intervention. He's indicted for bribery in three States. I cant even imagine what his legal bills look like.

Western smiled. Are you a character witness?

Hardly. If anything it sort of went the other way.

How is that?

His lawyer's name is Jack Wasserman. He's an immigration lawyer from Washington. About three years ago Wasserman came over to my table and sat down. He pulled a moneyclip out of his pocket and began counting hundred dollar bills onto the tablecloth. He counted out thirty-two hundred dollars and shuffled it up and pushed it over. He said: That's thirty-two hundred dollars. No particular reason for the amount. What I'd like for you to do is to write me a check for it.

What did you do?

I got out my checkbook.

I dont understand.

If he had a check from me he could use it as evidence that I had retained him as counsel and that in turn would give us attorney-client privileges.

Why did he think that you'd need them?

He didnt. He just didnt know that we wouldnt. These people dont like to leave things to chance.

You wouldnt have to have a contract or anything?

Anybody can draw up a contract and predate it. But a check goes to the bank. I wrote him the check and put the cash in a bank in Florida. Here comes the food.

They ate quietly. Kline was a frugal wine-drinker and they would leave half the bottle on the table. They ordered coffee.

Have you been by the bar?

No. I called.

No one looking for you.

They check in occasionally.

You dont believe they're going away I hope.

No. Probably I dont. They just know that I'm not there.

They. Them.

Yes.

What is it that you think is going to happen?

To me.

To you.

I dont know.

Well, you're probably not going to be assassinated.

That's reassuring.

You're just going to jail.

I keep waiting for you to tell me something helpful.

I wish I could.

How many people have you helped to change identities?

Two.

Where are they now?

They're dead now.

Wonderful.

Not much to do with me. One of them was a relative. The other was a drug user who od'd. Probably a hotshot. They were buying time but time is hard to buy and it tends to be expensive.

Why were you helping them?

Family. Always trouble.

Sorry.

The Kennedys.

Yes. You dont believe that Oswald killed JFK.

It's not a matter of belief.

Was this a matter of sleuthing? Or inside information.

Both. You start at the beginning. Fundamental facts. In this case the most fundamental facts are the ballistics of Oswald's rifle. A cheap mail-order rifle with a cheap scope sight. No evidence that Oswald ever even sighted it in. Or even that he knew how to. We know that one of the rounds missed the limousine entirely and struck the curb. Supposedly it hit a wire. Which is questionable of course. There's no evidence that Oswald knew anything about guns. Including how to shoot one. He had a marksman rating but marksman means they make you stand out there until you hit something. Expert is the rating that actually means something. I dont know what power the scope was. Four. Six. It's not important. What we know is that it was a piece of junk. In keeping with the rifle. The rifle was a 6.5 Mannlicher-Carcano. They couldnt even get the name right. Carcano is the name of the manufacturer. A mannlicher is a style of rifle where the forestock extends pretty much the length of the barrel. Presumably to keep you from burning your hand. So it's like calling a Colt revolver a revolver Colt. Maybe you could say it like that in Italian, I dont know. Prior to the shooting no one had ever even heard of this wretched piece of gear. The fact that it fires a bullet of about .25 caliber doesnt really mean anything. Military rounds have been getting smaller for some time. But they've also been getting faster. And faster is what counts. Speed kills.

Energy increases equally with mass but it increases with the square of the speed.

Yes. I keep forgetting that you know all this stuff. The Carcano has a muzzle velocity of something less than two thousand feet per second. You could handload a rimfire .22 to pretty close to that speed. Not that you'd want to. I've studied the autopsy photos. A lot of people have seen them. Of course there's no doubt that it's Kennedy. You can see his face clearly. The whole back of his skull is gone and the cerebellum is hanging out on the table. The drawings on the other hand are different. They show the section of skull that the round took out as more to the upper side. I think I'm going to go with the photos. If you look at frame 313 of the Zapruder film you will see a cloud of blood and brain-matter that half obscures the figures of the Kennedys. The material explodes up and to the right for a distance of quite a few feet. It even splattered some of the motorcycle cops. The Carcano could no more have done that than a BB gun could. The frames that follow show Jackie climbing onto the trunk of the limousine and a secret service agent climbing onto the trunk from the rear. They are reaching out to each other. But that's not what's going on. The story finally was that Jackie was trying to retrieve a handful of her husband's brains that had plopped down onto the decklid of the limousine. Which supposedly she does. Then she sits next to her dead husband covered in brains and blood and supposedly holding these brains cupped in her hands all the way to Parkland Hospital where she gives them to a doctor. Or so the doctor testified. You look troubled.

That's a pretty strange story.

Yes.

Is it a true story?

No.

What's the point?

The point is that people believe it. The point is that the more that emotion is tied up in an incident the less likely is any narration of it going to be accurate. I suppose there are incidents more dramatic than the assassination of a president but there cant be too many of them. I'd seen the Zapruder film of course. Multiple times. It wasnt released for ten years. By then it had been tampered with in ways that made no sense at all. I knew that Jackie had climbed out onto the decklid of the limousine. But I'd no idea why. So I sat down and watched it. There were three other films shot of the same scene but they were taken from the other side of the limousine and you cant see her hand. Plus Zapruder had a zoom lens on his Bell & Howell. How long do you think she was on the trunk of the limousine?

No idea.

Two point eight seconds.

All right.

She couldnt have scooped up some brains off the car. She crawled out, grabbed something, and turned and came back. You can see that she's not scooping anything up. She never even looks at what's in her hand. She has what she came for in her fingers and when she tries to scoot back she actually reaches down with this same hand and uses the heel of it to support herself and to push away to her left to get back to her seat. This is all on film. You can see it for yourself. What she's holding in her fingers is a piece of her husband's skull. At least one witness did actually report seeing where it sat rocking gently on the decklid of the limo. Like a teacup. Jackie had been bent over her husband. He'd already been shot. When the next round came through his head her face was about six inches away. It's what follows that's fairly extraordinary. From the time that her husband's head explodes in her face it is less than a second before she turns to climb up onto the deck of the limo to take possession of the piece of skull teetering there. You know what she's thinking. Or you should. She's thinking that if her husband is to be put back together she has to have all the parts.

That's even more bizarre.

Not really. For all the pain that he's inflicted on her if there is any unassailable evidence of her love and her dedication that is it. There's no argument. I find her to be a pretty astonishing woman.

He didnt deserve her.

If you look at the films taken from the driver's side of the limo she seems to be reaching all the way to the rear of the decklid but the Zapruder film shows that what she is picking up is still about a foot from the rear. She sprang into action because she thought that the piece of her husband's skull on the decklid was about to slide off into the street and be run over and crushed.

Western sat. After a while he looked up at Kline. You dont have a woman in your life.

No.

Why?

It's a long story.

But you like women.

I love women.

Western nodded.

Kennedy was killed with a highpower hunting rifle. Most likely a .30-06 but possibly something even hotter like a .270 Winchester or even a Holland and Holland .300 Magnum. But in any case a rifle with twice the muzzle velocity of the Carcano and a number of times the energy. As noted. It could even have been a .223—which is the NATO round. The bullet was a hollow point. What is called a frangible round. And it would have pretty much disintegrated. The bullets that Oswald fired were solid-jacketed. The one that was recovered was hardly even deformed. That fact alone tells you everything you need to know. The President's head literally exploded. This of course was not caused by the bullet but by the shockwave from the bullet. They looked at what was left of Kennedy's brains under a microscope and they were impacted with fragments of lead. But even that didnt give them pause. These after all are ballistics experts who actually refer to cartridges as bullets. And since the frangible rounds left no trace other than small pieces of lead then the only bullet found was the one from Oswald's rifle. But the so-called ballistics experts couldnt make anything of this.

All right.

Witness after witness was asked to change his—or her—testimony "for the good of the country."

All right, why?

The reason might appear to be simply that it was not a federal offense at that time to shoot a president. But it was a federal offense for two or more people to conspire to do so. Somebody had to know that. And that would dump the assassination into the lap of the US Attorney General.

Bobby Kennedy.

Yes. But even that doesnt really fly. The real problem was all the troublesome shit that the brothers had been up to. From Hoffa to Giancana to Castro. All of which would come to light if the assassination was actually looked into. So we have the Warren Report instead. The US Government persuaded everyone—all those witnesses who wound up recanting almost everything they had seen or heard—that their testimony would decide whether or not Russia was going to nuke us. There are literally millions of pages of documentation concerning Kennedy's death that have been filed away in a vault. To be seen when? The fatal round could have been fired from in front of the limousine. Contrary to the Warren Report of course. There are buildings there but no one bothered to look because they already had the book depository and the rifle and the empty shellcasings. And the actual sharpshooter could have been firing from an obscene distance. Marine snipers make kills at ranges of up to a mile. There's a set of equations that cross here. Where the distance the smallbore travels washes out the bullet's speed so that finally the energy and the shock of the heavier bullet supplant the smallbore's speed advantage. It's why long-distance snipers often prefer the fifty caliber. No matter how much it slows down it's still pretty much like a traveling brickbat.

You think that he was shot with a fifty caliber?

No. And I probably dont think he was shot at some great distance.

The farther away the sniper was stationed—in front of the car if he was—the more the windshield would come into play to block his shot. Anyway, the reason that Oswald said he was a patsy was because he found himself left to wander around, take a bus, go to a movie. Which I suppose was a designated backup meeting place. Waiting for a ride that was never coming. And if the ride wasnt coming then what was coming? Hence the shooting of police officer Tippit. Which is otherwise inexplicable. It may be inexplicable anyway. But even before that Oswald had seen something in the telescopic sight of his go-to-hell rifle that must have been extraordinary to him. The sight of the President's head exploding just as he was about to pull the trigger for the third time. Find me an instance of a man saying that he was a patsy who wasnt one. Anyway, the notion that anyone would conspire with a halfwit like Oswald to actually assassinate a sitting president is ludicrous on the face of it. They didnt expect that he would even hit Kennedy. That was just a fluke.

Where did you learn about guns?

I never knew much about guns until I got interested in the assassination. Then it took me about two days to learn everything. You could probably do it in one.

And the chap who set the whole thing up is having dinner with us. Why isnt this a dangerous thing to know?

It's pretty much an open secret. In some circles at least.

In some circles.

Yes.

Kline drained his cup and set it back in the saucer.

Are you ready?

I'm ready.

In the parkinglot Kline started to open the door of the car and then he stopped. He leaned with his elbows on the roof. How old are you?

Thirty-seven.

Yeah. I've got ten years on you. You asked me one time what I would do if I was in your shoes and I think I said something to the effect that I didnt know because I wasnt. But have you really thought about the practical issues of your situation? I have a feeling that the shape of your interior life is something you believe somehow exempts you from other considerations. Are you aware of the fact that you can go to jail? Are going, in fact?

Yes.

You cant work. In this country. You have no friends. What I think is that if I were you I would be wondering what was keeping me here. Or why I didnt give some thought to changing my identity. If you dont have the eighteen hundred dollars I'll front it to you.

I've got some money.

Well. In that case the position you've taken looks more or less jackassical.

He stepped back and opened the door. It's open, he said. This is one parkinglot where you dont have to lock your car.

He called Debussy in the morning but she didnt answer. He called the bar and Josie did answer. She said that the Feds came in to check on him about every two or three weeks. That's what she called them. The Feds.

What did you tell them?

Told them the truth. That we hadnt seen hide nor hair. They wanted to know who your friends were but I said that as far as I knew you didnt have any. No surprise there, I said. A bigger son of a bitch never wore shoeleather.

You just sort of kept to the facts.

You got a few pieces of mail here.

I'll send somebody for it.

What the fuck have you done anyways?

I dont know.

Rosie said she thought you'd gone to Cosby.

It may come to that. Thanks.

You take care.

He hung up the phone and went uptown to the Napoleon. When he walked in Borman was behind the bar. The place was empty and Borman was at the cash register counting money. Western watched him. One for you and one for the house.

Borman looked up and located him in the backbar mirror. Bobby boy, he said. Sit your ass down.

Western sat at the bar. Borman shut the cash drawer and came over. What are you drinking?

Club soda.

You got it.

He turned and tipped down a glass and reached and scooped it into the icebin and stood it under the soda faucet and pulled the handle.

I went lookin for you up at the Seven Seas. They said Bobby who?

He set the glass in front of Western. Please tell me they threw your ass out of there.

There's a bug in my glass.

Borman bent and squinted. Yeah. I think he's dead. Just dont drink all the way down.

Okay.

Western pushed the glass aside. How long have you been here?

Couple of weeks.

Where's the widow woman?

She keeps threatening to show up. I dont know, Bobby. I'm of two minds about this shit.

Two minds.

Yeah. I aint sure I'm cut out for domestic bliss.

Probably not. When have you seen Sheddan?

I havent see him since the funeral.

Since what funeral?

Sheddan's funeral.

John's dead?

He looked dead to me. They had him in a coffin.

When was this?

I dont know. Three weeks ago maybe.

You went to his funeral?

You think I'd have missed that? You didnt know, did you.

No.

Sorry, Bobby.

Did a lot of people come?

To the funeral? Sure they did. Give them what they want and they'll come in droves. All those old Knoxville hustlers. Most of them didnt look all that much better than John.

Damn.

Sorry, Bobby. I thought you knew.

He picked up the glass of soda and emptied it in the sink and scooped it full of ice and refilled it and put it back in front of Western.

All that crew from Comer's. I was kind of surprised to see them all show up.

Maybe they just wanted to be sure.

I thought of that.

Let me see your phone.

Sure.

He swung the phone over and placed it on the bar and Western picked up the receiver and dialed the Seven Seas. Janice answered.

It's Bobby. Josie said I had some mail. Is Harold there? Well tell him if he'll bring my mail down to the Napoleon I'll give him ten dollars.

He hung the phone up. You got anything to eat?

I think there's some redbeans and rice in the reach-in.

How long's it been in there?

I dont know. I dont remember it bein there back in the summer.

Well let me have a bowl of it.

You got it. You want crackers?

Sure. Let me have a Pearl. Whose paper is that?

Yours.

Sheddan. Goddamn it.

Sorry Bobby.

Just goddamn it.

He was sitting eating the redbeans and rice and drinking his beer and reading the paper when Harold showed up out of breath.

Damn, Harold. You didnt have to run.

I thought for ten dollars I ought to get down here pretty quick.

What have we got?

You didnt have anything. Just an ad from Sears and Roebuck.

You are shitting me.

Yeah. Here.

Western took the mail and handed him the ten. Thanks, Harold.

Anytime Bobby.

He sorted through the envelopes and came upon Sheddan's letter dated two months ago from Johnson City Tennessee and put the corner in his teeth and tore it open.

Dear Squire,

This comes to you from the veteran's hospital in Johnson City where the news is not good. The horseman it would seem has chalked my door and by the time this reaches you—assuming that it does—I may be well on my way to shuffling off this mortal coil. Together with any attendant condensers, transformers, and capacitors. Hepatitis C, with complications stemming from a mostly dysfunctional liver together with various inroads upon other organs traceable to age, alcohol, and a lengthy and eclectic menu of pharmaceuticals over the many years. Dykes has been up to see me several times. Believe me when I tell you there was no line to stand in. He commented to a mutual friend that I was going to find myself consigned to such deeps of the netherworld that you couldnt find me with an asbestos bloodhound. I think he plans an elaborate obituary for the Knoxville rag he scribbles for. Something he's only done before for one of Gene White's hunting dogs. I'd thought to give my body to science but obviously they draw the line somewhere. Dykes is on record that there can be no burial without an environmental impact study. One might think cremation an option but there is the danger of the toxins taking out their scrubbers and leaving a swath of death and disease among dogs and children downwind for an unforeseeable distance.

Several acquaintances have remarked upon my sangfroid at this turn of events but in all truth I cant see what the fuss is about. Wherever you debark was the train's destination all along. I've studied much and learned little. I think that at the least one might reasonably wish for a friendly face. Someone at your bedside who does not wish you in hell. More time would change nothing and that which you are poised to relinquish forever almost certainly was never what you thought it to be in the first place. Enough. I have never thought this life particularly salubrious or benign and I have never understood in the slightest why I was here. If there is an afterlife—and I pray most fervently that there is not—I can only hope that they wont sing. Be of good cheer, Squire. This was the ongoing adjuration of the early Christians and in this at least they were right. You know that I've always thought your history unnecessarily embittered. Suffering is a part of the human condition and must be borne. But misery is a choice. Thank you for your friendship. In twenty years I dont recall a word of criticism and for this alone deep blessings be upon you. If we should meet again I hope there will be something in the way of a wateringhole where I can stand you a round. Perhaps show you about the place. Look for a tall and somewhat raffish looking chap in a tailored robe.

Always
John

IX

In the last winter the Kid was already given to long absences. Sometimes she'd wake to a sense of someone having just quit the room and she would lie there in the quiet. Everything slowly taking shape in the gray light. Once a scent of flowers.

She went to Tennessee for what would be the last time. She called her grandmother and told her she was coming. They'd not spoken in months and there was a long silence.

Granellen?

She thought that her grandmother was crying.

Maybe you dont want me to come. It's all right.

Of course I want you to come. I cant tell you how much.

She didnt even have a coat. It had snowed and she walked in the woods. Her grandmother's boots. She was bundled in sweaters and she wore her grandmother's coat.

It's all right, Granellen. I dont really get cold.

Maybe you dont, Child. But I do.

A few flakes still falling. Gray against the gray sky. The great blocks of quarry stone among the barren trees. She knelt in the snow and traced with her hand a ropelike shape she took to be where possibly a snake had been caught out in the early cold.

She walked out to the quarry and stepped down onto the broad shelf of rock and crossed to the pool. A skim of clear ice over the dark water. She held out her arms and made of herself a figure frozen in dance and she tested with one boot the panes of ice.

•

In the morning she woke to the sound of snuffling and peered from under the quilt to see Miss Vivian huddled in the corner. She sat up with the quilt pulled about her. What is it? she said.

The old woman lifted the veil of her hat so that she could blow her nose. She clutched the balding ferrets of her stole and wadded the soiled handkerchief and held it to her nose and looked at the girl. I'm sorry, she said.

What is it?

I'm all right.

Why are you crying?

Because it's all so sad.

What's so sad?

Everything.

You're crying about everything?

It's the babies.

The babies?

Yes. It's just so sad.

She patted about her and came up with her lorgnette and put it to one eye and leaned to study the girl. They're just so unhappy. They were crying in the shopping center too.

The babies.

Yes.

Why were they crying?

We dont know, do we? We just know that it's unanimous.

No happy babies?

No. And they try so hard, bless their hearts.

Maybe they know what's coming.

The old woman blew her nose again, shaking her head. Powdered clay sifted from her face. It's very puzzling. That people seem to find it natural. Dont you think that's sad? That no one is concerned?

I dont know. Do they cry all the time?

No. I find them very brave. They want to be happy.

The girl studied her. Her burntlooking costume. The antique dress a deep and burnished purple. Like something left out in the sun. The hat piled with graveyard flowers. The laddered hose.

Are you all right? Are you cold?

I'm fine, my dear. She patted her nose and adjusted the stole about her shoulders and looked up. Maybe you're right. That they know what's coming. They seem to be of one mind. It's a troubling thing, isnt it?

I dont know what view of things babies could have.

The old woman nodded. I know. I think those of us approaching the middle years are often attracted to the young. We dont reckon on the heartache, of course.

Approaching the middle years?

Yes. One such as myself for example.

Of course. What do you think could be done? About the babies.

I dont know. You can distract them. For a while. You cant help but think that they bring their despair into the world with them. Still I cant imagine that they cry in the womb. Even though they might want to.

I'm not sure what the adaptive advantage could be to share an innate and collective misery.

The old woman sat composing herself. She seemed to be taking this under advisement. I'm just an old silly, she said. I dont know what it is that we've forgotten. How could anyone know without remembering? I only know that we dont want to remember it. Perhaps you're right. Perhaps it's just that they're afraid.

They're afraid of falling and loud noises. And drowning. Possibly snakes. I'm not sure how you would derive some atavistic angst out of that.

Well. It's difficult for us to come to grips with the nature of the problems that babies face. They dont know where they are, of course. They dont know who to trust. They could be in the woods somewhere. Waiting for the wolves.

Waiting for the wolves.

Yes.

I think creatures call out when there's no danger in doing so. Birds sing because they can fly. If the babies are crying it must mean that they are safe.

The old woman shook her head. Safe babies, she said. Oh how one would like to believe in such a thing.

Do you travel around by yourself?

Yes. No choice, really. I never married. If that's what you're asking.

I didnt mean to pry.

I'm not really one of them you know.

The entertainers.

Yes.

But sort of.

Well. One could say. I suppose. But I've never been fond of show-business people.

You rather keep to yourself I've noticed.

It's just that I'm not fond of make-believe.

Nor I.

Things said in jest are often cruel.

Yes they are.

In another life I'd have done things differently.

Another life.

It's not that I think so much that the babies have opinions. I think it's mostly that they just dont like it here. Of course you could ask as compared to where. They've never been anyplace before. Let alone here. And they've never seen people before and it might be a fair question to ask how it is that they would know that what they were seeing was people. Or if just any sort of creature would do. They've never seen themselves. If a baby was born in a house full of Martians I suppose it might take him a while to figure out that he was in the wrong house. What if he did look in the mirror and he had two eyes and everyone else had three?

Do you believe in Martians?

It wouldnt have to be Martians. They could find themselves among bears.

Gladly the crosseyed bear.

I'm sorry?

Bears.

Would that be so bad?

Not unless they ate you. As soon as they get here they start wailing.

The babies.

Yes. I dont think it has to be the here that's wrong. It could be us. For instance. What if we've become something repugnant to ourselves. That's not a happy thought, is it?

It seems an unlikely thing.

So is everything else.

Everything.

I think so. Of course, the most unlikely things arrive anyway.

Yes they do.

Did you cry when you were a baby?

As a baby. Yes.

But then you stopped.

Yes.

So what did you do then?

I didnt do anything.

You just laid there.

They thought there was something wrong with me. I would look up at them if they stuck their heads over the crib but that was about all. They'd sneak into my room at three oclock in the morning and I would just be lying there holding my feet. This went on for about two and a half years and then one day I got up and went down and got the mail.

That's not true.

No. But something like that.

Were there other babies around?

No. Just me.

What were you thinking about?

I dont remember. Apparently I didnt take all that much interest in the world. I had a couple of stuffed toys. I would suppose that the reason infants are not more horrified at being dumped into the world is simply that their capacity for horror and fear and outrage is not all that well developed. Yet. The child's brain the day before its birth is the same brain as the day after. But everything else is different. It probably takes them a while to accept that this thing which follows them around is them. After all, they've never seen it before. They have to hook up the visual to the tactile. The newborn are probably not that quick to ascribe reality to the visual. And ascribing reality is pretty much what they're being called upon to do.

What do they think the visual is?

They dont know. The womb is as black as it gets. I think when they close their eyes they might even imagine they've gone back. Or they hope. They need the respite. I'm sorry. I'm just thinking out loud.

I do that all the time.

But you think that they just dont want to be here.

I think after a while they want to hold someone responsible. It's what you learn when you learn about the world. Of course things can simply happen on their own. It's just that it's unusual.

You think we're disposed to look for someone to blame when things dont go well.

Yes. Dont you? If there's no one to blame how can you have justice?

I guess I hadnt thought of it like that.

If you'd never been anyplace before and you didnt know where it was that you were going or why it was that you were going there then how excited would you be about going?

Not very I suppose.

Babies early on come to believe that all the things that are happening to them are the work of others otherwise what are the others there for? Isnt that worth crying about?

Why cant they just be wet? Or hungry?

They can. But these are normally just things that you complain about and not things over which you scream in agony.

Maybe they just dont know the difference yet. My guess is that the reason they wail all the time is that they've been allowed to get away with it. Evolutionarily. If you want to eat a baby you should understand that they are watched over twenty-four hours a day by creatures with long spears and large clubs. Plus you'd probably have to move some pretty big rocks.

But you stopped crying.

As a baby.

Yes.

Yes. Actually I think I got pretty quiet.

Do you cry now?

Yes. I cry now.

He went to Arnaud's for dinner and sat sipping a chilled glass of brut champagne. He toasted Sheddan mutely. What do you say to the dead? You've few common interests. Your health? Should you answer their letters? They yours? When the waiter came to take the towel from the half bottle of champagne in the bucket Western waved him away.

Sir?

We like to pour our own champagne. We prefer it cold and effervescent as opposed to hot and flat. It's just a peculiarity.

Sir?

It's all right. I'll pour it if you dont mind. I didnt see lobster on the menu. What do you think?

Let me see.

When he came back he said that they did have lobster and Western ordered it broiled with a baked potato with sour cream and extra butter. The waiter thanked him and moved away. Western poured his glass and screwed the bottle back into the ice.

I'm sorry, John. I should have seen this coming. I should have seen a lot of things coming. Cheers.

Against his better judgment he stopped in at the Seven Seas. Josie was at the bar. Didnt expect to see you again, she said.

How you doing?

Good. You just missed them.

You're kidding.

Nope. About an hour ago.

Good timing. Why do you think they keep coming back? Why would they think I would be here?

I dont know. Of course I could point out that you are here. You want a beer?

No. I'm all right.

You dont look all right.

I lost some weight.

Yeah?

I look what?

I dont know.

Gaunt.

Whatever that is. You just look sort of down. Maybe just thoughtful. Moreso than usual. Which maybe aint so unusual.

A friend died.

Sorry to hear it. A good friend?

An unusual guy.

Somebody you're going to miss.

Yes.

You got some more mail here. These dudes dont believe me when I tell them I dont know where you are. They always ask. But it's just by way of saying that I dont want to know. I dont want them throwing my ass in jail for harboring a fugitive.

You could adopt me.

Adopt you.

Yes. Then I'd be an immediate relative and you wouldnt be required by law to rat my ass out.

You're shitting me.

I dont know. It varies by States. Hand me the phone.

She swung the phone over and set it on the bar and he picked up the receiver and dialed Kline's number. No answer. He put the receiver back. Then he picked it up again and dialed Debussy.

Hi Darling.

How did you know it was me?

I have this fancy new phone that tells you who's calling.

What are you doing tonight?

I'm working.

What time do you get off?

One. You're asking me out.

I want you to do something for me.

All right. Is it a girl thing?

I want you to read a letter from my sister and then tell me about it.

All right.

You dont want to know why or anything like that?

No.

So you can meet me tonight?

Somehow I thought we'd already made a date.

One thirty?

I cant get there by one thirty. Makeup takes longer to get off than to put on. I could do two.

Okay. Where?

You say.

How about the Absinthe House?

Okay.

We can get something to eat if you like.

I know. Are you okay?

I'm all right. I'll see you at two?

Yes.

Thanks Debbie.

He hung up the phone and went upstairs to the hall bathroom and locked the door and lifted down the medicine cabinet.

He got to the Absinthe House early and stood outside waiting for her. He knew that she hated walking through a door unescorted but he neednt have worried. She was coming across Bienville Street on the arm of a grayhaired gentleman in a suit. The man shook hands briefly with Western and kissed her on both cheeks and turned and went back across the street. Western and Debussy went in. The place was full, taken over largely by British paratroopers.

Mercy, she said.

Maybe this wasnt such a good idea.

She took his arm and looked out down the bar. We'll be fine. Come on.

A waiter was making his way toward them. The troopers whistled and catcalled. And look at the lucky charlie that's with her. The waiter reached them and herded them to the rear.

Thanks, Alex.

I'm going to put you back here. We can close the door.

Thank you, Darling. Alex this is Bobby. Bobby Alex.

We should have called.

It's not a problem, Sir. What can I bring you?

I'll just have what she's having.

You know she doesnt drink.

That's fine.

You got it.

He vanished into the smoke and noise and pulled the door shut.

I meant to ask him for a bar menu.

That's all right. I'm okay if you are. Although I may change my mind about that drink.

Did you want to go somewhere else?

No. Anyway, noise is the enemy of surveillance.

Are we being surveilled? Is that a word?

Yes. So tell me your news. I dont want to hear something horrible.

There's a lot of stuff I havent told you.

I know.

How do you know?

You're kidding.

All right. I think I'm about to become someone else.

It's about time.

Western smiled.

The waiter brought their drinks. Tall glasses of soda slightly colored with triple sec. Then bitters, and a twist. Western looked up. I've changed my mind, he said.

The waiter took one of the glasses and put it back on the tray. Western reached and took it back. Just bring me a double gin.

Neat.

Yes.

Debussy sipped her drink. You need support.

I dont know what I need.

Just jump in.

Okay.

He took the letter out of his shirt and laid it on the table. This is the letter. I've never opened it. I have a number of her letters and part of her diary for 1972 and I may ask you to keep them for me.

All right. Although I have to say it makes me a bit nervous.

You dont have to.

Who is it that's after you?

I dont know. I dont know that it makes any difference.

How can it not make any difference?

Because no matter who they are the only option you have is to run.

Are you going to run?

Yes.

I wont see you again.

That's another question. We'll work on it.

I dont want to lose your friendship.

You'll never lose my friendship.

She got out her cigarette case. I have your word on that.

Yes.

Do you want me to open the letter?

Wait a minute till my drink gets here. I'll take it out to the bar. I'd like for you to see if there's any mention of her violin. Where it might be. That and where she might have had a bank account.

All right. I can do that.

The waiter set the glass of gin on the table and Western took a sip out of the tall glass and poured in the gin and stirred it with a straw. Take your time. I've no idea what's in there.

All right.

I'm sorry, Debbie. I dont have anybody else to saddle with this.

It's all right.

All right.

Dont get in a fight out there.

I wont.

I'll send Alex out.

Okay.

Can I ask you something?

Of course.

Is that all right with you? To have no one?

Western stared at his hand. Flat on the table. After a while he said: I wasnt asked. I wasnt consulted.

You have no say in your own life.

If all that I loved in the world is gone what difference does it make if I'm free to go to the grocery store?

And this is for always.

Yes.

He looked up at her. Her eyes were brimming.

I'm sorry. I didnt mean to make you sad.

Why dont I just read the letter.

Maybe this is a bad idea.

Why dont I just read it.

All right. Thank you.

He took his drink and went out through the bar and stood in the street. Pretty quiet. Two young chaps sallied past and the taller of them gave him the once-over and then they looked into the bar.

I wouldnt go in there if I were you.

The other one turned at the door. You're not, he said.

The taller one had already looked inside and he came back out onto the sidewalk. Come on, he said.

What is it?

He turned to Western. Thank you, Sweetheart.

My pleasure.

He went in. Alex was looking for him. What did you say to her?

I didnt say anything to her. Why?

Because she's crying her eyes out.

Damn. All right. I'm sorry.

He pushed into the room and shut the door. The letter was lying open on the table. She looked at him and looked away again. Oh Bobby.

I'm sorry.

Poor baby. Poor baby.

I'm sorry. I'm just so stupid.

It's not your fault. I did it to myself. God. I'm just a mess. I have a sister you know. I'm sorry. I'm ruining your letter. She opened her purse and took out a tissue and blotted the letter where a watery streak of mascara had run on the page.

Dont worry about that.

She dabbed at her eyes.

I almost came in to tell you not to do it.

It's all right. I'm such a baby.

I'm really sorry.

The waiter opened the door and looked in. Are you all right?

It's okay, Alex. Thank you. It's just some bad news in a letter. We'll be okay.

He looked doubtful but he pulled the door shut.

I must be a mess. Do you really want me to keep the letters? How many are there?

Not a lot. I dont want you to do it if it will make you uncomfortable.

But I wouldnt have to read any more of them.

No.

All right.

Go ahead.

The violin is at the shop where she bought it. I hope you know where that is because she doesnt say.

I didnt know she bought it in a shop. I thought she bought it at auction.

Is it worth a lot of money? I'm guessing it is.

I think so. She bought it with the inheritance from her grandmother. I thought it was a bit extravagant to spend her inheritance on a fiddle. The money was supposed to go for her education but she said that somebody else would pay for that. And of course she was right. And she said that whatever you paid for an Amati violin it would still be pennies on the dollar in a very few years.

Where did she go to school?

The University of Chicago.

And she was what? Twelve?

She was thirteen.

How did she know what violin to buy?

She was pretty much a world authority on Cremona violins. She knew the history of a hundred of them. She used to get letters from museums asking for advice on pieces in their collection. She made mathematical models of their acoustics. Sine-wave patterns of the plates. She finally worked out a topological model that would tell you how to make the perfect violin. The Amatis were just sort of loosely glued together and she finally took it completely apart. She worked with a woman in New Jersey named Hutchins. A guy named Burgess in Ann Arbor. People are still trying to find her. She really didnt need a lot of help in picking out a violin. That Amati was a pretty rare find. I dont think it had been sold in years.

She folded the letter and put it back into the envelope.

I'm really sorry, Debbie. I didnt have anyone else to ask.

It's all right.

She opened her compact and looked at her face in the mirror. God, she said.

Should we go?

I need to go to the loo. Try and repair some of the damage.

All right. I'll get the check.

There wont be a check. Just leave a tip.

A five?

How about a ten.

All right. Thank you, Debbie.

They walked out through the bar but the troops by now seemed too inebriated to pay them much attention. Someone did call out to her to ditch that poof but that was about it. Western hailed a cab. They went up Dumaine Street to her apartment and he walked her to the gate.

I feel like I've encroached on your friendship.

It's just there, Bobby. It always was. No erasing. No encroaching.

All right.

Clara is going to be here in two weeks. I want you to meet her. You'll fall in love.

Are you excited?

Very.

She leaned and kissed him on both cheeks.

Do you want me to see you in?

No. I'm fine.

Do you have someone here?

Yes. Is that okay?

Yes. Of course. I dont mean to be a nosey parker.

She put the key in the gate and turned it and swung the gate open.

Call me.

I will.

And take care.

I will. And you.

Good night.

Good night.

Bobby?

Yes.

You know I love you.

I know. Another time. Another world.

I know. Good night.

X

He'd spent the day in town and he crossed back on the ferry in the evening. Standing on the upper deck and watching a boy and girl below passing a joint between them. The ferryboat was named the *Joven Dolores*. He called it the *Young Sorrows*. The horn blew a last time and the deckhands threw off the hawsers fore and aft and they began to move off into the quiet waters of the strait. The water slapping off the hull. The clocktower above the old walled town turning slowly and drawing away.

They trudged past the islands in the gathering dusk. Los Ahorcados, El Pou. Espardell. Separdello. The lighthouse at Los Freos. He'd bought a small ruled notebook at the stationer's in Ibiza. Cheap pulp paper that would soon yellow and crumble. He took it out and wrote in it with his pencil. Vor mir keine Zeit, nach mir wird keine Sein. He put the notebook away in the string bag with his few groceries and stood watching the gulls in the lights of the rigging where they swung out and back over the sternway. Turning their heads, watching the water below and watching each other, then falling away one by one back toward the lights of the town.

He went forward and stood at the iron rail with his face to the wind. Deep throb of the diesel in the decking underfoot. The island of Formentera a low stretch of bight and headland in the distance. The dark little archipelagos. A launch was crossing the shadowline from the sea into the heavens as the ancients in their small stone boats had once aspired to do.

He got his bicycle from the courtyard of the bodega at Cala Sabina and hung the bag over the handlebars and set out up the road toward San Javier and the headlands at La Mola. Fields of new wheat slashing softly in the roadside dark. Up through the pine forest. Pushing the bike. Alone in the world.

There was an iron lock to the heavy wooden door and a black iron handforged key planished with hammer marks and this Guillermo did not want to let him have. Is okay, he said. No one will come.

Bueno. Pero si va a venir nadie, por qué está cerrada?

Ah. No sé. Pero la llave es muy vieja. Es propiedad de la familia. Me entiendes?

Sí. Por supuesto. Está bien.

He pushed the door open and pushed the bike in before him and stood it against the wall and closed the door and took the lamp from the low table and lit it and set back the glass chimney and raised the lamp to see. Stone stairs up the inner wall. Musty smell of grain. The great bedstone lying in the dark and the enormous wooden gears and shafts, the great planetary. All of it hewn from olivewood and joined with iron fittings hammered out on some antique forge and all of it rising up into the dark vault of the mill like a great wooden orrery. He knew every part of it. Windshaft and brakewheel. The miller's damsel. He climbed the stairs through the shadows lamp in hand to the wooden loft where he slept.

His bed was a sheet of plywood propped up on wooden blocks and laid over with a straw tick sacked up in coarse linen and covered with a pair of black and gray Italian Army blankets. Overhead he'd stretched a plastic tarpaulin against the leaky roof and the bird droppings from the pigeons. He set the lamp on the low table along with the string bag and kicked off his sandals and stretched out on the bed. The pigeons stirred and wisps of straw drifted down in the yellow light. There was a small window set in the heavy stone wall where sometimes at night he'd sit and watch for ships. Their lights in the distance.

He slept and in the night he woke to a low flare of light in the tower. The lamp had burned down and was smoking. He reached and turned down the wick. A ship's horn. He never slept more than a few hours. Sometimes it was just the wind. Sometimes the rattle of the door below.

As if someone were trying the latch. He'd kicked a wedge of wood beneath it with his heel but now he liked the sound of it. He sat with the blanket around him and watched the distant dark of the sea with its shifting cape of stars where they lifted and fell. It came again, the pale ignition of a storm that shaped out the window and cast it brief and shuddering upon the farther wall. A sheet of light flaring silently over the storied sea, the thunderheads along the horizon shaped in the rim lightning and the slow leaden lap like slag in a vat and the slight smell of ozone. Brief season of storms. He slept to the patter of raindrops on the tarp overhead and when he woke it was day.

In the morning he walked on the beach hooded against the rain in his good oiled English anorak. The air was filled with almond blossoms. They lay drifted in the ruts of the road and shelved along the shoreline where they rode the slow black swells. Two dogs came racing down the strand toward him and then saw that they didnt know him and turned away. Great eskers of seaweed had washed up in the storm and the gatherers were on the beach with their wooden pitchforks heaping it onto their carts. They nodded to him as they passed, the little mules leaning into the traces.

He walked out to the headland in the fine rain. Floats of cork, bits of glass. Driftwood. Beyond the point the marbly rocks clattering down the strand, the long seething of the surf drawing away. Ancient. Tireless. Across the sound the rocky keep of Vedrà just visible. The stone spires black in the rain.

The ancient people here were called Talayot. After the towers they left. Then came the Phoenicians, Carthaginians. Romans. Vandals. Byzantine and then Muslim cultures. In the fourteenth century Aragon. Down the beach lay a dead dolphin. The long jawbone bared and the flesh in gray ribbons. He'd collected half a handful of bits of seaworn glass, frosted pale green and opaque. He formed them into a small cairn on the flat wet sand where they would soon tumble out to sea again.

In the years to come he would walk the beach all but daily. Sometimes he'd lie at night in the dry sand above the wrack-line and like the mariners of old study the stars. Perhaps to see how he might plot his course. Or to see what enterprise might be read as favorable in their slow crawl over the black and eternal vastness. He walked out to where he could see the lights of Figuretas strung along the far shore. The black sea lapping. He rolled his trousers to his knees and waded out. The Carolina coast on such a night. The lights at the inn and along the drive. Her breath against his cheek as she kissed him good night. The terror in his heart.

Sheddan once said that evil has no alternate plan. It is simply incapable of assuming failure.

And when they come through the walls howling?

In her white gown carrying the barnlantern out through the trees. Holding the hem of her gown, her slender form candled in the sheeting. The shadows of the trees, then just the dark. The cold in the stone amphitheatre and the slow turning of the stars overhead.

Here is a story. The last of all men who stands alone in the universe while it darkens about him. Who sorrows all things with a single sorrow. Out of the pitiable and exhausted remnants of what was once his soul he'll find nothing from which to craft the least thing godlike to guide him in these last of days.

In later years he'd go over to Ibiza on the ferry and have dinner with Geert Vis and his wife Sonia at Porroig. There would be a car waiting for him at the dock and at the house they would have drinks and good Spanish dishes of shellfish and chicken with rich sauces and good red wine from the mainland. Geert's driver took him back to the ferry in the evening. He sat on a bollard and watched the lights. Laughter from a cafe across the road. Out there in the dark of the bay the dull plonk plonk of a donkeyengined smack. Vis urged him to find a woman. He spoke with concern, leaning forward and pressing Western's arm. A rich tourist woman, Robert, he whispered. You will see.

Someone in the town had died. He'd heard the bells toll before it was even day. A certain sobriety among the darksuited men at the bodega. They nodded to him. He sat with his glass of wine. Pale woodslave lizards circled the rings of light cast upon the ceiling by the tablelamps. Stalking the moths like predators at a waterhole. Their tufted feet. Van der Waals forces. He nodded to the men and raised his glass. Coming home the sky was clear and the moon rose and squatted in the road before him. Walking up the long dark headland where the windmill stood in silhouette against the sky. He stood in the wind and studied the sweep of stars in the blackness. The lights of the distant village. Climbing the stairs, lamp in hand. Hello, he called. This cup. This bitter cup.

His father spoke little to them of Trinity. Mostly he'd read it in the literature. Lying face down in the bunker. Their voices low in the darkness. Two. One. Zero. Then the sudden whited meridian. Out there the rocks dissolving into a slag that pooled over the melting sands of the desert. Small creatures crouched aghast in that sudden and unholy day and then were no more. What appeared to be some vast violetcolored creature rising up out of the earth where it had thought to sleep its deathless sleep and wait its hour of hours.

It was his father who took her to see all those doctors. Who sat at the kitchen table in the old farmhouse and stared out across the fields to the creek and the woods beyond. He'd written in a notebook things she had said that he could not understand and he read them over and read them over until in the end perhaps he came to realize that her illness—as he called it—was less a condition than a message. He'd turned more than once to see her in the doorway watching him. Fräulein Gottestochter bearing gifts of which she herself would at last be no advocate.

His father. Who had created out of the absolute dust of the earth an evil sun by whose light men saw like some hideous adumbration of their own ends through cloth and flesh the bones in one another's bodies.

He'd looked for his father's grave in the ratlands of northern Mexico but he never found it. Talking in his bad Spanish with officials in soiled shirts who watched him wordlessly and did not even pretend to think him sane. On the streets of Knoxville he met someone from his childhood who asked with no apparent malice if he thought that his father was in hell. No, he said. Not anymore.

He'd sit sometimes in the little church at San Javier. The long quiet afternoons. The women in their black shawls would try their best not to steal a look at him. A stone font with stone infants. The cheap boards behind the altar had been painted gold and the plastered walls of the church were painted with flowers which were visited by mothlike creatures, drifting through the paneled light, one, the next. He'd thought at first they might be hummingbirds but then he remembered that there were no old world species of them. He lit a candle and dropped a peseta into the tin box.

He walked out along the headlands. In the distance the thunder rolled across the dark horizon with a sound like boxes falling. Unusual weather. Lightning thin and quick. The inland sea. Cradle of the west. A frail candle tottering in the darkness. All of history a rehearsal for its own extinction.

In the morning there was a spider on his blanket. Its sesame eyes. He blew at it and it scuttled away. Some dream of his father. Later in the day he remembered. A wasted figure shuffling along the corridor of the shabby clinic. Pushing a wheeled stand before him with his tubes and vials. Days perhaps from death and a nameless burial in the hard caliche of a potter's field in a foreign land. Who stopped and turned with his watery eyes. Paper slippers and a stained white gown. Where is my son? Why doesnt he come?

He cycled through the small port. Down the thin graveled estuary road and out along the flats. Where salt was once evaporated for the city of Carthage. Frumentaria. The Roman word. The lights of Ibiza coming up off to the north. He sat on a stone that held an ancient iron ring and worked on a flat tire against the coming darkness. His bike standing on its forks against the wall. He listened as he fed the rubber tube past his ear. He sorted a patch from the small leather satchel that hung from the underside of the bicycle seat.

One day he met an American girl from Baltimore and they walked through the old town. They walked among the stones in the little cemetery. He told her that he would be buried here but she looked dubious. Maybe, she said. People dont always get what they want. There were razor marks on her arms. He looked away but not in time. I have to go, she said.

In the evening he gathered wood and tarballs along the beach and built a fire and sat by the warmth of it in the sand. A dog came up the beach in the dark. Just the red eyes. It paused and stood. Then it went around by the rocks and continued on. The flames sawed in the wind and he slept wrapped in his blanket and woke to a fire burned down almost to coals. Green mineral flames and embers scuttling away down the beach. He pushed fresh wood into the fire and sat listening to the slow black lap of the waters in the dark. Rush boats dragged up onto the sand. The clang of bronze or iron in those ancient nights. The moans of the dying. If you burrin away the key to the codex yet against what like tablet can this loss then be measured?

Dont be afraid, she would say. Most frightening of words. What did she see? For whom blood was all. And nothing. A man of gifts without consequence. As a child she would make up games that even then were difficult for him to follow. She took him up to the attic where in later years she would at least for a while hold her own against a world heretofore unknown. They sat crouched beneath the eaves and she took his hand. She said that they were meant to find something hidden from them. What is it? he said. And she said it is us. It is us that they are hiding from us.

What she believed ultimately was that the very stones of the earth had been wronged.

Why can you not bury him? Are his hands so red? Fathers are always forgiven. In the end they are forgiven. Had it been women who dragged the world through these horrors there would be a bounty on them.

When he got back to the windmill it was still dark and he climbed the stairs and sat at his little table. He sat with his forehead pressed into his hands and he sat for a long time. Finally he got out his notebook and wrote a letter to her. He wanted to tell her what was in his heart but in the end he only wrote a few words about his life on the island. Except for the last line. I miss you more than I can bear. Then he signed his name.

They sat in the winter sun in the hospital window at Berkeley. His father wore a plastic nametag on his thin wrist. He'd grown a wispy white beard and he kept touching it. Oppenheimer, he said. It would be Oppenheimer. He would answer your questions before you asked them. You could take a problem you'd been working on for weeks and he would sit there puffing on his pipe while you put your work up on the board and he'd look at it for a minute and say: Yes. I think I see how we can do this. And get up and erase your work and put up the right equations and sit down and smile at you. I dont know how many people he did that to. It didnt make any difference what the problem was. If you're just talking about mathematics maybe Grothendieck. Gödel of course. Von Neumann was never in that company. Or Einstein for that matter. He was the better physicist of course. He had this extraordinary physical intuition, but he had trouble solving his own equations. Later, his problem was that he wanted to. He thought that it was a shortcut. I think it led him down the garden path. After General Relativity he never did anything again. I knew him, sure. In the sense that anybody knew him. Maybe Gödel did. His friends from Europe. Besso. Marcel Grossmann. Before he became Einstein.

He cycled to San Javier in the evening and drank a single glass of wine at the bodega.

An old man came shuffling along the road in his ropesoled shoes. A smile that held a single yellow tooth. The poppies along the road bright as paper flowers. In the evening he carried his blankets down to the beach and slept in the sand. What are you afraid of? she said. What can you fear that has not already come to pass?

The owner of the bodega was a man named João who spoke good English. He'd learned it working in hotels along the Costa Brava. It was his friend Pau who had died. An older man who used to sit quietly at one of the small wooden tables with his glass of wine. The skin of his cheeks dark and drawn and polished and his wrists brown against the white of his cotton shirt. He sipped his wine with a certain gravity and he had a white scar across his forearm that you could see when his shirtsleeves were rolled. It was put there by a thirty caliber machinegun and there were four more of them across his lower chest. His hands had been tied behind his back and the bullet which had broken his arm had already passed through him. He said that it was a matter for philosophy whether he had been shot five times or four.

Did he ever show them to you?

No.

He was too modest.

I think he was ashamed.

Why would he be ashamed?

I dont know. That's what I think. I think he did not believe it to be so noble a thing to be stood against a wall and shot down like a dog. The thing he told me was waking among the dead. Some hour of the night. The bodies already beginning to stink. Waking in the night in a pile of corpses and then crawling away. He crawled into the road and other patriots found him. I think he was ashamed. That was another world. He'd fought for a lost cause and his friends had died in silence and in blood all about him and he had lived. That was all. He waited for many years to hear from God what it was that was expected of him. What he was to do with this life. But God never said.

Western asked him what were his own views but João only shrugged and said that he did not know. Anyway, dont speak to me of God. We are no longer friends. As for being stood against a wall and shot down with a machinegun this was a thing which Pau did not outlive. In the end it became who he was. It is what we are discussing now. For instance. A calamity can be erased by no amount of good. It can only be erased by a worse calamity. He never married. He was treated with respect, of course. But in the end you must remember he was shot for nothing. The defeated have their cause and the victors have their victory. Were there times he wished he'd died along with his friends? Doubtless. He was from the north. A small town. What did he know of revolution? He came here years ago. He had no family. He was the sexton at the church. Sexton? Is that the word? I dont know why he came here. He had a small room. He rang the bells. I dont know why he came here. Perhaps he was like you.

In Ibiza the Holy Week parade. Horns and drums and lanterns. Masked figures. Coming down through the old city. The figures were clad in black with coneshaped hats and behind them came pallbearers carrying the corpse of their dead God on a litter through the cobbled streets. The dark stigmata of his upturned plaster palms.

He sat at a sidewalk table and drank a coffee. Someone was watching him. He turned but by then the man had risen and was coming over. Bobby? he said.

Yes.

You dont remember me.

I remember you.

What are you doing here?

Drinking coffee. Sit down.

Let me get my drink.

He came back with his glass and a paperback guidebook and pulled out the chair and sat. I couldnt believe that was you. Are you by yourself?

Yes.

What are you doing here?

I live here.

You live here?

Yes.

What do you do?

Not much. I just live here.

You're shitting me.

Western shrugged.

You ever get back to Knoxville?

No.

Did you know that Seals died?

Yes. I did. And Sheddan.

Darlin Dave?

No. I didnt know that.

I cant believe you're living here. Let me get you a drink. Jesus, where do all these damn dogs come from? What are you having?

I'll have a white wine.

White wine it is. Where's the waiter?

Hiss at him.

Hiss at him?

Yes. Here he comes.

What's it called?

Vino blanco.

Vino blanco, por favor.

The waiter nodded and padded away.

Who do these things belong to?

The dogs? They dont belong to anybody. They're just dogs.

One of them pissed in my wife's purse.

Did what?

Pissed in her purse. We were having lunch and when the food came she took her purse off the table and put it down on the sidewalk by the side of her chair and this damn thing came over and raised its leg and pissed in it. No particular reason. She tried to wash it out back at the hotel but it smelled so bad she had to throw it out. Along with most of the stuff in it. How long have you been living here?

About a year. Some of the racers used to hang out here. Back in the seventies.

Do they still hang out here?

No. I suppose this place is not what it was. There used to be some interesting criminals living here. A first class art forger. One of the greats. A concert pianist who murdered his wife. The police finally rounded them all up. The Americans here mostly visit each other and drink. I wouldnt recommend it.

What about you?

I live in a windmill. I light candles for the dead and I'm trying to learn how to pray.

What do you pray for?

I dont pray for anything, I just pray.

I thought you were an atheist.

No. I dont have any religion.

And you live in a windmill.

Yes.

You're jerking my fucking chain.

No.

The waiter came with the glass of wine. Salud, Western said.

Salud.

What is that you're drinking?

Fernet-Branca.

Stomach problems.

Yeah. Anything that tastes like this has got to be good for you.

Western smiled. He sipped the wine.

You're not kidding me.

No.

Well. You were always a puzzle. Which I'm sure you know. Are you a puzzle to yourself?

Sure. Arent you?

No. Not really. Anyway, I better go. My old lady's going to be waiting for me. You sure you're okay?

I'm okay.

Yeah. All right.

He rode his bicycle back up the island in the dark. The tail light that ran off the rear wheel dimming on the slow pull up La Mola. He left the bike at the door and walked out on the bluff and stood in the wind. The dark lap of the sea and the lights of Figueretas along the far shore. Faint taste of salt from the sea.

Sheddan would come to see him one last time and then no more. They sat in an empty theatre. Is that you, John? he said.

The long one was slouched in an upper seat. He didnt answer for a while. Then he said: It is, Squire. In a manner of speaking.

The breath of but one in the silence. He listened. What to say? It's good to see you, John.

Thank you, Squire. It's good to be seen.

I've missed our little chats.

And I. How did you wind up here?

In a theatre.

Yes.

Not sure. Maybe something to do with the fact that a theatre can never be dark. Something few people know.

A theatre can never be dark?

No. See the light behind you?

Yes?

It is always on. No matter what. Do you know what it's called?

No.

It's called a ghost light.

And what. There's one in every theatre?

Yes. One in every theatre.

And it's always on. Night or day?

Night or day. Yes. One takes no chances.

No.

Years of wandering all caught in the recollection of a moment. An empty theatre you may have also noticed is empty of everything. It is a metaphor for the vacated world of the past. At any rate it seems an unlikely place to come to for news. Are you well?

I think so.

Why are you here?

I'm not sure.

Nothing has changed.

No.

You wont be offended if I tell you that I find that heartening? You of the iron sphincter. The noble resolve.

No.

I suppose in the end what we have to offer is only what we've lost. It's not that I love paradoxes. It's just that they've increasingly come to seem the last factual reality. I suppose that's hardly a novel observation.

No.

But let me continue.

Of course.

You called me a visionary of universal ruin. But there was no vision to it. It was at best a hope. You were the visionary. You had the tools for it. I'd no grief in my heart, Squire. That was what was missing. I was always envious of you. For that among other reasons. God it's cold in here. I'm never warm anymore. You called me Beelzebubba.

I called you what?

Beelzebubba. You dont remember.

I remember. You were not amused.

No. A fake God and you shrug your shoulders. But a fake Satan can only be laughable. And then there's the implied bumpkinhood.

I'm sorry.

Consider it forgotten.

Thank you. What else?

Ah.

You should say.

I should have said. I was lost in thought, apt metaphor. I've little to lay at your door, Squire, but I wasnt treated well. All in all. A bit late for complaints I suppose. To some extent you wrote me off as a parlor intellectual. And it's true that I never got far from my raising. As I'm sure I've said before. I could always appreciate a cold glass of buttermilk. But that's not a bad thing.

No.

I'd like to have been in better graces with you. I dont think I was ungenerous. Even if it was with other people's money.

No. You were not.

I always thought you would drown yourself. You didnt.

No.

I had this recurring dream of you. One of two. Alone on the ocean floor in your indiarubber unionsuit. Fleeing some yawning subduction. You struggled in those hadal deeps like a man wading through mucilage while the pugs of your leaden shoes closed slowly in the loam behind you. The plates creaking. The clouds of silt rolling slowly up to engulf you. Your lamp had eked out and you were left to make your way in the eerie light of the ancient fumaroles smoking in the distance like standing candles. There was something more than poetic in your flight before those hellish sealamps out of whose sulphurous womb it well may be that life itself was brokered in the long ago.

You told me.

Did I? I forget. In their recollections dream and life acquire an oddly merging egality. And I've come to suspect that the ground we walk is less of our choosing than we imagine. And all the while a past we hardly even knew is rolled over into our lives like a dubious investment. The history of these times will be long in the sorting, Squire. But if there is a common keel to our understanding it is that we are flawed. At our core that is what we know.

You think that we loathe ourselves.

I do. Insufficient to our deserts, of course. But yes.

So how bad is the world?

How bad. The world's truth constitutes a vision so terrifying as to beggar the prophecies of the bleakest seer who ever walked it. Once you accept that then the idea that all of this will one day be ground to powder and blown into the void becomes not a prophecy but a promise. So allow me in turn to ask you this question: When we and all our works are gone together with every memory of them and every machine in which such memory could be encoded and stored and the earth is not even a cinder, for whom then will this be a tragedy? Where would such a being be found? And by whom?

I dont know, John.

The bore of one's life closes down like a collet. A final pin of light and then nothing. We should have talked more.

We talked a lot.

We might have come to synchronize our dreams. Like the periods of sorority sisters. In spite of the occasional causticities I'm compelled to say that I've always grudgingly admired the way in which you carried bereavement to such high station. The elevation of grief to a status transcending that which it sorrows. No, Squire. Hear me out. It's the idea of loss. It subsumes the class of all possible lost things. It's our primal fear, and you get to assign to it what you will. It doesnt invade your life. It was always there. Awaiting your indulgence. Awaiting your concession. And still I feel I sold you short. How to sort your tale from out the commons. It must surely be true that there is no such collective domain of joy as there is of sorrow. You cant be sure that another man's happiness resembles your own. But where the collective of pain is concerned there can be little doubt at all. If we are not after the essence, Squire, then what are we after? And I'll defer to your view that we cannot uncover such a thing without putting our stamp upon it. And I'll even grant you that you may have drawn the darker cards. But listen to me, Squire. Where the substance of a thing is an uncertain business the form can hardly command more ground. All reality is loss and all loss is eternal. There is no other kind. And that reality into which we inquire must first contain ourselves. And what are we? Ten percent biology and ninety percent nightrumor.

What was the other dream?

The other dream was this. There was a riderless horse standing at a gate at dawn. Some other country, some other time. The news that the horse brings is a day's ride old, no more. The horse's dreams were once of mares and grass and water. The sun. But those dreams are no more. His is a world of blood and slaughter and the screams of men and animals all of which he has little understanding of. The horse stands at the gate with his head bowed while the day breaks. He wears a cloak of knitted steel dark with blood and he stands with one forefoot tilted upon the stones. No one comes. The news does not arrive. This scene may be a painting. I dont know. I dont know what it means. Perhaps I saw it in a book. As a child. But this is what I dreamed. I wish I had other words for you, Squire. To prepare for any struggle is largely a work of unburdening oneself. If you carry your past into battle you are riding to your death. Austerity lifts the heart and focuses the vision. Travel light. A few ideas are enough. Every remedy for loneliness only postpones it. And that day is coming in which there will be no remedy at all. I wish you calm waters, Squire. I always did.

Thank you, John.

I have to go. We shant see each other again.

I know. I'm sorry.

And I. Dont let them talk about me, Squire. They'll say ugly things.

I know. I'll see what I can do.

He stood at the little wooden bar while João poured his wine. Whose cat has eaten a dragon and is dead. He set the bottle on the bar and he pushed Western's pesetas back across the bar to him. Salud, he said.

Salud. Gracias.

I should have been more kind about old Pau. I've been thinking about him.

I didnt think you were unkind.

One cant speak for the dead. Who knows their lives? In any case it is the nature of people to imagine that the defeated must have done something to deserve their undoing. People want the world to be just. But the world is silent on this subject. To win a war or a revolution does not validate the cause. You see what I am saying?

Yes.

Do you know the works of Carlos Roche?

No.

He was my brother. Older than me. He died in the war.

I'm sorry.

It's all right. He was the fortunate one.

To die in the war?

To die in the war. To die in a state of belief. Yes.

Belief in what?

In what. How to say it. Belief in himself as a man in a land under arms for a cause that was just for a people he loved and the fathers of those people and their poetry and their pain and their God.

I take it you've no such beliefs.

No.

Any beliefs at all?

João pursed his lips. He wiped the bar. Well. Of course a man has beliefs. But I dont believe in ghosts. I believe in the reality of the world. The harder and the sharper the edges the more you believe. The world is here. It is not someplace else. I dont believe in traveling about. I believe that the dead are in the ground. I suppose at one time I was like old Pau. I waited to hear from God and I never did. Yet he remained a believer and I did not. He would shake his head at me. He said that a Godless life would not prepare one for a Godless death. To that I have no answer.

Nor I. I have to go.

Hasta luego, compadre.

A small mule danced in a flowered field. He stopped to watch it. It rose on its hind legs like a satyr and sawed its head about. It whinnied and hauled at its rope and kicked and it stopped and stood splayfooted and stared at Western and then went hopping and howling. It had browsed through a nest of wasps but Western didnt know how to help it and he went on.

He found a coin on the beach. An illformed disc of bronze washed all but barren by the centuries. He put it in his pocket. Remnants of vanished worlds in these outposts. Like the bones of ships among the rocks of remote northern seas. The bones of men.

He sent to Paris for a collection of Grothendieck's papers and he sat by lamplight working the problems. After a while they began to make sense, but that was not the issue. Nor the French. The issue was the deep core of the world as number. He tried to trace his way back. Find a logical beginning. Riemann's dark geometry. His christawful symbols she had called them. Gödel's boxes of notes in Gabelsberger.

The weather had warmed and on these nights he'd strip out of his clothes and leave them folded over his sandals on the beach and wade out into the soft black water and dive and swim out beyond the slow lope of the surf and turn and loll on his back in the swells and watch the stars where some few came adrift of their moorings and dropped down that vast midnight hall from dark to dark.

He'd no photograph of her. He tried to see her face but he knew he was losing her. He thought that some stranger not yet born might come upon her photo in a school album in some dusty shop and be stopped in his place by her beauty. Turn back the page. Look again into those eyes. A world at once antique and never to be. After she left the quarry he sat alone until the small flames in their tins had guttered out one by one. Then just the dark of the countryside, the silence of it. The faint drone of a truck out on the highway.

He wrote in his little black book by the light of the oil lamp. Mercy is the province of the person alone. There is mass hatred and there is mass grief. Mass vengeance and even mass suicide. But there is no mass forgiveness. There is only you.

We pour water upon the child and name it. Not to fix it in our hearts but in our clutches. The daughters of men sit in half darkened closets inscribing messages upon their arms with razorblades and sleep is no part of their life.

After the long dry summer had passed he woke one night to see the high window in the wall of the grainmill appear out of the darkness. And then again. He sat at the window and watched out there beyond the blackest reaches of the sea the soundless thunder and the shuddering light beyond the rimlit clouds.

He sat at the bodega, at the small scrubbed wooden table. Reading the papers that Vis had sent on the boat from Ibiza. João went down the bar and came back with another letter and handed it to Western. Western sat looking at it. It was postmarked Akron Ohio and it was dirty and stained and looked at some point to have been stepped on. Un momento, he said. João turned and he handed him the letter back.

No es suyo?

No.

He turned the letter in his hand and studied it. Es su nombre, he said.

Western leaned back in his chair. He said that he didnt know anybody in America anymore and that he didnt want any cartas from them. João weighed this. He tapped the letter in his palm. Finally he said that he would keep it because people change their minds.

He pedaled home in the dusk. The tower was dark and damp when he entered and stood his bike against the wall. He climbed the steps with the lamp and set it on the table and sat and listened to the quiet. Sometimes at night when the winds came over the headlands he could feel something move deep in the ancient works, a low groan from the heavy olivewood complications and then silence again save for the wind circling the tower and rustling the straw overhead.

Late one evening he saw before him on the beach a small figure cloaked against the cold. He quickened his step but it was only an old woman walking the beach. Scarcely four feet tall. He passed her and wished her a good evening and then he stopped and asked if she was all right and she said that she was. She said that she was going to visit her daughter and he nodded and went on. He knew that he still hoped for that small and half forgotten figure to fall in beside him. Leaning into the salt wind with his hands in his pockets and his clothes flapping. He'd seen him one final time in a dream. God's own mudlark trudging cloaked and muttering the barren selvage of some nameless desolation where the cold sidereal sea breaks and seethes and the storms howl in from out of that black and heaving alcahest. Trudging the shingles of the universe, his thin shoulders turned to the stellar winds and the suck of alien moons dark as stones. A lonely shoreloper hurrying against the night, small and friendless and brave.

He climbed into the loft and sat at the tower window wrapped in his blanket. Spits of rain on the sill. Summer lightning far out to sea. Like the flare of distant fieldpieces. The patter on the tarp he'd stretched over his bed. He turned up the wick of the lamp at his elbow and took the notebook from its box and opened it. Then he stopped. He sat for a long time. In the end, she had said, there will be nothing that cannot be simulated. And this will be the final abridgment of privilege. This is the world to come. Not some other. The only alternate is the surprise in those antic shapes burned into the concrete.

The ages of men stretching grave to grave. An accounting on a slate. Blood, darkness. The washing of dead children on a board. The stone laminations of the world with their fossil prints unreckonable in form and number. My father's latterday petroglyphs and the people upon the road naked and howling.

The storm passed and the dark sea lay cold and heavy. In the cool metallic waters the hammered shapes of great fishes. The reflection in the swells of a molten bolide trundling across the firmament like a burning train.

He bent over his grammar in the light of the oil lamp. The straw roof hissing in the bellshaped dark above him and his shadow on the roughtroweled wall. Like those scholars of old in their cold stone rooms toiling at their scrolls. The lenses of their lamps that were made of tortoiseshell boiled and scraped and formed in a press and the fortuitous geographies they cast upon the tower walls of lands unknown alike to men or to their gods.

Finally he leaned and cupped his hand to the glass chimney and blew out the lamp and lay back in the dark. He knew that on the day of his death he would see her face and he could hope to carry that beauty into the darkness with him, the last pagan on earth, singing softly upon his pallet in an unknown tongue.